DAY OF THE WOLF

FOUR NOVELLAS

TERRY SPEAR

Cover design by Stephanie Rocha/Sourcebooks

Published by Sourcebooks Casablanca, an imprint of Sourcebooks
P.O. Box 4410, Naperville, Illinois 60567-4410
(630) 961-3900
sourcebooks.com

"Night of the Wolf" originally published in 2018 in *Heart of the Wolf*; "Day of the Wolf" originally published in 2019 in *Destiny of the Wolf*; "SEAL Wolf Pursuit" originally published in 2021 in *Silence of the Wolf*; "Tangling with the Wolf" originally published in 2021 in *Dreaming of the Wolf*, in the United States of America by Sourcebooks Casablanca, an imprint of Sourcebooks.

Cataloging-in-Publication Data is on file with the Library of Congress.

Printed and bound in the United States of America.
POD

Contents

NIGHT OF THE WOLF

A Heart of the Wolf Novella

Prologue

1840
Colorado Rockies

The weather was so dry—too dry. Though the red wolf pack lived in stone or log cabin homes near the river, Serena Wilder's father had warned that anything—a campfire, an electrical storm—could set off a wildfire and destroy their lives.

Today was that day, the fire catching hold so fast that no one had time to locate each other. She'd been gathering thimbleberries for a pie, but tossed her basket aside, the berries spilling out onto the dry pine needles as the winds carried the flames through the dry brush. The pine needles and leaves discarded at the base of the trees added fuel to the already out-of-control fire.

Serena was alone. Her twin sister, Bella, was gathering kindling somewhere else; her cousins, uncle and aunt, and her parents, were all doing chores. The men had been hunting for food. Her mother and cousins? She didn't know. As a six-year-old girl, she couldn't run as fast as a wolf to escape the fury behind her, so she stripped and shifted into her wolf pup form and ran toward the river. The smoke was so thick, she could barely breathe, and the flames danced from tree to tree high above her, the wind carrying the crackling sound like a warning: *Run little wolf, or you'll get burned.*

But the smoke could kill her first.

The last few feet to the river, she leapt as far as her small legs could, landing in the wet reeds. Finding a beaver's den, she buried herself in the sodden wood. She howled for her family, but didn't hear any sign of them, just the river splashing over her hiding place. She prayed the flames wouldn't catch hold on the wet wood, but as hot as it was, she feared it could. The wind blew and fire snapped and popped as it burned everything in its path.

Crying wolf's tears, she felt a lump the size of her home lodged in her throat. She prayed her family had found refuge somewhere safe.

The fires raged, the ground too hot to cross, small fires still eating away at larger trees. Her clothes and her basket she'd woven were gone, burned up along with everything else. Rains came after that, putting out the fires, and once they'd stopped, she left the river and made her way to her stone house as a wolf. The roof and everything that had been inside, the furniture her father and uncle had made, was nothing but soggy, charred remains.

She discovered her mother, still fully dressed, lying beneath a rock ledge, protected from the fire a short distance from the house. But Serena couldn't wake her. She sat and howled for the loss of her mother, for her family. Slept there beside her, until Serena knew she had to eat and drink and find a way to survive. She never found anyone else—Bella, her father, or the rest of her family—but one day she heard a wagon coming, and, hating to do it, she shifted into her human form. Covered in soot, teary-eyed, and naked, she stood on the wagon trail, hoping someone would take care of her until she could fend for herself.

CHAPTER 1

Present Day
Omaha, Nebraska

Serena Wilder packed up her belongings at the library where she had worked for four years. This was her last day because she and two other women were no longer needed on staff. Between funding cuts and the newly-installed automations—automatic book check-ins and self-checkouts—she knew she had to find another job, but she hadn't had any success. She packed away her remaining wolf postcards—not of any wolves she knew, but just the generic kind her friends had given her, because they knew how much she loved wolves, though not the reason why—that she had tacked to the board above her desk.

Her other two laid-off coworkers—strictly human—had already left. Serena had always worked around books, from being a teacher in the early days, to working in the first libraries. She loved books. But she'd had to move so many times over the years, and she was always starting over. How could she not? Once she hit her late teens, she had aged so slowly. People would wonder.

Now she'd applied for unemployment compensation, but she had a "waiting week" before she could be paid for subsequent weeks. After that, the amount of her highest quarterly earnings would be divided by thirteen and then again by two. So her compensation would be half of what she was already earning and wouldn't be enough to support her.

Serena was worried about paying her share of the house she was renting with a male gray wolf, Harold Gaston, but he'd assured her she'd get back on her feet and could pay him later. As a telephone line repairman, he made more money than she did. They'd met at a local diner, the first shifter she'd met in all her years of moving about. They didn't feel anything for each other in the way wolves who wanted to mate would. Her momma had often shared the story of how she had met Serena's dad. How they'd fallen in love from the beginning. And how she and her sister would have the same wolfish interest in another wolf when they were older—just like that. When she met Harold, she didn't feel any of the romantic feelings she thought she should have; nothing about him made her heartbeat quicken.

Serena was an avid romance reader, but she'd never been madly in love or even intrigued by a human, either, though her mother and father would have frowned at her even considering such a thing, if they'd still lived. Wolves mated with wolves for life. Not with humans, though she'd had a few human lovers over the years. With their sensitive shifter hearing, she found sharing a house with another wolf sure beat living in a noisy apartment complex.

And she liked being able to talk to Harold about wolf shifter things that she couldn't with anyone else.

She had the rest of her day planned—go home, run, shower, and hit the road to apply for yet another round of jobs. Anything would do for now.

When she got home, she was surprised to find Harold standing inside, his sandy hair tousled, his small, black eyes studying her. She thought he'd had to work. He smiled at her, but he shoved his hands in his pockets. He seemed tense, troubled. "I had some business to attend to, so I took the day off. How are you doing?"

"I've left the library for good." She set her bag of wolf cards on the dining room table. "I'm going for a run. Wanna go with me?"

It would make her feel better to run off some of the frustration she was feeling.

"No, I've really got to take care of some business."

He didn't say what his business was, but then again, they were just roommates; he had a right to privacy.

Then she realized why she had been so surprised to see him home, besides the fact that he was supposed to be working. No brand-new red pickup truck was parked out front.

"Having trouble again with your truck?"

"Yeah, pain in the ass. Total lemon."

"Is that the business you have to take care of?"

"It is."

"Did you want me to drive you then? I need to apply for some more jobs, but I'd be happy to help you out."

"No, I've got a friend coming by to take me to the dealership shortly."

But it was all a lie. *He* was all a lie. Maybe not the truck being a lemon part, but everything else…

When Serena returned home from running, she saw her car was gone. She panicked. Had someone stolen it? She raced through the house, looking for Harold, calling out to him. He was gone. So was her wallet and her car keys from where she'd left them on the dresser.

It didn't mean Harold had taken the car, but then she smelled the scent of a female gray wolf. He wasn't supposed to know any other wolves. Warning bells began going off. She told herself that he could have just met her. But why had her wallet, keys and car vanished?

She hurried to his room—everything was gone. She tried calling him, the call going to voicemail.

She pulled out her laptop and logged into his email—thanking providence that he'd given her his password six months ago to look up something for him when his phone went out on him at work and he desperately had needed the information.

She barely breathed when she saw he had a plane trip scheduled for him and a woman named Velvet Jamison this afternoon for Grand Cayman Island. Then she received an email on her phone from her bank thanking her for having an account with them and hoping she would consider opening another with them in the future. *What the hell?*

She immediately called the bank and was told that her account was closed.

"Tell me again how Harold Gaston could have cleaned out my bank account *without* my authorization."

"Whoever closed your account had two forms of valid ID. We'll notify the proper authorities, Miss Wilder."

A lot of good that would do Serena. The bastard would be on Grand Cayman Island with *her* money, sipping a fruity cocktail with one of those flipping colorful umbrellas and enjoying the sun, while she was stuck here on this cold spring day in Omaha, Nebraska. He'd be beyond anyone's legal jurisdiction. And all her hard-earned money would be sitting safely in *his* Cayman account. Or he'd spend it all. At least she'd learned where he'd gone. She was glad he hadn't thought to change his password.

"What do I do now? He took everything I own!" Serena said to the bank clerk. *Well, not everything, but close to it.* "I have $150 in cash and that's it. He stole my car even!" Without enough money to pay $1,050 for this month's rent, Serena would lose the rental home too. At least it had come furnished, so she didn't have too much to leave behind when she packed up and vacated the place.

She again thought of *home.* She'd been thinking of returning to the old homestead, wondering if there were any shifter wolf packs out there. She kept feeling like there might be, like there had been in the past. There also might not be, but she hadn't had any luck in finding wolves in the places she'd been living—Tennessee, Georgia, Oklahoma, Arkansas, here. She hadn't returned to Colorado since the human family had taken her from there and raised her. She yearned to find a wolf to love, who would love her in return like her mother and father had loved each other. Like her aunt and uncle had loved one another too.

A distant memory stirred faintly. The walls of her family's stone house had still been standing. What if her family's home was still there? A dilapidated building, maybe? What if she could claim the land for her own? She remembered catching her father putting something beneath the basement's stone floor one Christmas Eve. He'd explained to her the importance of the documents there—money for a rainy day, although for most things they bartered; a will; a deed to the house. Even if the house wasn't salvageable, maybe the land was worth something.

She shuddered. She had never returned there. Not after the wildfire killed her family. All she remembered was the smell of smoke hanging thick in the air, gray ash covering everything. And she had never gotten the sight of her dead mother out of her mind, assuming, years later, that her mother had succumbed to smoke inhalation.

"Miss Wilder, we could give you a bank loan," the clerk said.

"A bank loan." Giving a bitter laugh, Serena wanted to kill Harold. "That would be the day." She wouldn't even be able to get that once they learned she'd lost her job. Thank God, she had a credit card phone case, and had her phone with her when she went running, but she didn't want to get herself in debt in the event going after Harold and her money didn't pan out.

She ended the call. *Harold, the snake.* She wanted every penny he'd stolen from her.

Except she needed money to get to him. And since they were

both wolves, she really couldn't go to the police. Though the bank was sure to call them.

The only money she figured she could get her hands on quickly was her family's savings—if any of it was buried beneath the stone floor. It would be old money though; then again, maybe worth a mint—if her home was still there and hadn't been torn down. If it was, after all this time, surely someone else would have taken her property for their own. Not one of her red wolf kind. A human usurper.

She ground her teeth.

She didn't want to see the woods where she had romped as a child. Or relive the horror she'd experienced when she had found shelter in the beavers' lodgings. She didn't want to set eyes on the home she had loved—not after her family had died so horribly there.

But she couldn't think of any other option for now. She had to have money, and then she'd go after the bigger prize. *Harold.* Teach him to mess with one of her kind. He'd never do it again.

First, she had to find her car. Taking a taxi to the airport in hopes her car was there, she discovered his scent in the long-term parking area closest to the entrance he would have used to reach his gate and backtracked to where he must have parked her car. Between that and using her spare keys, she finally located it, her driver's license and other set of keys sitting on the console.

Now, it was time to take the next step—return home after all these years.

Two days later in the Colorado Rockies, someone or something stalked Serena as she left her car behind on the gravel road. She headed in what she thought was the right direction of her family's home, after going through the small town near where they'd lived, though it had grown some in size. The livery was now a museum; the old hotel, renovated; the feed store was still a feed store; the post office, a shop. And myriads of other buildings that were once homes along Main Street were now shops, bed and breakfasts, or art galleries. But the town was still quaint, no large department store chains. A couple of gas stations, a grocery store, a bank, and a few other shops had been added. A few more homes spread out from the town. But it was still a sleepy Colorado country town.

Beyond the town, she'd located the rock formations she and her sister used to climb that reminded her of giant stepping stones, a monument to an earlier time. In her day, the road that traveled past the stones had been dirt. Now it was gravel, not even paved yet.

Serena slipped between pine trees, barely making a sound as her hiking boots padded along the pine needle–covered floor. Whatever followed her proved clever, always keeping downwind of her, no matter how many times she circled, trying to locate it.

Keep cool, Serena. Don't let it rattle you.

Yet, she couldn't help the way her skin crawled. Every fine hair on her arms stood at attention. Her heart beat wildly and the sound of her blood pumping hammered in her ears.

She'd lived among humans way too long and had forgotten how to use her wolf instincts. *Listen to the sounds of nature*, she warned herself. *What do you hear? Ignore your panic. Listen.*

The rustle of the new green oak leaves shivered in the cool spring breeze. A distant creek gurgled over rounded stones as it had for thousands of years. A woodpecker pecked at rotting wood and a gray squirrel scampered up a nearby birch.

Something, whatever *it* was, watched and waited for her to make a move, as silent and cold as falling snow, as dangerously sneaky as a forest fire.

Damn *it*. Nothing would intimidate her in her woods. She hadn't thought they would be so green, as if the forest fire had never happened. She wasn't sure how she felt about that—as life went on without them.

She breathed in the wildness, enjoying the fragrance of spring. It stirred happy memories—sad ones, too. She'd only planned to find her home, the hidden money, a will, and the deed, but already she was feeling a pang of regret for not having returned sooner, for not taking back her family's heritage, if she could. She shook her head at the sentimental human part of the equation. All she came for was her money, the will, and the deed, so she could put the property up for sale after she took care of Harold and got what was left of the money he'd stolen from her. Afterward, she could live here until she sold off the property. But she'd been so upset over him, she realized she wasn't thinking clearly. How would she prove she was the descendent of the family who had owned the property in the first place?

A distant howl caught her attention. A wild gray wolf returned to the Rockies? She'd heard the Sinapu had reintroduced some into the area. *Sinapu* was the Ute word for wolves, and they were dedicated to the protection of the wild wolves and their habitat.

She stared in the direction, listening until she heard his mate call to him. Taking a deep breath, she wondered what it would be like to coexist with wild gray wolves in this day and age.

Would men ever be able to live with wolves in peace?

She hadn't lived in the wild for so long, she couldn't get the feel of it.

The fickle breeze switched directions. She turned her head to smell the scents. Nothing but the heavenly aroma of earth, pine needles, and oak leaves.

The sun withdrew from the tree-shaded sky, and her skin grew chilled. She rolled down the sleeves of her green sweater, annoyed she hadn't made any headway in locating her family's home.

The house had to be close by, she assumed.

She skipped over a fallen tree, then spied a clearing as the sky grew darker. Her heart sped up, and she dashed for the clearing.

A few more steps and she entered a landscaped yard. Not

wild like it had been when her family had lived here. The natural earth-toned stone blocks still protected the home's exterior, though she assumed someone had scrubbed away the black soot that had covered it after the fire. She stood in awe, overwhelmed for a moment, tears filling her eyes. Memories of playing in the woods, her mother calling to her sister and her to return home, the aroma of apple cobbler and fresh fish coming to her all at once.

The roof…

She stared at it. Green metal? She wrinkled her nose. And…and the place had been extended out the sides and back. She growled under her breath and moved in closer to get a peek inside the windows. Aluminum-framed windows replaced the wood ones and were now adorned with forest green shutters, which were pleasing to the eye. What was that on the roof? A skylight?

A light flickered on in the living room. She stopped dead in her tracks. The warm yellow glow filled the big picture window, but she couldn't make out any sign of a person moving about inside.

Forever, it seemed she stood in the clearing, staring at her home, frozen with indecision. She wanted to check out the cellar. The moneybox, if still hidden, was down there, and the only way to get to it was by going inside the house.

On the other hand, the house belonged to her, and not just the hidden money, making her feel whoever lived here now had to go. They had no right to her home.

Mostly, she needed the deed and will to prove it was hers. Her fists clenched and her jaw tightened. She wanted to scream,

"Come out at once, or I'll huff and I'll puff and I'll…"

The faint snap of a twig coming from the woods behind her garnered her full and immediate attention.

She whipped around. In the dark woods, the iridescent eyes of a wolf shown.

Nothing else…just the eyes. A gray? Had to be.

She glared at it, showing she wouldn't be intimidated, or frightened or…

The front door of her house squeaked open, and she jerked her head around.

"Whoa," a man said, stepping onto her front porch, his hand still on the doorknob. "What have we here?"

One very pissed-off homeowner whose home had been stolen by this person. Not to mention all the changes that had been made to the property when it didn't belong to him.

A black SUV drove up on the gravel driveway and skidded to a stop. Two males got out, who looked eerily like the man on the front porch. If she had to fathom a guess, the three were more than just brothers—they were triplets. Both looked her over as if she was prime meat, taking in every inch of her, from her hiking boots to the top of her head with her red hair pulled on top in a chignon with copper clips.

"Jeez, Shawn, you didn't tell us you'd invited Devlyn's mate to the pizza party. What would he say?"

"Hey, Fisher, she was feeling well enough to go with Devlyn to attend that woman's wedding in Portland, Oregon," Shawn said, smiling broadly. "*This* little lady is someone else."

The men all stared at her, then the other shook his head. "Hot damn, we got another one of them in our midst."

"I'll say, Heath," Shawn said.

"Sure is going to cause some troubles," Fisher said. "Got any more sisters?" He directed the question to Serena.

She took a step away from them and away from the wolf. Fisher turned his attention to the wolf, but no one said a word. She wasn't afraid of the beast, but instead kept her focus on the men in front of her. *They* were her enemy.

"Are you lost?" Shawn asked, his voice deeply sensual, but a tad concerned. He tilted his head to the side slightly. "She sure looks like her, doesn't she?"

Did he have a clue she'd come for her house? That he didn't have long to live here? The crap about looking familiar was a guy line for sure.

She studied him back, trying to determine if she had met him somewhere before. Dark-brown hair curled behind his ears and hung just below the bottom edge of his denim shirt collar. Her eyes drifted to his jeans—well-worn, stonewashed, faded, soft and hugging his muscled thighs, and…

"Miss?" Shawn said. "Are you lost?"

"Hell, come on in, miss, and share a beer and pizza with us. We've got plenty for all of us. I'm Heath. If you couldn't tell, we're all brothers." He lifted three pizza boxes, then motioned with his head to the other man. "That's Fisher, our youngest brother by five minutes." Heath was darker haired, amber eyed, and wore a plaid shirt, jeans, and hiking boots—the lumberjack look.

Blue-eyed Fisher grinned and raised three six packs of beer. He looked more like a cowboy, with a Stetson, well-worn cowboy boots, jeans, and chambray shirt with the western trimmings. His hair was a much lighter brown with golden highlights.

"And our oldest brother, Tanner, is…" Heath gave a small smile. "Well, he's roaming the woods right now."

Quadruplets? It took every ounce of effort for her to break free from her dilemma.

The hair at the nape of her neck stood on end. She knew the wolf was still behind her. Not close. Still hidden in the woods, still watching her.

The brothers' half-wild, half-pet wolf maybe?

"Would you like to come inside and use a phone?" Shawn asked.

She swallowed hard, the tears stinging her eyes. For now, she'd leave her beloved home behind. *For now.*

She turned and glanced in the direction of the woods. Her

vehicle was off the road two miles through the woods. She'd have to search her house when Shawn and his brothers weren't around. She was certain they wouldn't agree to her looking for the deed while they were in the house. Unless…unless she came back later when they were sleeping off the beer.

The wolf, gray and blond pelted, his eyes a beautiful dark amber, had drawn several yards closer, watching every move she made. He was a large gray. His ears perked up, twisted back and forth, listening to the sound of her breathing, judging how panicked she might be.

He sniffed the air, but she was downwind of *him*. Her lips lifted at the corners slightly. Then she bolted in the direction of the creek, hoping to return when they were asleep. She didn't want them seeing her car and license plate, possibly learning who she was, yet.

"Miss!" Shawn yelled. "Miss! Shit!"

The men ran after her, but humans were so unattuned to the wild. She'd soon lose them in her territory. The wind kept shifting and she couldn't detect their scents.

The land seemed so familiar, coming back to her as she made her way through it—the terrain, the trees, maybe taller than before, closer to the house than before.

For now, she dreaded meeting up with the wolf that bounded after her in hot pursuit. Not because she couldn't hold her own against him, but because she feared being tracked. She'd do this her own way. She had no intention of being forced to tell them why she'd been studying the house…or who she was. If she could get her deed, a lawyer, and file her claim, she'd get rid of the squatters without much trouble. Except, she'd have to prove she was her family's descendent too. She was afraid if she didn't find the deed and will first, they could destroy them, and she wouldn't have any recourse. Then she'd have to use her credit card and go after Harold.

"Damn it, where'd she go?" Shawn yelled.

"Hell, Shawn, we've got to let Devlyn know about her right away," Heath said. "He'll want a report at once."

She scrambled into the creek, then made her way downstream several hundred yards. Around a bend in the river, she climbed into an oak tree, certain the wolf would lose her scent.

For some time, the men and the wolf searched for her, splashing through the creek. Their boots knocked rocks on the shoreline together occasionally, then their noisy search faded away. The wolf circled beneath her tree, then headed after the men.

She would have smiled when they passed right beneath her leafy perch twenty minutes later, unaware she sat right above them. She would have gloated at her cleverness. But tonight, Shawn and his brothers would return to her home, eat pizza, drink beer, and sleep in comfort in her home while she had no place to call her own.

"Come on. Let's call it a night." Shawn trudged back to the opposite side of the creek's bank.

Fisher chuckled. "I know she's somewhere close by. But Red's not about to let us catch her tonight."

Her blood warmed. They thought themselves hunters and she was their prey?

No. This was her land. *Hers.* And she'd have it back one way or…

"All right, stay out here," Fisher said to the wolf. He shook his head. "You always did have a thing for a redheaded, long-legged beauty. See you in the morning."

"Ah, hell," Heath said. "We all do. And there'll be trouble. You know it. Then Devlyn's going to be pissed."

"Wouldn't you know she'd show up when our cousin's gone," Shawn said.

Shawn and his brothers tromped off. Serena fumed. If the wolf had gone into the house with its master, she would have waited until everyone went to sleep.

Now she was stuck in a tree like a raccoon cornered by a hound. For a while, the wolf sat. When she didn't move, he laid down, watching, listening, his ears twitching back and forth. She took in a deep breath and smelled the fishy stream, a hint of snow in the air, and realized how foolish she'd been to leave her jacket in the car. But if she left the tree, the wolf would hear her. Ah, hell. She rubbed her arms, her pants and boots wet from trudging through the creek. If she didn't get out of the cold, she'd freeze to death.

She began the climb down, and the wolf sat up and watched her. She swore the dumb beast smiled at her.

Before she could race off for her car, he leapt at her, and her heart nearly died a frantic death. He knocked her down, his paws on her back, his heavy weight effectively pinning her to the pine needle–covered ground.

She growled. "Get off me."

For several seconds, he held her there, not moving, though she tried to squirm out from underneath him. And then he leaned down, and she thought he was going to bite, but instead he licked her cheek.

"Get off me!" she screamed. She instinctively knew he hadn't meant to hurt her, but was playing with her like a big, friendly dog. Only he was all wolf.

To her surprise, he moved off. For a second, she sat up and stared at him. Then she jumped to her feet and bolted. He ran after her, but didn't tackle her again, though she expected it. When she reached her car, he paused.

"Afraid of cars and roads. Good. They can kill wolves." She jammed her hand in her jeans pocket. Then in the other. Panic coursed through her icy veins. Ohmigod, what happened to the car keys? If she'd lost them when she was running, she'd never find them now. Not unless she shifted into her wolf and, with her nose to the ground, could find her scent on them.

The wolf watched her, his eyes fixed on her, waiting for her to do something. She snorted. Her only other option was walking twenty miles to town. Fat chance. Or joining Shawn and his brothers for pizza and beer. *Great. Just great.* She wanted to take her property back in an impersonal way. The less she associated with these men, the less she'd care about having them evicted.

The snow began to fall. She was out of options.

Cold, wet, and hungry, her hands jammed in her jeans pockets, she headed back toward the house, the wolf trailing her like a puppy would its mother. "You know, you're supposed to go home with your master," she said, glancing over her shoulder at the beast. He woofed at her. If she hadn't avoided making trips to the wilderness with a wolf for so long, she would have recognized the warning in his bark. But it was too late.

The land gave way and she tumbled down a steep incline, branches slapping at her, tugging at her hair and shirt, her hands reaching out to grab something that would stop her fall down the rocky terrain. She swore she'd kill Harold for all the trouble he'd put her through. She felt the impact with the immovable tree before she saw it, felt the pain in her ribs. She smacked her head before the night turned into a hazy gray, then faded to black.

Chapter 2

Former Army Ranger Tanner Greystoke made his way down the steep incline easily in his wolf coat.

When he reached the base of the hill, he shifted, shivered, and prayed the woman wasn't injured too severely. She was lying on her back, passed out, her red hair splayed across the brush. She was beautiful, ivory skin, red cheeks from the cold and the walk. When she was glowering at him, she had beautiful blue-green eyes, bluer than Bella's.

After seeing she was breathing normally and her heart rate was steady, he crouched down to lift her off the cold ground. She opened her eyes and studied him, every bit of him—from his muscles to his package. She was definitely a wolf, and he smiled.

He cradled Red in his arms and hoped he wouldn't injure her further, but he had to get her out of the cold. It didn't help that her pants and boots were wet.

"What's your name?"

"Serena," she said.

"I'm Tanner."

He struggled to make his way up the narrow wolf trails he and his brothers had made, and when he reached the top of the hill where it leveled off, he headed straight for the house. Changing out of his wolf form and running around as a naked human in the freezing cold wasn't the smartest way to travel, but he couldn't carry her any other way. He could have howled for his brothers, but damn if he wanted them to come to her rescue. When she opened her eyes again, he wanted her to see him, not one of his brothers.

He took in a deep breath, inhaling her sweet scent. Earlier, he kept tracking her smell and knew she had to be one of Bella's kind: a red wolf, maybe even a relative, who looked a hell of a lot like her. He'd say they were sisters, but Bella had said her sister had died in the fire many years ago.

Now every one of his brothers would want her. Could they even convince her to stay here? They had to get hold of Bella. Maybe she could encourage her to stay with their pack. That still left the problem with his brothers. And Devlyn, their pack leader. If the brothers fought over her, Devlyn would decide what to do.

Which meant Tanner had to make sure Red wanted him, not his brothers. He smiled and quickened his pace. As long as she didn't have as quick a temper as Bella, no problem. He was glad Heath was here; as the pack's doctor, he'd check her out.

Her eyes fluttered open and she stared at Tanner's bare chest for a minute, took a shallow breath, groaned, and closed them again. She'd heal. Their kind always did. But it might take a while. He listened to her steady breathing and heart rate. He shook his head, not believing how fortunate they were to have her here with them tonight. He was still concerned about her injuries.

Like what had happened between Devlyn and Bella, Tanner had rescued his own little red wolf now. He smiled broadly, perfectly pleased with himself. Until he approached the front door of the house. He knew as soon as Shawn opened the front door, Tanner would have a fight over keeping her for himself. Not that she wouldn't have a say in it. Which meant he had to prove just how perfect a match they could be. At least he hoped so.

"What the hell happened?" Shawn asked, his brow furrowing, and Tanner knew his brother thought *he* had caused her injuries.

"She was returning to the house—at least she was headed this way—but lost her footing and fell down a steep incline. I tried to warn her. She hit a tree on the way down, smacked her head, and passed out."

Fisher and Heath came out of the den, then both crowded around while Tanner carried her to his bedroom.

"Hey, not in there," Shawn said.

Tanner gave him a look like he'd better cool it.

Shawn folded his arms. "Devlyn won't like it if you make a claim to her without his say."

"I'm in charge of his leather goods factory whenever he's gone. I'm the eldest of the four of us, and next in line to be the alpha leader if anything happens to our cousin."

Heath whistled. "Already tempers are flaring and we don't even know who she is or why she's here. Just because she's here doesn't mean she wants to stay. Let me take a look at her."

"She's come home," Tanner said, laying her on his bed. "I think she might be Bella's twin sister."

The Greystoke brothers drove to the pack clinic with the mystery red she-wolf lying in the middle bench seat, her head on Tanner's lap. Fisher was sitting in the third seat in back, Shawn was driving, and Heath was sitting in the passenger seat up front.

"She's got to be Bella's sister," Shawn said, driving through the woods on the winding road to the clinic.

"Or a distant cousin," Tanner warned, her head sitting squarely on his crotch, heating him up. "We don't want Bella to rush home thinking we've found her twin sister when we haven't."

"You don't want her rushing home so she can say no to you having the red," Shawn said.

As if Bella would have any say in it, or would even be inclined to say no. The choice was strictly the she-wolf's.

"We called Devlyn," Heath said, "as soon as we saw the lady here. Either they have no reception or they're doing their usual thing and they have their phones turned off."

Shawn shook his head. "Knowing them, they're at it again."

The she-wolf finally roused enough to speak. "Where are you taking me?"

"To my clinic," Heath said. "I'm the doctor for the Greystoke wolf pack. Are you related to Bella Wilder? You're the spitting image of her, except your hair is a little lighter red, and your eyes are bluer. If you're not her twin sister, I'd venture to say you're a first cousin."

She tried to sit up and groaned.

"Where are you hurt?" Tanner asked, half holding her up, half wanting her to lie back down.

"My ribs. I think I bruised them."

"And your head? You passed out," Heath said. "I don't remember."

Tanner wanted her to rest, but she struggled to sit up. He helped her, and then was going to buckle her seat belt, but as soon as he tried to lock the shoulder strap over her chest, she cried out. "Hell, sorry," he said, hating that he'd hurt her.

"Kill her before we get to the clinic, will you?" Shawn asked, sounding annoyed.

"I'm just bruised," she said, as if defending Tanner.

"What's your name?" Tanner held her hand to protect her if Shawn had to suddenly stop the car. Deer ran through the woods and sometimes they had to make sudden stops.

"Serena Wilder. You say my sister is alive?" Tears had filled her eyes and she looked as though she was fighting to hold them back. "Hot damn!" Fisher said. "Bella's going to be ecstatic to hear the news."

"Yeah, our gray pack raised her. Devlyn rescued her when they were both pups, and she mated him when they grew up," Tanner said.

Serena sobbed. "A gray wolf?" She sounded like she couldn't believe her sister would do something so crazy.

Maybe getting to know the she-wolf would be harder than Tanner suspected. She hadn't grown up with them. She didn't know them. Had she even been raised by wolves after she left the area?

"Yeah, gray wolf. Why didn't you return before this?" Tanner figured she probably believed everyone in her family had died, just like Bella had believed, and had never wanted to return and relive the horrific memories. He rubbed her shoulder gently, trying to calm her.

"I made it to the river and managed to survive while buried under wet branches of a dam. My dad had said beavers had built part of it. A rainstorm put the rest of the fire out, and when I couldn't find any of my family, I finally made it to the dirt trail. A couple of days later, a human family passing through in a covered wagon picked me up. They took me back east and cared for me until I was old enough to be on my own."

"So you felt nostalgic and came back to the old homestead," Tanner said. "We're eager to have you in the pack. Bella will be thrilled to learn you are alive and well."

"I..." She frowned and wiped tears away. Heath handed her a tissue box from the console. "How come you're living in our home?" she asked, still sniffling.

"Bella inherited the..." Shawn paused. "Uhm, well, she thought she was the only one who had survived. She gave the home to us."

"She found the deed?" Her eyes widened, still filled with tears.

"Yes, in the basement. And the will, too." Tanner realized then that Serena must have been shocked to learn gray wolves had taken over her home. "We can move out. It's yours, Serena." Tanner wasn't going to get a consensus from his brothers on the issue. The house had belonged to both Bella and her sister. Serena had every right to live there now.

Trying to get her emotions under control, Serena couldn't believe how nice the gray wolves were—at least Tanner. She wasn't sure if his brothers would agree to give the house to her, making them all have to move. She was so shocked her sister had been alive all these years, and furious with herself that she had never come to learn that until now, missing all the time they could have been together.

One by one, the other gray wolf brothers agreed. "Hell yeah," Fisher said. "It's yours. We can stay with others in the pack until we build a place of our own."

"Agreed," the doctor said. "I've been meaning to build a place next to the clinic so I'll be right there if we have any injuries or sickness I need to take care of."

Shawn cleared his throat. "But if you need anyone to stay around and protect you—"

"I'm volunteering," Tanner said.

She smiled through her tears. "Thanks. I have to admit I thought I'd have to get growly with all of you to chase you out of the house."

They laughed, but Tanner suspected she wasn't joking.

Shawn pulled into the parking lot of the clinic, built all of stone, the roof metal like her home's. Tanner hurried out of the car to help lift Serena out, but Heath was right there for her. His light-amber eyes looked worried.

"It's nothing major, Doctor," she said, taking his hand, but holding her ribs lightly with the other and groaning when she got out of the car. "Where is Bella?"

"She and Devlyn went to a friend's wedding. It's in Oregon and out in the country. They might not have reception," Tanner said. "We'll keep trying to reach them."

"I...need money."

Tanner frowned, looking like he was afraid that meant she intended to leave again soon. "I'd be happy to give you however much money you need."

"All of us would," Fisher hastily said.

She couldn't have appreciated them more for their offer. "Someone stole mine."

Tanner was now dressed in jeans, hiking boots, and a black T-shirt that molded to his sculpted muscles—the perfect balance, not the overdone kind. She recalled in vivid detail all those muscles she had gotten an eyeful of when he'd been naked, before he carried her to the house. His package was just as noteworthy, though she'd never admit she'd been peeking. He reminded her of hot baked buns, his wolfish scent woodsy, wet, and wild. And totally appealing.

Heath helped her to the front door of the clinic, while Shawn hurried to unlock it and turn on the lights inside.

"Who stole your money?" Tanner was immediately a growly wolf, and she thought he would tear into the man who did this if he could.

Hmm, that gave her an idea. She had thought she'd be dealing with this all on her own. But what if she had a male wolf to back her? She could pretend he was her new roommate and he could be there to lend some male muscle. Even better was that he seemed so eager to please.

Heath helped her to an exam room, but the brothers all crowded in at the door.

"Do you mind?" Heath asked.

"Tanner can stay," she said, wanting to talk further to him about Harold. If he was willing to pay for her trip and even come with her, she would go along with it.

Fisher and Shawn slapped him good-naturedly on the back. "Hell, he has her hoodwinked already," Shawn said, and he and his brother walked off toward the waiting area.

Tanner folded his arms. "Okay, tell me what this is all about." Heath examined her ribs. "They feel okay, nothing broken.

Let's take some X-rays."

He moved her into the X-ray room, set her on a table, and took the photos. While he developed them, Tanner came in and held her hand, his amber eyes concerned. "What's going on? Why did you return here?"

"I needed money to go after my roommate who was sharing a rental house with me. He took all my savings. Over one hundred and sixty thousand dollars' worth. He had grabbed my wallet that had my driver's license and debit card in it when I went running. He must have used a girlfriend to take out the money and even took off in my car. I'd just lost my job due to layoffs at the library where I'd worked. Luckily, I had some cash stuffed in a sock for emergencies, and kept my passport in there too. I used some of the cash on taxi fare to get to the airport, and then finally found my car. Between gas, meals, and lodging on the way out here, I used most of the money I had left." She sighed. "I didn't know if the house would still be standing, or if the basement was still there. I thought my dad hid some cash in a strongbox in the basement."

"You were headed to the car parked in the woods like you were planning to leave, but didn't. Why?" Tanner asked.

She ground her teeth. "I dropped the damn keys somewhere in the woods."

He smiled. She growled.

He laughed. "We'll find them. We'll take care of you so you don't have to worry about anything."

"I want to get my money back. I worked hard for all that money over the years."

"I understand. Do you have a photo of him?"

"I do. I kept one so I could show it to people while I try to find him." She pulled out her phone and located one. They'd taken a road trip a month after they began rooming together a few months ago and he was standing close to the edge of a cliff. She should have had him step back a little bit when she took that picture of him.

They'd met at a diner, realized they were both wolves, and began to talk. What a mistake that was.

"Okay, so square jaw, small black eyes, sandy-colored hair, cleft chin, and looks like a wily wolf." Tanner gave her phone back to her. "We have cousins, Vaughn and his brother, Brock, who are Navy SEALs turned PIs. My brothers and I are Army Rangers, now working at our pack's leather good factory. As PIs, our cousins can help us locate Harold, if we can't."

"Oh, I know where he is. He's on Grand Cayman Island. I want to fly out there and get my money. *Now.* I don't want him spending it all before I can catch up to him and make him give it back."

Heath returned and showed her the X-rays. "Good news. No breaks. No hairline fractures even. It appears you have a couple of bruised ribs. With our faster healing abilities, you should be good in a couple of days."

"Thanks, Doctor."

"Heath. If you don't mind."

"Thanks, Heath."

"What do you plan to do when you catch up to this guy?" Tanner asked.

She snorted. "I'd love to end his miserable life. But he just took all my money, didn't injure me or anything. If I can get all he took from me, plus enough money to pay for the trip out there, then I'd be satisfied."

"You're sure he's on Grand Cayman Island?"

"I am." She reached down to pull out the confirmation paper from her jeans pocket, but her ribs hurt every time she moved.

"Here. Let me." Tanner helped her down off the table.

He reached in her pocket—she tried not to squirm at the way

his heated touch was doing amazing things to her body—and pulled out the folded piece of paper showing the resort Harold was staying at and the flight he was taking. "Looks like we don't need to use Vaughn and Brock's services. If you want, when we return to the house, we can book a flight out first thing."

Things were definitely looking up! She couldn't wait to see Bella, but she didn't want to ruin her sister's chance to celebrate her friend's wedding. In the meantime, Serena had to get her money back before this scumbag ex-roommate spent all of it.

More than that, she wondered just what it would be like to kiss the hot wolf who was signing on for this mission. An Army Ranger? *Beat that Harold, the telephone line repairman.*

Chapter 3

Tanner was ready to rip Serena's ex-roommate to shreds for stealing her money, though he was thankful Harold's actions had caused her to leave wherever she'd been living and return home. "Do you want to show Harold's picture to my brothers and cousins?"

"Uh, yeah, sure." She handed her phone to Tanner and he leaned forward and handed it to Heath. "Everyone can stay at the house until we resolve this money situation with my ex-roommate," she told the brothers as they drove her home.

"Are you sure you don't need more muscle?" Fisher asked. "Four of us should be able to convince the bastard what a mistake he'd made."

"Who would be left to run the factory?" Shawn asked. "Tanner's in charge there."

"I'll leave you in charge," Tanner said.

The brothers smiled. Never in a millennium would he think to give up his position as the manager of the facility to one of his brothers for anything other than being near death.

"I've got to stay in case we have any medical emergencies," Heath said, handing the phone back to Tanner.

He passed it back to Fisher.

Fisher gave an exaggerated sigh. "The plant needs me. Unless Devlyn declared a holiday for the staff and we could shut down for a few days."

"We have too many outstanding orders to do that," Tanner warned.

"Okay, so you're it. But if you need any help, we'll be out there in a heartbeat," Fisher said.

"Deal." Tanner got the phone back from Fisher. "Do you mind if I share the photo in a text to some members of the pack?"

"Sure. And thanks," Serena said, and for the first time, she seemed to relax.

"Are you sure you don't mind us staying at the house longer?" Fisher asked.

"We'll be gone and when we get back, we'll see what happens then."

"You can't mean to leave the pack after you return," Shawn said. "Bella would be devastated."

"I don't want to leave my sister. We need to catch up on everything that's happened over the years. Has she had any kids yet?"

Heath said, "I wasn't sure if she wanted to be the one to give you the news first. But since you asked, she's due to have triplets in a few months."

"Ohmigod, that's wonderful. Well, that decides it. I'm not leaving."

Everyone whooped and hollered, and she laughed.

The whole pack would be damned glad she was sticking around. They'd all make her feel welcome.

"Are you sure you're all right with us staying at the house tonight?" Shawn asked.

"I'd like the company."

"And you need to be watched in case you're in further pain or have any complications from your fall," Heath said.

Tanner and his brothers agreed.

As soon as they arrived back at the house, all the brothers coddled her—setting her up on one of the brown velvet couches with pillows and blankets and providing a steak dinner for two that Tanner prepared himself, since they'd both missed out on the beer and pizza. She seemed to appreciate that he'd fixed it for her, though she'd said she didn't want him to go to all the trouble.

He wanted to. What better way to prove he could be the right wolf for her? "Tell us all about this ex-roommate. Is he a wolf?"

"He is. And so is the woman he took off with. I smelled her scent in the house when I returned from the library, my last day after they gave me my layoff notice. I suspect he waited until the last minute to leave because he was always that way. He knew he didn't have any time left. Once I was home, I could have caught him at whatever he was up to. I'd asked him if he wanted to go for a run, but he hadn't. When I returned, I saw he'd taken my car without my permission. And I smelled the unfamiliar she-wolf who had been in the house. I tried calling him, then texting him, but he didn't answer. I assumed he took my car because his truck was in the shop and I was without a job. But I felt something was off. He would have told me he needed to borrow the car and asked me for permission to use it. That's when I checked the closet and realized he'd taken his clothes and a couple of suitcases. I started checking his email and learned where he'd gone. Grand Cayman Island. The bastard."

"And the woman?"

She hmpfed. "A gray wolf like him." The brothers exchanged looks.

She sighed. "Okay, yeah, after the experience I had with him, gray wolves were on my blacklist. But you all have been great and I can't thank you enough for everything you've done for me already." Tanner showed her his phone. "The earliest flight out for us here tomorrow is at 8:30 a.m., arriving there at 3:27 p.m. It'll take us an hour and a half to get to the airport from here."

"Okay, I'm game."

"Do you want us to drive you?" Fisher asked.

"No. That's a three-hour round trip for you. We'll just leave the car in long-term parking in case it takes a while," Tanner said.

His brothers smiled at him, sure that he wanted her all to himself. Which he did.

Early the next morning, Shawn handed Serena her car keys while she and Tanner had breakfast before they left for the airport. "We all looked for the keys last night so we could move the car and carry your bags into the house," Shawn said.

"Oh, thanks so much for all your help."

"How are you feeling?" Heath asked. "Much, much better, thanks."

"We'll have to look the part when we get there. Do you have anything that you can wear there?" Tanner asked.

"Sure. I had to vacate my rental house. I brought everything I owned."

"You can leave what you don't need here and just pack up what you need for a summer vacation. Do you have a bathing suit?"

She smiled at him.

"If you don't have one, I'll have to buy you one."

"I have a bathing suit, though this is *not* a vacation," she reminded him. "What about you?" Swimming in the surf total appealed, if they could swing it.

"Absolutely. Sunscreen. Flip flops. Board shorts. Sunglasses. We'll need to look the part of tourists. ACP—an automatic Colt pistol, just for backup. I'll get in close to where they're staying to do surveillance. We'll rent a car. You can wait for me at the bungalow since Harold knows you. I can scope out the situation and then we can make plans."

"All right. Sounds like that will work." As soon as she finished eating breakfast, she hurried to repack her suitcases, so she had her laptop and camera in a carry-on, and her clothes and other essentials in a midsize bag.

Tanner had already packed and the guys were waiting for her to finish, then Shawn carried out her bags to Shawn's SUV.

The three brothers gave Serena hugs and wished her luck, slapped Tanner on the back, and then she and Tanner headed out. "I wish we could have reached my sister before we left," she said.

"I agree. She'll be glad to hear from you as soon as she's able." Serena was feeling much better, both physically and mentally, about everything. Their faster healing abilities really were a godsend. And with the support of a pack, she felt she could manage anything. Even letting this go, if she had to. Family and friends were more important than anything, but she still had to give this her best shot or she'd forever regret that she'd let Harold get away with it.

She was certain Tanner could convince Harold to give up her money if she couldn't access his accounts covertly. And she felt good about getting to know the brothers better, even though she hadn't met the rest of the pack yet. Would she have trouble with any of them? No sense in borrowing trouble.

With her sister having triplets, she was excited about being part of that. Wolves naturally helped take care of other wolves' pups, and she was thrilled to be there for her sister. She couldn't wait to see her.

"I made reservations at a resort down the beach from Harold. Their place was full, but I thought it was better for us to have a little distance between us anyway; this way we can do some surveillance before we confront them."

"Sounds good. You won't be in trouble for taking off like this when your pack leader left you in charge at the leather goods factory, will you?"

"I don't believe Devlyn will fault me too much. Your sister is a different story. I can just imagine her being irritated with me for taking you with me in the event this guy fights back. What kind of a wolf is he? Alpha? Beta? Omega? A lone wolf?"

"He's a lone wolf, no pack. He's alpha, except when he did his cowardly, beta act of stealing my money and slipping away like a thief in the night."

"What about the woman?"

"I never met her. I have no idea where he picked her up. It makes me wonder if he'd planned this all along."

"Wolves don't have sexual relations unless they agree to mate because we make a lifetime commitment to one another. Had he led you to believe that he wanted that with you?"

"No. Neither of us had. For the time being, we just needed each other to share the cost of a furnished rental house. I couldn't afford a place of my own in Omaha, not on a library clerk's hourly wage. Renting an apartment would have cost more than splitting the cost of a rental house. I couldn't live in an apartment anyway. You know how it is with our enhanced hearing. Since he was a wolf, he was more compatible as a roommate than a human. I couldn't find any female wolves to room with. And Harold and I became friends. With us, there was more of a friendly vibe rather than anything physical." She shrugged. "I hadn't been around wolves for eons, and when I met him, it was the first time since the fire. I didn't know what it was like to feel anything like…" She hesitated.

"Carnal pleasure between wolves?" She smiled at him. "Yeah."

"How long were you together?"

"Three months. Which makes me wonder if he planned this or if it was something that just happened. He met another she-wolf, decided to mate with her, and help himself to my savings before they left? Or maybe she's a relation."

"So, the plane reservations were for two."

"They were. The woman's name is Velvet Jamison. Different last names, but that could be for any number of reasons."

"Velvet?"

"That was the name on the reservation. One male, one female."

After arriving at the airport, Serena and Tanner checked their bags and hauled their carry-ons onto the plane. She and Tanner had both taken laptops. Thankfully, Harold hadn't stolen that.

They finally settled in their seats on the plane, but they'd have two stops and would have to change planes both times before reaching their destination.

"What if he says he didn't take any of my money?" she asked Tanner.

"Why would you travel all the way to Colorado to look for a buried treasure in your parents' basement if you hadn't been robbed of all your savings?"

"I can show the account was closed, but he could just say I did that. I don't have any hard evidence it was him."

"Bastard."

Serena glanced out the window. "Makes me feel like doing what I initially wanted to do."

"Take 'em out permanently."

She squeezed his hand. "I know I shouldn't feel that way, but—"

"Not only did he take all your money, he hooked up with another she-wolf to pull it off."

"Right." She let out her breath on a heavy sigh. "I was angry. Then you and your brothers treated me so nicely, and it helped me to feel a little better."

"To know you weren't the only wolf left in the world with no one to watch your back?"

"I admit, I was feeling that way. You think you know somebody, and then you learn just how much that isn't so."

"Well, one thing about the pack, if anyone did that to another pack member, there would be hell to pay."

"I never thought there'd be a pack in the area where we'd lived. Not a shifter pack. And that gray wolves would be living in my home, or that my own sister would be alive and mated to the pack leader. It's all still a shock."

"All good, right?" He leaned over and pulled her against his shoulder so she could rest.

She smiled, then frowned. "Until we get to the island." Yet, this was nice, she thought. Resting her head on the hot wolf's shoulder, she breathed in his spicy, male wolf scent, listening to his steady heartbeat, feeling his warm touch. *Really nice.*

Chapter 4

From the flight schedule Serena had found for Harold and Velvet in the email, they had only arrived the night before, and their return flight was scheduled ten days from then, but they were traveling to Raleigh, North Carolina, instead of returning to Omaha. Tanner was surprised Harold hadn't changed his identity, probably figuring Serena wouldn't catch him because she wouldn't have any money to do anything about it. He couldn't go to jail as a wolf, because it was too dangerous for their kind if he needed to shift during the phase of the full moon. Not to mention that taking on two gray wolves when she was a smaller red wouldn't have been a good idea.

Harold would never suspect an Army Ranger wolf shifter would be hot on his tail.

Tanner and Serena had lunch between flights. When they arrived at the island, they picked up their luggage, got their rental car, and, before they went to their lodging, Serena directed him to go to a bank. There, she opened an account. If Harold could do it, Tanner figured, she could do it too. Then they headed for their lodging. In retrospect, he probably should have asked her if she wanted a separate place. He'd reserved a two-bedroom bungalow on the beach so that they'd be together, share meals, and he could watch over her. Not only was it something he'd do for any she-wolf who was part of the pack, but he also wanted to get to know her better. Plus, Harold might just want to try and scare her off, or worse.

He might have been sneaky about running off with her money, but no telling what might happen if she began stalking him to get it back.

When they walked into the bungalow, she took a deep breath and looked around. There was a cute little kitchen with sunshiny decor, and stairs leading to the bedrooms and one bathroom.

She set her bags down on the tile floor. Tanner set his bags by the stairs.

"What if Harold had done this before to women he's hooked up with?" Serena asked.

"I was thinking the same thing. There's a good bet that he has."

"And that he'll do it again. Easy money."

"I agree."

She walked over to the living room window that looked out on the beach. "That makes me want to wring his neck again."

"Wait until we get your money back from him first. It would be different if he had some charitable reason why he took the money. Coming to the island to have fun with some new she-wolf? I don't think so. I need to run out and pick up some groceries and some dinner for us. Unless you want to have something delivered?"

"Go ahead and order something for us, then you can get some groceries and the takeout. Anything's fine with me."

He pulled out his phone and searched for a restaurant close by that served takeout. "Chinese?" He joined her and showed her the menu.

"Sure. The spicy broccoli and beef for me."

"All right. I'd take you with me, but…"

"We might run into them. I feel like I'm on house arrest."

"Because of me?" He didn't want her to feel as though he was calling all the shots. He just wanted to make sure they didn't tip off Harold unless she had to.

"No. Because of them. I suspect she knows what I look like

if she had to disguise herself as me when she went to the bank. Though it was a big bank, and I didn't know anyone personally. I didn't go in very much, just used the drive-through or made automatic deposits."

"Why don't we take a run tonight when it gets nice and dark?"

"As wolves?"

"Yeah. What do you think?"

"I'd like that. I'm glad you're with me. I was so mad, I was ready to tear into the two of them all by myself. I wasn't concerned about my own well-being. I didn't figure I had anything to lose at that point."

"I don't blame you. And I'm glad to help you in any way that I can. All right. I'll call in the order and pick it up when it's ready."

"I hope trying to get the money doesn't take more than a couple of days."

He hoped it did. Then he'd be able to spend more time alone with her on a tropical island without his brothers or anyone else's interference. He carried her bags up the stairs, then he called in the order to the Chinese restaurant. Afterward, he carried his bags up and put them in his room.

He heard her setting the table for dinner. "View of the beach up there?"

"Yep. Both bedrooms. Food's ordered." He headed back down the stairs. "What are you going to do?"

She opened her laptop on the kitchen table and turned it on. "I'm looking for the layout of their cabana. I'm checking his email also. Okay, he received a confirmation for dinner for two at a Chinese restaurant for tonight—like now."

"Not the same one we're getting takeout from though, correct?"

"It's the same one. It's the closest one to both our places. If they see you, they won't know you anyway."

"But if they smell me, they might be able to smell you on me."

"Oh. Sorry. No more hugs for you."

"Hell, I'll kill the SOB for all he's done to you myself. I'll have them deliver the food here and I'll run to the grocery store while they're at the restaurant."

"Thanks for doing this and for everything you've already done for me."

He thought she was going to give him a hug for stepping in to be her hero. He must have looked hopeful, or eager, or something. She smiled broadly, closed the distance between them, and gave him a warm hug. Warmer than she'd given his brothers when they'd said goodbye. And that told him she just might be interested in something more between them. He meant to give her a simple, sweet kiss; as much as he was craving something wilder, more passionate, wolfish even.

She began to kiss him back, as if searching for the truth. Was she just as passionate a wolf as he hoped she would be? *Hell yeah.* He gave into the moment, holding her tight, kissing her soft lips, enjoying the heat of her body, the softness of her curves, and the sweet scent of the human and she-wolf combined. Her kisses became more insistent, needier, more passionate.

When they broke free of the kiss, they were breathing harder and their heartbeats were drumming. Her eyes darkened and she appeared dazed. Her arms were still wrapped around his back, and he was holding her close, the two of them gazing into each other's eyes. He knew by the way their pheromones were singing to each other that she had been affected by the intimacy just as much as he had. Not to mention he was fully aroused.

There was something between them, a connection between wolves they could build on.

"I'd tell you I shouldn't have done that with you because I don't really know you, but…I have to admit I've never felt that way with anyone I've ever kissed," Serena said.

"The heat? The desire?" He smiled. "Ditto for me."

Then she sighed and released him. "I'm going to unpack and change into something a little cooler."

"Save a swim date. We can go swimming and running after that long flight. I'll get the groceries and be right back."

"I would love to go swimming and unwind a bit before we take care of business." She gave him a short list of what she'd like to eat—oatmeal for breakfast, dark-brown sugar, tea, and sandwich fixings.

When Tanner left, Serena unpacked her bags, and then changed into shorts, sandals, and a halter top. Returning to the kitchen, she opened up her laptop to try to learn anything more about Harold from his emails.

She still couldn't believe the way she'd felt when she had kissed Tanner. She'd had a few flings with humans over the years, which were fine as long as she wasn't mated to a wolf. But the craving to make a human hers? Or to take this all the way with a wolf like Harold?

Never.

Back in Omaha, she'd observed a male blue jay courting a female in spring, fluffing out his chest, his wings spread, trying to impress her. The female had been watching him, interested. Appreciative of all his hard work. In Tanner's case, he'd stayed near her when he was a wolf, had tried to warn her of danger, and had taken care of her after she'd hurt herself.

He didn't have wings to spread, but he was definitely in courtship mode, showing how protective he could be, and helping in any way to take case of this business too.

Drawn to him, she tried to tell herself she only kissed him to see if all wolves were the same as humans. Nothing to write home about. She had quickly learned that wasn't the case with Tanner. If she'd had someone to write home to, she would have told her she had found one hot wolf.

She checked more of Harold's emails. She kept thinking he'd

remember she had used it once, and he would have changed his password. Maybe he didn't think she was that bright. He would never suspect she was just down the road from him, a beach's run from his cabana.

Then she saw another couple of email confirmations.

Harold and Velvet had paid for a stingray snorkeling excursion tomorrow afternoon and were going on a sunset catamaran cruise tomorrow night. They would be gone for five hours for the snorkeling trip. The catamaran cruise would take about three hours. She and Tanner should be able to... Shoot. She was thinking they could sneak into their place, find his laptop to see if she could hack into it and learn about his bank accounts, but Harold would smell their scent. Even if only Tanner went, Harold would wonder why a male wolf had been there.

The food arrived and she tipped the delivery man, then carried the food into the kitchen to serve it. She received a text from Tanner: Did the food arrive?

She texted back: It did.

She told him about Harold and his girlfriend going out on the two trips.

Tanner texted back: Why don't we eat out for lunch and dinner tomorrow since they'll be gone for so many hours?

She texted back: We could.

She really didn't plan to stay on the island long. They could have a quick lunch, then break into the cabana. Or Tanner could. He could find the laptop and bring it out to the rental car where she could learn what she could on it. They'd still have the problem with leaving Tanner's scent behind. She suspected they might have to just threaten Harold to force him to give up her money.

Tanner texted: I'll be right there. The grocery store is nearby.

She replied: See you.

She fixed them glasses of ice water, then looked out at the beach.

She was a take-charge person, and sitting here doing nothing was driving her nuts. While Harold and Velvet were at the Chinese restaurant, she wanted to check them out and learn what the woman looked like. Was she similar in coloring and build, or just the opposite? Serena wanted to see how the two of them reacted to each other—intimate or just getting to know each other? Hotly craving each other?

She should have been angry that he'd used another she-wolf to help steal from her, but his actions had forced her into new circumstances—learning about her sister and finding a whole pack of eligible male wolves to choose from—which thrilled her. Harold had done her a favor.

Even though the Greystoke brothers said they'd take care of her and she didn't have to worry about money, she couldn't allow Harold and the she-wolf to get away with stealing her savings. Only an omega or beta wolf would let another wolf abuse her trust and do nothing about it.

She heard Tanner park the rental car out front, and she hurried to help him with the groceries. He only had a couple sacks of groceries and took the opportunity to wrap his arms around her, bags still in hand, and kiss her as if she'd come outside to welcome him back home after he'd been away for eons.

She laughed and kissed him back, and did something so uncharacteristic for her when it came to a man—*but he was all wolf.* She rubbed her body against him in a way that said she was interested in being *more* than just one of his pack mates. That got him smiling in a hot, sexy way. After the official greeting, they entered the bungalow and shut and locked the door.

"Okay, I didn't want to text about all this stuff, but I was thinking we could search his place for any clues about where he might be keeping my money and how to access it. But then he'd smell that we'd been in his place."

"I have hunter's spray I brought with me."

Her jaw dropped, then she frowned at him as he put the groceries away. "Do you often use it to conceal your scent?"

"Only when necessary."

"Okay, then good. They're going to be gone for about eight hours on excursions tomorrow, so I figure we'll be able to slip into his place one of those times." She began to serve the Chinese food.

"I've got lock picks we can use. Standard *lupus garou* issue."

"What if we run into them when we're running or swimming?"

"I'll tear into him and make him wish he hadn't taken your money and your car."

That made her worry. She didn't want Tanner injured. And for what? Money? His life was too important. But she didn't want to emasculate Tanner by mentioning it, reminding herself that he was an Army Ranger. She'd jump in and fight the bastard though, if Harold got a lucky strike and Tanner needed her help.

After eating and washing up, they stripped out of their clothes, opened the door to the patio on the beach, and shifted, intending to enjoy the beach and ocean that night, the sun already having set. The dark was perfect for their night vision, but humans wouldn't be able to make them out.

They ran as wolves, then shifted and ran into the water as humans. She never imagined skinny dipping as a human with a wolf. She and Tanner swam, the full moon shining on the waves. She'd never been in the Caribbean or even to a beach before—lakes, ponds, rivers, yes—but this was beyond beautiful, and she loved it here. Too bad she wasn't on a vacation with the handsome wolf, not worrying about getting her money back from a crook.

Tanner took hold of her arm, pulled her close, and kissed her. Now this she'd never tried before—kissing a naked man in the ocean, the warm swell of water lapping at their waists, the sultry breeze ruffling their hair, the silky sand under their feet. It made her nearly forget her purpose here.

He nuzzled her cheek. "Are you ready to run past the cabana and check it out?"

"Yeah, let's go. I wish we could check out their place early, but they might—"

They saw movement on the beach, two gray wolves racing down the white sandy beach, and Tanner quickly turned Serena away from their view. Since he was half a foot taller than her at six feet tall, he sufficiently blocked their view of her. He wrapped his arms around her and kissed her then, as if that was part of the charade. Though she had to admit Harold would never suspect she would be here with one hot wolf.

She kissed him back, her arms wrapping around his waist, her wet body pressed against his, and felt his cock stirring to life. For the moment, she didn't give a damn about Harold and the she-wolf.

But then Tanner pulled his hot lips away from hers and said, "Can you access his computer if he has it at their cabana?"

"I can."

"The Grand Cayman account would be new, wouldn't it?"

"He might have had it for a while. He uses the same three passwords for everything. He had them written down on a slip of paper in a drawer. I came across it one day while looking for a pen in his desk drawer."

"What if he's changed the passwords?"

"I can try to hack into the account."

"You're a hacker?" Tanner looked amused.

"Just a hobby. It came in handy when my coworkers at the library forgot their passwords on their computers. It was hush-hush, and we never breathed a word of it to management. If that doesn't work, we'll go to plan B: force him to tell us to give up the money."

He glanced over his shoulder. "We'll have time to search for his laptop when they go on the snorkeling trip. They're gone now and way down the beach. We should return to the bungalow. I don't want to run into them as wolves on the beach."

"Agreed. Let's go." She glanced down the beach and didn't see any sign of them. "Should we make a run for it as naked humans or furry wolves?"

"Wolves. We'll reach the bungalow faster. If we can't see them, they can't see us from this distance either."

They moved through the waves to get closer to shore, then shifted and ran for the bungalow's porch. Tanner shifted again, opened the door, and then Serena shifted and walked inside with him. He shut and locked the door.

"Now what?" he asked.

Her phone rang then, and she wondered who would be calling her. "Gotta get that." She grabbed her phone and saw that it was Bella; she was glad Tanner had added her name and number into her list of contacts for her. "It's my sister." She felt overjoyed at once. Not wanting to try and dress while talking to her sister on the phone, she climbed the stairs to the bedroom. "Omigod, Bella!" Tears filled Serena's eyes. "I can't believe you're alive! Or mated to a gray wolf." She slipped under the covers. "Or that you're having triplets!"

"I can't believe you're alive either, and now you're risking your neck, trying to get your money back from your ex-roommate?" Bella sounded annoyed with her, but she was sniffling too.

"In my place, you would have done the same thing." Serena knew her sister would have. She was too stubborn not to.

"I don't want you to risk your life over the money. We have plenty in the pack, and you don't have any concerns in that respect."

"At first, I felt I didn't have a choice. But it didn't change my feelings about him stealing my savings. It's mine. I worked hard for it. And I don't want him to feel he got away with what he did."

"Okay, I understand. I'm glad Tanner's with you. Devlyn is ready to send more than half the pack there to take the wolf down."

"We're fine. For now. If we have trouble, we'll be sure to call you." Serena heard Tanner talking on his phone downstairs and wondered if he was still naked like she was.

"I can't believe I'm really talking to you. Everyone's been trying to reach us. We finally arrived at a location where we had cell phone reception. You don't know how thrilled I am." Bella began to cry.

So did Serena. "I can't wait to see you, Sis. We'll"—Serena sniffled—"be home soon. I can't wait to hear all about your life."

"Same here. Don't do anything that will get you killed over there. I will never forgive you."

Serena smiled. "We'll be there soon. And I promise I'll be careful." But she'd also promised herself she was getting her money back, and she always kept her promises.

Still, they talked for two hours straight, and when they finally hung up, Serena felt as though they had barely been apart all those years. She wanted to know more, but it was time to call it a night. Though she was certain Tanner understood her need to reconnect with her sister, she didn't want him to feel neglected either. Not when he was willing to help her like this.

She threw on some shorts and a T-shirt and headed downstairs. He was dressed in shorts, watching out the window. "See anything?" she asked.

"I saw them return as wolves headed in the direction of their cabana. Did you have a nice talk with your sister?"

"I did. But we need to talk about so much more."

"I'm not surprised. Devlyn called me."

She'd wondered who Tanner had been speaking with. "Checking to see if we're all right?"

"Giving me hell."

Her lips parted. She was surprised Devlyn was angry with his cousin. "Because you didn't ask his permission first?"

Tanner closed the distance between them and pulled her into

his arms. "Because I brought you here, risking your life without a solid plan and no backup."

"We're going to get the money by accessing his account."

"He wants us to wait. He's sending two of my brothers and our cousins Vaughn and Brock."

She didn't want to delay what she and Tanner intended to do while Harold and his girlfriend were on the stingray feeding excursion, especially when Serena only knew about that trip and the night cruise for certain. This was their best opportunity to grab the money surreptitiously.

She let out her breath. "When are they arriving?"

"Two days from now. The flight in was booked. They're going to try flying standby in the meantime."

"Okay, this is what we're going to do. We have Harold's itinerary for most of tomorrow. Beyond that, we have no idea when they're going to leave the cabana, or when they're going to return. To do this as covertly as possible, this is the best shot we have. If we get the money, the guys don't have to fly out here, unless they want to. And we can return to Colorado."

He smiled down at her. "You and Bella will really keep Devlyn on his toes."

She smiled up at Tanner. "Are you going to call him and tell him the plan?"

"Nope. If we're successful tomorrow, we'll tell him then. If we're not, we'll go with a new plan B. Wolf pack muscle."

"Okay, it's a deal. Thanks, Tanner. I hope you won't get into too much trouble."

"I'll just tell him you made me do it." She laughed. "I doubt he'll believe that."

"He will. He'll know I'm trying to persuade a wolf to court me, and I'll do whatever it takes, within reason. As long as your life isn't on the line."

Chapter 5

The next morning, Tanner and Serena prepared breakfast at the bungalow. Tanner made the works—omelets, bacon, hash browns, toast, and coffee. She had her oatmeal. But all he could think of as he prepared breakfast was that he hoped Harold and the she-wolf wouldn't cancel their plans so he and Serena had time to do what they needed to do.

"You said his laptop was in the shop." Tanner took his seat at the kitchen table with Serena to eat.

"It was. He picked it up two days before he left."

Tanner had a nightmare last night that he and Serena would arrive at the cabana and the wolves would be there. If it did happen, it just meant they'd have to force the truth out of them.

Movement outside the kitchen window caught his eye, and he noticed the palm tree fronds were flapping wildly in the wind and the waves were covered in white caps, larger than they were last night. He checked the weather app on his phone. "Hell." A tropical storm was approaching the islands.

"What's wrong?" Serena asked.

"Storm's coming in with gale-force winds of up to sixty miles per hour. It might veer off, but it might not."

"Oh great." She checked Harold's emails. "Damn it. The tour group has cancelled the excursions for both this afternoon and their catamaran dinner cruise. It's understandable, just not something I wanted to hear."

"Have they rescheduled for a later date?"

"No. They'll have to wait out the storm. If the docks are torn up, it might be canceled for the duration of their stay here." Serena sounded disappointed.

Tanner hoped they didn't have more trouble than that. "Says here, no flights in or out of the islands until further notice. So the guys will be delayed coming here to back us up also."

"What will we do?" She looked so disappointed that she couldn't just take care of this and be done with it. He reached across the table and took her hand, giving it a reassuring squeeze. "We'll get it done." Though Tanner couldn't be sure how. If the storm destroyed their lodging, and Harold's laptop with it, then what? Not to mention a real risk to themselves if the storm was bad enough. "The tropical storm has developed about thirty miles offshore. We've got some food, but I need to return to the grocery store and pick up some more items just in case we lose electricity."

"I'll go with you."

"What if Harold and the she-wolf have the same idea?" Tanner really didn't want Harold to see Serena. Harold couldn't leave the island right away, but he might leave as soon as he could if he saw Serena was here, before she could get her hands on the money.

"All right. Get plenty of water, some spare gallons for cooking and washing up, and canned goods."

"Got it."

"I'll clean up our breakfast dishes. You go before everyone cleans out the grocery store."

"All right." He carried his dishes and coffee mug into the kitchen, then pulled her in for a warm hug and kissed her, already feeling possessive and needing her to know he was there for her.

She kissed him back in a way that said she appreciated it, their mouths open to each other, their tongues sliding against each other's. He groaned when she pulled away. "More later," she assured him.

"Then I'd better hurry."

It took him only ten minutes to get to the grocery store, and Serena was right; the place was packed. People, mostly locals, were stocking up. He smelled the panic, everyone in a rush to grab what they could.

Wheeling a cart in front of him, he picked up a couple of camp lanterns, flashlights, candles, several packs of bottled spring water, several extra gallons of water, canned goods, other nonperishable food items, a radio, and a propane stove. Tanner smelled a male wolf had just been down the aisle where he was picking up some chips, and he didn't believe there would be a lot of wolves vacationing on the island. He rolled his cart around the corner and saw a man and a woman clinging to him. Covertly, Tanner snapped a quick photo of them to show to Serena, wanting to know if she had ever seen the woman before, and he sent it to his brothers and cousins.

The guy had sandy, dishwater-colored hair; the woman, mousy brown hair. She pulled free from him and began wringing her hands, looking worried. He was laid back, smirking, his hand rubbing her back underneath her shirt. From the picture Serena had shown Tanner, that was Harold.

"I think we should leave," the woman said, most likely Velvet. She was about the same petite build as Serena.

"All flights have been cancelled because of the storm. We'll be fine. I've been through two of these here already. No big deal." Harold pulled her in for a kiss.

Tanner thought they'd known each other for a while. Or maybe the two of them felt something for each other that Harold hadn't felt for Serena and vice versa. Something that went deeper than just a physical attraction between wolves. Still, Harold hadn't needed to steal Serena's money or leave without telling her he'd found a she-wolf who meant everything to him. Which made Tanner suspect Harold was a scam artist and had planned this out in advance. And that the woman meant something more to him than someone he just used to grab Serena's money.

Tanner was glad Serena wasn't here to witness their display of affection.

He stayed out of the wolves' way, grabbing what he needed, hoping they wouldn't notice his wolf scent.

As wary as wolves were, he hoped they didn't catch sight of him halfway watching them. Though if they did, they'd probably believe he was just curious about them because he was a wolf too. They finally checked out and left, not noticing Tanner, thankfully. Then he waited until their headlights turned on and they backed out of their parking space. Already the blue morning skies filled with white fluffy clouds had turned ominously dark gray, and spatters of raindrops began to fall as Tanner hurried to load the groceries in the car, then returned the cart to the store.

He received a call from Serena. "Headed back, just getting into the car," he said.

"Okay, I was worried. It's fixing to let loose at any moment. I looked into the emergency shelters. We'd have to bring our passports, ID, money, nonperishable food for three days, and three gallons of water per person. They take children, the sick, and the elderly as priority. They don't have room for a lot of people, so I figure we'll just stick it out here. I already closed all the outdoor shutters."

The winds were blowing him all over the road, and the rain was coming down in a torrent, so he was glad when he finally pulled into their parking space and cut the engine. "Okay, why don't you fill the bathtub with water? We can boil it if we need it. I picked up a small battery-operated radio and extra batteries in case the electricity goes out."

"I've been filling the tub. I've got the TV on and am watching the weather channel. Good idea on the radio."

"I'm here. I'll grab our stuff and be inside in a minute."

She headed outside to help him. "I never expected this." Neither of them had brought rain gear, so they were getting soaked as they hurried to carry the bags into the bungalow. "But I should have. We're in Hurricane Alley. The program I was just watching said this island has been hit or brushed by a tropical storm or hurricane every year and a half or so."

"I checked the weather report before we came, just to see if we had any bad weather coming. It showed nothing."

"I guess they pop up without warning sometimes. Suddenly there's a tropical depression that worsens, and then if you're in its path, watch out. We won't have to take a shower." She set the wet plastic bags on the counter and hurried after him to get the rest of the stuff.

He glanced back at her, considered her T-shirt plastered to her breasts, and smiled.

She chuckled and helped him get the gallons of water into the bungalow. Once they were done, he locked the door and pulled her in for a hug. "I like the wet look on you."

She smiled and rubbed her hand on his wet shirt covering hard abs. "I like the look on you too. What are we going to do while we wait out the storm?"

"I found some board games in the cabinet underneath the TV. We can keep tuned into the weather report while we're playing some of the games." He set the flashlights on the table while she made them some tea and coffee.

"Oh, the big set of dominoes. Ever play chicken foot dominoes?"

"Nope. I'm game." Tanner showed her the photo of Harold and Velvet. "I took this of them in the store. Recognize them?"

"That's definitely Harold. I've never seen the woman before." He was glad she didn't seem perturbed about the woman.

They set up the dominoes, then sat down to play, the wind howling outside their shuttered windows. The news was updated periodically on the TV, the lights flickering.

"Hmm," she said, placing her double domino next to his single domino, making a "T." She glanced at the shuttered windows. "If we lose electricity, we may have to play a different game." Though they had enhanced night vision as wolves.

"We can. Tired of this one already?"

"No. I'm winning."

He laughed. "We just began."

The strength of the wind whipped everything into a frenzy.

The roof started vibrating violently.

Tanner reached over, pulled Serena close, and kissed her cheek. "If it gets too bad, we can move under the stairwell. It has no windows and a narrow space that would offer the best protection."

"We should move blankets and pillows in there now."

"Let's do it, to be on the safe side."

They headed up the stairs to get the bedding, and she entered her room, while he gathered the pillows and blankets from his.

After they set up their makeshift shelter underneath the stairs, complete with bottles of water and a flashlight, they looked at it for a moment. Tanner wrapped his arms around her. "Are you ready for me to beat you at dominoes?"

She rubbed his arms, thinking of running to Harold's cabana to see if they had gone somewhere else to ride out the storm. "What if Harold and Velvet went to a shelter?"

"Children, the sick, and the elderly have priority. Remember?"

"Right. And he's an alpha wolf."

"And we're supposed to stay put during the storm." She sighed. "All right. Back to dominoes."

The shutters rattled and so did the walls and roof. It was eerie sounding and gave her a chill. They settled on the couch and half watched the news as the weatherman reported the tropical storm was growing closer and picking up steam.

And then they were kissing. She wasn't sure how it happened.

But she'd blocked his next move, taking the spot where he wanted to go next with his domino, and he tackled her. She squealed, then laughed as he pinned her to the couch and began to kiss her.

She gave into the kiss, forgetting about the howling wind and rattling bungalow. About Harold and her money. This is what she'd needed in her life, and no money could buy what she was feeling for the wolf—the hot yearning, the wolfish need.

"I think I could fall for you." She smiled up at him.

"I want to make that happen." Tanner sounded so sure of himself, she thought he might just be right.

Then the TV and overhead light flickered and went out, plunging them into darkness.

"Time to go to our shelter," she said.

"Agreed." He got off her, grabbed the flashlight and the radio off the coffee table, and she slipped her arm through his.

She and Tanner couldn't have sex or they'd be mated wolves, but that didn't mean they couldn't fool around. And she'd only do that with a wolf she really, really liked.

"So what do we do now?" she asked as they moved into the narrow hall.

"This small space isn't very accommodating for games or much else."

"We just got up, so taking a nap seems kind of silly." She joined him on their blanket bed on the floor.

"There's only one thing I can think of." He smiled at her and cupped her face.

"When the lights go out..."

Tanner began to kiss her again, and the way the bungalow was rattling, she really did wonder if they were going to make it through this okay.

But then he was on top of her, whispering, "I'll protect you." And she knew he would do anything to make that happen.

Serena never expected to be having afternoon delight with a hot wolf, hunkered down in a makeshift shelter with a tropical storm bearing down on their location. God, how she wanted this, the hot passion erupting between them, their bodies naked and rubbing against each other.

Their kisses became more insistent as the winds became more violent. What if this was the last chance she'd ever have at making love to a wolf? And the first. But consummating the relationship would mean a mating.

Still, they stripped off their clothes, and then she concentrated on every aspect of what they were doing: his hand massaging her breast; the sexy, sea-salt smell of his skin; the way his heart beat as rapidly as hers.

He was hard—from his arousal to his toned muscles—but his mouth was soft against hers, nipping and kissing, then pressuring until his tongue came into play with hers. Their tongues teased and stroked each other's.

Then his hand moved between her legs, and he began to stroke her clit. Her hands grasped his shoulders as she clung to sanity, her breath short. She was barely breathing as he rocked her world. But then he rubbed his engorged cock against her mons, the aching need compelling her to grab his hips and pull him harder against her. She shouldn't want him thrusting between her legs, but she sure as hell did. Her belly tightened, her blood on fire. He slid a finger inside her. The climax was so close, she could taste it, and then she let go and cried out with wild pleasure, right before he closed his mouth over hers again.

He rubbed his cock against her belly, her hands gliding up his arms. "Do you want me to—"

"Shhh."

So she moved against him, her hips rising, pushing against him, until he groaned, and she felt him spill his seed on her belly.

"Sorry," he whispered, kissing her forehead.

"Don't be. That was amazing." And she knew it wouldn't end there.

The storm raged on for hours, and finally sounded like it was beginning to die down a little. Serena and Tanner cleaned up, then dressed and went into the kitchen to make tuna sandwiches, adding chips and pickles and bottled water for lunch. They listened to the radio reporting that the storm was moving onward, but the winds and rain continued to pelt the bungalow until later that night. And then it was calm, everything quieting. The storm had moved out to sea.

The electricity suddenly came back on, and they went outside to see the damage. The waves were still huge, perfect for surfing. A few palm fronds were scattered about and red tiles missing on some roofs, but no major damage that they could see.

"Looks like we made it safely through that one."

"If we can weather a storm like that, we should be able to manage anything." Tanner pulled her in close, resting his head on the top of hers, his arms wrapped around her waist as they looked out to sea.

"Do you want to see how their cabana fared?"

"Yeah, sure. Let's go."

They headed down the beach toward the cabanas and everything there looked fine too. "I wonder if the docks and boats are all right," she whispered.

"We'll have to check the news and see what was damaged on the island. They might not report it until daylight tomorrow."

They returned to the bungalow, and she was glad the storm was over and that at least where they were, it hadn't been too bad. She didn't know what they would do if the excursions Harold and Velvet were going to take were canceled for the duration of their stay here.

"At this point, I don't see any reason for us to have separate bedrooms, do you?" Tanner asked.

She snagged his hand and hauled him up the stairs. "Wait, our pillows and blankets are still under the stairs."

They retrieved the bedding, then he chased her up the stairs.

At the top, she hesitated. "Let's use your room."

He looked like one satisfied wolf. She figured she looked like one too.

Early the next morning, Tanner checked Harold's email, wanting to know if the excursions were rescheduled or not, while Serena was taking a shower.

Wearing shorts and a T-shirt, her hair still wet, she joined him, and he kissed her as if they were already a couple. "You are the perfect wolf to wake up next to in the morning, and ride out a storm with too."

"I only screamed once."

He laughed. "I jumped too, when I heard that big bang."

She saw he had his laptop out and was checking emails. "What's the verdict?"

"A few trees were down, some vehicles flipped in the high winds, some roofs were badly damaged. But the docks and boats on that side of the island are fine, and the trips were rescheduled. Harold received confirmation emails for this afternoon and tonight."

"Yes!"

He was hoping they'd get this done and maybe skip over to one of the Sister Islands, as long as they hadn't sustained a lot of damage. "Flights have commenced also, but the guys were delayed because of the flights getting backed up yesterday."

"We'll be okay."

Tanner sure the hell hoped so. He made it through a tropical storm on a small island with the she-wolf, and he sure as hell didn't want to lose her now.

Chapter 6

As the looming hour approached, Serena fought the nervousness she was experiencing, trying not to show it outwardly, but Tanner could smell it on her.

After hastily eating lunch, her stomach in knots, she spread her legs and arms so Tanner could spray the hunter concealer all over her, then she did the same to Tanner.

"Ready?" he asked.

"Yeah, let's do this." She thought he looked like he'd hoped she might have changed her mind. She wasn't giving this up for anything.

They drove over in the rental car and parked nearby. "I'll knock on the door to ensure they really have gone on the stingray snorkeling trip. If no one answers, I'll use the lock pick and you can join me."

"When he's on trips, he always hides his laptop under the sofa."

"All right. See you in a minute." Tanner gave her a hug and kiss, and then he walked to the door with purpose. The cabanas were separated by vegetation, and he didn't hear anyone about. He knocked on the door, and when no one answered, he texted Serena.

He pulled out his lock pick. As soon as he opened the door, Serena hurried to join him. "So far, so good," he said.

But anything could go wrong.

She quickly checked underneath the floral couch, but it sat so high, it probably didn't look like a safe place for Harold to hide his laptop. "Not here," she whispered.

"Checking the bedroom."

"He wouldn't have taken it with him. Not snorkeling. So it's got to be here somewhere." She looked in the kitchen. "Not in here." He looked in the two bedrooms, smelled that both Harold and Velvet were staying together, which was no surprise there, but smelled they'd had sex here, or sexual activity. "The safe in one of the closets is too small for a laptop, unless it's really small."

She joined him. "I can't imagine he would have locked it in the rental car." She eyed the safe. "You're right. The safe is too small for his laptop. Unless he bought a new one for traveling. I can't figure him out. He always had plenty of money. Why would he have stolen mine?"

"Some people never have enough."

Harold's clothes were neatly hung up in the closet, Velvet's piled on a chair, but Tanner noticed the suitcase behind his shoes. "In there, maybe?"

Serena grabbed the mostly empty black bag and set it on the bed. An airline security–approved lock protected it. She used her own key that would work on it and the lock clicked open. After she unzipped the bag, she found a leather case, his laptop. She pulled his laptop out and set it on the desk in the bedroom.

Tanner appeared as relieved as she was that it was there. Now if she could only get into his computer. "I'll watch for any sign of them returning," Tanner said.

"Okay, good. I'm into his computer."

"Anything yet?"

"He's so predictable. He has all his bank account links set up on his toolbar for one-click access. I'm trying the variations of his passwords to see if I can—holy cow."

"You got into one?"

"Yeah, and boy, has he got the money. I wonder how much of it he earned and how much of it he stole. Over two and a half million dollars. Why would he need my one hundred and sixty thousand?"

"Like I said, some people never have enough. It could be he has an addiction to stealing too. Gets a thrill out of the game. Why don't you grab your money, and let's go. Are you done yet?"

"Almost."

Once she was done, she packed the laptop back into his suitcase, zipped, and locked it, then tucked it behind his shoes in the closet. She took one of his tennis shoes and shook it out. Then another.

"What are you looking for?" Tanner asked, glancing over his shoulder at her.

"Looking for his credit card." She found it and stuck it in her pocket. "He'll find it missing at some point and have to call it in to cancel it."

"Then he can't use it until they send him another."

"Exactly. He doesn't have another card and he never carries cash."

Tanner smiled at her. "Are you done?"

"Yep."

"Did you get your money?" he asked, hurrying her out of the cabana. They locked the door after them.

"Plus, a little extra to pay for the expense of us flying out here and the cost of the accommodations. That way it won't look like it was me just taking back my money. It would throw him off track. I changed his passwords on the accounts too. He'll have to prove he owns them to be able to change them himself."

Tanner smiled at her. "I had an idea, but was waiting until we learned if we could manage this."

"Yeah?" she asked as they returned to the rental car and got in. "We're already here. We can't get a flight out to Colorado right away either. If we can get one, why don't we take one of those thirty-minute flights to one of the smaller islands? Cayman Brac or Little

Cayman? They're quieter, but perfect for swimming, snorkeling, and running. Then we won't have to worry about running into Harold or his girlfriend. They haven't made any reservations to fly over there or stay there, have they?"

"No. He always has receipts for all his activities sent to his emails, and nothing's popped up. I like the idea."

"Okay, I'll make reservations. First, I need to call and make sure that my brothers and cousins don't come here."

When they arrived home, Tanner called Devlyn and put it on speaker so Serena could listen in. "Serena's got her money, but we can't get a flight out for a couple of days."

"She had no trouble getting it back at all?" Devlyn sounded surprised.

"She accessed his bank accounts. We're flying out to one of the smaller islands to stay out of the way until we can get a flight home. Just so we don't cross paths."

"You think you won't need your brothers? Or our cousins for backup?"

"We should be good."

Devlyn didn't say anything for a moment. Then he said, "I'm sending them anyway. A few days on the beach, watching your backs, and then you can all return home."

Tanner wanted to groan out loud. All his brothers and cousins were bachelor wolves, and he knew, though they would be eager to watch out for him and Serena, they would also be vying for her attention. She might have wanted to experiment with Tanner, but it didn't mean she had decided to mate him. Yet.

But Devlyn was right. Better to be safe than sorry, though Serena and he could leave about the time the others arrived. Maybe they'd hang around a little longer, then.

"All right."

"Everything else going all right?"

Tanner thought his cousin meant about how he was getting along with Serena. "We're doing great. I need to make reservations for the other island. We'll let you know how things are going a little later."

"Okay, stay safe."

When they ended the call, Tanner made reservations for a flight and accommodations to Cayman Brac. "Two hundred feet of sandy beachfront, four bedroom, three and a half bath villa. That will be enough room for the four guys, you, and me. We can enjoy the botanical gardens, Rum Point, blow holes, restaurants, and of course all the swimming we'd like." Tanner wished the guys could stay somewhere else but he knew they wouldn't. How could they protect them if they were at some other location? Though Tanner really didn't believe they needed protection.

"Sounds great. I'm going up to pack. When are we leaving?"

"As soon as we get packed. We'll head on over to the airport."

"Do you have a pair of scissors?"

"For a credit card?" Tanner smiled at her. "He should never have messed with you. Here I thought you were going to need me."

"You never know when a little muscle can turn the tide."

After they packed up the car, they headed for the airport, turned in the rental car, and waited for their plane.

Tanner wrapped his arm around her shoulders as they sat next to each other in the airport. "I wonder how long it will take him to notice some of his money is gone. As much as he had, maybe he won't notice right away."

"He probably will notice. He's tight with his money."

"Do you feel better about everything now?"

"I do. Payback can cause some major heartburn—for him. I wonder if now that he's not as wealthy as before, his girlfriend will want to stick with him."

"I believe they might be mated," Tanner said. "I agree."

"One hundred and sixty plus some change is only a drop in the bucket if Howard has that much money. Too bad we couldn't have made more of a statement." Tanner rubbed her back.

"If I'd known that he'd swindled others like me, I would love to give the money back. But without knowing that for certain, I won't be a thief like him."

"He swindled the wrong she-wolf."

An hour and a half later, they landed on Cayman Brac, grabbed their bags, rented a car, and headed to the villa. Serena loved the other island and would have enjoyed exploring some of the fun things they had to do there, but now that they'd finished the business she'd come for, she didn't want to chance running into Harold or his new girlfriend—and she was ready to have some fun.

"Did you want to keep the pretense that we're just friends?" Tanner asked as they entered the sunny villa.

"You mean as far as the bedrooms go? Nah. Not unless you're worried about what the other guys will think about us rooming together."

He laughed. "I would hope they would think they have no chance with the beautiful she-wolf."

"They don't. This is really nice. Not that the other place wasn't also. But it's nice to know we're here to just have fun now. Do you want to go swimming?"

"I'd love to. Then for lunch, I'm taking you to a restaurant.

Seafood sound good?"

"In the islands, absolutely. They have caves here we could explore too. Right now, the ocean is calling to me."

Tanner finished removing his clothes and pulled on his board shorts.

She pulled on her bikini bottoms, then pulled off her bra, but before she could fasten the bikini top, Tanner was doing it for her.

"Are you worried he might figure out I did it and track us here?" she asked.

"Not here. If he believes we flew out of here, I'm sure he'll assume you went home with a wolf. He'll probably be looking for you on Grand Cayman for a while though. They have some flights back to the States, even if they didn't have the one we needed, so we could have been on any one of those. Did you ever tell him where you were from originally?" He grabbed a couple of beach towels and set them on loungers on the back patio.

"No. I never talked to anyone about it." They headed out into the tropical warmth, a sea breeze carrying the scent of fish, brine, seaweed, and salt water.

"If he finds us, I'll take care of him. As to whether he'd figure out you had a hand in this, maybe, since you had his email password. And he might realize you could have seen his bank passwords in the drawer."

"True." She dashed for the water. She smiled back at Tanner as he chased after her. "The sand is so white and so soft underfoot." She dug her feet into the warm sand, then reached the water's edge. He swept her up in his arms and ran into the stirred-up surf, the waves cresting still higher than when they went swimming the first night. "Are you serious about not seeing any of the other wolves when we return?"

"After you stayed with me when I was in the woods, carried me to the house when I was injured, brought me here and helped me to break into his place, protected me during a tropical storm, let me beat you at dominoes, and now…this?"

"If you put it that way…" He smiled down at her, still holding her in his arms, braving the impact of the waves as they rolled against his legs.

"But it's a lot more than that. I've never felt this way for another man. A wolf. With you, it goes a lot deeper. I love you and I didn't think I'd ever feel that way for someone."

"I fell in love with you the moment you showed up and I began to follow you as a wolf. I was ready to claim you for my own from the beginning. Wolves sense when they've found their mate. And I knew I had to convince you in any way I could that I was yours. I love you right back, Serena." He leaned down to kiss her, but just as his mouth touched hers, a rogue wave crashed into them, sweeping them off their feet, and they were pulled under.

He was out of the water first, grabbing her hand and pulling her from the water. She laughed and wrapped her arms around his neck, kissing him back.

The waves tugged back and forth at them, but they only broke free of the kiss when they were ready. Then they swam out beyond the breakers and floated together, loving sharing this time on the island before she met the rest of the pack and learned what her role would be.

She would no longer be on her own, but a contributing member of the pack. "I could create a small library, if you don't already have one," she suddenly said.

He smiled, and kissed her cheek. "I was thinking about returning to the villa and mating. You're thinking of going to work."

She chuckled. "Sorry. I know it's important to contribute to a pack."

"A library would be welcome."

After walking along the beach while holding hands, she said, "I want to come here again sometime. Not just to this island, but to Grand Cayman, to take the excursions Harold is going on with his mate."

"Anytime."

She wrapped her arm around his waist as they headed to the villa. "What do you want to do for the rest of the day?"

"I'm taking you to the seafood restaurant for dinner, but before that, we need to finish some other business."

"You're eager to be a mated wolf, I take it."

"Hell yeah."

She loved the way he wanted her, as if nothing could please him more. And she wanted him just as much—a new beginning, a return to her lands, and becoming close to her twin sister again.

They rinsed off outside under the shower and then dried off quickly. Then he opened the door, scooped her up, and carried her over the threshold. He paused to shut the door with his hip, and she reached down and locked it. Then he headed for their bedroom.

"Oh heavens, put me down," she said, as he reached the stairs. He just leaned down, kissed her, and carried her up the stairs.

Tanner figured his brothers would ask him how he managed to convince Serena he was the right wolf for her. Loving the she-wolf came easy. Protecting her could be a challenge, but he would always be there for her no matter what.

He set her on the floor before helping her out of her bikini. She reciprocated, pulling off his board shorts. Then he joined her in the bed, cupping her face and kissing her mouth, her hands wrapping around his waist, and pulling him closer. "I've waited for you all my life."

She smiled. "I feel the same for you."

Then they were kissing again, his hands molding to her breasts, feeling her nipples tighten. He rubbed his hard cock against her belly, a way of sharing his scent with her and carrying her scent with him. She was his and he was hers.

"You are one hot wolf," she breathed against his chest before she licked his nipple, sending shivers of pleasure to his core. She pulled gently on his nipple with her lips, then moved to the other. She was breathing harder, her pheromones heating and triggering his own.

"Beautiful," he whispered as he trailed kisses down to her breast and licked one nipple, then tugged gently on it with his mouth, just as she had done to him.

She moaned softly, running her hands over his biceps.

He moved his mouth over her left breast to the right one and licked the nipple, his hand cupping the left, his thumb rubbing the nipple.

He couldn't believe how lucky he was.

He reached between them and began to stroke her, kissing her belly. He rubbed harder, more vigorously. She clutched at his arms, her face tight with concentration. He could see when the climax was about to hit, smell her sexy arousal, loved hearing her cry out with pleasure.

He began to kiss her mouth, and then she reached for his hips, grabbing hold, and pulled him closer.

"Do it," she said.

He slipped his cock into her, and once he was seated fully, he began to thrust. She was hot, wet, and tight, perfect for him. He hoped she felt he was just as perfect for her as she gyrated her hips and he thrust harder.

He paused to kiss her throat, her chin, her mouth, wanting desperately to prolong this. Then he drove his cock in deeply. Striving to make it last, he rubbed against her, but he couldn't hold off any longer and groaned with release.

She thrust her pelvis at him as he finished, then still joined with her, he pulled back enough to coax another climax out of her. She clutched at his hair, tightening, then let go. "Oh. My. God."

He smiled, slipped out of her, and pulled her into his arms. "I love you, Serena."

"I love you right back, you beautiful, *big* wolf."

They were enjoying the afterglow of making love, of being mated wolves, when Serena's phone rang. Thinking Bella was calling, she rolled over to grab her phone off the bedside table and saw it was Harold. Her heartbeat quickened.

"Harold," she whispered, as if she had answered the call already and he could hear her.

"You want me to talk to him, or just hang up?"

She let out her breath. "I could block his calls, but I think it's important to hear what he has to say." She sat up, answered the phone, and put it on speaker.

"When I find you, you'll give me every cent back. Or you're dead."

Then he hung up on her.

CHAPTER 7

Tanner was livid. No one threatened a pack member, let alone his very own mate, and got away with it. Harold might have just been mouthing off about deadly retribution, but Tanner assumed he wasn't. What made it so unbelievable was that Serena had only taken back what was hers.

The wolf had the chance to live, maybe a few thousand dollars poorer, but at least he had his life. Not now. Serena wasn't going to have to worry about looking over her shoulder all the time. Living in a pack, she'd most likely be perfectly safe, but all the bastard would need was one chance to get at her.

"I'm sorry," Serena said.

"Don't be. How much do you want to bet that he would have been just as much of a bastard if you'd taken only a fraction of your own money? You were able to access his accounts and make him feel vulnerable, yet you were gracious enough not to take his money too."

She frowned. "Right. Just like he violated my trust and my privacy by accessing my accounts."

"Correct. But I suspect he doesn't see it that way. He can do it to you, but no one gets away with doing it to him."

She let out her breath. "Okay, so we return to Colorado?"

"No. I suspect if he doesn't learn where we've gone, he'll be waiting at the airport, watching for us. We'll wait for my brothers and cousins to get here and make further plans then."

"He didn't say he was going to kill you also. Do you think he believes I'm alone?"

Tanner pondered that for a moment. "I think you're right. Which would make sense. How would you have found another wolf so quickly when you weren't seeing any and didn't know any in the area? He would have known about it. Everything happened so quickly, he most likely wouldn't suspect you'd be here with a male who would protect you with his life."

"I'm sorry I got you into this."

"This has all worked out for the best. I got you." Tanner grabbed his phone and called Devlyn. "We might have trouble. Harold discovered the money's missing and threatened to kill Serena. We're at a villa in Cayman Brac, and from the sound of it, he thinks she acted alone."

"Damn it. Okay, the guys are on their way. Vaughn and Brock got on a flight flying standby. They'll be in tomorrow morning. Your brothers are still waiting for a flight. Vaughn and Brock will help you put the guy out of his misery if it comes to it."

"Okay, thanks."

"You keep your heads low. Don't take any risks."

"We're going to be here. We're eating at a seafood restaurant, but otherwise, we're staying here." Tanner gave him the location of the villa.

Serena had quickly gotten on her cell phone, and he wondered what she was doing.

Devlyn responded, "All right. I'll let your brothers know what's going on. The other guys are on their flight, and we won't be able to reach them for a few hours. Anything else?"

"No. I'll call you if we learn anything further."

When he ended the call, Serena put her cell down on the bedside table. "Harold doesn't have any reservations for anything. Not for a flight out here either."

"He must know you used his computer to get into his bank accounts. Maybe he remembers you accessed his email for him before."

"Then he changed his email account and made up a new one so any reservations would go to that instead of just changing his password. That way he'd give us a false sense of security if he reserved a flight out here. Now we won't know about it."

"That's a good bet. We won't be able to monitor what he's up to. But he can't monitor us either. Brock and Vaughn are on their way. They should be here by tomorrow. Fisher and Shawn are stuck at the airport. They're still trying to get a flight out."

"Is Devlyn mad about it?"

"Hell yeah. No one threatens his pack members and gets away with it." Tanner pulled her into his arms and they snuggled together.

"I mean, that I got us in this predicament?"

"No, he respects you for what you did. Let's rest for a while, then go to eat."

They fell asleep for a while, then woke to go to the restaurant. Serena so wanted to do this, but she was upset about Harold.

She was trying not to show it, but she worried he might discover she was here and try to kill both Tanner and her. She felt they needed to stay put and just wait for the guys to arrive.

"We're going out to eat," Tanner said, pulling her from the bed. "We'll deal with him if he shows up."

Tanner set up triggers that would reveal if anyone had come into the villa: sand left at the back door so that if anyone entered that way, they'd have to walk through it. Harold couldn't jump far enough to avoid it and if it was disturbed, they'd know. At the front door, he secured a strand of Serena's red hair at the bottom of the door with a little brown sugar and water solution. If anyone opened the door, it would pull loose.

They packed their laptops and her camera in the car and kept all their important documents with them. All they left were their suitcases and clothes, nothing they'd miss if Harold decided to take them.

They were off to the restaurant after that, ordering lobster tails and shrimp, her favorite food. In the islands, they were really fresh and tasty. "I think we need to take turns on guard duty tonight, don't you? Until your cousins get here?" She pulled another piece of lobster meat from its shell and dipped it in lemon butter sauce.

"I think it's a good idea, but we're staying together." He drank from his fruity rum drink.

"In the living room? We could set up the sofa bed."

"That's what we'll do."

"This was the nicest dinner I've ever had, the nicest company too."

He leaned over and kissed her. "It's been great. Ready to go back to the villa?"

"I am." She could tell he was tense too, not enjoying the meal as much as they would have liked. Not when they had to worry about Harold.

Tanner paid the bill and they returned to the villa. But he checked the front door, found her hair was still in place, indicating no one had been through the door, and she checked the back door. The sand hadn't been touched. No smell of Harold or the she-wolf either. They wouldn't have hunter concealment here, so Tanner was confident if they arrived, he'd smell them.

"Looks good. No problems yet, and we might not have any. Let's make up that sofa bed, we need to finish off this day right."

They quickly made the bed and fell into it, tearing off each other's clothes, half dressed and kissing. What a way to end their first day of mated bliss.

Tanner wanted Serena to pull first watch so he didn't have to wake her in the middle of the night. He assumed if Harold found where they were located, he would try to approach them in the middle of the night, figuring they'd be asleep. He had his gun nearby, but when he took out the wolf, he didn't want to show he'd shot the man. Better to have a wolf kill him; no one would be able to explain that.

Serena had shifted to be able to take him on if he showed up. Tanner told her if Harold did, he wanted her to come get him. They had no way of knowing if Harold's mate would take part in a fight or not.

An hour later, he heard Serena growl low. Tanner was out of bed in a flash, shifting, and joining her. He nuzzled her with his cheek against hers. And she turned and licked his face.

Then he heard movement outside the villa. Something moving quietly.

He stayed where he heard the movement while Serena headed to the back door.

The sounds moved away. They waited for a good half hour, then Serena shifted. "We need to see if it was them."

Tanner shifted. "We can't leave the villa. We're safer here. If they break in, we have the advantage. Besides, he won't want to kill you right away, if that was him out there. He'll have to force you to give up your money first. Why don't you try to sleep for now? I'll shift again and keep watch."

"All right. If someone comes again, tell me and I'll shift."

"Believe me, I will. If it is them, he might be regrouping, realizing you're not alone, not when a male wolf has left his scent here also."

"I hadn't thought of that. You're probably right." She shifted again and climbed on the sofa bed.

He smiled at her for shifting back into her wolf form, and while she curled up to sleep, he checked out the whole of the villa inside, listening for any indication someone might be trying to find a way in. He heard the wind and waves, but nothing else. As soon as it was light out, he'd check to see if the wolves had left their scent behind.

As soon as she heard a kitchen window break, Serena was off the sofa bed in a flash, not running for the kitchen as a wolf, but heading in the opposite direction to the front of the villa. She suspected the window was a diversion. She was right. Harold used his lock pick on the front door, but a chain lock prevented him from opening it. He used bolt cutters to cut the lock and then barged inside as a naked human. She lunged for him before he could shift, knowing she couldn't take on the heavier male wolf once he shifted. But Tanner slammed into him first, biting him hard in the arm, forcing him to drop the bolt cutters.

Harold shifted, growled, and struggled to get the aggressive wolf off him, snapping his jaws, unable to get to his feet. He'd made the tactical mistake of entering the house before he shifted, of thinking whoever was with her wasn't as powerful as him. His arrogance could be his downfall. She only hoped.

She was half watching the two wolves fight—though Tanner was winning the battle—and keeping a lookout for Harold's mate in case she tried to come in the back way. Serena couldn't believe Velvet wasn't already here. Maybe she wasn't as alpha as her mate. Then Serena heard something crunching on glass, and she prayed Tanner would take care of Harold quickly, while she raced off to stop Velvet from helping Harold. The gray she-wolf was bigger than Serena, but what the gray had over her in size, Serena had in pure aggressive adrenaline. Like Tanner, she didn't hesitate to take the wolf on. Serena might not have fought with wolves for some time, she imagined neither did this she-wolf. But Serena had killed a couple of real wolves who hadn't liked that she'd crossed their territory. What could she have done? As much as she'd hated to kill the wolves, it was either that or be killed herself.

Thankfully, the two grays hadn't ganged up on her, so she fought one and then the other. So one gray she-wolf wouldn't be an issue.

She still heard growling in the front room when she tore into Velvet. The woman growled just as loudly back, which made Serena even angrier. She hadn't wanted Tanner to hear her fighting with a wolf. He needed to concentrate on his own fight and not worry about her.

The wolf came so close to her throat, Serena nearly panicked. She had to quit thinking about Tanner and concentrate on the menace before her. She lunged forward, snapping her jaws, tearing at the wolf. She didn't want to kill her, but if she left Serena no choice, she would do what she had to do.

She tasted Velvet's blood and the wolf squeaked and dodged away from her. Serena waited to see if the wolf would quit. It was quiet in the other room, and she glanced behind her to see Tanner standing there, panting, watching what the gray she-wolf would do.

A male gray and a smaller red female were too much for the gray she-wolf to handle. She jumped out through the kitchen window and tore off down the beach. She wouldn't report this to the police. She couldn't.

Serena licked her mate's face, and they both shifted. He took her in his arms and hugged her tight.

"Do you think she'll return?" Serena asked.

"She would be crazy to. I'm going to take a swim."

"I'll go with you."

"I'd rather you—"

She raised her brows at him.

He let out his breath. "—go with me and we'll take your ex-roommate swimming."

She thought of them bleeding—Tanner had suffered some bite marks, and the she-wolf had managed to claw Serena—but neither were badly wounded. Harold was bloodied too, and all she could think of was that sharks feed at night and they all would be bleeding in the water.

"There's a boat rental place not far from here. I'll get a boat and we'll take the body out," Tanner said, changing his mind.

"They have to be closed for now."

"Exactly. Will you be all right?"

"Yes. I doubt Velvet will stick around to see what we do next.

While you're gone, I'll be a wolf."

Serena shifted as Tanner left, and it took him so long, she didn't think he'd ever return with the boat. Finally, he returned and brought a fishing net, too, and carried Harold's human body out to the boat.

"You can stay here."

"I'll help you." Wolves helped their mates out, always.

They went out as far as they could, where divers wouldn't be diving to see the coral reefs, and after weighing him down, they heaved Harold into the ocean. Once they were done, Tanner dropped Serena off at the villa beach. He'd been torn between taking her with him just in case Velvet visited again and dropping her at the villa in case he got caught returning the borrowed boat. Serena had worried about the same thing, anxious that the she-wolf might come back. She'd shifted to wait and watch for her.

When Tanner finally returned, they locked the front door, and would call management in the morning about the vandalism to the window and security chain at the door. Which meant they had to keep up the guard watch until then in case Velvet snuck back.

But she didn't.

The next morning, Tanner called Devlyn with an update on what had happened. "We don't need my brothers' help, if they can't get a flight out."

"They got one earlier this morning. They're afraid they'll miss out on a chance to get to know Serena."

Tanner pulled Serena into his arms and said, "It's too late for that, unless they mean in a brotherly way."

Devlyn laughed. "Is this news I can share with the pack?" Serena smiled and nodded.

"It sure is. It's a done deal. Hey, I've got an incoming call. Get back with you in a bit." Tanner took the call from Vaughn. "Are you arriving soon?"

"At the airport on Grand Cayman now. We're boarding the flight for Grand Brac, but we passed a woman—a gray wolf—with bags in hand, headed for a flight leaving for the States. She had light-brown hair and looked just like the picture you sent to us of the two of them when they were at the grocery store."

"Okay, that's Harold's mate, and he's dead."

"Hell, don't tell me we flew all the way out here just to miss out on all the action."

"You can help us celebrate the mating."

And that's just what they did. Tanner's brothers joined them several hours later, and while all of them sat on loungers on the beach, rum drinks in hand, they watched the sunset go down over the aqua waters.

"Next time a new she-wolf shows up, I want to be the one doing the protecting," Brock said, sipping from his rum and cola.

Tanner smiled. "The SEAL wolves always think *they* should get the girl."

Serena snuggled up to Tanner. "Not this time. An Army Ranger won out. Are you ready for bed?"

All the guys looked at Tanner and laughed.

"With the pretty she-wolf of my dreams?" Tanner swept her up in his arms and headed for the house. "You don't *ever* have to ask."

Epilogue

Devlyn didn't trust that Velvet wouldn't try to steal from another wolf, so Brock and Vaughn located her to see what she was up to after she'd left Grand Cayman Island. Ironically, she hadn't married the wolf and he'd never given her access to his accounts, so she was penniless. Which meant all that money was still sitting in a Grand Cayman account. She'd run off with another wolf and was living in Virginia and it seemed that was end of the story for her.

Serena couldn't wait for Bella to have her babies, though Bella hadn't wanted to know their sexes, so Serena was waiting for the babies to be born before she bought anything for them. They got together all the time, whenever Tanner was at work, or when she wasn't working hard to set up her lending library.

She and Tanner had set up housekeeping in her family's home and hoped to have their own children one day, while Heath was building a home behind the clinic. Fisher and Shawn were building a place of their own, though all of the brothers often came over for pizza parties once a week at Serena and Tanner's home. Serena enjoyed being part of a wolf pack again.

"It was way too many years for us to be apart," she told Bella, hugging her lightly, not wanting to squish the babies.

"Every day I can't believe our good fortune to have you home again."

Serena couldn't have been happier to be home with her sister again and to see her as a pack leader with her loving mate.

And Tanner had been the greatest, as if he'd been her red-hot lover for an eternity. She loved him for it.

Tanner was reminded daily that he had stolen the red wolf from his brothers just because he was the eldest. But he knew that no matter how it happened, in the end, he and Serena had been meant to be together.

And no one could have been more right for the vivacious and protective alpha red wolf he would cherish always.

Day of the Wolf

A Heart of the Wolf Novella

Chapter 1

Retired army Special Forces officer and gray wolf Michael Hoffman had stopped at a service station on the way to check out a gray wolf pack in Colorado, run by a Bella and Devlyn Greystoke, when an attractive blond captured his eye. Her hair was swept up in a bun, strands falling loose around the nape of her neck and framing her face. She was wearing skintight black jeans, a soft, light-blue sweater, and black suede boots on this cool, fall day, but what really caught his attention was her sweet scent. She was a wolf. And he thought he recognized her and her scent. If so, it had been a long damn time since he'd seen her, and it had to have been a really brief encounter, because he didn't remember having really talked to her at all.

Michael had served all over the world providing foreign internal defenses, special reconnaissance, counterterrorism, and yeah, unconventional warfare when the mission required it. Running into she-wolves he was attracted to rarely happened. Mostly because they just weren't where he was at the time or were ineligible—mated, too old, or too young. He wondered if she was part of a pack here. Hell, maybe *she* was mated. Before he could ask her if she belonged to a pack locally—since he was here now and might as well check it out—she got into her car and drove off in a hurry.

Thinking he could follow her and still learn if she was part of a local pack in this part of Colorado, he finished gassing up when he saw three men jump into a black pickup, yelling to each other that they had to catch the woman. The driver gunned the engine, and they tore off after her. Michael could be wrong, but he sure thought it looked like trouble was headed the she-wolf's way. After replacing the gas nozzle on the pump, Michael jumped into his Jeep and slammed his foot on the gas pedal in hot pursuit, ready to provide some Green Beret muscle if the little lady needed it.

Retired army officer and red wolf Carmela Wildhaven couldn't believe a stop at the service station outside of her pack's territory on the way to her home from the airport could potentially prove to be dangerous. She'd headed toward the store to buy a bottled water when she saw three male wolves near the glass door inside whom she thought she recognized. A chill ran up her spine just thinking about them. She'd hoped they hadn't seen her before she high-tailed it out of there.

She couldn't believe the former army sergeants were here, so close to the Silver Town wolf pack's territory. Unless they were from here originally. She sure hoped not.

She didn't regret that she'd sat on the board that had eliminated them from the service for smoking pot in a government van while in uniform and on post, right before she'd retired from the army. The looks they had given her when they left the hearing warned her that they'd pay her back, because as a wolf, she should have been voting in their favor to allow them to stay on active duty. But she really hadn't thought she'd ever see them again.

If they had just been given an official reprimand that had stayed in their records but they had faced no other consequences, she could see them pulling something like that again or worse. Then what would happen? They'd be incarcerated? As wolves? Not good. Besides, she hadn't been the only one who had voted them out of the service—all the combat officers and the noncommissioned officers on the board had too.

She'd quickly turned around and climbed into her car. She'd hoped she'd managed to leave before they saw her. She drove out of there as fast as she could without running over anyone or hitting another vehicle and headed toward home again, realizing if they hadn't seen her, they might still smell her scent in the area. Why were they here? That was what bothered her the most. She hoped they hadn't been trying to track her down, but it seemed to be too much of a coincidence that they were here.

She'd just returned from Germany where she'd participated in a crossbow competition that she nearly won, but she'd just missed out, and her bags were still in the car. Her crossbow and quiver of arrows also. Unfortunately, she'd lost her phone somewhere between the States and Germany. She had no idea when or where she'd lost it because her cell phone had died and she couldn't use it until she had a chance to charge it. She'd wondered if someone had stolen it from her or if she'd left it behind somewhere. She really could use it now to call the sheriff for help.

She glanced at her rearview mirror and saw a black pickup truck following her some distance behind. If she could just reach her turnoff a couple of miles ahead and drive for three more miles, she'd be in the Silver Town wolf pack's territory.

A couple of weeks ago, she'd joined them and started her job as the receptionist at the clinic that served the pack before she had to leave for Germany. Thankfully, Darien and Lelandi Silver, the pack leaders, had been fine with her taking off right after she had been hired on. They'd been impressed with all her wins in archery competitions, and they'd even set up an archery range so she could teach anyone who wanted to learn how to use a crossbow and so that she could continue to practice her skill and win more competitions.

She sure hoped the wolves from the army *weren't* members of the Silver Town wolf pack and she just hadn't met them yet. She wasn't even sure how the pack leaders would handle that, since she was new to the pack and they might have been with the pack much earlier on, so who would they side with?

She glanced up at her rearview mirror again and saw the black pickup was now barreling down the highway, speeding, growing closer. It might not be the men from the army. It could be someone else who was driving recklessly and not trying to chase her down.

Not that she really believed that. Her blood chilled, and she tightened her hands on her steering wheel.

She was speeding on the two-lane road, but they were still catching up to her, hell-bent on reaching her, intimidating her, or, if she was lucky, just planned to pass her.

She thought of turning around and going back to the service station. She didn't see anywhere to pull off and turn the car around though. Maybe she could slow down and let them pass if that was their intent, but they were driving so fast, she was afraid they might hit her car anyway.

They were so close now, they were practically on her bumper. Angry and frustrated, she could do nothing about it. They nudged her car, once, and then twice. The last time, they backed off a bit, and she thought maybe they were going to give it up. But then they sped up again. Only this time, they struck her car hard. A loud bang resounded, of metal on metal. Her heart practically seized. The road curved, but she couldn't make the turn. At the high rate of speed she was going, the car flew off the road. It landed hard on the ground, the sound of explosions filling the air. She realized all four of her tires had blown.

The car traveled through branches and fall leaves, slowing it down some. She hit the brakes, trying to stop from hitting the huge, oak tree in her path. The car still slammed into the tree, jolting her hard. Her airbag instantly inflated and deflated. She was glad she always wore her seat belt. She felt okay, a little sore, but nothing that would slow her down. She could stay in the car and hopefully remain protected. She glanced out the back window while struggling to unfasten her seat belt. Stay calm, she told herself.

The driver had parked the truck on the road, and all three of the men were exiting their vehicle. It was them. The three sergeants, all rogue wolves. One of the men had a tire iron in his hand. They meant business.

She was afraid her car wouldn't protect her.

The seat belt released, and she threw open the driver's door, grabbed her crossbow and her quiver of arrows, and jumped out of her car. Panicked, she stumbled on a couple of tree roots, regained her footing, and ran in the direction that would take her to her pack's territory and hopefully safety.

She glanced back and saw the men were stripping off their clothes. God, they were going to run as wolves, and she couldn't outrun them as a human. She wouldn't have enough time to take down all three men with her bow either. As a wolf, she could move faster, but fighting three male wolves? She wouldn't stand a chance.

Michael saw the pickup slam into the red Ford Escort, sending it flying off the road. His heart practically stopped. He'd kill the men with his bare hands. Or better yet, his teeth. He jerked his Jeep to a stop behind the pickup and saw the woman disappear into the woods. The way she was sprinting indicated she hadn't been injured badly in the crash. But a pack of three male wolves were chasing her, their clothes scattered in a couple of piles on top of the leaves, and a tire iron was lying nearby. From the way her car had slammed into the tree, he could see the vehicle was totaled. He was glad she didn't appear to be injured.

He had to remind himself that she could be the one in the wrong. What if she'd killed one of their family members? And they were intent on eliminating a rogue wolf?

Wolves had to take care of their own. He was well aware of that. They couldn't go to prison regardless of the crime committed, because during the full moon, the man might shift into a wolf, and that would cause a world of trouble. He jumped out of his Jeep, raced down the incline, and stripped off his clothes. He couldn't reach the wolves while running as a human, and he stood a better chance fighting them wolf-to-wolf. Not a really great chance. They were all big males and would give him a run for his money.

Even if she had wronged someone, he wanted to know the details before he let them take the matter into their own hands. She was still running as a human, and she'd never outrun the wolves before they caught up to her.

Maybe he could distract them long enough so she could get away.

He stopped and howled, telling her to keep running and he'd take care of these wolves, hoping his howl would delay them too. They all stopped. The three male wolves turned to see who was following them. The woman was standing slack-jawed not that far ahead of them. Michael bared his teeth at his prey. He was taking the wolves on, *even* if the woman was in the wrong. They could sort it out later.

Armed with her crossbow, Carmela still couldn't believe the three male wolves had found her and were chasing after her. Once they'd wrecked her car, she'd run about a half a mile through the woods from there, hoping she'd find help. No such luck. She really, really didn't want to shoot them, but she didn't think they had any intention of just airing their griefs with her or they wouldn't have wrecked her car and come after her. Not after they had cast her growly looks, threatening her they'd pay her back at the end of the hearing.

Now, there was a new male wolf on the scene, aggressive, baring his canines at the three males that he'd brought to a stop with his howl. She prayed if anyone was in the area, they might hear the mystery wolf's howl and come to investigate what he was doing here.

He barked at her, telling her in no uncertain terms to get the hell out of there.

But if he was there to serve as her hero—maybe he was with the Silver Town wolf pack and she just had never seen him before—she wasn't leaving him to fight these wolves on his own. He might be big and tough, growly and capable, but there were still three of them he had to fight.

She considered stripping and shifting, but she was a female and a red wolf, which made her a smaller wolf, and there wasn't any way she could successfully win against any of the males. Her crossbow gave her the only chance she had. She nocked an arrow and aimed at one of the wolves, the biggest one, who was in the middle of the three, the one she thought was the leader of the pack, and she'd thought he was the leader when they went before the army board. He had a darker, more mottled coat of blacks and grays, a little bit of beige, and a white belly. One of the gray wolves was gray and white and the other pure black. She didn't think she had anything to worry about with the wolf challenging the others, his saddle reddish, his back gray, his belly blond, and his mask reddish.

The leader bared his teeth at the lone wolf, but the leader didn't race in to attack the other wolf. She was surprised he wouldn't, because the lone male wouldn't be much of a contest for three males in their prime. Still, she was certain they wouldn't want to be injured either if the wolf could do some real damage.

She hoped she could even the odds somewhat.

Then the lone wolf circled around in her direction, the whole time watching the other wolves for any sign of aggression on their part, his jaw set, his eyes narrowed at them. She assumed he was trying to reach her before the other wolves attacked, attempting to provide better protection for her instead of trying to draw them away from her, because she wasn't leaving. She was surprised he'd risk taking her side in this if he didn't belong to the Silver Town wolf pack.

He lifted his chin, and she knew he was going to howl. For help this time? For his Silver pack mates? She so hoped he was one of them, but his call earlier hadn't brought anyone else to their aid. She was afraid no one was close enough to hear his howls.

Before he could get much more than the start of a howl, the leader of the pack raced forward to stop him. The other two ran forth to aid their leader, and she aimed her bow and shot the leader, aiming for his chest, but he ducked, something a regular wolf wouldn't have done, but a wary human would, and her arrow sailed over his back. He was moving so fast, she quickly nocked another arrow and nailed him in the hip this time. It wasn't in her nature to kill a wolf. A *lupus garou*. She wanted to disable him and let the pack handle it. But she wasn't going to allow the wolves to kill the lone wolf who was standing by her side. She had hoped that would stop the aggressor wolf and the others would turn tail and run back to their truck.

The leader stumbled but then kept moving toward the lone wolf as if her arrow was doing nothing to slow him down, and the other two wolves were nearly upon them. She didn't have time to nock another arrow. She lifted her chin and howled as a human. Her howl would carry some distance, though in the woods, it wouldn't travel as far as she'd like. Maybe she could alert her pack members, if any were in the area, to come save them.

The lone wolf tore into one of the other wolves. The leader collapsed before he reached her, the arrow finally having an effect, and the other wolf came at her before she could nock another arrow. She slammed her bow against the wolf's head as he lunged at her, his teeth bared, and she smelled onion on his breath as he tried to bite her.

CHAPTER 2

MICHAEL WAS TRYING TO kill the black wolf so he could tear into the other wolf next and protect the woman, a red wolf. He really thought he recognized her now that he saw her up close. From the army? A brief encounter when he was at Fort Sam Houston but leaving for his next assignment? He hoped she wasn't in the wrong, but he couldn't help himself when a woman was in need of a hero.

That was only *if* he could protect her! She was fighting the wolf with her crossbow and trying to nail him with an arrow in her other hand. The wolf was dodging her efforts, growling and snarling and snapping. Michael had done a lot of damage to the black wolf he was fighting, but the wolf was just as big as him, and the black wolf had bitten him in several places too.

He and the other wolf were snarling and growling and biting, but then the gray wolf lunged at the woman, and she tripped and fell over some exposed tree roots. Michael had to leave his flank open to the black wolf so he could attack the gray wolf before he killed the woman.

The black wolf took advantage of Michael's maneuver and jumped at his flank. Michael was afraid he'd made the worst mistake of his life, but he had to stop the gray wolf. Michael managed to tackle the gray wolf, forcing him to the ground and stopping him from hurting the woman. She was on her feet in an instant, and with both wolves tearing into Michael, he noticed she was able to nock another arrow.

She aimed and shot the gray-colored wolf. The wolf was in such a rage, the arrow didn't appear to be slowing him down. Michael bit into the black wolf again, and this time, he managed to grab him by the back of the neck, bit down hard, and killed him.

She fired another arrow, and it just missed Michael's ear. He turned to see the gray wolf lunging at him. The arrow went winging by Michael and hit the last aggressor wolf. Another arrow and then another flew past Michael until the gray wolf was wearing four arrows, and he sank to the ground, unable to fight any further.

His own injuries bad, Michael was unable to stand any longer, and he collapsed on the leaf-littered ground.

The woman ran to him and yanked off her jacket and pressed it against one of his wounds. "Live, brave wolf, so that you can be a hero another day." She pressed a kiss on his cheek, and he noticed then she was bleeding too, both of her arms, where the gray wolf had bitten and clawed at her when she fended him off with her crossbow and arrow.

She sat on the forest floor, lifted Michael's head onto her lap, and stroked his head. "*Don't* die on me."

He wanted to know her name. When he'd seen her so many years ago, the way she was standing, he hadn't been able to see her name tag on her uniform.

He wanted to ask if she was part of a local pack. He wanted to join that pack, and he wanted her to date only him. Because she thought he was her hero. Though she hadn't said he was *her* hero. And she had been the one to take down two of the wolves with her arrows.

He let out his breath. He had to get up and take her back to his Jeep to get help for them. But the longer he lay there, the weaker he felt. Damn it. Heroes continued to be heroic. They didn't collapse in a bloody heap while the heroine ministered to them.

He tried to get up again, but his body wouldn't listen to his brain.

"No, lie down." She lifted her chin and howled again. But then, as if afraid her howls weren't going far enough, she rested his head on the forest floor. "I'm Carmela Wildhaven, by the way." Then she began to strip off her clothes. Wolves did that in front of other wolves all the time when they went running as wolves, so it was no big deal. Normally. Unless the wolf was a she-wolf and not known to the male wolf. Was she an eligible wolf? As in not mated to another wolf? He glanced at the other wolves. The two had turned into their human forms. It appeared they had expired. Good, fewer to have to deal with in the future, except for disposing of the bodies. Michael tried to look around further for the alpha wolf. He was gone. Hell. Maybe the rogue wolf had crawled off and died in the woods. Michael could only hope.

They needed to do something with the remaining bodies as soon as they could and search for the other wolf also. As if Michael could do anything right now. He sure hoped she wasn't a rogue wolf. And he hoped she was a member of a pack nearby that could help them out.

She pulled off her black lace panties and bra last, and all he could think of was how exquisite she looked. Beautiful creamy breasts that had him staring a bit. She smiled a little at him. "You are looking a lot less heroic and perfectly wolfish now."

He managed a small smile back, and then she shifted into a beautiful cinnamon-colored red wolf. She licked his cheek, and then she howled. And howled. And howled.

Her wolf's song was the most beautiful voice he'd ever heard. For the moment, she was all his. Unless a pack full of hungry bachelor males came to rescue her, and then he was history.

She howled again. And this time, he managed to lift his head and rolled over on his belly. He howled to join her wolf's song, and he thought they had the most beautiful symphony in the world, right before he heard a responding howl. And another. And then several more. He felt guarded relief.

The wolves were coming. And he knew they would take his place as her hero when they took care of her injuries.

Carmela was thrilled that so many of the Silver Town male pack members showed up to aid them, some in their wolf coats and some as humans armed with guns. The pack's veterinarian, Doc Mitchell, was with them, carrying a bag of medical supplies. He quickly applied a field dressing to the male wolf's wounds. Then Doc Mitchell did the same thing for her wounds. She thought she could run as a wolf back to the vehicles they must have parked on the road near where her car had left the pavement. But some of the men brought a field stretcher for both the injured wolf and her. Doc Mitchell kept trying to rouse the man.

Jake Silver, subleader of the pack and brother to the pack leader, Darien, jogged through the woods to join them.

"Can you hear me?" Doc Mitchell asked the injured wolf over and over again.

Several men were also taking care of the two rogue wolves' bodies, for which she was grateful. She'd been glad that she was one of the members of the Silver Town wolf pack, because everyone was so helpful in a crisis. They seemed to genuinely care about the injured man and were worried that he wouldn't make it. Though their kind healed faster than humans, they could still die if they lost too much blood before their enhanced genetics could kick in and heal them.

They'd covered Carmela and Michael each with blankets. She shifted so she could talk to the injured wolf as Jake and his younger triplet brother, Tom, carried her stretcher. She needed to tell the men about the wounded rogue wolf that had vanished also. And she belatedly realized she needed to tell them this one was a good guy. "He saved my life," she said.

On the other stretcher, the wolf shifted, and for a moment, she stared at him, worried he'd died and that was why he'd shifted. His eyes were still closed, and she wasn't close enough to hear his heart beating.

"Stop! He's shifted," she called out, her eyes filled with tears.

Doc Mitchell checked on the injured wolf. "He's breathing, and his heart's beating. He's fine. Keep moving, Peter and Trevor." Doc Mitchell winked at her with a small smile lifting the corners of his mouth.

But she couldn't relax. Not when she knew the wolf was in such bad shape.

"What happened?" Jake finally asked her.

"Those men ran their pickup truck into my car, causing me to leave the road and crash it into a tree. Then I ran, and they stripped, shifted, and tore after me. Thankfully, I'd had the presence of mind to take my crossbow with me."

Jake said, "There wasn't a pickup on the road. Just a Jeep and your car off the road."

Carmela closed her eyes in exasperation. "The leader got away then? I shot him in the hip. Or…or maybe someone stole the truck sitting on the road? I was hoping he might have crawled off and died somewhere else."

Jake called out to some of the other men, "Search the woods for an injured wolf."

"I helped eliminate him and the other sergeants from the army. The one that got away was the alpha, the leader of the pack. His name is Raymond Hayworth. Anyway, the lone wolf came out of nowhere. He wasn't with the other wolves, but he had been intent on protecting me. I thought maybe he was a member of the Silver Town wolf pack but I hadn't met him before."

Jake glanced back at the wolf. "He's not one of ours. I don't know him."

Tom agreed. Everyone with them said the same.

"I—I saw him once. At Fort Sam Houston, but I didn't get a chance to meet him. He was in a hurry to get somewhere, but I smelled his wolf scent."

"So he was in the military like you? Or a civilian?" Jake asked.

"He's a Green Beret."

Jake glanced at the injured man. She could tell he was impressed. *She* was impressed.

"One wolf facing three wolves, it figures," Jake said, shaking his head.

"Two of us, not just him!" Carmela said.

Jake smiled at her. "Hell, yeah, here I thought you were kind of a sweet beta and had a cool hobby of shooting a crossbow in competitions. I didn't know you were so badass."

She never considered herself that way. Sweet when she wanted something. Beta? No way. And her crossbow had been her life since she was little. Even while she was in the army.

"This wolf could be real trouble," Jake said, "with the kind of training he has if he's a problem wolf."

He wasn't trouble. He was her hero. She loved being with the pack. Loved the warm and welcoming Silver Town wolves. But if they kicked her savior out of here, she had half a mind to go with him. Not that he'd even want her to tag along. But what if he had a great pack? And he was interested in a little courtship on the side? If he wasn't mated.

"I recognize one of the dead men," Tom said. "He was questioning Bertha Hastings at her bed and breakfast about whether you were a member of the pack or not. By then, you had already left for Germany to compete in the crossbow competition. She said you were living here, and he asked where your place was exactly, that he was a cousin and wanted to see you. She called me, and I came over to see what was up. He smelled like a gray wolf though, not a red."

"I don't have any close cousins that I know of. And none that are gray wolves," Carmela said.

"We didn't know that," Jake said. "We need to know who else might have a vendetta against you because of your army background."

"No one. At least no one who is a wolf. Those men were the only three I had encountered who were wolves and had done something illegal while serving in the military."

They finally reached the road and found a bunch of piles of clothes, the lone wolf's fiery-red Jeep, and her poor smashed car. She wanted to cry. She'd saved up for two years to buy it. Her first new car. She'd bought used cars over the years. But missing was the black pickup truck. "The black pickup isn't here," Carmela said, disappointed. Though she recalled them saying it was gone, she had to see it for herself. She'd so hoped the wolf had crawled off and died. "They were parked right there."

"The truck left skid marks," Jake said.

"The injured wolf's name is Michael Hoffman," Mason, the bank president, said, holding up a wallet and driver's license. He pulled out another plastic card from the wallet, and she could see it was Michael's military ID. "Retired lieutenant colonel, U.S. Army."

They lived so many years but aged so slowly, he looked like he was a really young LTC, maybe thirty in human years. Of course, she looked like that too. "And a Green Beret," she said, wanting *everyone* in the pack to know that he was.

And then she was helped into Jake's SUV, the blanket still wrapped around her. One of the men set her clothes, crossbow, and quiver of arrows on the seat beside her. She thought of getting dressed, but she knew they'd just make her strip when she got to the clinic and start her on an IV to fight infection from the wolf bites and claw marks.

They carried Michael into another vehicle, and she wished she could be with him instead as Jake and Tom drove her to the clinic.

Once she was in a hospital bed at the clinic, her arms freshly bandaged and an IV dripping antibiotics into her veins, a concerned nurse checked her vital signs again. Nurse Charlotte Grey was a middle-aged woman, smiling at her, but the worried look in her expression told Carmela that things were not good. Carmela was anxious then that the wolves they killed were some of the Silver Town wolf pack's. No one had said anything about it, and she'd been so concerned about Michael, she hadn't even thought to ask. Then again, Tom said that the one wolf had been trying to locate her, so they couldn't be part of the pack.

Maybe Michael was in distress and he wouldn't pull through. That made her sick to her stomach. "How is Michael doing?"

"He'll live," Nurse Grey said, smiling. "Can I see him?"

"Not yet. He's in surgery." That didn't sound good.

"How come he came upon the scene so quickly? Did it seem a little…convenient?" Nurse Grey asked.

Carmela frowned at her. She understood the wolves in the pack had to be wary of other wolves coming into their territory and causing trouble for them, but she knew Michael was one of the good guys. "He was heroic. I owe him my life. I was just lucky he was there, so close at hand."

"It's a good thing that you compete in crossbow target shooting competitions and have won several national and local championships," Nurse Grey said. "I imagine, after how you handled yourself, you'll find more of our pack members wanting to take lessons from you on how to use a crossbow."

"I've never used it as a weapon before." Which made Carmela think of how she'd abused the bow and an arrow while trying to beat off the one wolf who had been too close to her to shoot. Not that she'd had any other choice.

Carmela glanced at the doorway and realized she had an audience. A dark-haired man with amber eyes, wearing a badge, jeans, and a tan shirt, was standing there taking down notes. *Sheriff Peter Jorgenson.*

"Do you mind if I ask you a few questions?" Peter asked. Hadn't he already overheard enough? Not only that, but he'd helped carry Michael's stretcher, and she told him what happened to them then too.

She explained everything to him again. She sighed. She owed it to Michael to help him out in any way that she could. He might need some time to recover, though she suspected many members of the pack would be offering him assistance after he had helped to save her life. While she'd been in the army, she could never "be" with wolves in a pack, so that was her goal once she'd retired. She'd actually been on her way to check out a pack near Denver, the pack leaders Devlyn and Bella Greystoke, when she'd gotten a flat tire and some wolves of the pack of Silver Town had fixed it, free of charge. She'd learned then that the Silver pack ran the town, and they needed a receptionist. Not to mention the pack leader, Lelandi, was a red wolf like her. They'd even found they were related, distant cousins, and that had been great news. She was eager to get to know Lelandi better. She was surprised to learn that their families had begun in Colorado, but hers had ended up in Texas, and they had lost contact with the earlier families. Carmela had even had several dates with some of the bachelor males in the short time she'd been here, but she was trying to date a wolf only once to leave her options open. And she wanted to make sure she truly loved being here with the pack before she set down permanent roots.

Then she heard someone being wheeled into the room down the hall, and she thought it must be Michael.

"Can I see him? Michael?"

CHAPTER 3

Michael felt like hell, like when he'd been wounded in a firefight on a combat mission. Though having a bullet rip through him was a lot different than having a wolf chewing on him. He was all bandaged up and hooked up to an IV while being transferred to another bed in one of the clinic rooms.

One of the wolves who had helped load him into a vehicle to bring him here, Jake Silver, subleader of the wolf pack, said, "Darien and Lelandi Silver run the pack, and I am sure they'll be delighted to meet you after you helped to save one of our own wolves."

Then a man joined them who was wearing a sheriff 's badge. "Sheriff Peter Jorgenson," he said, reaching over to shake Michael's hand. "We have a ton of folks offering to put you up once you can leave the clinic. Bertha Hastings's Bed and Breakfast will even accommodate you for free until you can get on your feet."

"What about the huntress?"

Peter frowned a little. "I'm not sure about you staying at Carmela's place."

"No, I mean, how's she doing? I saw the bite marks on her arms."

"She'll be fine. She's being taken care of at the clinic also," Jake said.

"What...what about the men?" Michael asked, still not knowing if they had been part of the pack or not.

"We're looking into it," Peter said. "We have two of them in the morgue for now. We brought your Jeep in and impounded it, just to protect it until you can leave the clinic. Carmela's car was totaled. We're taking care of it also."

"Wait, what about the other man? The leader of the three? He was wearing one of Carmela's arrows too."

"No sign of him. The guy's name is Raymond Hayworth. He must have made it back to the truck and left. The truck was gone. We found the clothes of the other two men and their IDs. No sign of Raymond's clothes. According to Carmela, they'd been in the army. She had been on an army board that gave them other than honorable discharges, and they'd threatened her for not voting in their favor, so we're certain they were after her for that reason. What we need to know is how you happened to arrive in time to help Carmela," Peter said.

Michael was wondering when they were going to question him about that. He would be a mystery to them. Except he was certain they would have found his ID and could check into his background.

"I saw Carmela at the service station near there. I was going to ask her if there was a wolf pack in the area that she belonged to that I could check out. I'm looking to settle down with a pack since I retired from the army. She was headed for the store, but she suddenly whipped around, got in her car, and tore off as if she saw some kind of trouble headed her way. The three men came rushing out of the store, said they had to catch her, jumped into their new model black pickup, and took off after her. I didn't realize they were wolves at first. I couldn't smell their scent, the way the breeze was blowing. I followed, concerned that she must have known them—which was the reason for her quick turnaround—and that they were hassling her. A few miles down the road, I saw them hit her car, and it sailed off the road. I pulled in behind them, saw they were shifting and racing after her. That's when I knew they were wolves. My only thought was to help protect her. That was my job."

"You did a good job," Peter said. "You saved her life. Now we need to know if the injured wolf survived his injury and if he belongs to a pack. Carmela is new to our pack, if you didn't know."

Now it sounded like the sheriff thought she might be trouble and had brought this trouble to their pack. Michael could understand their concern. If the rogue wolves had family, friends, other pack members, any one of them could want revenge.

Then he heard footfalls and saw Nurse Grey poke her head into the room. "Do you mind having a visitor? Carmela Wildhaven would like to visit with you for a little while if you're feeling up to it."

His whole outlook brightened. "Yeah, sure."

Carmela came into the room then, and he was so glad to see her alive and well. Her arms were bandaged, and she was attached to an IV like he was. She was wearing a hospital gown featuring gray wolves on a snowy background like his also, except she was wearing a pair of matching pants too. Jake pulled a chair over for her so she could sit closer to the bed.

When Carmela was seated, another woman entered the room without invitation. Everyone looked to see what she had to say, and Michael assumed she was a pack leader. "I'm Lelandi Silver, and my mate, Darien, and I run the pack.

We want to personally thank you for saving our brand-new member, Carmela, from the wolves. She happens to be my distant cousin also."

That could be good news for him if it gave him an in to join the pack, or bad news if they wanted her to mate someone who was more important in the pack already. Though Carmela could already be interested in someone, he reminded himself.

"Do you need me for anything else?" Peter asked Lelandi. Lelandi patted his shoulder. "Not here. Keep trying to find out what you can about the three men. We need to learn where the other wolf got off to and discover if we're going to have any more trouble for the pack."

"I will." Peter left the room then.

"When you have a chance, you can decide where you want to stay, Michael, until you're all healed up," Lelandi said. "Of course, Darien and I would love to have you stay with us."

Michael glanced at Carmela, and she blushed. He smiled. Yeah, she was the one he'd like to stay with. He thought she must not be mated or some male wolf would have been coddling her about now. "I'd like that, Lelandi, thank you." He might not be able to stay with Carmela, but he had the notion he'd visit with the pack for now, get to know the leaders better, and see if he could help learn what he could about the missing, injured, male wolf. Of course, he was all for providing protection for Carmela if they'd let him. And maybe he would remain with the pack if it looked like a good place to be.

Lelandi said, "Okay, good. Doc Weber said he would release you in a couple of days, depending on how fast you heal. Your dressings will still need to be changed, and we have to make sure you don't have any infections and fever resulting from the bite wounds too. Carmela, Doc said you could leave tomorrow, as long as you're not having any fever."

"Okay, great," Carmela said.

"I'll check in on you later." Then Lelandi took Jake's arm and led him out of the room.

Carmela thought Michael was a handsome wolf, his hair dark brown and army-regulation cut. He had a chiseled face, vivid blue eyes, a nice, warm smile, but his skin was pale, and he wore several bandages on his arms. Thankfully, the wolves had missed tearing at his legs. She hated to think how injured he was under the gown.

"Hey, Michael." She took his hand and held it. "Thank you for saving me."

"I should be thanking you."

"Without you, I couldn't have done it. But I agree. We did it together. I remember seeing you briefly at Fort Sam Houston. You were leaving when I was arriving." She remembered thinking he was hot for a human. Her interest had been piqued when she saw he was Special Forces and even more so when she'd realized he was a wolf. She hadn't seen him in wolf form before, and she'd never seen him again, so her memory of his scent had faded over the years. "Yeah. I couldn't believe you were a wolf, but I had to catch a flight out of there to my next assignment at Fort Sill, Oklahoma. Man, I thought about you the whole way there, wishing I'd at least known your name."

She smiled. "You were a captain then. Congratulations on making LTC."

"Thanks. You were a captain too. Did you stay in?" he asked. "Yeah, and I retired at the same rank as you."

He smiled. "Congratulations are in order for you too."

"Thanks. So do you plan to stay with the pack for a while?"

"I'm looking for a pack to join, actually."

She brightened. "Oh, well, good. I did the same thing when I was retired and wanted to check out another pack in Colorado, then had a flat tire near here, and…" She shrugged. "I found this pack, and they were so helpful and welcoming, I just stayed." She explained the business about the men, her car, and why she was armed with a bow.

"That's great on the crossbow competitions. As to the man who got away, you're going to need some extra protection," Michael said. "Since the guy came after you and you physically injured him, I suspect he'll be coming after you again."

"Are…you offering to protect me? You need further medical

attention." She knew he was interested in courting her then. Not that she was surprised. There was a shortage of eligible she-wolves in the pack, and she was very eligible. They also had a common background with the military.

"Yeah, I'm combat-trained and tested."

"You did great out there against the two wolves. Thanks for giving me a chance to run off, but I didn't believe you'd be able to manage that many wolves at one time. I suspect Peter will have someone watching over me."

"He can be the outside guy." She chuckled. "*You* are injured."

"Believe me, if any rogue wolf tries to get into your house, I'll be there to take him down."

"I believe it. So you're applying for the inside protection."

"Yeah."

"I have to warn you my house isn't all the way set up. I just moved here. I'm a little way out in the woods so I can run as a wolf when I like. I've got the kitchen set up, but I still have a lot of boxes I haven't unpacked yet. I haven't hung up any pictures or made the bed up in the guestroom."

"I can help. I'm not an idle kind of guy."

She tilted her chin down. "*You* are injured," she reminded him.

"I heal fast."

She sighed. It wasn't that she didn't want him in her house. She would love to help him recover. And she would enjoy the company if her house wasn't such a mess. She didn't want him overdoing it if he chose to help her unpack a bit. She assumed he'd be doing way too much to prove to her he was all macho and he could handle a few bites.

Still, she got on her phone and called Peter. "I assume you're going to have someone watching my house when I'm there."

"Yeah, and someone will be following you around wherever you need to go to make sure you stay safe."

"I have a bodyguard staying at my house when he's able to," she told Peter, watching Michael smile to hear her words. Even if he couldn't do much to protect her, she thought he would get better sooner if he was at her place, getting some tender loving care.

"Don't tell me you mean the Green Beret," Peter said. "Yeah."

"He's wounded."

As if she didn't know that. "Yeah, but he's a Green Beret." She smiled at Michael. "I'll help change his bandages for him."

"You know this is going to cause quite a stir," Peter said. "You mean I might lose my job?"

Peter laughed. "No. Just that if you begin courting him… Well, you know what I mean. And actually, this will help save us on guard duty. We were going to have to put someone on guard duty for him also. Deputy Sheriff Trevor Osgood will be watching over you on the first shift. A bunch of us will be taking turns—on outside duty, wishing we were on inside duty with you."

She chuckled. "Okay, thanks." They ended the call.

"Is it going to be a problem for me to stay with you?" Michael asked.

"Nope. Would you mind if I stay in here with you overnight?"

"No, I'd be glad for the company."

"Okay, good. You just stay there. I'll be right back." As if she really thought he was going anywhere. She left the room and got hold of Nurse Grey. "Is it okay if I move to a bed in Michael's room?"

Nurse Grey gave an exaggerated sigh. "You do know that many of our bachelor males were hopeful they had a chance with you."

Carmela smiled. "They may still have a chance."

"Somehow, I don't think so. And yes, you can move into his room. Your clothes and crossbow and arrows are in the closet in your room. Oh, and don't worry about your job. Lelandi said you have two weeks to heal up. If you want to return to work sooner, that's fine, but there's no need to. I overheard that Michael is going to be staying at your place. He might need your care for longer, so you'll be all set."

"Okay, thanks. I'll grab my stuff and move then." Feeling better about this business as far as Michael staying with her, considering how badly he'd been hurt because of her issues when he hadn't had anything to do with it, Carmela saw Tom was serving on guard duty here at the clinic. This was a decided advantage of living with a pack. Not that she'd ever thought she'd really have this kind of trouble.

She soon joined Michael and put her clothes in the closet in there. She set her bow and arrows under her bed, then climbed under the covers of her bed.

Michael was watching her. "Do you think we'll have some trouble here?"

"No. But you know it's always a good idea to be prepared, just in case. Tom Silver is serving on guard duty for now. And if you didn't hear what I was talking to Nurse Grey about, she said I've got a couple of weeks off from work. So once you feel better, you can help me hang pictures."

"I can certainly do that." He closed his eyes then, and she knew he needed to sleep.

She hoped her being in his room made him feel more comfortable. He wouldn't be worrying about her being down the hall if they did have any trouble. Not that she expected him to leap out of bed to protect her. She was doing all the leaping to protect him if it came to it.

Chapter 4

The black wolf bit at Michael, and the other wolf came in for the attack. Michael groaned and woke himself from the nightmare he was having of fighting a couple of wolves and doing his best not to lose the battle. He glanced around the room and realized he was lying in the clinic bed. He remembered he'd been injured in a fight with the two wolves and was recovering from his injuries. He looked at the bed nearby where Carmela was sound asleep. He was glad she was here with him. He didn't know what kind of shape he'd be in if he had to leave the bed to protect her, but he'd have done it. It appeared they hadn't had any trouble during the night. A nurse had come in to check on them some hours earlier. Other than that, Michael had slept fairly well.

Michael studied Carmela further and frowned. Her face appeared flushed. He was feeling better, but he was concerned she was running a fever. He pushed the call button to get the nurse's attention.

Nurse Grey was back on duty, and she hurried to see him. "Yes, are you okay?"

"Yeah, but Carmela looks awfully flushed."

Nurse Grey brought out a thermometer and checked Carmela's temperature. "Okay, thanks, Michael. She's running a fever."

Carmela opened her pretty green eyes and groaned. "Don't tell me I've got an infection from that bastard wolf's bites."

"It appears that way. We'll give you some stronger antibiotics until your body can deal with this. It's Doctor Weber's call, but I'd say you'll be staying with us another day."

When Carmela and Michael were finally released from the clinic the following day, she was glad she could go home and take Michael with her. Thankfully, he hadn't incurred an infection, but since she had, they both were planning on taking it easy at her house. He had his Jeep, and she could use it for as long as she needed it until she could get a new car, he'd told her. But she didn't want him to feel obligated, and as soon as she could settle with the insurance company, she was getting a new car. And she was thrilled that someone had gotten her bags out of her totaled car and put them in Michael's Jeep.

Trevor, one of the deputy sheriffs, was at the house, making sure it was secure. He tipped his hat to them in greeting and hurried to grab some bags out of Michael's Jeep. She was so grateful for the way everyone was helping them out.

Michael pulled two of his own bags out of the Jeep, but he groaned with the effort.

"What did Doc say? No heavy lifting for you," Carmela cautioned him.

Trevor cast him a warning look that said he'd report any infraction of the doctor's orders. "I'll grab the rest of the bags. You can just get settled in the house." He carried Carmela's bow and arrows and one of her bags into the house for her. "We've had someone watching the place but haven't seen anyone approach it while you've been in the clinic."

"*If* he returns. With any luck, he'll have died from his wound, but I suspect if he was able to get someone to remove the arrow from his hip and take care of him, he'll live." Carmela dropped her carry-on bag on the floor and collapsed on her sofa, hating feeling so wiped out. Boxes she hadn't unpacked were stacked around the living room and dining area, a few others opened where she'd pulled out some things and didn't have time to put the rest of the stuff away. Her priority had been getting the kitchen and her bedroom in order. It made her tired just looking at them. "Even so, it might take him a while to return if he intends to. He might figure he'll have some other wolves to deal with."

"I agree," Trevor said.

Michael set his medicines and Carmela's on the kitchen counter. "Does anyone want some coffee?"

"Black coffee would be great, Michael." Carmela laid her head back against the couch.

"Thanks. Black coffee works for me. I'll get the rest of your bags. Be back in a minute." Trevor soon brought in the rest of the bags and set them on the floor in the living room. "Did you want me to take any of these back to the bedrooms?" Trevor motioned to the black bags and the purple ones.

"The purple ones can go to my bedroom, please, and thanks," Carmela said. "My bedroom is the last room down the hall on the left. Michael's black bags can go in the first spare bedroom on the right."

Once Trevor had moved all the bags into the bedrooms, he rejoined them in the living room. "Is there anything else you need me to do for you before I begin my guard watch?"

Michael handed him and Carmela cups of coffee.

"I think we'll be okay. We'll call Doc Weber if we begin feeling poorly or Lelandi if we need anything else." Carmela knew that Lelandi would organize any help they might need.

"I'm good, thanks, Trevor," Michael said.

"All right. Well, I'll be outside until my shift ends."

"Thanks, Trevor, for everything," Carmela said.

Trevor finished his coffee and put the cup on the kitchen counter. "Sure thing." He headed outside.

Michael locked the door and joined Carmela on the couch. "Maybe we should have stayed another day at the clinic. You look as wiped out as I feel."

"Thanks."

He smiled and drank some of his coffee.

"Okay, I should have thought this through a bit further." She sipped some of her coffee, then motioned to all the boxes. "Somewhere in one of those boxes are more linens. I don't think either of us is ready to tackle a bunch of boxes, searching for them."

"I can look for them."

"You could. I can, but I think it would be better if we just rest." She finished the remainder of her coffee and set the mug on her coffee table. "We both need to lie down. Doctor's orders. And we know that's the best way for us to recover faster." She rose to her feet, and he finished his coffee, setting his mug near hers, and stood.

"Are you sure you don't want me to look for the sheets? I can manage," Michael said.

She smiled and took his hand. "Tomorrow." Or the next day or whenever she had more energy. She led him to her bedroom and began stripping off her clothes.

"You want me to sleep in here?"

"If it doesn't bother you. Some wolves don't like to sleep with others if they're used to sleeping alone, but it's the only bed that's made up, and the sheets are fresh. I changed them before I left for Germany."

"That works for me." He began stripping out of his clothes, but though he was trying not to wince or groan, he did both, and she knew the only place for them was in bed, resting.

She pulled a nightshirt out of her drawer and slipped it over her head.

He left his boxer briefs on and joined her. "I had hoped you weren't mated and we might court if the pack allowed me to stay. I never thought I'd be in bed with you this fast."

She laughed. "Only because of the circumstances we're in. Courting, eh?"

"Yeah. But I'll also help you hang pictures and unpack your boxes."

She reached over and took hold of his hand, squeezed it, and released it. "That works for me."

"We're courting?"

"Yeah, except we might need to get our strength back first." He chuckled, leaned over, and kissed her cheek, then lay back down on the mattress. He was smiling, looking at the ceiling, and she thought he was one sexy Green Beret, covered in battle wounds and bandages, all because he'd come to a mystery woman's defense. Yeah, she was dating him. A she-wolf couldn't ask for more. And in the end, he might even be the wolf for her.

In the middle of the night, Carmela hit Michael, waking him from a dead sleep, and he found her sound asleep, flailing her arms, fighting an enemy, he suspected. He leaned over and held her arms. "It's okay, Carmela. You're safe." When she'd socked him, he'd thought he was under attack at first. Luckily, she hit his chest where he hadn't been bitten.

Then she calmed and rolled onto her side, her blond hair falling over her shoulder in a silky caress, just beautiful. He lay back down and fell asleep again. When she rolled over again later that morning, she woke him, and he glanced at her. She opened her eyes and smiled at him, but she appeared flushed again.

"Your fever appears to be back." He reached over and felt her forehead. "Yeah. Just stay here. I'll get some of your medicine for you."

"Thanks, Michael. What an awful way to begin our courtship."

He smiled and kissed her hot forehead. "This helps us to see if we're right for each other, through sickness and health."

She smiled.

"I'll be right back." He returned with water, orange juice, and her medicine. "Do you think you can handle some eggs?"

"Sure. Over easy, shredded cheese sprinkled on top, if you think you can manage making them. I usually overcook my eggs due to inattention."

He chuckled. "I'll do my best."

Her brows knit into a frown. "How are you feeling?"

"Much better. I'm ready to tackle some of those boxes."

"Ugh. Don't even mention it." She sat up and took her medicine and drank some of her water, then finished the orange juice and lay back down.

"After you've eaten, if you're feeling any better, you can sit or lie on the couch, and I can unpack some of the boxes and organize the contents the way you want." He really did feel better, and he was ready to earn his keep and help her out at the same time.

She pulled his pillow over her head, and he smiled. He decided to wait on making her breakfast and let her get some more sleep if she could. In the meantime, he went into the guest bedroom and fished some clean clothes out of one of his bags. Once he was dressed, he went into the living room and looked out the front window. Tom was standing on the front porch, serving on guard duty.

Michael opened the front door. "Hey, Tom, would you like some coffee?"

"Yeah, sure. How are you both doing today?"

"I'm good, feeling much more myself. Carmela's running a fever again. She's been having them on and off."

Tom came inside, and Michael made them some coffee. "Does she need help unpacking?" Tom motioned to the stacks of boxes.

"Not for now. I offered to help, but she went back to sleep. Have you had any word about Raymond?"

"We've learned his father lives in Bend, Oregon, according to military records. His mother is deceased," Tom said, taking the mug of coffee Michael offered him. "Peter contacted the dad, and he said his son was still in the army as far as he knew. He wasn't surprised to learn Raymond had gotten in trouble in the army and had been kicked out. The dad had issues with his son also over the years. He said Raymond was strong-headed, doing his own thing, right or wrong. Mostly wrong. But his dad said the other two men were his pals and they were the ones who got him into trouble. I didn't mention that Carmela said Raymond was serving as the leader of the three wolves. The other two were from Bend, Oregon, also, but their families are gone."

"No pack out there?"

"No. Thankfully. So if Raymond returns, he'll hopefully be on his own, but he'll have to heal up. His dad said if Raymond goes to see him, he'll let us know. He won't take part in giving his son a safe haven when he's tried to murder a woman for doing her job. And the thing of it is, she wasn't the only one who was on the board. He understands that. He retired from the army, and he thought his son could learn something from it."

"Do you think he really will turn him over to us?" Michael asked, unable to believe the father would.

Tom shrugged. "He may have the best intentions, but when he sees his son, he could very well change his mind and try to straighten him out or protect him. Peter told him the other wolves are dead. Raymond's dad said he was glad for that but didn't ask how they died. Peter didn't want to tell him that you and Carmela fought them. Darien would rather it sounded as though the whole pack took them down just to keep either of you from being involved in any of this further."

"Okay, thanks. Did you want some breakfast? I was going to fix some eggs for Carmela."

Tom cast him a small smile. "It sounds like you moved right in."

Michael pulled a skillet out of a cabinet. "Yeah, you know it helps to be a hero. Of course, it helps when the lady is the heroine and takes care of some of the bad guys too."

Smiling, Tom shook his head.

They heard Carmela padding down the hall in a pair of slipper boots. She was wearing a robe over PJs now and still looked a bit flushed. "Hey, Tom."

"How are you feeling?" Tom asked, frowning.

"Oh, getting better. As soon as I can kick this fever, I'll be all set. I guess you don't have any good news about Raymond."

Michael began breaking the eggs over the skillet. "Did you want some eggs, Tom?" he asked him again.

"I've already eaten, thanks." Tom said to Carmela, "We've had no luck in finding him. When you shot him, do you think he was playing possum until you wouldn't notice him leaving and then he took off? We're wondering how badly wounded he was."

"Yeah, that's just what I believe happened. I think he was waiting to see if his buddies would take us out, but when it looked like they weren't going to win against Michael and my bow, he ran off as fast as he could in his condition. I believe he knew that arrow was going to really slow him down in a fight. I was surprised when he keeled over on the ground as if the arrow had killed him, then when the fight was over, he had vanished." Carmela took a seat at the kitchen counter.

"We wondered about that. His dad said he *wasn't* the ring-leader," Tom said.

She scoffed. "He was. Even in the army, he was the one who convinced the other guys they wouldn't get caught smoking dope in the van because he'd done it a number of times. He was the one who led the attack too."

"Yeah, he was the leader," Michael agreed, adding shredded cheese on top of the eggs cooking in the skillet. "He was eyeing me, trying to intimidate me, but it wasn't working. Maybe he was testing my resolve before he attacked."

"If you're wondering if Raymond could have died without getting medical treatment, yes," Carmela said. "Were there any reports at any area hospitals of an individual shot with an arrow?"

"No. We checked all the local hospitals." Tom finished his coffee and set the mug on the counter. "Darien says he really doesn't think the guy will be in any shape to come here for some time. Doc Weber said depending on where the arrow struck the wolf, it could take him a couple of weeks to heal from it. We're going to safeguard you until the two of you are feeling better yourselves and then call the guard detail off. We will have someone drive by to check on things, just no 24/7 guard force watching the place."

"That sounds good to me. I really think the 24/7 guard force detail isn't necessary right now either," she said.

"Well, Darien and Lelandi said it is until both of you are back on your feet. I'm headed out. Just let me know if you need anything," Tom said.

"Thanks, Tom. We will," Carmela said. "Thanks," Michael said.

Tom left the house, and Carmela locked the door behind him, then set out the silverware. Michael served up the eggs, toast, and fresh cups of coffee.

After they finished eating, Michael heard someone else arrive outside. He didn't recognize the sound of the vehicle. Darien Silver dropped by with a casserole for them to eat later. "We've come to tell you that you can join the pack if you'd like," he told Michael. "We can always use another good wolf in our ranks. You proved you have the mettle to help our pack members out in a pinch."

Michael shook his hand. "Thanks, Darien. You can count on

me to help out wherever and whenever you need me to." Michael suspected the offer was as much an attempt to keep him here so that if he and Carmela mated, they wouldn't lose her.

Carmela thanked him for the casserole too.

After Darien left, Michael started looking over the boxes. Carmela retreated to the bedroom, and he thought she was going back to bed, but then she returned with a pillow and a blanket. "I know that look in your eyes. You want to help sort out this mess. Are you OCD, by the way?"

He chuckled. "I guess I'd moved so many times while I served in the army that the only way I could feel settled was to get rid of the boxes and put everything away as quickly as I can." Even if the house wasn't his or the boxes filled with stuff weren't either.

She settled on the couch. "Go ahead."

"Files and office supplies?" He cut open the first box stacked in front of him.

"In the office, second room down the hall on the right." He went to lift it, and she said, "Uh, uh," in a way that said no! "Behind the boxes stacked over there, you can find a dolly."

He smiled. "Okay. Filing cabinet is in the office, I take it?" He retrieved the dolly and placed the box on top of it. Then found another box of files and added it to the dolly.

"Yes."

"Any order?"

"Important stuff in top two drawers. They have the blue tabs. Third drawer down, yellow-tab files, and last is the drawer with the green tabs."

"Got it."

Then she closed her eyes and he headed off with his first two boxes. He hoped it would be all this easy so he could unpack the rest of the boxes in short order. He hoped she'd feel better if she didn't have all this work ahead of her once she fully recovered.

He began filing all her files in the oak chest, eager to get it done and then tackle the next few boxes. He envisioned having everything put away pronto.

Chapter 5

Carmela hadn't really expected Michael to sort out her boxes, but she appreciated that he wanted to. She just hoped he didn't pull out any of his stitches or get sick from doing all this work. She closed her eyes while she heard him placing files in the drawers, and she must have drifted off to sleep. The next sound she heard was Michael in the guest bedroom.

She glanced over at the stacks of boxes and saw six more had vanished. Maybe he found the sheets and comforter for the guest bed. He might need his own space to sleep in while he healed up, but she'd miss him in her bed. She vaguely recalled hitting a wolf with her bow in the middle of the night and then Michael's hands on her arms, restraining her and kissing her and telling her she was safe. She'd just gone back to sleep and had half wondered this morning upon waking if she'd imagined all of it or if it had happened. If it had, she didn't want to be beating on him while he was trying to heal up. Or at any other time. Here she'd worried he might not be used to sleeping with anyone else, and then she had to attack him in the middle of the night, if she had.

When she woke again, she didn't feel feverish, thank goodness. She smelled the chicken and broccoli casserole in the oven, noticed a whole stack of boxes was gone, and Michael was dozing on the recliner.

She smiled at him. He looked so peaceful. She thought he was so sweet to join her in the living room and be with her and not retire to bed where he could have had a better sleep. But she did wonder if she'd find everything he put away. Which meant she'd have to keep him around longer so she could ask him where things were and hope he'd remember.

She carefully left the couch, trying not to disturb him, then headed down the hall to check out the guest room. He'd made the bed. In the linen closet, she found all her towels, extra pillows, and linens all stacked neatly on each of the shelves. She decided he needed to live with her if he was always this organized. She checked her office and found he'd brought all the boxes with office supplies in here. All but one was empty. In her oak supply cabinet, he'd neatly organized her printer paper and the rest of her office supplies. She let out her breath in relief. He was a wonder.

She finished emptying the last box and sorting the office stuff, then carried a couple of the empty boxes out of the office. The timer on the oven dinged, and she dropped the boxes on the floor of the hall and ran to the kitchen to turn it off so it wouldn't disturb Michael, but he was already getting up to take care of it.

"Are you feeling better? It looks like you no longer have a fever." Michael turned off the oven and the timer. Then he used an oven mitt to pull out the casserole dish and set it on top of the stove.

"Yes, and thanks for everything." As soon as his hands were free, she gave him a warm hug, hoping she didn't hurt any of his injuries.

As if he wasn't hurting at all, he pulled her tight against him and she smelled his hotness, his maleness, his wolfishness, his turned-on pheromones, all making her feel feverish again, though she knew it was only from the heat he was generating in her and not from her wounds.

He kissed her mouth then, soft and gently at first, then pressuring a little, waiting for her to respond by opening her mouth to him. And she did, wanting to open her whole body to him.

She hadn't felt this wrapped up in a wolf ever, and she had to curb her fascination in him to allow them time to get to know each other. Though from everything he'd done for her already and the way her feminine parts were so eager to get to know his male parts even better, she suspected she was fighting a losing battle.

They finally separated and sat down to eat lunch.

After they finished their meal and cleaned up, they tackled some more of the boxes together, setting pictures aside against one of the walls until they could find her tools. Once he found the box, he held up the hammer in one hand and a nail in the other in victory.

She laughed. He was cute. She had figured it would take her weeks to get the pictures hung up, but they spent the rest of the afternoon putting her tools in the tool chest in the garage and then hanging up pictures.

That evening, they had casserole leftovers for dinner and settled on the couch to watch something on TV. They picked a true story about a Dutch banker financing the resistance during WWII, and she liked how Michael and she were trying to decide on one of a great number of shows they were both interested in—action, adventure, historical, true stories, fantasy, thrillers.

After the movie, it was past time for bed, and she wondered about offering for him to join her in bed, but she didn't want to sound too needy.

"I made up the bed in the guest room to empty some of the boxes, but if you need me to chase away your nightmares..." He left his offer hanging, waiting for her to take him up on it or to decline.

She sighed and took hold of his hand. "I hit you in the middle of the night, didn't I?"

"Not me. You were striking out at a big, bad wolf, I imagine. No worries. You didn't hurt me."

"You don't mind if I'm fighting more monster wolves in my sleep tonight?"

"Nope. And it saves me having to race down the hall from the guest room to protect you." He smiled down at her, rubbing her back.

"Okay, that decides it then." She hauled him back to her bedroom, but then she wondered how he'd known to come to protect her in the woods. "You sure showed up at the right time when I needed a hero."

"I saw you at the service station. I was filling up, and then you looked…spooked. I smelled your scent and thought you were the same woman as the one I had met at Fort Sam Houston and hoped you were with a pack I could check out locally."

"You mean, you wanted to date me already?"

"You could very well have been mated. But then you tore off and I saw the men going after you. I thought you might need some backup."

"Okay, I was belatedly making sure you weren't a stalker." She kicked off her slippers, removed her robe, and slipped under the covers.

He smiled, stripped out of everything but his black boxer briefs, and climbed under the covers. "No, just a man with a mission—looking for a pack to belong to."

"Do you have any siblings?"

"A twin brother, who's also in the army."

"Green Beret?"

"Yep. We were always confusing our trainers. On a regular basis, they threatened to kick one of us out of the program. Daniel wants to stay in to make full bird colonel if he can. Then he hoped to join me if I was a member of a wolf pack he liked. It was just a good thing our roles weren't reversed and he came here instead."

"He'll probably be glad he didn't get chewed up."

"Oh, I'm sure he'll be regretting his decision. I'm just glad he's not here at the same time or you'd get us mixed up."

"No. Way. You might look similar, but I'd know you anywhere

from your growls, howls, voice, and scent." She drew close and kissed his cheek. "And…kisses."

He pulled her into his arms, and she stiffened a little. "Are you sure you're not hurting?" she asked.

"Believe me, this makes all the hurts go away."

And then she really knew she'd lost her mind when she began to pull off her PJ shirt and he helped her out of it the rest of the way. Then he was tugging off her bottoms and she was tackling his boxer briefs, trying to be careful not to hurt any of his bandaged wounds.

Both of them naked now, she was kissing him again, their mouths nuzzling, their tongues licking each other's, and then he was deepening the kiss. Their pheromones were going crazy. She was so wet and ready for him that she spread her legs over his, just wanting to join with him in the worst way. Yet for wolves, that would mean mating for life, and she knew they couldn't go that far.

He rolled her over onto her back, and for a moment, she was afraid his wounds were hurting and that he'd had to move her off him to find relief. But then he plundered her mouth with his tongue, and his finger began to stroke her feminine nub. He was one hot wolf, ready for action, no matter what condition he was in! She certainly could learn to love a wolf like that.

They continued to kiss, her hands touching his skin wherever he wasn't bandaged. She couldn't believe they were doing this now, and yet everything about it seemed right between them.

His muscles rippled with his moves, his tongue tasting and teasing her tongue and lips. Her climax was building with every stroke of his finger against her swollen nub. His touch was tantalizing, pushing her closer and closer to the edge. And then he slid his finger between her feminine lips as far as he could go. She cried out with release, not believing that simple thrust of his finger would bring her to the end. The sensation lifted her and at the same time cloaked her in a warm blanket of belonging.

Wanting to give him the same pleasure, she began to stroke his rigid cock then, slowly, enjoying the ridges, the head, the weeping tip, varying the pressure, watching his tense face as he collapsed back on the bed, his hand caressing her shoulder.

And then she maneuvered around on the mattress so she could take advantage of his kissable mouth, tonguing him, deepening the kiss, stroking him as he cupped her face, and this time, he plunged his tongue into her mouth.

His hips involuntarily thrust, and she knew he was ready to release. He was beautiful, his body tense with need, his expression focused, his brows knit together, his sexy mouth parted, and then he moved her hand faster on his cock right before he exploded. "Hot damn, Carmela."

He said her name in a way that was wolfish and sexy, and she loved hearing him say it.

Then he sighed and ran his hand through her hair. "I'm going to jump in the shower and—"

"I'll take care of your bandages afterward."

"What about yours?"

"I think I'm ready to remove mine for good."

Michael left the bed and snagged her hand. "Then that means we can shower together."

She really hadn't expected to be soaping up the colonel's body with her pearl bodywash, but she loved moving the soapsuds all over his hot body. He removed the bandages from her arms, and her wounds were fading, courtesy of their faster healing genetics. He kissed her skin around the injuries. And then she removed his bandages from his back and arms. She thought his wounds were healing nicely also. A couple of his worst bites would need bandages again.

She left the shower to dry off, and he dried areas he could reach. Then she carefully dried him off around his wounds on his back and flank. After she bandaged him again, they kissed and returned to bed. She was glad to see that his wounds were on the mend and that her fever hadn't returned.

This time, when they climbed into bed, they snuggled together.

"You didn't say whether you had any siblings or not," he said, stroking her back with a light touch.

"A brother, like yours, staying in longer to make the next rank and a Green Beret. My dad had been Special Forces also, my mother a personnel officer in the army, which is how she met him. We were military all the way. What about yours?"

"At first, my parents objected to my brother and I going on active duty. They felt our place was at home, but they finally accepted that we loved the military. My paternal and maternal grandfathers had been in, and hearing their war stories, they convinced both my brother and me to join up," Michael said.

"I think that's why you caught my eye, because my brother and dad had been Special Forces. I have the utmost respect for them."

"Thanks. What about you? I didn't catch which branch of the army you were with."

"Adjutant General Corp, like my mom. I had a lot of different jobs while I was in."

"Including sitting on an elimination board." He sounded all growly about it.

She didn't blame him. She felt the same way after what they'd had to deal with. "Right. Who would have ever thought the men would seek revenge because I helped to get rid of them from the service. It makes me wonder what else they could have been involved in. I wondered that at the time. And of course, since then."

"Trying to track you down, so it seems. How long ago was it?"

"A little over two weeks."

"And you've been here how long now?"

"Two weeks. Except I was in Germany for a few days at the crossbow competition. Have you ever used a bow?"

"Hell, yeah. But for friendly competition, not the real thing. I bet you could teach me a thing or two." His cell phone rang, and he groaned. "Be right back."

She moved off him so he could get his phone out of his pants pocket, his jeans on the bedroom floor. She wondered if someone in the pack was calling him. More trouble?

Chapter 6

"Hey, Daniel. Man, have I got some news for you." Michael climbed into the bed, and he loved that Carmela snuggled with him again as if this was meant to be. He sure could get used to this. "I found a pack in Colorado. Not the Greystokes' pack like I told you I was going to see but another out of Silver Town, Colorado. They run the whole town."

"Hell, that's great, brother. If I don't make the cut for the promotion in the next few years, I'll join you. They run a whole town, eh? Any sexy, available she-wolves?"

"About that—"

"No way could you have found a wolf this soon."

"She's army like us, but we ran into some trouble. We got bit up pretty bad, but we're healing well now."

"Wolves attacked you? Are they dead? I know it has to have been more than one wolf if you were injured that badly."

"There were three of them, but one escaped. The pack's helping us to look for them."

"I'm putting in for leave. I'll join you there soon."

"No. You don't have to. I know you're busy trying to earn brownie points with your boss."

"Not when my twin brother's been injured. Does she have a sister who's available?"

Michael chuckled. "No. A brother though. He's one of us too."

"Bryan Wildhaven," Carmela said, kissed Michael's chest, closed her eyes, and snuggled up tighter to him.

"A Bryan Wildhaven," Michael told his brother.

"Hell, Bryan? He's a red wolf. She's a red wolf? Send me a picture. The guy's working at the post here with me now. Does he know his sister has been in trouble?"

"Does your brother know about the trouble we've had?" Michael asked her.

She shook her head. "I don't want him to know either.

He's a hothead when it comes to my safety."

"He doesn't know, Carmela said. And she doesn't want him to know for now," Michael said to Daniel.

Daniel snorted. "Give me the address and I'll be there as soon as I can get away."

"You really don't have to—"

"You're my brother, and I might have a sister-in-law soon *if* you put your heart into it, and I know you well enough to know you will. If there's another bastard out there itching to put you and the lady six feet under, I'll be there to eliminate him first. So how did this all go down?"

Michael explained everything that had happened. He didn't want to tell Daniel that he really didn't need to come to take care of him. He suspected Daniel wanted to check out the pack as much as anything, and he definitely wanted to check out Carmela and give his seal of approval. Michael wanted to ask how Daniel knew Bryan and what he thought of him, though he didn't want to ask his brother in front of Carmela. Michael gave Carmela's home address to his brother.

"I'll talk to you soon," Daniel said.

"Talk soon." Michael set his phone on the bedside table.

"He better not tell my brother about the trouble I was in.

Or tell him about you."

Michael smiled and caressed her arm. "You mean about this?"

"Right. About *this*. Bryan planned to come to see the pack when he had some time off in the summer, but if he learns a wolf injured me and could still be after me, he'll want blood."

"My brother too, believe me."

"Great. And my brother will most likely give you the third degree too."

Michael sighed and kissed her forehead. "I don't know about your brother concerning me, but my brother will love you."

She smiled up at him.

"I may have to remind him he's staying in the service and *not* joining the pack right away though if he thinks he has any chance with you."

She chuckled. "If I beat on you again, wake me, and tell me to behave myself."

He smiled and kissed her. "All right." But if that happened again tonight, he only wanted to make love to her, all the way this time. Though he knew he was jumping the gun a bit on that. He hadn't felt this intrigued with a she-wolf ever though. He was also cognizant of the fact that other male bachelors in the pack were most likely interested in getting to know her, and even his brother would be just as intrigued.

He sighed and closed his eyes, needing to sleep, to get better, and to get on with this courtship business—in the most pleasurable way, though he did enjoy helping her organize her place too. He liked neat and orderly. Chaos didn't work for him.

Early the next morning, Michael was just waking, glad that Carmela's nightmare hadn't returned, when her phone rang. She moaned, sighed, and grabbed her cell off her bedside tale. "Ohmigod, it's my brother. He wouldn't be calling unless your brother told him about the trouble we were in." Sounding cross with Michael, she answered the call.

Michael ran his hands through his hair. No way had he wanted to upset her. He thought of letting her have some privacy but thought she might need him to back her up. She didn't motion for him to leave, so he stayed.

"Okay, listen, Bryan…no, *you* listen. Michael's brother wasn't supposed to tell you—"

Michael instantly knew that wouldn't go over well with her own brother.

"All right, all right, but Michael and I are okay… Good grief. I'm a wolf. And I know how to use a crossbow. And I was armed. We're both healing just fine." She glanced at Michael, and her lips curved in a small smile. Then she frowned again. "We're courting. We met a number of years ago, briefly. He's living with me now… I'm fine, Bryan. Give it a rest."

She smiled again at Michael. "Yeah, well, you go easy on him. He helped save my life, and he paid dearly for it, but we're well on the road to recovery. And believe me, if the other wolves in the pack don't take Raymond down first, we will. Besides, I shot him with one of my arrows, and he's not going to be feeling in the greatest shape for a while, if he's even alive… All right, fine. Love you too. Bye." She set her phone done on the table, then began to get dressed. "Okay, so both our brothers are coming, but they are in charge of a major field training exercise, and they can't get away right now."

"Good." Michael knew they didn't need their brothers' interference in either the pack politics or their courting business. He got out of bed and began dressing.

"You probably got the gist of the situation from our conversation, but Bryan was giving me grief for taking you in. As if he would have done anything differently if he had met a woman he liked and they were sharing a place while they recuperated from a battle."

Michael glanced at her arms while she was dressing. They were looking much better, the wounds barely visible. She didn't look feverish either, and that was good. "Does he get along with my brother? I didn't ask my brother about his relationship with Bryan."

"They are enemies, at least for the training exercise."

"Well, at least you and I are on the same team."

"I agree. I don't think I had any nightmares. At least that I recall." She pulled her shirt over her head. "Did I beat on you any last night?"

"No. We were good."

"Good. I was going to ask you what you'd like to do today," she said as they headed for the kitchen.

"Unpacking more boxes works for me."

"Are you sure? After all you've done for me? Wouldn't you like to do something that's more…fun?"

"Yeah, I'm sure about unpacking things." He didn't mind at all, and he'd really prefer getting rid of the clutter so they could just enjoy the time together before she felt she had to return to work.

She sighed. "I always thought a man who cooked would make for the perfect dream mate, but a man who unpacks boxes and puts things away in a neat and orderly fashion after a move? Even better!"

He smiled. "I know how annoying it can be to start a new assignment when my house is in disarray, half of my stuff still packed, and I can't find anything. And it takes months to sort everything out. Sometimes even longer. I figure while you don't have to go in to do your receptionist job, we'll take care of all this, sooner rather than later. When you begin working again, you'll be able return to home-cooked meals and a night of relaxing or whatever else you want to do."

"That sounds like a real deal. Are you going to get a job here?" She looked through her cabinet and asked before he could answer her, "Would you like to have chocolate chip pancakes for breakfast?"

"That would hit the spot. Absolutely. As to what I'll be doing, I'm not sure about the job market around here. I'll have to see what the pack members need. My skill set might not be needed here for much of anything." He made them some coffee and set the table.

"True. There might be no need for counterterrorism or warfare, except for taking care of Raymond, but you've been a manager as an officer in the army, and I'm sure you have all kinds of other skills." She scooped the pancakes off the skillet and set them on two plates.

He took her in his arms and smiled down at her. "*Oh, yeah*, all kinds of *other* skills."

"That you can earn a living at," she clarified. She wrapped her arms around him and kissed his mouth.

Man, he could so get used to this. He kissed her right back, and the way her sexy body was pressed against his, she was already stirring up his other head. "I do have a retirement income from the army. Which means I can help pay the bills even if I'm not working right away. And I've saved a lot of money over the years and invested a good chunk of it wisely."

"I have my retirement check also and investments. So it sounds like we'll be doing great financially." They took their plates and mugs of coffee to the table. "I may have to keep you here for good just so you can tell me where everything is that you put away."

"Hell, I should have unpacked more boxes *without* your supervision."

She laughed. "Okay, so I've been thinking about where this guy would go."

"To see someone who could remove an arrow. He could break it off and push the arrowhead through if it had been in a limb, and the arrowhead might have even exited on its own, but not when it was in his hip. Pulling it straight out would do more damage, and he couldn't push it through the body."

"Right. And if it was next to a large blood vessel or severed one, if someone pulled it out, it could cause him to bleed to death. Which would solve our problem," she said.

Michael buttered his pancakes and then poured waffle syrup over them. "True. He'd really need a CT scan to see exactly where the arrowhead is located. He'd need a surgeon to remove it. He could have internal injuries and an infection. Even with running off like he did, the arrowhead is sharp and could continue to injure and inflame the tissues around it. Hell, it could have even lodged in a bone."

"Or bent and could snag on more tissue. Well, we can always hope for the best," she said. "Though if someone else found him dead with an embedded arrow in his hip, I might be in trouble."

"You have a whole pack of wolves to back up your story. Besides, it's a local sheriff 's matter. I wonder if he could have dressed once he shifted and then driven out of here." Michael knew Raymond couldn't have put on his pants. He might not have taken the time or even been capable of dressing the rest of himself.

"Huh. I hadn't even considered that. I keep feeling like we should look for him. And take him out before he can come after us again."

"Yeah, now that I'm feeling better, I was thinking the same thing." Michael let out his breath. "Once we take care of him, we can finish up the boxes." He knew it sounded kind of cavalier, but the wolf had signed his own death warrant. He wouldn't be allowed to live after he and his friends had tried to kill Carmela and him. "But how do we find him?"

She carried her plate into the kitchen. "Why don't we learn all we can about him? I'm certain Peter has an all-points bulletin out on his vehicle and is continuing to check any reports of a wounded man being cared for at a medical facility. But maybe we can check some other sources."

"Social media," Michael said, carrying his plate into the kitchen. He was going to clean up the dishes since she had made breakfast, but she shook her head at him.

"I'll take care of this. I bet you can learn more than me about his background with the training you've had."

He smiled. "Yeah. I was a computer science major, went to the brand-new cyberwarfare training, and even taught there. Learned to hack into computers to be able to learn how to stop hackers." He went back to his bedroom and grabbed his laptop, then sat down in the living room and began doing searches.

"Get out of here. Really? Cyberwarfare training. Wow." She finished cleaning up the kitchen and got her laptop out. "This will be great. Teach me all you know, and I'll teach you how to win in crossbow competitions."

When she sat next to him, he said, "Do you want to mate?" She laughed.

"I think it's a prerequisite before I can teach you everything I know," Michael said.

She kissed his shoulder. "Just keep thinking those thoughts. So what are you looking for?"

"Check out all the social media sites you can think of. We're looking to see if this guy has posted anywhere about needing help with removing an arrow. Okay, here's a guy asking how to remove an arrow."

"You're kidding." She leaned over to see what Michael had found.

"Nope, totally serious. He says he can't go to the ER because he doesn't have any medical insurance."

"He might not have, once he was kicked out of the service. When was it posted?" She answered her own question. "Two days ago. On a site for people looking for answers to questions they have and signed 'A Wolf.' This was posted shortly after he was shot."

"But then someone posted that a doctor would have to take care of his injuries."

She showed Michael her laptop. "And someone sent him a link to a YouTube video telling him how to remove an arrow."

He glanced at her find and shook his head. "It figures you could find just about any kind of lesson on YouTube."

"Right. He changed his story when someone asked who shot him, and he said he was writing a book about his character who was shot in the wilderness by a hunter, and the arrow was embedded in his hip. But the wolf said it was just an accident."

Michael shook his head. "That's our wolf. It's gotta be."

"He asked if a guy was shot in the hip and was bleeding pretty bad and the arrow was still stuck in the guy, how could he remove it safely? Someone left him a link of an archery site that outlines how to deal with a hunting accident—applying pressure, not removing the arrowhead, and stabilizing it. You know, like with tape or something. Which wouldn't have happened because he was running as a wolf. And then it says it helps if the caregivers, as in the other bow hunters with him, gave a duplicate arrow to the doctor so he knows what he's dealing with. However, it does say the wounded guy has to seek medical attention."

Michael snorted. "With any luck, no one took care of it, but if he did expire, hopefully it won't be traced back to us."

"Right. He has my arrow in him. And my fingerprints if police could get them off the arrow. Okay, so we know that he was alive at least two days ago. For the kind of injury he had, he'd have to see a doctor. And I'm sure he couldn't have traveled too far away before the pain would hit. He would have to hide his black pickup so no one would find it too."

"Yeah."

Someone called Carmela, and she looked at her phone. "Got to take this. It's the insurance adjuster, calling me back for an appointment about my wrecked car."

Chapter 7

Carmela's insurance adjuster, Desmond Reynolds, a wolf and a longtime friend of hers, arrived on time to take her statement, have her fill out forms, and sign a release for her vehicle for disposal. She was glad the guys had removed everything from her car already. Wait, she had an audiobook in her CD player in the car. They might have missed that. "Michael, would you mind calling Peter and asking if they pulled the disk for *Heart of the Wolf* out of the player in the car?"

"Yeah, sure thing." Michael quickly called Peter while she began filling out the forms.

She told Desmond what had happened and that it was a hit and run.

"The police haven't caught him yet then?" Desmond asked.

"No, but it was a black pickup truck, and the guy's name is Raymond Hayworth." She wrote down his license plate number for the adjuster. "He was a sergeant in the army. A lot of us use the same insurance company. He might also."

"I can sure check on that. Okay, so, this was an accident?" Desmond asked.

"He hit her car on purpose," Michael said. "I saw the whole thing. He'd torn after her at the service station where she'd just gassed up. I went after them because I was afraid the guy was intent on doing something reckless."

The adjuster handed Michael a form to fill out. "If you could, just write your statement on that. I'll see if I can get hold of Sergeant

Hayworth. I've already seen the condition of the car, and the mechanic gave me his opinion," Desmond said.

"It's totaled," Michael said as if the adjuster better not come to any other conclusion.

The adjuster gave him a small smile. "Yes. It's totaled."

"What's the bottom line?" Michael asked as if it was his car. She loved him for it, but he had no worries from Desmond. He would fully cover the cost of her car.

"We'll cover the actual cost of the car, since it's only a couple of weeks old. Since you paid it off, we'll make the check out to you, Carmela." Desmond wrote it out right then and there, and she was surprised and glad.

Then he shook their hands and left.

"He's been my adjuster from the beginning, and he's been a friend for years. Like a brother. I sure wish we could have gotten Raymond's address from him if he learned what it was, but I know he couldn't give it to us," Carmela said.

"Yeah, not legally. But I can try to hack into the insurance company's records and see if I can find his address."

"I'll need to deposit the check in the bank," she said. "Okay, we'll go together."

"And then I need to buy a replacement car." She was so excited to get a car again. "Did you want to go shopping for a car? If you don't mind taking me. They don't have any dealerships in Silver Town though."

"Yeah, I'd be glad to. I've been feeling a bit cooped up." Michael got on his laptop.

"What are you looking for?"

"Raymond's address and the best value for your money on a new car."

"Oh, super! I'm not really all that great about dickering for the best price."

"Yeah, it's amazing how much money you can get taken off the price if you know something about what the value is to begin with. Are you going to get the same kind of vehicle or something different?"

"A tank?" She sighed. "I loved my car. I want another one just like it."

"All right." He found some places for them to check out, and she called Darien.

"We're going to look at some cars to find a replacement for mine," Carmela told the pack leader.

"I'll call Peter and have someone take you. If you find a vehicle you like, you and Michael can drive it home and whoever your guard is will follow you back," Darien said.

"Thanks, Darien."

Within the hour, Peter Jorgenson had come to pick them up to take them to go to some of the car dealerships. "We found your *Heart of the Wolf* disk. It's in my glove compartment."

"Thanks, and sorry for you having to take us to look for cars, Peter," Carmela said.

"Are you kidding? I've been wanting to look for another vehicle for myself, but I've never taken the time to do it. You're doing me a favor," Peter said.

"Good."

Michael was still trying to find Raymond's address on his laptop in Peter's car.

"We need to drop by the bank so I can deposit this check," she said to Peter before they left town.

"Sure thing."

After she deposited the check at the bank, Peter drove them out of town to the first dealership on their list.

When they reached the place, Peter headed for the body repair shop first. "Come with me."

"I thought he said he was looking for a new vehicle to buy," Carmela said to Michael as they followed him.

"He's probably looking to see if Raymond's truck is here being repaired by chance. It's a new model truck too."

"I am," Peter said, glancing back at them.

"Which proves how irrational he was to have run it into my car," she said, looking at where the new cars were parked that she wanted to check out.

"I doubt he would have had much damage, not with the heavy-duty front bumper his truck was outfitted with. But someone like that, who had a vendetta in mind, wouldn't stop at anything to take care of it, it appears."

Then they saw Peter leaving the auto body shop, and he shook his head at them, indicating Raymond's black truck hadn't been repaired there.

Peter began looking at pickups, but he was still keeping an eye on them as Carmela looked at different models of the car she wanted. But the one she liked wasn't in the red color she had her heart set on. She didn't want to wait for it to be delivered if another dealership had it. Even though Michael had said she could use his Jeep, she needed to have her own car so he could be free to drive his own vehicle whenever he had to.

They went to two more dealerships, and at the last one, Carmela found just the car she wanted, though she told Michael she wasn't sure about this one in an attempt to work with Michael to get the guy to come down even more on the price. Between the two of them, they got the lowest price they could get. Which meant she actually had extra money left over after her insurance company had paid for her totaled car. She couldn't believe how much Michael had saved her money, and she was thrilled and knew for that reason, and a ton of others, he was a keeper.

Peter came to speak to them in the salesman's office while the salesman was off getting a contract printed out. Peter was smiling at her, and she thought it was because she'd picked out her new car. Then she thought maybe he had found Raymond's black pickup. "Don't tell me Raymond's truck is here." She was hoping it was and that Peter could impound it and Raymond wouldn't be able to go anywhere.

"No. But he came in to buy a new bumper. The 'old' one is damaged with scrapes and dents and is wearing some of your car's red paint. He also had the truck detailed. The man who serviced it said he'd removed blood from the front seat. Raymond had explained to the guy that he'd been in a hunting accident and one of his friends drove him to a hospital to get the arrow removed. The auto repair guy said he believed it. Either that or he didn't want to get the police involved. I'm confiscating the bumper for proof of the accident. Best of all, I have his local address."

"Good. I could only find the last residence Raymond was living at while he must have been on active duty in San Antonio," Michael said.

"I can't believe he managed to drive over here after being injured like he was. Okay, I'll finish buying my car, and then we can get out of here," Carmela said.

The salesman returned with the contract, and she hurriedly wrote a check and got the keys for the new car.

They left the showroom to talk more privately in the new car lot while someone removed the stickers off her new car and cleaned the windows.

"The two of you can't be involved in arresting him. I'll call for backup and check his place out. Do you think you can head on home with your new car without getting into any trouble?" Peter asked.

"We're here with you now," Carmela said. "Is his home close by? By the time you get some more men out here, he could be gone."

"You were armed with a bow the last time. Neither of you have a gun, right?" Peter asked.

They shook their heads.

"You can't tear into him with wolf teeth if he's living in a housing development. And neither of you are cops."

"Deputize us," Carmela said.

"Even if I did, you still don't have any weapons on you. It would be reckless of me to allow you to help in this case."

Carmela let out her breath in exasperation. "I'm sure Michael knows a few combat moves."

Peter called his deputy sheriff. "Trevor, get five of our deputized men to this address pronto." He gave him the address and then turned to Carmela and Michael. "I'm heading over there."

"Without backup," Carmela said.

Michael smiled at her, but Peter looked exasperated. "Okay, listen, I'm supposed to watch over you too. Come on. You can follow me over there, but *don't* get involved."

Michael rubbed her back and leaned down and kissed her cheek. "We'll do that."

She didn't know about Michael, but she was ready to take care of the wolf on her own.

A car salesman brought her car out for her, leaving the key in the ignition, and thanked her for purchasing it, then headed back into the salesroom.

Then she sat in the driver's seat and gripped the steering wheel before she started the engine. She instantly had a flashback about her car being hit from behind with a loud, grinding bang and then her car sailing through the air. She hated that she felt tense and anxious about driving the new car.

"Do you want me to drive?" Michael asked, sounding sympathetic, standing beside the driver's door while Peter was watching her too.

"Sure. Thanks. Did you find a truck you want?" she asked Peter.

"Not yet. I have to keep thinking on it."

"I know what you mean. It took me weeks to decide on my car the first time around." She got out of the car and climbed into the passenger seat and loved smelling the newness all over again. She couldn't believe she felt so horribly stressed over driving her new car though.

"It's okay," Michael said as he programmed her Bluetooth for her phone before they drove to Raymond's house. "That happened to me once. I was in a six-car pile up and broke my leg. I kept feeling like everyone was going to plow into me at a second's notice the first time I drove my new car. Before the accident, I was driving on a clear day when some maniac barreled past me. He raced up to an eighteen-wheeler, and the truck had to slam on his brakes in front of him. The guy jerked his vehicle in front of the van ahead of me, but he hit the corner of the van's front fender, spun out of control, and hit the eighteen-wheeler. After that, it was chaos. I slammed on my brakes and headed for the shoulder to avoid hitting the smashed-up vehicles in front of me. The guy behind me had the same notion and crashed into me, knocking me into the van. My car was totaled. After several weeks of driving the new car, I was finally able to let go of the anxiety. It's been years ago now, but just the same, if I hear tires squealing and someone's slamming on their brakes, I still brace for impact."

"Wow, Michael. Maybe I *should* have gotten a tank."

He smiled. "You'll be fine. But anytime you want me to drive you anywhere, you just let me know."

She appreciated that he wanted to make her feel better about it. She'd never been in a bad accident like that before, so she hadn't realized she might feel that way. Still, she was thrilled to have her new car and apprehensive about seeing Raymond again.

"Peter's right, you know," Michael said to her. "It was one thing to fight Raymond and his friends off in the woods, but another to do so in a situation like this."

"Yeah, but Peter couldn't go by himself either. He needs backup."

"I agree wholeheartedly with you."

"Sorry for offering your services when I should have let you make that choice."

Peter and another man loaded Raymond's damaged bumper into the bed of Peter's pickup truck, then Michael followed Peter out of the parking lot. "I would have reminded Peter I could handle the man with my bare hands, but you were doing a great job of it. You know, we're going to have to mate. I've never met a woman who thinks so much of my combat skills."

She chuckled. "Well, you were amazing as a wolf, and I can only imagine what you'd be like without your wolf coat."

"Pretty amazing."

She chuckled. "Why does it sound like you mean other than your fighting ability?"

He laughed.

They finally reached a place near where Raymond's house was located but far enough down the street that no one could see Peter's truck as he parked curbside. Michael parked some distance behind him to allow him room to maneuver quickly if he needed to.

Carmela pulled out her phone while they were waiting and checked on the address to see if Raymond was the only one who lived there. There was no sign of a vehicle, and she suspected Raymond had hidden his pickup in the garage, unless he was driving around.

"The house isn't his," she warned Michael, then she called Peter. "Raymond is living there, but the house belongs to a Denver Peterson."

"All right, thanks. I wonder if this Denver character took care of his injury. I showed a picture of Raymond's driver's license to the men who dealt with him, and they said it was him."

"Did he limp? I would think he'd at least be limping," Carmela said.

"I asked, but they said not that they had noticed. I figured it would be noticeable if he was injured badly enough and this soon after the fight," Peter said.

"What if it was someone who looked like him? A twin brother? A cousin?"

Peter let out his breath. "I'll call Raymond's dad back. My deputies should be here in about forty minutes," Peter said and signed off.

"That would make sense," Michael said, "if he had a relative aiding and abetting him. I wondered how he'd manage to buy or rent a place if he was out of work."

"Unless he's working and had money saved up from his time in the military."

Peter called them back a few minutes later on the Bluetooth. "His dad says he has a cousin by that name, but he didn't think of him because Denver had never been in any kind of trouble. And guess what? He's a surgical nurse practitioner."

"That would have been helpful to know. I guess my question about the dad turning his son over to us was answered. He was protecting him, probably knowing damn well where Raymond was staying," Michael said.

"Raymond could have lied to Denver," Peter said. "He could have told him just what Denver—if that's who dropped off Raymond's truck at the repair shop had said—that he'd been shot by a hunter. That could very easily have happened while he was running as a wolf, but they couldn't tell anyone that part."

"Okay, so that explains the blood in the truck and the arrow in the hip. What about the front bumper where it was scratched and wearing remnants of red paint from an obvious vehicle collision?" Carmela asked.

"That he'd had a minor accident some time back and he needed to get his car detailed anyway, he might as well replace the bumper," Peter offered. "There wouldn't be any reason for Denver to believe Raymond had run a car off the road, parked, shifted, and chased a bow hunter down."

"True. Let's just hope the guy remains a good wolf and you don't have to eliminate him too," she said.

"A red pickup is coming out of the garage," Peter said. Great. Their backup wasn't there yet.

"Do you want us to follow him, assuming that's Denver Peterson?" Michael asked.

"Yeah. I need to wait and watch the house, making sure Raymond doesn't leave if his truck is parked in the garage. I can't see it from here."

The red pickup drove down the street away from them, and Michael started the engine and began to follow the car.

"See? You did need our help, Peter," Carmela said.

"You were right all along. Keep the line open to keep me posted, will you?" Peter asked. "I hope the hell I don't regret my decision."

"Yeah, sure." She was glad they could help out further with this. She hated unfinished business, but especially in a case like this where her life, and Michael's, could still be in danger. "I'm going to check and see if he works at a local hospital."

"Already on it," Peter said. "It's Mercy Hospital. I asked if he was in, and they said no, he'd taken leave for a few days because of a cousin who had a medical emergency."

"Bingo," Michael said.

"So he's not going into work." Carmela located the hospital. "His workplace is in the opposite direction of where he's headed."

"You don't think Raymond's lying down in the back seat of the red pickup, do you?" Peter asked.

"Could be. I did wonder if someone at the dealership had a run-in with police at some time or another and called Raymond to warn him you've got his damaged truck bumper and were asking about him," Carmela said. "It looks like Denver's headed out of town. He's driving in the direction of Silver Town, though he's using a different route than we took."

"Maybe he wants to turn Raymond in to us, but I doubt that it would be that simple," Peter said.

They'd continued to drive, and Peter finally told them that his deputized men had gotten to his location. They were going in to search the house. "I have a search warrant—readymade for any emergency when it comes to wolves. Is Denver still headed toward Silver Town?"

"Yeah, he's now on the road where I had the accident. Ohmigod," Carmela said, looking in the rearview mirror. "We have a black pickup on our tail, and it looks suspiciously like Raymond's truck."

"It's Raymond's truck," Michael said, sounding angry. "I recognize the license plate, and he's speeding up to catch up to us."

"Hell, we're on our way," Peter said.

But she knew Peter and the other men would be too late.

Chapter 8

Michael wondered now if Denver and Raymond had set this up to take Carmela and him out. Or was Denver unwittingly involved in this action?

No matter what the circumstances, Michael had to protect Carmela at all costs. He knew she was going to be his mate sooner or later, and he didn't want to lose her to some bastard seeking revenge.

"I wish I had my bow," she said, watching the sideview mirror.

"It wouldn't help against his truck. I wish I had my gun though."

"Me too. I mean, mine too." She was gripping the dashboard, bracing for the worst.

Michael knew the black pickup was about to ram them from behind, and he was hoping he could move fast enough to avoid the impact. Though he was thinking of saving their lives, he also was thinking about Carmela's car and the trauma she would feel from driving it again if she suffered another bad car accident. If they lived through this.

The truck was getting ready to slam into them, and Michael pulled into the oncoming lane, only because there was no traffic coming. But the truck followed them and again tried to slam into them. Michael turned the car into his own lane, the truck matching his maneuver. Michael knew they'd never make it. The truck was too well protected, weighed a ton, and the car was going to be a casualty.

Michael was already flooring it and heading straight for the red pickup. He could imagine Raymond sending them crashing into the other truck and then hitting them from behind, turning Carmela's car into an accordion.

"He's going to hit us. I can't avoid it. If I get too close to the red pickup, we're going to be sandwiched between the two vehicles."

"Can you just leave the road?" she asked. "We'll crash."

"We're going to anyway. Once he hits you, you won't have any control over the car. If you slowed down and he hit you, the same thing would happen."

"I can't do it, Carmela. If I leave the road and get us killed, it will all be my doing."

She ran her hand over his arm. "I'm ready." She closed her eyes.

"Here goes." Michael felt the truck slam into their bumper, the jolt slamming into him, and he tried—without success—to stay on the road.

She cried out.

The car flew off the road and headed for a stand of trees. He slammed on the brakes, trying to stop the car from reaching the trees. "Are you okay?" They were still traveling at too high a speed through the leaves and brush.

"Yeah, the red pickup truck parked down the road," she said, peering through the window behind them. "Raymond parked his truck, and now he's coming after us down the incline. He's limping, but he's got a rifle."

Michael tried turning the car to avoid hitting the trees so the airbags wouldn't inflate and break through the windshield, but the car slid sideways into the trees. "Shit." He'd made it impossible for Carmela to get out of the car on her side. "Come on. Let's get out of here." He opened his door, and she scrambled out after him. He grabbed her hand, and they ran behind the stand of trees and her car. They hurriedly stripped off their clothes.

The red pickup was backing up along the road to reach them. Michael hoped Denver wasn't armed with a rifle also.

At least Raymond was having a difficult time coming after them. Raymond stopped to aim his rifle, and Michael and Carmela shifted, then ran as wolves, turning sharply to keep the cover of the trees between them, zigzagging like the army had taught them. Even so, Raymond was running after them as if he was so determined to get them, he was feeling no pain, and he kept stopping to fire rounds at them.

Chips of wood went flying near Michael as a round hit a birch, and he thought as soon as the maniac ran out of bullets, he was coming around and killing him as a wolf.

But Raymond must have had the same thought, and when he stopped shooting at them, Michael shifted and said to Carmela, "I'm going after him. The others might not make it in time to reach us, and we can't let him get away."

She nodded.

He knew she would go with him. He just hoped Denver didn't cause trouble for them too.

Then he shifted back into his wolf form, and they ran in a semicircle to reach Raymond. The mottled-colored wolf was ready for them, his emptied rifle and clothes in a pile on the leaf-littered forest floor.

"Raymond! Come on, man, give it up!" someone shouted from closer to the highway, and Michael suspected it was his cousin, Denver.

Michael just hoped Denver wouldn't show up to protect his cousin. Michael might not be able to take out the two males if they were both wolves, but he'd do his damnedest to protect himself and Carmela, knowing she'd get into the fight to help out too.

Michael couldn't wait for Raymond to initiate the fight and tore into him.

Carmela was observing the two wolves fighting, and she wasn't interfering, for which he was glad. But he realized she was also watching for the person who was drawing closer to their location. Michael knew she'd tear into Denver if he acted threatening in the least. Michael just hoped the guy wouldn't get involved. If he was a good guy, like his uncle had said he was, he wouldn't. Then again, when it came to family...

Despite Raymond's hip wound, the bastard was a tough wolf to nail, though Michael repeatedly tried to take him down before the other guy showed up. Michael felt his own stitches ripping loose, damn it. He and Raymond were snarling and biting each other, each trying to get the advantage.

Carmela suddenly growled low. Michael wanted to see what she was growling about, figuring it was Denver, but he had to keep his focus on the wolf who was trying to kill him and prayed that Carmela stayed safe.

"I don't know what this is all about," the other man suddenly said, sounding desperate, but at least for the moment, he wasn't getting involved. "Can't we work something out?" *Hell, no.* Michael suspected that Denver didn't know the truth of what had happened then. He might have thought that his cousin wasn't in the wrong initially, except that Raymond had hit their vehicle and crashed it. Still, Denver might think that Michael had been the one at fault for some reason. Hopefully, Denver wouldn't be naïve enough to believe it.

Michael kept biting, trying to get a fatal hold on the wolf. Denver must have moved in their direction because Carmela raced at him growling and barking, her stance showing complete aggression, yet she was trying to stop him without tearing into him.

Michael couldn't be more grateful to her for being here for him...again. Then they heard vehicles slamming their brakes on the road. Men were shouting.

With the other men coming, it was as if Raymond knew this

was the end for him, and he wanted to finish Michael off now. He charged in with even more vigor and ripped opened another of Michael's wounds. Michael retaliated, this time getting a bite onto Raymond's throat that finished off the bastard. The wolf collapsed, and Denver cried out. Michael growled at Denver to stay back just in case he intended violence, but the man just ran his hands through his hair, tears trailing down his cheeks.

Carmela started licking Michael with affection and concern. He was bleeding, but he could still walk, unlike the last time. This was the last time he was going to be involved in a wolf fight with one of these wolves, he thought with satisfaction.

A couple of wolves howled, and Carmela lifted her chin and howled back to let them know they were safe. It didn't take long before the wolves showed up. They nudged both Carmela and Michael and then howled to let the others know they had reached them and it was good news.

Looking like he was in shock, Denver sank to his butt on the ground, staring at his dead cousin. Raymond was lying there in his human form now.

Suddenly, Peter and Trevor were running as humans to see them, Jake and his brother Tom right behind him also.

"Hell, it looks like you're headed back to the hospital, Michael," Jake said, carrying a bag of medical supplies. "Can you make it on your own this time?"

Michael barked at him. No way did he need a stretcher, though he was certain he'd need some more stitches.

Jake nodded, and Denver said, "Here, let me take care of him." He gently wrapped Michael's wounds as best he could.

"You must be Denver, Raymond's cousin," Peter said as they headed back to the road and the vehicles. "I'm Sheriff Peter Jorgenson, and we'll take care of Raymond's body, unless you want to take him home to bury him."

Denver shook his head. Then he looked worried. "What happened exactly? He told me that a hunter had shot him with an arrow when he was running as a wolf. Raymond couldn't do anything but try and make it home to me. Then I removed the arrow and put him on antibiotics. I didn't report it to the police or take him to the hospital because he'd been running as a wolf. He said it was no problem. And we heal faster. He didn't seem to have any sign of infection, so I thought everything was good. I took his truck in to have it detailed."

"And his truck's front bumper had sustained damage, and red paint marks were left on the metal," Peter said.

"Yeah, he explained that someone had run into him in a parking lot and he wanted to replace the bumper at the same time."

Peter explained what had really happened.

Denver frowned. "I didn't know about any of it. I swear."

"Your uncle vouched for you," Peter said. "He said you were a good man. But why were you headed in this direction? And how come Raymond followed you or knew to follow Carmela?"

"His friends had been staying with me, and suddenly, they weren't. I…I guess I was suspicious. They hadn't packed up their stuff or anything. They just left everything behind, and they'd been with Raymond in his truck that day. He said he dropped them off at the bus station. Something just didn't add up. I wondered if the other men had been running as wolves when he was shot. I asked him the location where he'd been shot, and he told me in this vicinity. He was on some powerful painkillers or I'm sure he wouldn't have told me the location. I came out to check the area, just to see if he'd been telling me the truth."

"Michael told me he and Carmela found notes on the internet asking for help to remove an arrow from his hip. If he had you to extract it, why would he have asked for a way to deal with it?" Peter asked.

Denver let out his breath. "I was the one who posted about it. I've helped with a lot of surgeries, but I've never removed an arrow from anybody. I was checking to see if anyone knew how to do it successfully. I found an interview for an ER doctor who was asked how to take care of an arrow wound, and he said to just apply the regular lifesaving techniques. He'd never had a patient like that, so he really didn't know for sure. And then there were ancient documents on how to deal with an arrow wound, but those weren't really useful. Too antiquated. So I did the best I could, and with our healing genetics..." Denver paused. "Well, if he'd lived, I think he would have come through just fine. He might have had a slight limp though.

"I...I just can't believe I was taken in by Raymond's lies. I'd met the other men and didn't like them. When I saw my cousin hit your car, I backed up to see if I could help you and couldn't believe he was in a wolf fight to the death."

"What do you want us to do about his body?" Peter asked.

"He wronged your pack members. It would be hard for me to take him back and have a regular funeral for him after he'd been chewed up by a wolf. My thanks for taking care of him, like I suspect you did with the others."

"What about his truck?" Peter asked.

"I'll ask my uncle if he could use Raymond's new truck if you can hold onto it for a bit," Denver said.

"We'll impound it, and you can pick it up anytime you like," Jake said.

They reached the vehicles, and Jake shook Denver's hand and wished him well while some of the other men carried Raymond to the back of Peter's pickup truck where Raymond's damaged bumper rested. Others gathered Michael's, Carmela's, and Raymond's clothes, and then a tow truck had been dispatched to retrieve Carmela's car. This time, she jumped into the back seat of Jake's vehicle with Michael. He was glad they were together on the ride to the hospital. And he was relieved that Raymond was dead. But he hated that her brand-new car was damaged.

Carmela shifted and began getting dressed. They would drive around to the back of the clinic to take Michael in as a wolf—easier that way.

When they finally arrived at the clinic and slipped in the back way, Michael gently grabbed Carmela's hand with his teeth and pulled her toward an exam room, not waiting for a nurse to tell him which way to go. He didn't want to risk any human who might be at the clinic seeing him, and he wanted Carmela with him. She was carrying his clothes so he could dress after Doc sewed him up.

Nurse Grey came into the room and placed a gown on the chair for Michael. "Doctor Weber is coming."

Michael had barely shifted when Doctor Weber came into the exam room and shook his head. Michael sat on the exam table and placed the gown on his lap. He felt the stinging and burning of fresh bites and the older ones all over his back.

Doctor Weber said, "When I patch up my patients, I don't expect them to return with all kinds of new wounds. And the old wounds are not to be reopened."

"I promise I won't let it happen again, Doc," Michael said, winking at a worried-looking Carmela, who left his clothes on the chair and came over to hold his hand and stroked it, giving him comfort while the doc sewed up his wounds. He appreciated her for it, but he wanted to take her into his arms and let her know just how ready he was for other business. His wounds wouldn't slow him down.

"Is the rogue wolf dead for good this time?" Doc asked. "Hell, yeah." Michael was damn glad of it too.

"Good." Then Doc smiled.

"We can't keep courting like this," Michael said to Carmela, kissing her hand.

She leaned over and kissed Michael's mouth with a tender touch. The doctor cleared his throat. "I'm trying to take his mind off you sewing him up," she said.

"Just get it over with and mate her," Doc said to Michael. "Okay, we will." She gave Michael a beautiful smile with a hint of sassiness.

"Hurry up, Doc. Are you sure you need to sew all those wounds up?" Michael was impatient to get to the really important business at hand.

"You're Special Forces, so I've been told on numerous different occasions. Grin and bear it," Doc said.

Michael frowned. "That's not what I meant." But he suspected the doctor very well knew that. He seemed to have a really dry sense of humor.

"No charge for either visit. Darien said the pack has got it covered," Doc said.

"Thanks." Michael should have joined the pack a long time ago.

When they were done, Michael and Carmela went home *without* a guard escort this time, except Peter had to drop them off while Carmela's car was being repaired.

They thanked Peter, who gave her the CD, and then went inside the house, and she locked the door. "I could unpack some more boxes while you sit and take it easy for another day or so," she said. "You need to rest after suffering all your new injuries." She sounded so serious.

He pulled her into his arms. At least the wolf hadn't managed to injure his chest. "You mentioned a mating. That's all I need to hear. Believe me, I'll be better than new in no time." She was too important to him to wait even another hour before she was all his. She'd agreed, and he was ready.

She looked skeptically at him, but she led him back to the bedroom. "You know if we get too vigorous and any of your stitches pull out—"

"Doc will completely understand."

She smiled up at Michael. "I love that you are who you are, one adorable, sexy wolf."

CHAPTER 9

"I LOVE YOU RIGHT back," Michael said, walking Carmela to the bedroom, and she couldn't have been happier.

She'd had her career, and now she was going to have her wolf. And she knew she wouldn't regret a moment of it. Well, sure, they'd have their ups and downs, just like any other couple—wolf or otherwise—but, man, she was taking advantage of Michael's hotness. Of course, that was *after* he was fully healed. For now, she would take it easy on him.

She helped him out of his clothes and then made him sit on the bed. He opened his mouth to object, but she was running the show. "Sit. And stay."

He smiled up at her as she started to remove her clothes. The way he was watching her made her feel like she was doing a striptease in front of him, though she was just removing her clothes in the most expeditious manner, not provocatively. But his riveted attention told her he thought otherwise.

He pulled her between his legs and slid her panties down, the last article of clothing she was wearing, and kissed her bare tummy. She took hold of his head and kissed it.

"What works best for you?" She realized after she said the words, it sounded suspiciously like she didn't think he could manage making love to her. She knew he could, but she didn't want him being in all that much pain.

"If you insist on babying me—"

"Only when you've been injured again—"

"I'll be on top."

His back. She knew he had to be feeling some pain. She quickly climbed into bed and then smiled at him as he joined her. He began kissing her mouth, the passion quickly igniting a firestorm between them. He truly was hotness personified. Tasting him, breathing in his masculine and wolfish scent, she felt the familiar pang of need, of want. But this time, they'd go all the way, make the mating for life, watch each other's backs for now through eternity. Bring their own little ones into the world.

She kissed him again, so damn thankful he'd survived the fight with Raymond. She felt the way Michael was moving against her, rubbing his cock against her leg, wanting more. He was already hard with wanting, and their pheromones were kicking butt.

He moved his mouth down her jaw, caressing with his hot lips, moving lower until he captured a taut nipple in his mouth, his hand capturing her other breast and massaging it. She was wet and achy between her legs, her fingers touching his scalp gently.

His hand slid down her belly and reached her nub. He began stroking her with urgency, and she practically jumped, as sensitive and swollen as her nub had become. She wanted to stroke him too and said, "Move so I can do it to you."

His voice was ragged with lust when he said, "I'll never last."

She smiled. She thought he'd have better control than that. But when she began stroking his cock, he groaned and slipped his finger between her folds and swirled it around. She practically screamed with climax, and he pulled away from her, then slid his cock inside her.

Once he was fully seated inside her, he pulled out most of the way and then pushed in, thrusting, their skin sweaty, his eyes darkened like she was sure hers were. She wanted to hook her heels around his hips in the worst way or rest them over his shoulders to allow him the deepest penetration. But she was cognizant of his injuries. For now, she moved her feet so her knees were up, and she arched against his thrusts, loving the intimacy between them and the love they had for each other.

The rapturous moments between them stretched out, propelling her to the top of the mountain peak again. He clutched her hands, their fingers threaded together, and he kissed her mouth, his pelvis undulating against hers, and she fell from the mountaintop, every resolve to make this last as long as they could shattering into a million seconds of ecstasy. "Colonel," she breathed out, and he smiled against her mouth, kissing and licking, and then he groaned with release.

"Colonel," he mouthed against her lips. "Hot…damn," he whispered.

She smiled, and he pulled out of her and sank down beside her on the bed, lying on his chest this time, his arm draped over her, saying he wanted the intimacy to continue but he couldn't lie on his back because of his injuries.

"You are such a wolf," she said. "I can't believe you didn't want to wait until tomorrow at least."

He kissed her shoulder. "Are you kidding? No. Way. I love you, Carmela, all the way to the wolf's moon and back."

She turned onto her side to face him and kissed his forehead. "I love you just as much, but you will stay in bed for the rest of the day and night."

And she meant what she said. Though making love again hadn't been in the plans, they didn't make a move to unpack one more box. Not that night anyway. They were wolves in love.

Epilogue

Two weeks later, both Carmela's and Michael's brothers were due in to see them, to meet with the pack, and give their approval of Carmela and Michael's mating. Not that the two of them were waiting for their brothers' approval. And her latest new car had been repaired. She was working again, but her whole house was in order—once Michael had recovered further from his injuries and they'd unpacked the rest of the boxes—and she couldn't have been happier.

She'd been teaching Michael a lot about archery, and she thought he might even have a chance to compete and win in a competition, as dedicated as he was to learning. In fact, that was one of the things she loved about him. He never did anything halfway. And he'd been teaching her a little bit about hacking just in case they ever had to track down a rogue wolf again.

Michael was eager to see his brother, hoping Carmela's brother wouldn't be too put out that he hadn't given his seal of approval to the mating beforehand, though Michael and Carmela would have mated anyway. It had about killed him not to put the house into order sooner than they had, but she'd insisted he heal up because she didn't want to face Doctor Weber's stern condemnation if Michael had pulled stitches loose before they were supposed to come out. Michael loved how concerned she'd been over him though. He hadn't had anyone act that way since he lived at home and his mother took care of him as a boy. Being with the guys meant they just toughed it out and got business done as usual.

His household goods were coming today too, and they'd have to sort everything out and see what they needed to get rid of. Or get a bigger place. Maybe they would—as soon as little ones were on the way.

"Hey," Carmela said, finishing up the dusting before the brothers arrived. "They won't be here for another hour and a half." She raised her brows and smiled at Michael.

He didn't need for her to spell it out to him, and he scooped her up and carried her back to the bedroom. They had stripped and were in the middle of making love when they heard car doors slam out front.

Aw hell. That was the trouble with being in the military—punctuality. Except that meant his brother was always early. It appeared so was Carmela's.

"They can wait," Carmela said, growling at Michael.

He laughed and made love to his mate. The rest of the world could just wait.

SEAL WOLF PURSUIT

A SEAL Wolf / Silver Town Novella

Chapter 1

Becky Woolworth was busy scheduling a dinner engagement for her employer, liquor heiress Pamela Tynan, so she was surprised when Pamela barged into her office with a proposition that had nothing to do with her own life or commitments but instead Becky's! She couldn't believe it when Pamela said, "Becky, dear, how long have you worked for me?"

Pamela was wearing one of her royal-blue business pantsuits. She always looked so together, and the pantsuit's color complemented her warm blue eyes and short blond hair in a chin-grazing bob. Becky often went shopping with her, and her boss was always telling her to grab anything she liked at the most expensive dress shop. Becky never felt she needed to dress as smartly as her boss, but Pamela insisted with a wave of her hand, saying Becky needed to look her best in her employ. Which was a way of saying Pamela wanted her to have expensive clothes too, not that she was embarrassed with her hired help's couture. Pamela was just nice that way.

"Over three years, ma'am," Becky said, putting the restaurant owner on hold. The owner or manager of restaurants where Pamela was a guest often wanted to be the one called to ensure they reserved the best seating for the heiress.

"Yes, over three years, three months, and so many days. Yet in all that time, you haven't once dated anyone," Pamela said.

Which had all to do with Becky's wolfishness. She was a gray wolf shifter, and finding a wolf like herself to date was a problem, especially in Mountain View. But also, she really didn't have a lot of free time off from work to just enjoy herself. Every time Pamela told her to take some time off, she called Becky in a fluster, wondering about this problem or that. Becky was always there to help sort out her life. And she loved working for Pamela.

The perks were great. A lovely guesthouse on the estate, very private in the woods. All paid health and dental insurance, and a lovely forest to run in as a wolf. Becky even had her own garden she loved to cultivate. Great pay. A great boss. She couldn't have asked for more. Pamela might be an heiress with money to burn, but she was also very down-to-earth, and when it came to charities, she had a big heart.

"I haven't really found anyone I want to date," Becky said, hoping to get back to the owner of the restaurant to finish the reservation. She imagined he had plenty of work to do and couldn't sit on hold forever.

"Right. And it's all my fault," Pamela said.

Becky had to smile. It was no one's fault that there weren't any wolves around here to date, but she quickly lost the smile and cleared her throat. "I've got Rizzo's owner on the line—"

Pamela waved her hand in dismissal. It wasn't that she didn't appreciate that people had other things they needed to do with their time, but when she decided something, she wanted it done now. "I will take care of it."

"The reservation?" That would be a first.

"No, no, *you* deal with that. Dating. I'll make sure you have a date and time off for it." Then Pamela smiled as if she were making the best charitable plan of the year and headed out of Becky's office.

Becky's jaw dropped. Not only did she not want to go out with any old human, but she didn't want to disappoint Pamela when she had to tell her it wasn't working out between her and said human. No one knew she was a wolf shifter, and she had to keep it that way.

And there was no turning a human, even if she really, really liked one, because then he would have trouble shifting during the full moon, and if he had a family, well, the repercussions would have a rippling effect. "Hello, Mr. Binghamton, I'm so sorry to keep you waiting. Yes, six tonight, and Pamela said she will decide on her meal when she gets there. Yes, one guest."

"The guest's name?" the owner asked, which was par for the course because they wished to greet their VIPs by name when they could.

"Uh, no name." Pamela rarely said who she was taking with her or who was taking her to a restaurant or some social engagement. It lent a bit of mystery to her and that made it fun. But the owner or manager always asked, and when Pamela told her to do so, Becky would let the person know too.

Sometimes, Pamela even took Becky as her guest, which made it extra special for her.

Max Browning couldn't believe it when his boss at the PI agency, Ryan McKinley, also his wolf pack leader and the mayor of Green Valley, Colorado, called him into his office, told him to shut the door, and said he had a job for him—a blind date with a woman. No particulars at all. Not what she did for a living, her name, who she worked for. Nada. The thing was that if he had a name, it *wouldn't* be a blind date. Max could learn almost anything about a person if he knew his or her real name. Aliases took a bit more work to run down the real person's identity, but he was good at doing that too.

"For real? Okay, so is this an agency job?" Max asked.

"Yes. The client asked for one of you to take a woman out on a blind date. *You*, in particular." Max opened his mouth to object, but Ryan waved his hand in dismissal. "Don't ask Asher.

She specifically checked you out apparently, liked what she saw, and wanted you to take out the woman."

Asher Wells was one of Max's coworkers and a friend. Max let out his breath in exasperation. He would do anything for his pack leaders—Ryan and his mate, Carol—but this wasn't something he'd ever thought he'd have to do, or he might just have to set some limits next time on the terms of his employment. "When and where?"

"Tonight, at six at a restaurant in Mountain View, so it'll take you about twenty-five minutes to get there. The client is paying for both of your meals. Take a raincoat. It's supposed to pour tonight. Take an umbrella for the lady, just in case she's unprepared. The woman's name is Becky, and the client said that was all you needed to know."

Max shook his head. "How many years have I known you now?"

"Plenty. There's a first time for everything. Have fun, enjoy yourself, make the most of it.

Remember, it's a free dinner out."

"Where?"

"Rizzo's Italian Restaurant. They're high class, so don't dress down too much."

Max saluted him. "I've got a case I'm looking into. A missing German shepherd, but I'll be ready when I need to be with raincoat and umbrella—for the lady, just in case."

Max took off to do another neighborhood search for the dog, posting more flyers, checking with animal clinics to see if anyone had contacted them. At least the dog was chipped, so if someone took him in to have the vet check it, they would locate the owners. The dog had been wearing a collar with his name and address and vet clinic name on it, but the owner had found the collar hung up on a low-hanging branch and realized the dog wasn't wearing it when he got out. If the yardman hadn't opened the gate at the wrong time, just when Bear was out doing his business, none of this would have happened.

Max loved animals, and he was always taking the cases of missing pets. Not that Asher or Phoenix, their newest PI agent, didn't like animals, but Max jumped on the cases. Everyone he talked to was sympathetic to his cause when he went looking for the missing pets. Well, except for the occasional pet thief but that was a different story.

When Max arrived at the restaurant that night, he didn't know what to expect. A woman who was so shy she couldn't meet anyone on her own. Or one who worked with mostly women and there were no work-related romances to be had. He wondered who had set up the woman for a blind date through a PI agency. A friend? A relative? How bizarre was that?

All these thoughts were running through his mind when he saw a woman who looked a little uncomfortable standing all alone. She was pretty, with short dark hair and green eyes that widened a bit when she saw him studying her. She was wearing a silky green dress, presenting an image of softness and curves, and the neckline dipped a little, showing a tiny bit of cleavage, enough to be enticing but not too much to be suggestive. The white sandals that completed the outfit were high-heeled and sexy, emphasizing her shapely legs. Was she the woman?

He just hoped they enjoyed the dinner and the night wouldn't drag on. The good thing was that she was here even before he arrived, and he'd come early. He hated late dates, as if the woman had to make a big entrance if he hadn't picked her up and brought her there in the first place.

He cleared his suddenly gravelly throat and realized he was feeling a bit awkward, when he rarely felt that way. He was a Navy SEAL after all. He headed over to her side of the entryway to see if she was his date since she wasn't making a move in his direction.

And as soon as he did, he smelled she was a gray wolf like him. He was shocked, thrilled, and he smiled broadly at her, hoping she *was* his date. He'd never met her before, probably due to her living in a different city that he didn't come to very often, and they probably didn't travel in the same circles.

She looked shocked to smell that he was a wolf. She didn't smile, just quickly clamped her lips closed, took another deep breath of him as if to reassure herself he truly was a wolf, and then gave him an almost imperceptible smile—of relief, he thought.

"Well, this is a pleasant surprise," he said, trying not to sound totally gobsmacked that he had a much more appealing dinner guest than he thought possible. And then he wondered if his pack leader Carol had set this up. She was much more likely to try her hand at matchmaking than her mate, Ryan.

"I, uh, agree," his date said and stuck her hand out to shake his with a formality he hadn't expected. "I'm Becky Woolworth."

"Max Browning." He shook her hand with a gentle firmness.

He wondered if she'd ever gone on blind dates before. He'd gone on one a time or two, nothing that had ever worked out, but those had been with wolves. He had never expected her to be a wolf. At least they had a chance to make something of it if they liked each other.

Max was beginning to wonder if this had been a job at all.

"So who set you up on a date?" he asked Becky as the hostess seated them at a booth. "My boss."

He laughed. "My boss did the same to me. He's like us, but he didn't say you were too. I just assumed you weren't."

"Oh, me too about you. My boss isn't one of us, so I really figured you weren't—" She quit talking when the server brought them menus.

"Thanks," they both told the server, then opened their menus to check out the selections.

"So why did he think you needed to go on a blind date? And what does your boss do?" Max wanted to learn more about Becky in a social way, but he couldn't help also using his PI training to learn all there was about her and her boss.

"Um, Pamela Tynan is my boss's name and I'm her personal assistant. I thought I was scheduling an appointment for *her* for dinner with a guest tonight, but it turned out I was the one she wanted the table saved for, and you are *my* guest."

Max smiled. "She has good taste in restaurants."

"She can afford them." Becky set her menu aside. "So what do you do?"

"I work for Ryan McKinley as a PI in his investigative agency, and he's the one who set me up. Now, if I'd known you were a…well, one like us, I would have believed my boss's wife, Carol, was behind it."

"She's kind of a matchmaker, I take it."

"Yeah. So why did your boss think you needed to have a date for tonight?"

"I've been working for her for over three years and not been on a date for all that time. I mean, it's not easy finding one of our kind just anywhere, and I do have a job that keeps me busy. I don't understand why she would have contacted your boss to arrange this through a PI agency though."

"I don't know. And the thing of it is, she chose me, no one else. We have four other guys who work at the agency. One is recently married, but truthfully, I had thought of passing this off to another single guy."

Becky smiled. "I'm glad you didn't. Not that I know anything about the other guy, but this is fun. Now that I know you're a wolf too," she said, when no one else was around to overhear them. The server came back and Becky ordered veal scallopini. Max decided to order the same thing.

And glasses of red wine.

"If you have the time, maybe we could go to Green Valley tonight and run, and then I'll return you here after that," he said.

"Or I could follow you there so you wouldn't have to drive me back here. Sure, I would love that. I'll have to make sure my boss doesn't need me. She's pretty good about letting me have my nights off, but there are times when she's got all kinds of things she wants me to do, so I never know. Then too, sometimes she'll give me the time off and then need me to take care of business that just came up or look for things she can't find."

"Okay, so we'll ask her first."

"Right."

"I hope your drive to her place isn't too out of the way if you have to be at her beck and call all the time," he said.

"No. She has a veritable mansion, and I live in one of the guest-houses on the property. It's really nice and I love it. She has a lot of acreage so I can run as a wolf when it gets dark."

"I don't blame you. Ryan and Carol have a lot of acreage, so we'll be safe there." Their wine, glasses of water, bread, and salads were served.

"Have you ever been here before?" Becky asked Max when their server left. "No. It's expensive. Not that I can't afford it, but I generally stick to—"

"Fast-food places?" she asked.

He chuckled. "Not on a date. But this wouldn't have been my first choice. It's great though." He clinked his wineglass with hers. "To your first blind date, right?"

"Yeah. Is this yours?"

"I've gone on a couple that friends set up. Always wolves though. Nothing panned out."

"So what do you do as a PI?"

"Serve as a bodyguard when I need to. Search backgrounds. Look for missing pets, children, wives, and husbands. Investigate to see if someone's cheating a company out of money or cheating on a spouse. Determine the truth in paternity suits. Just a whole lot of different stuff. And I can add blind dates to the list."

Becky smiled.

"And you? What does your boss have you doing?"

"Oh, everything from keeping up with her financial advisors and lawyers to maintaining her social and business engagements. The list goes on, kind of like yours, but in a different way."

"Did she make the dinner reservation for us?"

Becky chuckled. "No. I always set them up. Talk about a surprise when she said she was sending me to the restaurant to meet my blind date. The owner was here to greet her and her important guest. Imagine *his* shock when he saw me and no boss. I was afraid he would think I had played a trick on him to get the best seating in the house for a date of my own."

"I hope he greeted you with as much respect."

"He did. Because he knows it would get back to my employer if he hadn't and she would not be happy about it."

"Well, at least that's good. I would have a word with him otherwise."

"And that would have been reported back to my boss. No thanks! I really like working with her and want to keep it that way. What about your boss?"

"Yeah, I like him and the other guys I work with." But Max couldn't quit thinking about why Becky's boss had singled him out to go out with her. Why not someone else? Someone who lived in Mountain View? Puzzles always made him want to unravel them. Why, if Ms. Tynan thought a PI would be a good guy or match for Becky, not one who was located closer to home? Maybe Ms. Tynan thought Becky needed to meet someone somewhere else since the pool of eligible bachelors was not as acceptable? Who knew? He had to just enjoy dinner with the she-wolf and then he would run with her.

Their meal was served to their table then.

He carved off a bite of veal and ate it. "This sure is good."

"It's my favorite when I've come here with my boss. So what are you working on right now?

Anything exciting? If it's okay for you to talk about it."

"I'm trying to track down a missing German shepherd. He raced out of his backyard when the yardmen came in to mow."

"Any leads?"

"No. I'm afraid someone found him and just kept him. According to his family, he's super friendly and will go to anyone who has a kind word to say to him."

"Oh dear. I love animals, so I know how hard that would be for a family to lose one. Maybe I could help you look for him after we run. With our enhanced sense of smell, we would make a great team."

"Sure, if you don't mind looking for a missing dog on a date."

"No, I'd love to help you."

He appreciated the offer, and it would be nice to have the company. They finally finished their meals and Max said, "I'll need to thank your Ms. Tynan for both a delightful dinner and dinner companion."

"She'll be thrilled it worked out. Not that anything more will come of this..." Becky quickly said, as if she was afraid to sound like it was a given that he would want to see her again. Especially if it was on his own money.

"Yeah, well, I was thinking about that. No time like the present to make another date. How about... Well, I guess we need to see if your boss can release you for another date first."

Becky smiled. "I'll text her now to ask her. Don't pay a tip," she quickly said when he pulled his wallet out of his pocket. "She has already done so." Becky got a response right away. "My boss is okay with it, but she insists that the only time she can afford to lose me this coming week is tomorrow night. Is that too soon? I just need to make a reservation for her and a companion at this restaurant for tomorrow night and I'll be free. She also said to enjoy my time with you tonight. I hope she doesn't think I'm into one-night stands."

He chuckled. "I know that's not the case, not when we are what we are. Are you ready to go?"

"Oh, yes, I can't wait to run."

Just as she said she would, she followed him home in her car, and he wondered if she was surprised he owned a place with acreage that adjoined his boss's place. Then he showed her the guest room where she could strip and shift, and he went to his bedroom to do so. He met her in the living room where she was waiting for him, a pretty black wolf, her tongue hanging out, appearing to be eager to run with him. Just as much as he was eager to run with her as a wolf.

They took off through the wolf door and raced through the woods to the river beyond. The property had wildlife cameras all over it, and anyone monitoring them could see that wolves were running on the property. They would know him, but they wouldn't have a clue who the pretty black wolf was. He was so glad Ryan had told him he *couldn't* swap with Asher to take the assignment. Asher would be disappointed that he hadn't gotten the job, once he learned of it. Who would ever have thought it would have turned out this well?

They ran with each other, him leading the way, her exploring and smelling the scents of rabbits and deer, of other wolves, and he imagined she would be surprised to smell all the wolves in the area. Was there a wolf pack in Mountain View? He wondered too where her family was. He hadn't mentioned his either though. He had to remind himself they'd had just one date. He couldn't expect for them to know each other's life history after one dinner out.

Chapter 2

Becky really liked Max, and she hoped she could continue to date him without it interfering with their work. Cute smile, great dimples, dark hair and dark-brown eyes that melted her heart defined him. His hair was a little longish and he wore a trimmed beard. He looked like he was about six two, like her dad and brother were, while her mother and sister and she all were five seven.

His suit was light gray; his shirt was even lighter and complemented his hair and eyes. The shirt was open at the collar and a couple of buttons below were unfastened, which made him appear both dressy, casual, wolfish, and sexy.

He was the perfect gentleman at dinner…and then offering for her to run with him on his pack's property? She knew he liked her well enough to extend the date night a bit. She would never have thought a blind date could be this nice and lead to a wolf run.

She smelled all kinds of wolves that had been in the area, and that made her wonder how big the pack was. She'd belonged to one when she was growing up, but they only had six other wolves in their pack. What would they think of her going on a blind date? They wouldn't have approved. But it turned out all right, hadn't it?

They were running toward a river. She could hear the sound of it flowing and smell the water when suddenly rain began pouring down. She loved the rain, so she didn't mind getting wet. Their outer coats would repel much of the moisture, their inner coats keeping them warm and dry, though it was a nice warm summer evening, so getting cold wasn't an issue.

She wondered if they would run into any other wolves out here.

But she also wondered why her employer had contacted Max's boss to hire just him. Pamela couldn't know he was a wolf, but she suspected, from the way Max spoke of them, that his boss hired only wolves. She was feeling great, excited about running with a wolf. Max's dark-gray saddle was surrounded by lighter gray fur, his belly fur and under his chin all blond and his muzzle a light gray, though he had a dark-gray mask on the top of his head and face. He seemed to enjoy running with her as much as she enjoyed running with him.

The rain didn't make any difference to her, and she was glad Max hadn't stopped to return her home as if she was so fragile she would melt. Maybe he was afraid she would end the date with him, but she was serious. She wanted to help him look for the missing dog first. She loved her job, but she didn't do anything like this, nothing where she could use her special wolf skills. Sometimes, she wished she worked for someone who was a wolf and would know how important that was to her.

They reached the river and drank from it, and then he nuzzled her in a way that said he was glad she was with him. She reciprocated, and then he indicated he was ready to return home if she was. She agreed and they raced off to see who could reach the house first. She hadn't raced with a male wolf on a date ever. He gave her the lead, and she thought he was cute for doing so. Though she was fast, so he might not have needed to. They would have to test their speed some other time.

For their first date, this was perfect.

As soon as they arrived at the house, they heard both their phones ringing. She'd known the bliss couldn't last long. She hurried into the guest room, shifted, and shut the door. She was so hoping Pamela didn't need her home right away. "Hello?"

"Hey, I didn't want to interrupt you about anything, but I was just checking on you to make sure you're all right."

Becky smiled. She'd be even better if her employer would give her the whole night off. "Yes, we're having fun. He's a PI and is looking into the disappearance of a family's German shepherd. I offered to help him look for the dog." After telling her boss that Max was a PI, she realized Pamela already knew that.

"Oh good. I just wanted to make sure I hadn't done anything wrong in setting you up on a blind date you hadn't enjoyed. Though I guess if you're having another date tomorrow night, things are working out."

"Yes, thanks, Pamela. We're having fun."

"Enjoy the rest of your time with your date. And good luck with finding the dog."

"Thanks." Then they ended the call and Becky sighed with relief.

As soon as she was dressed, she joined Max in the living room. She was eager to help him look for the dog.

"Here's Bear's scent." Max handed her the collar. "I kept it with me in case I find him, and I've got his leash in the car. We'll park at the homeowners' home and then take off on foot from there. I'll let them know we're coming so we can park in their circular drive."

"Okay, good idea." She so hoped they could find the dog. "When you find their dog, then what?

You'll have another assignment to work on?"

They climbed into his car and took off down the road.

"I always have several cases I'm dealing with at the same time. Like the missing dog case, the blind date mission—"

She laughed. "Hopefully, you'll see that as a mission accomplished."

"Yeah, in the best of ways, and I'm going to tell my boss to refund Ms. Tynan's fee for hiring me for the job, if Ryan had accepted one."

She laughed. "Pamela would not take a refund, believe me. She hired you in good faith."

"Was that a call from your boss?"

"Yeah, she was just checking to see if we were still enjoying our time together. What about your call?"

"From Ryan, asking the same thing of me. He was astounded and glad to hear you are a wolf." At least the rain had stopped when they finally reached the dog owners' two-story brick home and its big circular drive and parked. Becky was surprised they didn't have an ornate fence and electronic gate out front, but none of the other fancy homes in the area did either.

"Do you worry that a thief stole the dog to resell?" That was what she would be concerned about.

"I worry more about someone in the neighborhood calling the police because two people are roaming through the neighborhood looking for a dog."

"Oh, I hadn't thought of that."

"We have a couple of gray wolves on the police force, and everyone knows the mayor and that his investigators are good at their jobs—if the police get called to check us out. And I'm sure you have nothing to worry about since your employer is someone important."

"Right. I just don't want to drag her name into it if we are picked up for looking suspicious, if I can help it."

"I don't blame you."

After he texted the dog's owners, they got out of the car. With collar and leash in hand, Max and Becky began walking through the neighborhood, searching for Bear's scent.

"When did he go missing?" Becky asked.

"Just yesterday afternoon. I came right away, but I couldn't find any sign of him."

"Did they take him in any particular direction when they took him for walks?"

"No. They left food out for him, but raccoons ate it."

"Oh, that's not good."

They had walked about two miles around the houses, though all of them had fenced-in backyards. Unless the dog jumped one, he wouldn't be in someone else's yard. Unless someone took him into their yard or home.

Max finally said, "We could be at this all night—"

"Wait, I hear something. Scratching? Bear! Are you there?" She thought she heard some noise from the garage of the two-story stucco home they were approaching.

A dog yipped in the garage. "Bear!" Max called out.

The dog barked. But it wasn't alerting its owners that someone was trespassing on their property. It was a happy bark that said he recognized his name but couldn't reach them to greet them properly. "That's got to be him," Becky said. "I don't smell his scent here, but if they picked him up in a vehicle, they could have brought him here and left him in the garage."

"When I went by yesterday to ask all the neighbors if they'd seen any sign of the dog, these owners weren't home. I checked again earlier today, same thing. No one was home. No barking either though." Max went to the front door and knocked.

A dog in the house was barking, and so was the one in the garage. They sounded similar in breed and size.

No one answered, and Becky was afraid the owners didn't want to open their door to strangers. She didn't blame them.

Max called out, "I'm a private investigator searching for a missing German shepherd that goes by the name of Bear. I believe he's the dog in your garage."

A man came to the door then and frowned at him. "Have you got some ID?"

"Yes, sir." Max showed him his ID and a picture of Bear and his collar and leash with his name and address on them. "You can verify with the pet owners that they hired me to locate him." He gave the man the owner's number.

"You're with the mayor's PI agency?"

"Yes, sir."

"Come on in," he said. "I just brought my wife home from the hospital. The dogs were staying with friends. I didn't have time to locate the owners."

"No problem. They'll be thrilled to get him back."

The man led them into the garage and Bear greeted them all. Max put on his collar and leash. "Where's your vehicle?" the man asked.

"We've been walking through the neighborhood, searching for Bear, hoping he was still in the area." Max explained how the dog had gotten out of the family's yard.

The man shook his head. "My yardmen were here when Bear came into the yard to greet them. They thought the dog belonged to me so they shut him up in the yard. Imagine my surprise to find an extra German shepherd at my house. Sally, my German shepherd, was in the house at the time and she adores Bear."

Max and Becky smiled.

"I'm glad you came to get him. At my age, I'm too old to have a bunch of grand puppies." They laughed.

"Thanks for taking care of him," Max said. "Sure thing."

Then Max and Becky headed back to the owners' home about a mile away.

"I ought to take you on more of my cases. You're my good luck charm," Max said to Becky. "I'm glad we found him, and I can't wait to see the happy reunion." She couldn't think of a happier moment for all parties concerned.

But before that could happen, Max was texting the owners the good news. "I bet they're excited."

"Yeah. They wanted to drive out and pick him up, but I told them we're giving him a good walk home," Max said.

"He smells like he could use a bath," Becky said, wrinkling her nose.

Bear wagged his tail at her, looking to be having the time of his life. New friends, a nice long walk. Yeah, nothing could be better until he returned home to his family.

When they finally reached the house, the man and his wife and three boys of about seven through ten years of age rushed out of the house to greet Bear. He was just as happy to see them as they were to see him, his tail wagging hard, his tongue licking their faces, then all giving him affectionate hugs.

"We can't thank you enough," the man said. "We're just glad we finally found him," Max said.

Then they said their good nights and Max drove Becky back to his place. He got them some glasses of water, and after they had their fill, she had to head home.

"I've had a lovely time with you tonight, Max. It couldn't have been better."

"I agree." He kissed her lightly on the lips, and she kissed him back and smiled. "'Night, Becky."

"'Night." She got into her car and drove home feeling heavenly. She thoroughly enjoyed a fantastic dinner with Max and a lovely wolf run, and the perfect culmination of the events tonight? Finding and returning a beloved pet home to his family.

She finally arrived home and had barely gotten inside when Pamela called. Becky was so ready to just call it a night and bask in the delightful evening she'd spent with Max. She didn't want to think about work right now.

"Hello, Pamela."

"Did you find the dog?"

"Yes, we did. Seeing him with his family was truly heartwarming." But Becky suspected that wasn't why her employer had called her.

"Does he seem like a...good PI?"

"Of course. I'm sure that the mayor would hire only the best for his agency's reputation." Not to mention, Max was a wolf.

"You're sure?"

"Well, yes." Becky wondered what this was all about. Pamela seemed so serious. "Okay, I want you to hire him for a job for me."

That was why Pamela set Becky up on a blind date with a PI? So Becky could investigate the PI for her? That was hilarious. Wouldn't Max be amused that Becky had been investigating him even though she hadn't known it either!

"I need him to find the man who was to be my husband, but I don't want anyone to know about it. No one, all right? Can Max be fully trusted with this confidential information?"

"Husband?" When in the world did that happen?

"Yes, yes, it's something no one knows about. I'm an only child, and when I fell in love with Christopher Anderson, my parents were furious with the both of us. They said if I insisted on marrying him, I would lose all my inheritance in the event of their deaths. Well, I've finally received the rest of my inheritance, and I'm going to do what I have always wanted to do. Be with him. He's kind and generous, and I think he still loves me like I love him."

The first thing Becky wondered was if the man truly loved Pamela or if he was a gold digger, waiting in the wings for her to come into her inheritance.

"In heart we were all but married, but we couldn't risk actually getting married. If either of my parents learned the truth about it, they would have given all of my inheritance away to a cousin. Now, I know it sounds cavalier, if I truly loved him, I would have given up the inheritance to be with him—"

"But it was his idea for you not to throw it all away for him, right?" Becky hadn't meant to sound like she didn't trust the guy's motives, though she didn't in the least. When a woman fell in love with someone, she could easily be swayed into believing the guy loved her too. Becky had been down that road, so she knew something about it.

"Right. I know how it sounds. If he'd wanted to marry me without hesitation, casting aside the money, and all that mattered was me, it would seem more legitimate. I understand that. And I'm no dummy."

No, Pamela was shrewd in her business dealings.

"So you want Max to try to find him? He wasn't just waiting for you to get in touch with him and marry you?"

"Yes and no. He's been waiting for ten years. But in the last six weeks, I haven't been able to reach him. He says it all has to do with his work."

"Ah, so you want Max to not only locate your husband-to-be but also to ensure he's a safe bet to marry."

"Exactly. That's why I need to know if Max is going to be close-mouthed about this whole business. I don't want even the mayor to know about this job. I'll pay Max handsomely, rest assured, and he'll have to dedicate himself to just this high-priority case.

"Christopher waited so long for me that I can't, with a good conscience, end things between us without knowing what he's been up to and if he's seeing someone else and ready to move on or if he's truly ready to make a full commitment to me."

"Ten years is a long time, and you haven't been seeing each other in all that time?" Becky couldn't imagine the relationship they'd had. If she was hooked on a guy, no way would she be able to wait to be with him, money or no. And if he wanted her to wait and marry her when she had the money instead, that made him suspect to Becky's way of thinking.

"We had been seeing each other up until six weeks ago. We stopped when Christopher thought someone was spying on us, but then I just couldn't get in touch with him. My dad could very well have had a PI watching either one of us earlier on."

"What if Max has other important cases he's working?" Becky couldn't expect him to drop everything for one person. It wasn't fair to the people whose cases he was already working on, nor to him or anyone else with the firm that would have to take over the cases.

"We'll come to that when we come to it."

"When was the last time you actually saw Christopher?"

"Six weeks ago to the day. I told him that the settlement would be through soon, back then, but he didn't believe it. He thought I was just stringing him along. He said he had a job in Europe for the next few weeks and then he would be home. As soon as I learned I would get the rest of the inheritance, I figured it was time to tell him, but something just doesn't feel right. Actually, I probably could use a full-time investigator."

Becky sighed. Max was a wolf and she suspected he would prefer working for Ryan since he was a wolf too. She could imagine how nice it would be to talk about cases when they were all wolves and could relate to one another so well.

"Okay, so you want me to ask Max to look into this boyfriend of yours, who was to be your husband, and see if there's anything fishy going on and report back to you. Max might need to talk to you further to see if he can learn any other details that you might not have told me." Either because her boss didn't want to say or she just didn't think the information was relevant, but it would help Max with the case. Becky hoped he would take the case and she'd see more of him.

"Yes. Call him tonight, if you don't mind, and let me know what he says."

"Yes, ma'am." Becky ended the call and called Max. "Hey, my boss wants to hire you for a job." Then she explained everything she knew about it.

"Seriously? Okay, no running it by my boss? He's going to get suspicious if I transfer my cases to the other agents and won't tell him why."

She chuckled. "You know? You're a wolf. Of course you'll tell him, and of course the word won't get out to anyone beyond those that need to know. I'm not worried about that. You have to do what you have to do to keep yourself from getting backed into a corner."

"True. I didn't want to lie and tell you I wouldn't. Ryan needs to know what's going on with the agents in his office. We have a daily briefing, letting him know about the more important cases we're working on, though sometimes what seems to be less important might be extremely so."

"Where does this case rate?"

"I'd say, considering who is hiring me for the job and the concern to her reputation, it's extremely important."

"Did you need to speak to her about Christopher?"

"I do. I'll give her a call."

"All right. I'm going to get ready for bed. 'Night, Max, and thanks so much for doing this."

"Wait, was our dinner a case of you checking me out to see if I was reliable enough?"

She smiled. "Well, for *me*, it was just a blind date. Apparently, Pamela had an agenda of her own. That's kind of a switch for you, isn't it?"

He laughed. "I would never have guessed it in a million years. She's great at this business."

"I think what sold her on you, besides my putting in a good word, was that you found the dog for the owners."

"And you had a lot to do with that."

"We make a great team. I'll see you tomorrow."

CHAPTER 3

MAX DIDN'T KNOW WHAT to think of this new mission of working for Ms. Tynan. He was certain his boss would be fine with it, but he still needed to check with him because Max would have to transfer all his cases to the other guys. And Ryan needed to know where Max was if he wasn't working on regular cases. He called Ryan right away and explained what he needed to do.

"All right, Max, you sure got yourself into something that sounds intriguing. Mum's the word. Tell the other guys they need to take over your cases, and if anyone gives you grief, have them come to me. I would rather this stay between you, me, Becky, and Ms. Tynan."

"Yes, sir."

"How did the date go? I guess Ms. Tynan was checking you out."

Max smiled. "Becky and I had fun. And yeah, that was sure a surprise to both of us." Ryan chuckled. "That's good. See you tomorrow morning then."

"Thanks, Ryan." Then Max called Asher. "Hey, I've got a job to do—boss approved—and it means not working on any other cases."

"Well, hell," Asher said. "I bet the pay is better than the cases you were working on. So what do I need to take on now?"

Max was glad his friends at the agency agreed to take his other cases on such short notice. He really wanted to do this right, and he couldn't have if he'd been worrying about taking care of cases he'd set aside, though he knew Ryan would have made sure someone did them. They all worked together, and if someone was having trouble with something, they all chipped in to assist. It helped that they were wolves and belonged to the same pack.

The good news was he was going to be seeing more of Becky, and that really played into his plans perfectly. He would enjoy every minute he could with the she-wolf!

Then Max called Becky back. "We're all good. I made arrangements with Asher and the others to take the rest of my cases, and I've talked to the boss and he's fine with it. Do I need to call your boss and tell her?"

"No. As her personal assistant, I handle all the stuff like that. If she feels differently about this, she can tell me if she wants to deal directly with you."

"That works for me."

"I'll tell her you're for sure working strictly on her case. She'll be pleased. Don't be surprised if you solve this for her in a way that makes her happy enough that she might just want to hire you full-time."

He chuckled. "She might not like to hear what I learn."

"I totally agree. I'll see you tomorrow then."

"You will. 'Night, Becky." This sure had been a strange turn of events that he'd never expected. He stripped off his clothes and took his shower, climbed into bed, pulled his covers up, then grabbed his laptop resting on his bedside table. He set it on his lap and checked his special databases for anything relating to Christopher. He had so many hits that he would have to speak with Ms. Tynan again to get some more details on him.

Max set his laptop aside and turned out his lamp, settled against his pillow, and closed his eyes. He suspected that if the other single guys ever met Becky, they would be hounding the boss for a blind-date assignment. But Max didn't believe they would ever get as lucky as he had on a blind date. And solving a case tonight with her? It couldn't have worked out any better, not only for the family, the dog, the ones who had found Bear, and him and Becky, but it probably helped him snag this new assignment that looked like it could get interesting really quick.

First thing in the morning, Max called Becky's boss. "Ms. Tynan, this is Max Browning. I don't have enough information for Christopher Anderson. Do you have any other details about him that will help me narrow the search? Birthplace? Birth date? Parents' names? High school attended? All these things will help with reducing the number of names I have to comb through."

"Yeah, sure. And please call me Pamela. Christopher and I went to school together. We graduated from Vander High School, class of 2008, and he was born June 21, 1990. I was in some of the same classes with him. He's a natural strawberry blond, has the nickname of Red, and his parents' names were Fred and June Anderson. Both of them still live in Mountain View, but they are adamant he shouldn't have anything to do with me since I wouldn't give up my fortune to marry him. It's a decade later and they could have had grandchildren by now. They felt that once I received my inheritance, I wouldn't marry him, so my relationship with them is as bad as it was with my parents with regard to Christopher. Also, he was born in Kansas City."

"I'll start the search on the databases again. I don't want to ruffle feathers, but I do want to speak with Christopher's parents to see if they have any clue where he might have gone."

"I don't believe they will be helpful at all with this. If anything, they will lie about his whereabouts so that I can't get ahold of him, if they know where he is."

"I'll let you know if this helps. Talk to you later." Max and

Pamela ended the call, and he began to narrow the search down. Using Christopher's parents' names, his birth date, and his high school, Max was able to narrow it down pretty quickly. Even though he'd thought this was going to take a lot longer, now it looked like it wouldn't take any time at all. But one of the things he learned was that Christopher's biological parents had died in a car accident when he was two in Kansas City. The Andersons were his adoptive parents. Max wondered if Christopher knew that.

Becky called him back. "Hey, I'm free for lunch if you want to come here, and you can tell me how things are going. Pamela is busy for most of the day, so she wanted you to update me if you have any news."

"Yeah, sure, I'd love that."

When it was time for lunch, Max arrived at Becky's home on Pamela's estate, a lovely little brick one-story home surrounded by woods, but Becky had planters around the house that were filled with flowers. He wondered if she loved gardening and had planted them.

Becky had made a delightful lunch of Indian spiced chickpea wraps, something he'd never had before.

They sat down to eat, and he told her how good the wraps were.

"Thanks. I should have asked if it was something you might like first. So what did you learn?" she asked.

"I called Christopher's parents, and they wouldn't tell me a thing about his whereabouts. Either they figured Pamela wants to know, or they're worried he's in some trouble and they don't want to give him up."

"Who did you say you were working for?"

"I say I'm a private investigator, and I don't name my client."

"Okay, that's good. But they still suspected something was wrong?"

"Sure, when a private investigator gets involved, usually something is up. Though if he has nothing to worry about, there shouldn't be any problem. I also learned the Andersons are his adoptive parents, and I don't know if Christopher realizes that or not. He was two when his parents died."

"Oh, that's sad. So what do you do next?"

"I'm trying to learn who his friends are and where he's worked in the past. I'm coming up with nothing. No current location for him."

"Hmm, I'll text Pamela and see." Becky quickly pulled her phone off the dining table and texted her boss, then waited. When she got a return text, she said, "Okay, she said no, that he was an investment counselor, did investments overseas, but he never told her which firm he worked for. I wonder if she didn't ask or look into it further when she was seeing him because she didn't want to believe he could be a con man or seeing another woman."

"She's more interested in learning the truth. Nobody likes to believe they're being conned, and when emotions and relationships get in the way, it can be really hard to keep reality and relationships separate," Max said.

"So gut feeling, what do you think?"

"I don't know enough about him to give a guess yet. Sure, I can speculate, but I would rather be more well informed first. Speculation won't help my investigation, unless it comes up with new leads I can look into."

"Pamela's really open about a lot of things, but when it comes to relationships, she is really tight-lipped about them. I had no idea she had been dating Christopher. Not that I blame her. She has been in the tabloids any number of times, and she really tries to avoid anything about her love life getting into them. Particularly while she was trying to get her inheritance. If her parents hadn't been so adamant about who she was seeing, she might not have been so secretive. In any event, I don't blame her. It's different for us. We are able to see each other when we can anytime, and we don't have to worry about paparazzi reporting our every move. Of course, they did report about Christopher early on, but then she was careful because her parents were so angry with her."

Later that afternoon, Max was back at the office, looking up news stories about the Tynans, and one caught his attention. He thought he might see some references to the boy Pamela Tynan had dated, but this was a story of when she was a little girl and she had cried wolf! According to the news story, she had broken through ice on the pond on her parents' property and a wolf saved her. Only the wolf shifted into a woman and fished her out before she drowned. And then she carried Pamela off to a cabin somewhere where she warmed the girl up and then took her back to her property and vanished. No one believed the young girl, but Max thought it was too much of a coincidence that Pamela had seen a wolf shifter who had saved her when she was young, hired a personal assistant later who was a wolf, and then picked Ryan's PI agency to hire a wolf to check into the missing boyfriend.

Knowing the woman who rescued her was a wolf shifter was one thing, but how did Pamela know about Becky, if she did?

Then what about the business with him and the other wolves in the Green Valley pack? He remembered the incident they'd had on their Green Valley pack land recently. The case where hunters had shot one of their wolves on the pack leaders' land. And the hunters had sworn they'd shot at wolves. Of course the wolves said they were walking along the river on a date when the hunters started shooting at them. It was in the news all over the place. Several of the wolves had been involved in the whole affair, including Max and the rest of the PI team as they tried to gather evidence against the hunters. Some had testified against the hunters; some had been in the courtroom watching the proceedings.

Pamela could have seen the news at any time since it was so widespread, given the nature of the hunters' accusation—that they'd been shooting at wolves who had turned out to be humans. He could see where she might have put two and two together and figured it out that the couple the hunters had said were wolves had truly been shifters too, since she'd had the earlier wolf experience at the frozen pond.

Then there was Becky. Why did Pamela assume Becky was a wolf, if his assumptions were correct? He called Becky up to ask her. "Do you ever run as a wolf on your employer's property? Somewhere you would feel safe?"

"Yes. She has hundreds of acres that are never used for anything. She doesn't allow hunting or anyone to trespass on the property. It's really pristine, and it makes for a great place to run in. Why?"

"I found an article about her when she was a young girl. She was rescued by a wolf."

"What?"

"Yes. I have no idea who the woman who rescued her might have been, but she pulled her out of the frozen pond on her parents' property when Pamela fell through. The wolf shifted to save her. The girl told everyone, but of course no one believed her."

"Ohmigod, the woman carried the girl to a cabin and warmed her up and—"

"Yes, you found the same article I was reading," Max said.

"No, my mother told me the story. She saved a young human girl, despite her people chastising her for doing so. She couldn't let the girl drown, even though she risked detection. She carried her toward home, but then my dad, who wasn't mated to her yet, came to help Mom and the girl, so my mother could shift back into the wolf. At the house, they warmed Pamela up, dried her clothes and hair, carried her back to her property, and told her to stay off the pond in winter or spring thaw and run along home.

"My dad said that he mated my mother shortly after that because she did what was right, and he would have done the same. Still, the other wolves in their pack didn't agree. My mother wouldn't have done anything differently, and my father was always proud of her. Then she had me, my sister, and brother, triplets, and it made her doubly glad she'd saved the girl. No one deserved to die like that."

"Pamela Tynan was the girl." It all fit.

"My boss," Becky said. "She knew who my mother was then? That was why she hired me?"

"I don't know. Not for sure. But, well, I don't believe in that many coincidences."

"Okay, I have to agree. Wow, now I don't know what to do. The others in the pack always said that humans who knew about us would have to be turned or eliminated. We couldn't risk that anyone would learn about us."

"I agree. But because of her wealth and how well known she is in the area, I don't think that's a viable option either way."

Chapter 4

Becky was so shocked to learn that a wolf had rescued Pamela when she was a girl that she didn't know what to think. That her mother was the one who had saved Pamela was even more of a surprise. That Pamela might know that Becky was a wolf just blew her mind.

She immediately wondered if Pamela had seen her running as a wolf on her property. But then Becky thought that maybe Pamela had wildlife cameras about. Becky had never realized they could be set up in the woods. *Great. Just great.* She would never be able to run as a wolf out there again. She hoped that Max wasn't right in his assumptions, but she didn't think he was wrong. It was just too much of a coincidence that Pamela set her up with Max and that she'd hired Becky after her mother had saved Pamela's life when she was a girl. Becky wondered just what Pamela had thought of her when she hired her. She'd had to wonder if Becky was a wolf too, unless Pamela's family had convinced her that werewolves were just imaginary creatures.

Becky wanted to talk to her about it. She wanted to quit her job and leave town. She felt conflicted. She loved her job and had never wanted to leave it. Pamela had made her feel like a friend and confidante, yet she knew so much more about her than Becky knew about Pamela. She couldn't believe it. She sighed and knew she had to just focus on the current job, learn what she could about the boyfriend and the new guy, and go from there. Becky wanted to tell Pamela she knew and understood and hoped Pamela would keep their secret. But maybe she would anyway. Maybe she realized that Becky needed someone in her life—a wolf—just like Pamela wanted someone in her own life. If that was the case, Becky appreciated her boss all the more.

"What do we do now?" Becky asked Max.

"We do just what we planned to do. We learn about Christopher, and beyond that, we talk to Ryan and Carol, my pack leaders, about what's going on. They need to learn the truth when it involves anyone knowing about wolf shifters in the pack, and in your case too."

"I just can't believe this."

"I can't believe your mother rescued her. But it sounds to me like Pamela wants to pay her back in some way by taking you in, giving you a job, and finding a mate for you."

Becky smiled. "She doesn't know anything about our kind. That we mate for life and relationships have to be for a lifetime."

"I agree, but I think that's what this is all about. The date bit and to see what you thought of me as far as looking into her relationship."

"Do you think that's all on the up and up? What if she doesn't really need anyone looked into?

That you can't find anything about this Christopher boyfriend?"

"In the kind of work I do, anything is possible."

"Okay. You're coming for dinner?"

"Yeah, sure. I can't wait."

That night, Max drove to Becky's house for dinner, eager to enjoy her company again, and she made pork chops, fried dollar potatoes, and a cauliflower and broccoli blend.

After dinner, she took away the dishes and put them in the

dishwasher. "What if Pamela has wildlife cameras set up on her property and she has recorded where I've been running as a wolf?"

Max frowned. "Wouldn't you have noticed that she was having them set up? You're in charge of all that, right?"

"Normally, yeah, but if she wanted to catch me at it, then maybe not. Maybe she had them set up before I interviewed for the job. Then again, it would have been smarter to have done so on the trail I normally take."

"Let's take a walk. You show me where you usually run. I don't see a dog door, so she didn't have one installed for you."

"No. But she's always said I could have a dog and have a dog door installed if I would like." Max raised a brow as they headed outside. "You made a trail where you walked?"

"Yeah, I never thought anyone would be watching me going on my runs. I would always shift way out in the woods."

"Always at the same place?"

"Yeah, I'm totally a creature of habit. I always felt safe there, never ran into any problems, and moving to another location might not have been the same for me. So I didn't want to chance going somewhere else."

He thought it was a nice night for a walk in the woods with Becky, though he would have loved to run here with her as a wolf too. Every chance he had at changing into his wolf form when he could do so safely was something he loved to do. He was looking up at the trees for any sign of trail cameras along the path Becky always took, the grass worn down here, evidence that a hiker's trail had been made.

He smelled her lingering scent in the woods, and if he'd come upon her scent before, he would have wanted to find the wolf that it belonged to. A she-wolf, sweet and saucy. He smiled down at her, but she was looking a little worried, and he realized this wasn't just a pleasant walk in the woods with him but an investigation into whether she'd been observed as a wolf running through the area. "Have you ever seen her on your runs through the woods as a wolf?" he asked. As wolves, they saw movement and were really observant of their surroundings. They had to be, since they were wary of danger to themselves, so he figured Becky wouldn't have just run through the property without thinking of that, no matter how vast the land was or how little it was tramped on by anyone else.

"No. And yes, I naturally watched for any sign of anyone. Even though it's posted all over that no hunting is allowed, it's always a concern that hunters will ignore the signs and try to hunt on the property. So I'm always cautious when I go out. I haven't seen anything that looks like a camera in a tree, have you?"

"No." But that didn't mean Pamela didn't have trail cameras watching for wildlife in other locations or just for security. Even if she just had them up to watch any wildlife—cougars, deer, anything that might move around on her property. "You could ask her."

"Then she might suspect that I realize she knows about me."

"You could smell her scent and see her reaction." As wolves, they were much more attuned to changes in people's behavior and their corresponding scent. "Um, not that I want to worry you, but I think I'll go over your home with a bug detector to make sure there are no listening devices in your place and no hidden cameras either."

"Oh, great. I never thought of that."

"I've been hired to check a home, office, vehicles over for that very thing." Becky's eyes widened. "Did you find any?"

"In one client's office and home, yes. But it wasn't what I thought."

"Like espionage? Someone trying to learn about their products or something?"

"FBI surveillance. They called me in and told me what was up. The surveillance was legit and what the client was doing wasn't."

She arched a brow, waiting to hear what the client had been doing that wasn't right.

"Drugs. He was running a big pharmaceutical drug ring, and I nearly messed up the sting operation."

"So what happened?"

"I had removed the devices and destroyed them, then the FBI took me into their confidence and had a little talk with me. I could be charged with obstruction, or I could agree to plant new devices."

"Did you?"

"Sure. I work for the good guys. I told the client that I needed to do another sweep in a few days to make sure I hadn't missed anything, then slipped in several more bugs than the FBI had managed to plant the first time around. I was off the hook and they arrested the bad guy, who had incriminated himself fully." Max shrugged. "All in a day's work."

"Wow. I'm glad you didn't get charged for a crime."

"Well, Ryan wasn't happy about it. He doesn't like it if we end up with a client who's a bad egg. It's bad news if we look like we're helping a scoundrel get away with illegal stuff. So yeah, we started screening clients better. Though they can slip through the cracks sometimes. Like with Pamela. Digging deeper, I found the connection with our kind. On the surface, she seems to be just a nice woman who cared about you having a date out. Then it morphed into me looking into a guy she'd been dating. And now? Maybe something even bigger—as it relates to us. Has she ever said anything to you that would lead you to believe she knows about you? Or us?"

"No, this is all a shock to me. I mean, she's always so nice to me. She can be a bear when it comes to other people who work for her. I don't mean in a bad way, but when people do her wrong, she doesn't let it slide. I admire her for it. It's not that she expects perfection. People make mistakes and she's forgiving, but man, if you knowingly do something to undermine her or steal from her, she will really come down on you. For instance, we had a maid who was selling Pamela's stories to a tabloid. It was hitting too close to home for it not to be coming from someone who was on staff. "Pamela trusted me, as if she thought I had a bigger moral compass, and I guess as a wolf, I do, because none of us want to end up in jail. So I set up a situation where I would give staff members different stories, nothing that would hurt Pamela but that sounded juicy and were so far-fetched that no one would believe them. But coming from me, the people who worked for her would. Only one person, the maid, knew the story I had shared with her, and it went straight to the tabloid. I gave her one more story, though by this point, I knew it had to be her, and then I followed her around, just out of sight like a wolf would, until she made the mistake of calling the tabloid on her phone. Our enhanced hearing being what it is, I was able to listen in beyond the wall. I looked up the man's name, Mr. Quinlin, and found him to be one of the reporters for the tabloid."

"The maid could have been talking to him about something else."

"No, she was sharing the story I had given her. Pamela was at a luncheon in town at the time, and I think the maid thought she was being covert about the whole thing. In truth, she had shared several stories before we caught her at it."

"Hell, you would make a great PI."

Becky laughed. "It only worked because I'm a wolf and I work for Pamela. Anyway, Pamela fired her. She wouldn't give her a referral, and if anyone asks her about her employment with Pamela, she'll tell them the truth. If a prospective hirer wants his or her life exposed to the tabloids, the maid is the one to hire."

Max smiled. "I doubt anyone of consequence will hire her. It's ironic that the maid wanted the extra money but was too shortsighted to realize she had a steady income all along."

"And lots of benefits. Pamela believes in educating her

employees. Some are high school dropouts. She doesn't care. She wants them to have the best opportunities in life they can have, like she had, when they leave her employ. One girl, who had been a maid for her, had dreamed of being a nurse. She's an RN now. Pamela made that happen."

"She sounds like a really great employer to work for." Max continued to search the area, walking with Becky to all the usual places she ran as a wolf. They reached the pond where Pamela could have died. "I could have missed trail cameras set up in areas where you don't go that frequently," he admitted. He didn't want Becky to believe he had been totally successful just because he hadn't found any cameras. He was hoping that Pamela hadn't set up any. If she had and she was willing to keep the secret, someone like the corrupt maid wouldn't. What a story for the tabloids—and actually for any of the news sources—that would be. He wrapped his arm around Becky as the air chilled.

"Well, I guess I'll just have to come to your place to go running from now on," Becky said.

Max smiled down at her and then leaned in and kissed her. She wrapped her arms around his waist and kissed him back, and they opened their mouths to each other, tasting the bouquet of the wine they'd had with their dinner. This was an even nicer end to a date. He hadn't expected to kiss her again.

Then they heard movement in the woods and Max turned. He saw a tan-colored cougar watching them, and he yelled at it to go away. But it just stood there with its amber eyes aglow, looking like it was eyeing them as a meal. "Remain standing upright. I'm going to grab a stone and throw it at him, but we don't both want to lean down. With a cougar, we need to look big and menacing."

"Then I'll get the rock and you remain standing tall. You're taller than me after all." He agreed. "Sure, go for it."

She moved a few paces away from him, but he followed her to

stay close, and she grabbed a big stone. Max yelled at the cougar again, but the big cat was keeping his distance and not moving a muscle to leave. Becky returned with the rock and Max pitched it at the cougar. The big cat jumped back but didn't run away like they had hoped. He was stubborn, hungry, and he probably thought humans should be on the menu. Becky got another couple of rocks and gave one to Max. This time, he ran at the cougar, throwing the rock, and she did the same. Hers didn't go as far as his, but still, with two wolves running at him, albeit in their human form, they scared the cat off. At least for the moment.

"Let's head back to your place, but keep a lookout for the cat. Sometimes they'll begin stalking someone once they have their back turned to them," Max said.

"I've never seen one here before."

"He might have come to drink from the pond and we're in his way, or he could be adding us to his meal-to-go along with a drink from the pond." Max gathered some rocks, and so did Becky.

"I would have smelled him before when I went for a run."

"He might be new to the territory."

"I'm definitely running as a wolf at your place."

Max began thinking about the issue with Pamela again. He had to learn the truth from her about whether she believed wolves were real or not.

"I think what you do is fascinating," Becky said. "It's remarkable how you connect all the dots between these news stories concerning wolf issues."

He smiled at her. "It has its ups and downs. But I do like what I do."

Max heard something moving through the woods behind them. They both glanced back at the same time, and he knew Becky had heard the same thing. The cougar was back. "I guess he wasn't looking for water like I had hoped," Max said.

They began walking backward, to keep an eye on the cat. They couldn't run, climb trees, or turn their backs as that could make him chase them down and kill one of them. He was eyeing Becky, the smaller of the two targets. They yelled at him but kept their ammunition in case he got too close. He was following them, keeping the same distance. Max wanted to change into his wolf coat and tackle the cougar, but then Becky would need to also. And he was afraid there still might be trail cameras. Before he could even mention that to her, Becky was stripping off her hiking boots, socks, and jeans. He watched the cougar while she stripped the rest of her clothes off and shifted in a blur of forms. As a wolf, she growled low at the cougar while Max quickly stripped out of his cargo pants, boots, socks, and T-shirt and shifted. Now the cougar had two much more ominous characters to threaten.

Still, the cougar didn't run off. Not until both Max and Becky ran at him. Max wasn't sure she wanted to at first, but then she charged, and he was ahead of her in a second, not wanting her to have to face the threat of the cat's wicked claws and teeth. The cat jumped straight in the air and took off running. Max thought they would run after the cat for a short distance until they figured it had enough of two wolves chasing him. But Becky wasn't stopping so Max kept up with her, racing through the tall grass and feathered, needled pines. They kept running until the cougar was well away from the pond, and then she slowed her run, and so did Max. He figured she was done now. He assumed the cougar would stay away and wouldn't try to follow them any farther. It was one thing to lob rocks at him. Another to give him a race with death. Not that they planned to kill him, but they had to impress upon him that this territory was theirs.

They licked each other's faces in camaraderie, telling each other they had done good. Then they watched for the cougar for a little bit longer, but it didn't seem to be returning. Max motioned with his head and a little woof to say they needed to get back, and Becky woofed at him. They both raced off, the wind in their fur, their tails straight out in an alpha posture as they headed back to their clothes. He realized even in the face of danger, they worked well as a team. Even as fast as they were running, it took them some time to return to where they'd stripped out of their clothes. Then they shifted and hurried to shake out their clothes and dress. Once they were done, they hugged and kissed each other.

"Outings with you are fun," he said.

"Ditto for me. I never thought I would run into another predator on the prowl out here. Thanks for helping me look for cameras and chasing off the cougar." Despite Becky saying so, she gathered her rocks back up. "Just in case."

"He would be dumb to return to stalk us." But Max picked up his rocks too, because it was better to be safe and prepared than sorry.

They finally reached her house and set the stones in a pile around a tree where Becky already appeared to be nurturing a sedum rock garden.

"I think we need to speak with Pamela about this wolf business," Max said.

"I was afraid you might say that, but are you sure? The notion of letting sleeping dogs lie comes to mind."

"I'm certain you're going to feel differently about her now. You can't help but think she might be watching your every move as a wolf. I propose we somehow bring up the situation with her nearly drowning at the pond. I'll run it past Ryan because wolf stuff like this needs to be discussed, but if you think we could do it, we will. If you think you would have a better chance at it alone or that I would, we can talk about that too. I just think from now on, you'll behave slightly different around her. We need to learn if she truly knows about us or not."

Chapter 5

Becky knew Max was right. Worrying that cameras could have caught their actions tonight, that listening bugs or cameras could be in her home—though Max said there weren't any—made her feel unnerved. And she didn't want to feel that way working for Pamela. But what if they did discuss what Pamela knew about wolves? She would still be an outsider, still have the ability to expose them if they let on that wolf shifters did exist and she wanted to share that news with the world. Becky just felt disquieted about the whole thing.

After Max left, she was going to call her mother and talk to her about the incident.

"I've got to be on my way," Max said. "I'm sure we'll have a pack meeting over this, because it does affect all wolves."

"I agree." This time when they kissed goodbye, it was a long, lingering tongue kiss. He warmed her to her toes and spread the warmth throughout her body to the tips of her fingers that were clinging to him.

He continued the kiss, and she was thinking that, if they could, she would like him to stay here with her tonight. Because of the way Pamela called on her so frequently, she was afraid staying at his place overnight would present a problem.

"You know, it's getting harder for me to give you up for the night," Max said, kissing her cheeks reverently.

"I was feeling the same way about you and wondering if it

would be better for you to stay here because of my job or safer for me to stay at your place, because of us both being wolves. But not tonight. I think you need to discuss this business with your pack leaders."

Max sighed. "Yeah, as much as I would love to just stay with you tonight, I agree."

Then they said good night, and he left her home and drove off. She really enjoyed being with Max, and she couldn't believe how swept up she'd become in his job too. She sighed and took a shower, but when she was coming out of it, her phone was ringing. Naturally.

She answered it, and yes, it was from her boss. "Yes, Pamela?"

"Invite Max to have lunch with us tomorrow. I want to hear what he has learned about Christopher."

"Okay, sure, I'll call him and see if that works for him." He was on Pamela's case after all, and Becky didn't know where he would be while he was in the middle of it. Maybe that was another reason Pamela wanted him to work only on her case. Because she was still pulling the matchmaking strings.

"When I said 'us,' I of course meant you too," Pamela said. "I just wanted to clarify that."

"Thanks, Pamela." Becky did eat with Pamela sometimes—because her boss enjoyed her company, Becky figured—and then they would discuss some of the ongoing situations Becky needed to be made aware of or that Becky needed to talk to Pamela about.

"Did he learn anything?" Pamela asked as if her curiosity was getting the best of her and she couldn't wait to hear about the investigation from Max.

"He might have. He had some promising new leads, and he wanted to check into them further."

"And you?"

"Me?" Becky's cheeks heated. She was certain her employer was referring to Max and her dating, but she didn't want to assume as much.

Pamela chuckled. "Coming along fine, I hope."

"We've been enjoying each other's company, yes, Pamela."

"Good. If you ever need any time off to have dates with him, just let me know."

"I will, thanks." But Becky didn't think she would. She would just do her job, and she and Max could be together around their work schedules for meals and maybe some overnight get-togethers. She didn't think she would have to take any extra time off to do that. Her boss really needed her to keep her schedule straight for her. It made Becky feel useful in a good way.

"Well, good night, and I'm glad things are working out. We're having chicken salad for lunch."

"I'll tell him. What time?"

"Noon. Maybe that will give him more time to learn more about the situation with Christopher. And, Becky? If Max needs to go to some other location to run more leads down, I'll send him, all expenses paid."

"I'll tell him. Thanks."

Once they ended their call, she called Max. "Lunch with Pamela at noon; a chicken salad is on the menu. And I'm invited. Also, she'll pay for your expenses if you need to go anywhere else to track Christopher down."

"I'm still trying to learn where he ended up. I'm calling Ryan now about this wolf situation. I'll talk to you later."

"Okay, good luck and good night."

On the way home from Mountain View, Max called Ryan and told him about the business with Pamela and the wolf who had rescued her.

"Becky's mom rescued her as a wolf?" Ryan let out his breath. "Okay, we need to talk to Carol about this and get her take on it. We'll have to decide with the rest of the pack how we're going to handle it. I'm sure Carol will want us to meet tonight about it. Then you'll have your decision when you have lunch with Becky and Pamela. If Pamela has any plans to mention the wolf business to you, we need you to be ready."

"Right, though I suspect the lunch date has to do with Christopher and not anything to do with wolves, but you never know. Already this has gone in so many different directions that it's hard to say."

"Correct. I'll give you call in a little bit." Ryan ended the call but called back only a few minutes later. "The meeting is scheduled in fifteen minutes. Everyone's headed to my place now."

"All right. I'm almost there." That was one thing Max loved about his pack leaders. They weren't wishy-washy about taking action. They got things done right away.

When he arrived at the pack leaders' house, several wolves were already there. Some lived close and others lived across the town, but it still would only take them about ten minutes to get there. No traffic issues in Green Valley, especially this late at night.

Max explained the situation to the pack members. Some of the older wolves shook their heads. He took that to mean they thought that Becky's mother shouldn't have rescued the human girl. But if it had been him, he would have done the same thing. Carol had been more recently bitten and turned, so she was more sympathetic to the human equation. They could very well have eliminated Carol after *she* had been bitten. She was also a nurse, so her goal was to save people and not let them die without doing everything she could in her bag of tricks to get them through. Ryan felt the same way.

Most everyone did, except for five of the elders, one female, four males.

"So we let Max tell her straight out that she was right all along? A wolf shifter saved her?" one of the elders asked.

"I think we'll let it ultimately be Max's call. He's seeing the woman tomorrow for lunch, and we assume they'll be discussing the case he's working on for her. But if the other situation comes up, we want everyone to be in agreement on how it's handled," Ryan said.

"Kill her or turn her?" the she-wolf elder asked.

"Or let her live among us as she has all along," Max said.

"Okay, so do we put it to a vote? Three different options. We let her live as she has before, we eliminate her, we turn her. I think everyone knows what the repercussions are for each of the options. She's not some drifter, so if she's turned and can't fight the shift, that's going to be an issue for someone as important as she is. The same if she somehow just vanishes. Or if we leave her be, she might tell on us," Ryan said.

"But she hasn't before," Carol said.

"She did in the beginning, but she was just a kid, scared, and nearly drowned," Max said, having to be perfectly honest about it. If she learned they were really wolves, if she only suspected so now, then what? Would she want to tell everyone who hadn't believed her before? They couldn't trust that she wouldn't. Then too, if she decided she wanted to marry Christopher, the husband would be her closest confident. Would she tell someone who had such a special place in her heart the truth? It was hard keeping secrets like that from someone you loved, even if it could protect them.

Carol passed around pieces of paper and pens for everyone to write down their choices. Then once everyone wrote a 1, 2, or 3 down to choose their selection—let her be, death, or turned—Carol collected them in a bowl. Then she said, "Okay, so this is only in the event that she truly knows what we are. If she doesn't or doesn't make any hint to Max and Becky that she does, we take no action."

Everyone agreed. That was one thing Max liked about their pack. They had a really tight-knit pack. Ryan and Carol made a good team. The pack members had been a little worried that Carol might be a problem with her shifting issues, but she was a nurse and well liked, so they couldn't have been more pleased with the way things had turned out between her and Ryan.

"So what about you and Becky?" Asher asked before Carol could read the votes off the papers in the bowl.

Max smiled and everyone laughed. Yeah, he wasn't giving her up to any bachelor wolf in the pack or anywhere else.

Then Carol began reading off the notes, and at the end, not one person voted to have her eliminated. Most wanted her turned. Five were willing to let her live as before.

If Pamela wanted to be turned, the good thing about that was Becky would be there to help her out. Max would too. Well, the whole pack would, if they turned her. But the boyfriend could be an issue unless someone who was in their pack appealed to her and became the boyfriend.

"Okay, so if we turn her, she would need to date one of us," Asher said, smiling. "Forget your quest to look into Christopher for her. She would have us there to watch over her every step of the way."

"Can we have another vote?" Stephan Wright, one of the single males, asked. He was only twenty and not old enough to be Pamela's mate, Max was thinking.

Carol smiled. "We'll have another vote as soon as we know what's going on with Pamela. For a decision that affects all of us, we want this to be unanimous."

Max agreed and so did everyone after a fact. Then the meeting ended, but Ryan and Carol wanted to talk to him further before he went home.

"Asher does have a point as far as turning her and then keeping her in the family, so to speak. If she knows about us or highly suspects, she has already set in motion a plan to work with us. Still, we have to cover all bases, and keeping her as one of our own would assure us she wouldn't talk. Unless she made a mistake in appearing in public when she couldn't stop the shift, she would be okay," Carol said.

"I agree," Ryan said. "For the sake of the pack, for the sake of our kind, I think that Asher is right, actually."

Max took a deep breath and let it out. "We have another issue. If she truly loves Christopher and wants to be with him, what do we do about him? Turn him too?"

"Well, if we talk to her about us being wolves, maybe we can convince her she wants to be one of us, and she shouldn't be with Christopher," Ryan said.

Carol shook her head. "If Pamela is in love with Christopher and she knows about us as wolves for sure, we've got another stumbling block in our path and it's back to the drawing board for us."

CHAPTER 6

BECKY WAS ALREADY APPREHENSIVE about having lunch with Pamela this afternoon, but when Max called her to say he had canceled with Pamela already, she just felt it was bad news.

"I'm still trying to get a lead on Christopher and hope to have some information for her soon.

Tonight or tomorrow," Max said. "Uh, sure."

"I'm so sorry, Becky. I know how difficult this is for you what with worrying if she knows about us."

"No problem. I'll ask if she wants to cancel lunch with me too. Hopefully she will." Becky had managed a number of tasks this morning for her employer, and so far, everything was fine. But sitting down with her at lunchtime? Becky was afraid it would be too tension-filled, since she now knew about Pamela's past experience with a wolf shifter. It was just something she couldn't forget. Then she called her boss. "Pamela, since Max is in the middle of chasing down leads on Christopher and can't make it for lunch, do you want to cancel our lunch date?"

"Heavens no. It's about that time. Why don't you join me in the dining room?"

Becky could imagine ominous music playing in the background as they had their lunch.

When she finally sat down with Pamela and the server set their dishes of chicken salad, a teapot and teacups, and glasses of water on the table, Pamela said, "I'm glad Max is working so hard on this case and might have some good news one way or another soon. Has he told you about any of what he has learned?"

The server left them to have their lunch in privacy.

"No, but I'm hopeful it all turns out the way you want it to." Talk about being put on the spot! Becky wanted to spill the whole story—that Max and she were wolves. That the wolf who saved Pamela as a girl *was* her mother and that her father and sister and brother were all wolves. Instead, Becky concentrated on eating her lunch, feeling uncomfortable when normally she enjoyed meals with her employer. Becky wondered if she would have felt any better if Max had been there explaining some of what he'd learned during his investigation.

"My staff has been dismissed for the lunch hour so they can go off and enjoy a lunch in town for a couple of hours."

Becky took a bite of her chicken salad, trying for nonchalant, but she was afraid of what that meant. Pamela wanted to discuss something private with her, and that probably meant about them being wolves.

"I wanted to mention the reason I'm always reticent about you going to the pond in winter. I fell through the ice there when I was six."

"Oh, that's awful." Becky's blood felt chilled. "Yes, and a woman saved me."

"A woman?" Becky hoped she was sounding as surprised as she was trying to let on that she was. "Yes. I learned later that she was your mother."

"My…mother?"

Pamela smiled. "Yes. It's not the reason why I hired you. Well, I mean, certainly, you were my choice over seven other candidates because of it. I can't lie about that. It did help me to make my decision." She took a sip of her water. "Did your mother ever tell you about it?"

"It must have been before I was born."

"So she never mentioned it?" Pamela asked again.

"I…I vaguely recall some talk of it. As a kid, I wasn't paying much attention, I guess. And she didn't boast about it or anything. I just remember her warning us when we were kids not to cross frozen lakes or ponds in the event they weren't all the way frozen. She didn't want us falling through the ice. We used to ice skate on a pond in a park, so she just made a point to remind us of it every winter. There was a case of two kids falling through the ice one year, about the time I was learning to ice-skate with my brother and sister and friends, so I had believed that's why she kept mentioning it to us."

"She had saved me before that. She took me to her home to warm me up and dry my clothes."

"Oh."

"Nobody believed me."

"That she saved you? Why wouldn't they?" Becky acted as sincerely as she could that she had no clue that a wolf had saved Pamela.

Pamela smiled. "I had a big imagination back then—according to family and friends."

"You are very creative. That's why your liquor line continues to be such a success."

"Right. I…" Pamela shook her head. "If it wasn't for my imagination going wild on me, I would swear that what I had seen was all true." She took another bite of her salad. "You went for a walk with Max in the woods yesterday."

"Yes. We had a great walk. Lots of fun." Becky was dying to ask if Pamela had any security cameras set up anywhere.

"Good. You'll have to swim in the pond together. When I was a kid, I swam there all the time." Becky smiled. "Sure, if you don't mind, we could do that."

Pamela sighed. "I just wish you knew something about Christopher's whereabouts and what he's doing."

"Hopefully, Max will have something substantial for you tonight."

"Do you believe in the paranormal?" Pamela asked.

"Uh, psychics? Sure. Not that all people are sensitive to things that some experience, but I believe some can see or hear things the rest of us can't." This was so not good. Paranormal as in werewolves? She bet that was what Pamela was getting at.

"Right."

"What about you?" Becky asked. Pamela had never said anything to her about any of this before. She always seemed the most levelheaded kind of person.

"Well, I do believe that there are those who sense things that the rest of us don't. Not me. I don't have a paranormal cell in my body. But what if what I thought I had experienced was real? That a werewolf saved me from the pond when I nearly drowned."

"A werewolf?" Becky's mouth dropped open. It wasn't an act either. She hadn't thought her employer would *really* come out and say that to her.

"Yeah, it was in all the papers when I was a kid. I told everyone I saw that a wolf had run to the edge of the pond and turned into a woman to save me."

Becky ate another bite of her food, unsure what to say.

"I have to admit, I wanted to see if you would turn into a wolf and run in the woods."

"Me?" Becky's heart hitched. It was a good thing Pamela couldn't smell her nervousness or hear her thumping heartbeat. "That would be scary." Not only that Pamela would see Becky do that but that Becky would learn she had. But then she frowned. How had Pamela known who had actually saved her? The woman could have been anyone.

"I always wanted to thank her," Pamela said.

"Why do you think she was my mother?" Becky had to ask, because in the article, it hadn't said.

"My parents hired a private investigator to find her. He found her home, though she denied she had done anything so heroic. But I had remembered the direction she had taken me from the lake. I used to play in the woods all the time. The investigator showed me a picture of their house and of her, and they were the same as I had remembered them. My father offered her fifty thousand dollars for saving my life. Your mother refused to accept the money, saying she hadn't done anything, and if she had, she wouldn't have asked for money for it.

"But my father could be just as stubborn. A year after the incident, your mother had triplets, and he set up an account to fund you and your brother and sister's education. He knew I wouldn't have been alive if it wasn't for your mother's brave heroics, and he wanted to do something for her children."

"And then you hired me because of that?"

Pamela smiled. "You have a great education, you're fun to be around, and you're really great at your job. I knew you would be. But what I still want to know is, can you shift into a wolf like your mother can?" Before Becky could answer her, Pamela got a call. She took it and said to Becky, "We'll talk later." Then she hurried out of the dining room.

All Becky wanted to do was get on her phone and tell Max what had happened. She had half expected it, dreaded it, and when she heard Pamela talk all about it, that changed everything for her.

Chapter 7

Once Becky had told Max what had happened during the lunch with Pamela, he felt bad that he hadn't been there to help her handle the issue. It wasn't easy dealing with someone who knew what wolf shifters were and finally admitting to it and being put on the spot. "I'm on my way over."

"No, you need to keep working on finding Christopher. That's your job."

"I should have been there for you."

"And done what? You couldn't have done anything more about it."

"I should have been there for moral support, and yes, I could have at least talked to her about this wolf business."

"Will you have enough information to share with her about Christopher tonight?"

"He's running me ragged. I'm not sure that I will have."

"Okay, well, I want you to come tonight and have dinner with me anyway. And if it's not too soon, stay the night."

He smiled. "Yeah, I'll do that."

"But for heaven's sake, learn something more about Christopher."

"I learned he's working for an investment broker at a bank."

"Where?"

"In a town in Kansas, but he's gone to Europe, so I don't know what that's all about. But this business with Pamela changes everything if she's totally hooked on him and doesn't want to give him up for anything."

"We can't turn him too. If we decide—the pack decides—Pamela needs to be turned for her own peace of mind and ours."

"I'll have to call Ryan about this latest development."

"Okay. I'll wait to hear what he has to say."

"He and Carol are busy with their jobs for now, so it will be a while before I can talk privately with them. I can't wait to see you tonight though."

"I'm glad you came into my life. I just wanted to tell you that in case you didn't know."

He smiled. "I feel the same way about you. And I've been trying to keep you a secret as much as I can."

"From whom?"

"The other bachelor males."

She laughed. "I'll see you tonight then."

"I might still be trying to track down Christopher while I'm at your house, if you don't mind."

"No. I might have to field a call or two from Pamela, if it doesn't bother you."

"Not in the least."

"Okay, good. Chicken for dinner?"

"You read my mind."

Then they ended the call and he was glad he had let her know how he'd felt about her going it alone with discussing the wolf business with Pamela. He talked to Asher about the situation at the PI agency after that.

"That's all the more reason for one of us single wolves to meet up with Pamela and tell her how much we're glad she understands us and can be our friend," Asher said.

"You would try to become her boyfriend, but I think she's still hung up on this Christopher."

"Right, but you know what a relief it is when we meet up with another wolf and we can talk openly about what we are? After all these years with living with what had happened to her, don't you think she's going to feel the same way? That she can finally discuss what she has had to bottle up for decades?"

"True. We'll just have to see what our pack leaders say about it." Max certainly didn't want to start encouraging the rest of their wolves to meet up with her and make friends when Pamela wasn't a wolf. What if she decided she'd made a big mistake? That she should have kept her mouth shut all this time?

They couldn't risk exposing more of their wolves' identities to a human. "Well, I want to be the first in line to offer my bite."

Max chuckled. "What if she isn't your type? You have no idea if the two of you would be compatible. Not that you would have to mate each other if you bit her, but still, what if she felt beholden to you, and you realized she wasn't the woman you were interested in mating? It could be a disaster."

"You're right. I wouldn't bite her. I just would get together with her for a date or two and see if there was any spark between us. Speaking of which, what about you and Becky?"

"We're enjoying some time together." Max didn't want to tell him he was staying over at her place tonight. That would sound like the beginning of something deeper, but he didn't want to take anything for granted. What if it didn't work out? Then Asher might be interested in dating her. Max just felt it was best to keep mum about it all.

"More than some time together, I suspect," Asher said, then got a call on a case he was working. "Yes, Mrs. Probst. I've got some photos to share with you if you think you're up for it."

Asher was working on a husband-cheating case where the wife had all the money, so she was ready to kick him to the curb if what she suspected was true. But she had to have proof so she wouldn't have to lose too much money on the deal. Luckily, she did have a prenuptial.

Max packed his overnight bag with a couple of days of clothes and his laptop to do his research. Then he headed over to Becky's place to have dinner with her. She'd already told Pamela he didn't have enough new information to discuss with her tonight, and Pamela had made other plans for dinner. Becky hadn't thought she would need to tell her boss when she was having dinner with a friend, but since he was working Pamela's case and would be on her property, he wanted Pamela to know that he was going to be there.

When he arrived at Becky's home, she gave him a warm hug and a big kiss, which he immediately deepened, wrapping his arms snugly around her. "I know we haven't been seeing each other for long, but this feels so right," he said.

"I agree, which is why I wanted you to stay the night. Not to mention that all this business with Pamela has me worried. I wanted to talk to you in person and not on the phone or be texting you all the time."

"I feel the same way." He carried his bag into the bedroom, and then he set his laptop in the living room. "I should have mentioned it, but the reason I might be doing a little bit of work on this case tonight is because of the time differences."

"Certainly. What did Ryan and Carol say about this whole matter?"

"They were both working at their jobs. I figured I would call them once we were together and we could all talk to one another on speakerphone, particularly since you were the one who actually spoke with Pamela about this."

"That's true. Are you ready for some chicken?"

"Yeah, and if you would like, and I'm not getting way ahead of myself, I could grill us some steaks tomorrow night. I noticed you have a grill on your back patio."

"Oh yes, I would love that. And a wolf run tonight? When I feel unsettled, I really like to run as a wolf. And now that there's a cougar on the property, I really want to do it with you and not by myself."

"Absolutely."

"Do you think we should go in a different direction? Just in case we missed seeing any cameras in that area?"

"Yeah. I mean, we've checked it over, but the chances she would have them all over the place, rather than where you always run, seems to be unrealistic. We'll have to scent-mark the new territory so the cougar knows he has got the two of us to deal with."

She smiled. "I never scent-mark my territory." He tsked. "That's half of who we are."

They sat down to eat the chicken and the Mediterranean vegetables she'd cooked in a spicy sauce—zucchini, potatoes, red bell peppers, peas. It was great.

"I love your cooking."

"Thanks. I can't wait to eat your grilled steaks."

"Corn on the cob sound good? Baked potatoes? I can make them with the steaks." He forked up some more potatoes.

"Sure, that sounds great."

"And for after we eat our chicken, I made us mocha treats topped with whipped cream and raspberries."

"Now that really sounds great."

Once they were done, they had dessert, and then Max needed to call Ryan and Carol. He'd already sent Ryan a text telling him that he needed to discuss the situation with them about Pamela after dinner.

"Okay, so here's the deal," Max said and then he motioned for Becky to tell them everything that she could recall that Pamela had told her.

"It sounds as though she wants to be one of us," Carol said.

"I agree, but is that prudent?" Ryan asked.

Max and Becky took a seat on the couch together to snuggle while they talked over the speakerphone.

"I think it all depends on Christopher," Becky said. "If she is truly in love with him and he is with her, then I don't think turning her is a great idea. Not unless you're ready to turn Christopher too."

"And Christopher does have parents who are living. That would be an issue," Max said. It could have a snowball effect. They didn't want to have that many newly turned wolves to deal with. It was bad enough turning just one person.

"If she wants to be turned," Ryan said, "her whole staff would have to be terminated in a financially acceptable way. She can't be around a bunch of humans on a daily basis if she has trouble shifting during the phase of the full moon. The only way it would work is if she hired all wolves from our pack to fill her various jobs. Some of her positions would be easy enough to fill, I'm sure. But some jobs could take some training. Still, she would have to agree to all that. She might be partial to some of her staff and not want that."

"Then it goes back to eliminating her," Carol said.

Everyone said no to that. Max knew that Carol was the most adamant about not doing that since she had been turned and still had difficulty at the time of the full moon. And she couldn't shift and play as a wolf with her mate or the rest of the pack members during the new moon either. But it was different for her because she had a loving wolf mate and she was part of a whole pack who watched out for her. Even her job as nurse meant she worked in her own clinic with only her own people. They were still trying to get a wolf doctor to work for them as they expanded their wolf base, but for now, sick or injured wolves who needed to be seen by a doctor went to Silver Town.

"So what do you want me to do?" Becky asked. "I think she

suspects how dangerous her knowledge of us is to both her and to the wolves in general. But we owe it to her to tell her what her options are."

"We still need to find Christopher. I'm hoping that if I can make contact with him, he'll tell me he's not interested in her any longer and has moved on. I haven't learned if he's in a relationship, but if he is, I hope that would help her to see that he has moved on. The thing of it is, if he really wanted her money, he could have approached her right after her parents died and she had inherited all the estate. Why wait?"

"To make it appear that he wasn't after her money?" Becky asked. "I mean, if he had jumped right in after their deaths, don't you think it would have looked like he had been waiting in the wings all that time for the day to come?"

"I agree," Carol said.

"All right, well, I want you to learn what you can about Christopher. Find him, talk to him, and then we'll go from there," Ryan said.

Ryan was one of the best investigators there was, and Max trusted his advice. The same thing went for being a great pack leader.

"You two enjoy your night," Ryan said, and Carol echoed the sentiment.

Then they ended the call and Becky sighed. "I will feel like I'm sitting on pins and needles until we resolve this."

"I'm doing everything I can to locate Christopher so I can start up a dialogue with him. I just hope he's honest with me when I'm able to talk to him."

Becky left the couch and began gathering up the dishes, and Max joined her to help clean up the kitchen.

"But about us," Becky said.

Max smiled. "That's more of a sure thing." She smiled, raising a brow.

"I wouldn't leave you hanging about whether I would want to be with you or not. I definitely am all for being with you."

She chuckled and put the dirty dishes and the silverware in the dishwasher while he cleaned the baking dish.

Becky sure hoped Max was ready to take their relationship further. Not all the way. They needed some time to get to know each other better. She was going to suggest a movie, but she wanted to make love to him—unconsummated, of course. Consummated meant mating for life, and they weren't ready for that.

She washed her hands and he followed suit. Then she cleared her throat, wanting to propose going to bed, and hoped he was thinking along the same lines.

She reached up and cupped his face, and he instantly placed his hands on her hips, pulled her close, and leaned down to kiss her. Yes! That was just what she had in mind.

They kissed, the heat building between them, but she wanted him to know she wanted more. Not just an after-dinner kiss. She ran her hands over his T-shirt. He was wearing shorts and a T-shirt, nice and casual, though she liked seeing him all dressed up too. He had nice legs, well-toned from running, and in shorts, he was hot.

She kicked off her sandals and he smiled. Yeah, he knew where this was going.

He nuzzled her cheek with his, his body pressed lightly against hers, but then he hugged her closer, letting her feel his burgeoning arousal. He was such a hot wolf. She shifted her hands down to his buttocks and pulled him even more firmly against her, wrapping one leg against the back of his, caressing him with her bare foot, offering herself to him in an erotic way.

He cupped her buttocks then and lifted her against him, and she wrapped her legs around him. Man, she wished they could just go all the way, the sweet, achy longing between her legs just coming to bear.

"To the bedroom?" he asked, kissing her cheek.

"Yeah," she said, her voice breathy, sounding sexier than she had thought it would.

He carried her into her bedroom, her legs still wrapped around his hips, and the whole time he was kissing her, hugging her tight, making her wet.

When he reached her bedroom, he set her down on the carpeted floor, then she removed his shirt, and he pulled her shirt up and over her head. He kissed the curve of her breasts and placed his hands on them, squeezing a little, then kissing her again, though he kept his hands on her breasts, massaging, making her feel sexy and irresistible.

He slid his hands down her bare tummy and found the fastener on her shorts, then undid the button and unzipped the shorts. She wriggled out of them before she began working on *his* shorts. She loved summer. Fewer clothes when she wasn't working, which meant less to have to peel off for making love to a wolf.

He kissed each of her breasts through the sheer bra cups. She wore them for support, not for padding, but she liked the sheerer ones on hot days. They made her feel cooler, and for being with a hot wolf, the bra was sexier than others she had.

He seemed to think so too and rubbed his thumbs over the fabric and her nipples and smiled as they peaked and poked at the fabric. She only wore bras like that when she wore T-shirts or other heavy materials that no one could see through, but when her shirt was off in the presence of a hot wolf that she was eager to seduce—perfect.

Then he dipped his head and licked a nipple through the fabric, and she sucked in her breath. She was already soaking wet for him, and if they could make love to each other all the way, she would just pull him into bed and get on with it.

He lightly scraped his teeth against one nipple, making her

groan with need, his thumb still rubbing the other as if to keep it satisfied. She was feeling the erotic ache in her groin grow. Then he reached down and unfastened the clip in the front of the bra, unsnapping it and freeing her breasts like she wanted to do with his erection.

Her bra straps were hanging off her arms, while she pulled down his unfastened shorts and released them. They slid to the floor, and she dropped her bra and started to pull down his boxer briefs. Then he was doing the same with her boy-shorts panties, and they were totally naked, their pheromones engaged and their hearts beating frantically.

They ended up on the bed, all skin and muscles and legs and arms, never-ending kisses and tongues and hands. Stroking and kneading, passionate longing claiming them both.

For a moment, he paused on top of her, his hands on the sides of her head, gazing at her with lust and—dare she say it?—love. Then he took a deep breath and kissed her again.

She kissed him back, tonguing him for entrance, and he gave way, took her in, and held on with his lips in a sexy way, sucking, making her even wetter down below.

She ran her hands over his back, and then he changed position again. This time, he was behind her, his hand reaching between her legs and stroking her. His body was angled over hers so he could still kiss her. This was better than nice.

He kissed her neck and back and stroked her and every erotic nerve he could reach. No man had ever pleasured her like this before. She was thinking he was really a keeper!

He was rubbing his body against her back, his erection swollen with readiness. She placed her hand over his and made him rub her nubbin harder, faster, eager for completion. She felt the momentum building, the anticipation driving her crazy, their arousal making it all the steamier. The orgasm was just beyond reach, so close, so far.

If only she could just grab hold and ride it to the moon. Then she shattered and cried out, feeling awash with pleasure.

Max pulled her over on her back and smiled down at her, his gaze filled with lust. He kissed her mouth and played with her breasts, skimming his hand over the nipples, teasing them with delicate sweeps of his hand. She didn't want to let go of the earth-shattering moment, wanting to remember it for always, just in case it never happened to her again.

But then she pushed him on his back and climbed on top of his legs. She took hold of his rigid arousal and then smiled as she began to stroke him, thinking just how beautiful he was lying against her pillow, her bed, and she would remember this always.

Max was so grateful it had come to this with Becky. He had hoped they could continue to make love to each other as they got to know one another. He swore she'd never climaxed with another guy before, and she seemed thrilled. Seeing her sitting on his legs, her own spread for his viewing pleasure, her breasts beckoning him to mold his hands around them again, he settled against the mattress, feeling the overwhelming need to climax as she continued to ply him with magic, one stroke at a time. She smelled divine, of musky woman and she-wolf, and he vowed to bring her to climax again—tonight, later.

But for now, he was caught up in the way she was stroking him, taking him to the top and bringing him to orgasm. She continued to milk him, and he wished they were further along in their relationship when they were mated, and they could go all the way. Yet this was great too, and he would be ready to do it again soon.

When they were finished, he climbed out of bed. "Man, Becky."

"Yeah, wow, Max."

He smiled. "I'm going to shower. Do you want to join me?"

"No, another time."

He smiled at her, leaned down and kissed her, and headed for the shower in the master bathroom. He thought she wanted to build up to all this. But someday, he hoped, he would shower with her and make love to her in there too.

He washed himself with her tangerine body wash, since his toiletry bag was still in the guest bedroom. Then he joined her in bed, and she was smiling at him, looking pleased, beautiful, sexy, and like she'd had a good romp. He wouldn't mind going another round with her later. When they both wanted to. And they did.

As to Pamela, she had dropped the issue of the wolves, to Becky's surprise, and when she had tried to talk to Pamela further about it, her boss had dismissed it as silliness on her part.

For two weeks, Becky and Max worked and played and made love, while Max searched for Christopher and she continued to do her job. Then Max learned Christopher was now living in Green Valley, to his astonishment.

"Christopher is in Green Valley, working as a librarian," he told Becky over the phone.

"What? He's no longer an investment counselor?" Becky sounded disheartened by it. "I'd kind of hoped he really had waited to be with her all this time and that he was doing well financially himself. Though we would still have the wolf issue."

"Right, but remember, that doesn't necessarily make him a bad guy."

"He might not want to share where he's working with her, believing she wouldn't want to be married to someone who wasn't in a higher income job."

"Correct. He might be embarrassed to tell her the truth. And if she knew that's what he did, he might be afraid she'd really think he was after her for her money, since he probably doesn't make that much on his own. But with this information, I can learn about his income, investments if he has any, and who he might be seeing."

The next morning, Max went to see Christopher at the library to learn what he could from him in person. When Max arrived there, he went inside and saw a tall, strawberry-blond-haired man sitting behind a desk, looking just like the picture on Christopher Anderson's driver's license. "Hi, I'm Max Browning, and you're Christopher Anderson?"

The man smiled at him. "I am. What can I do for you?"

That was when Max smelled that the man was a wolf. *Hell.* "I know an acquaintance of yours, and she was under the impression that you were in Europe as a financial advisor of some sort."

His expression turned dour. "Yeah, well, no longer."

"Pamela?"

"Yeah. There's nothing between us." He took a deep breath. "You're like me, and you know nothing could come between us, if you know what I mean."

"Okay, but you couldn't tell her you weren't interested in her any longer?"

"Listen, when we were young and dumb, I had the idea she could be mine. But it couldn't happen because we're not the same. Did you know about the accident she had when she was young? The near drowning incident?"

"Yeah, and she thought a shifter had saved her."

"Yeah, a shifter *had* saved her. So she loves wolves. She loved me, though she didn't know I was, um"—he spoke more softly—"one. Like I said, I was young and dumb. I wasn't in her social class, and that wasn't just because of how much money my parents made. It took a lot of time for me to get over her, but I finally realized that I couldn't do anything about it. We're just too…different. I couldn't…turn her. For years, I'd considered it."

"Okay, so you need to tell her it's not going to work out between you. You need to meet with her, tell her—"

"What? That I lied to her because of what I am? I can't. You know that. It's better if I just don't say anything." He frowned at Max. "Who are you anyway?"

"A private investigator she hired to find you."

"To tell me it's over?"

"Yeah, if you weren't who you said you were or you were seeing someone else, I figure." That made Christopher smile. "Well, then you've done your job."

"No. She needs to hear it from you. We have another issue though." He explained a little about their pack and Becky.

Christopher's eyes widened. "Are you certain?" He sounded a little uplifted to hear the news. "Yeah, I'm certain."

"What if I spoke with her?" Christopher asked.

It appeared Christopher still loved her. "She apparently doesn't know about you. And I'm not talking about your job situation," Max said.

"Right."

"You weren't waiting for her because of the money, correct?" Max didn't want to help an opportunistic wolf mate her just because of her wealth and prestige.

"What do you think?" Christopher asked, frowning at him in annoyance.

"I honestly don't know. But I do know she has waited for you all these years, and she still wanted to see you before she decided if it would work out between the two of you. She wouldn't have hired me if she hadn't wanted to find you. She could have just moved on, but she felt she had to make things right between the two of you first."

"And discover if I had waited around just to get her money? I didn't, you know. It was the…other issue. That's something you can't explain away."

"What about you? Have you been seeing anyone else? You're not part of our pack here."

"I just moved into town last weekend and started this job. I didn't realize there was a pack located here. But no. I haven't been dating anyone."

"Well, it's a great pack, so I'll make sure you can visit with the leaders and—"

"Learn what's expected of me?"

"They're very open-minded, but I'm sure they'll offer some advice about the lady in question too."

"All right. Thanks. Sorry I've been kind of brusque. This has been a sore spot for me for so long—"

"Because you love her?"

Christopher nodded. "I tried dating other women, but no one held a candle to Pamela."

Because she is an heiress?

"It's not about the money," Christopher said as if he knew just what Max was thinking. "I know that's something everyone will believe no matter what I say about it."

"That's true." Max wasn't going to sugarcoat it, but he suspected Asher was going to lose out before he even had a chance to speak to Pamela if she still loved Christopher too.

Max wanted to go with Christopher to speak with the pack leaders, to learn what they all had to say, but he suspected Christopher couldn't just take off from work. Maybe at lunchtime, if Christopher could go with him and if Max didn't have lunch scheduled with Pamela and Becky. Then he wondered if he could get the lunch switched to dinner and meet with the pack leaders and Christopher at lunchtime.

"I was meeting with Pamela for lunch to discuss what I've learned about you." Christopher looked saddened by the prospect.

"I think you need to speak with the pack leaders first, so I'm going to propose to Pamela that we have dinner instead, if she's free. At lunchtime, you and I can meet with Ryan and Carol, talk about the best way to handle this, then have dinner with Pamela this evening. You will have to meet us there too. What do you think?"

Christopher's expression brightened, then he looked glum again. "What if she doesn't believe me when she learns I don't make that much money but I still don't care anything about the inheritance?"

"I think her reaction to you and the way you respond to her will tell all. Are you free for lunch and dinner?"

"Yeah, I am."

"I'll have to make sure the mayor doesn't have anything planned for lunch also."

"All right." Christopher looked hopeful, but then he frowned again. "What if Ryan doesn't think I should do it? Or he thinks I should call it off?"

"Let's just see how this all goes. Who knows? She may be over you. I don't want to sound harsh, but we just won't know until we're there."

"Okay, let's do it."

"Oh, one other thing, I talked to your parents on the phone. They were against you marrying Pamela."

"They were my adoptive parents and didn't have any clue that I was a wolf. They'd raised me since I was two in Kansas City and moved with me at that time to Mountain View. I had to sneak out to run as a wolf whenever I had the chance. Not that the phases of the moon force me to do anything, but it's just in our blood. I never met any wolves there while I was growing up. But my parents felt that Pamela was just leading me on and never planned to marry me because I didn't have the kind of money she had."

"Okay, gotcha."

After he left Christopher, Max called Pamela. "Is there any way we can get together for dinner?

I'm still looking into the situation and should have more information by dinnertime."

"I have a dinner with a couple in town."

"Okay, can we switch it to tomorrow then? Lunch or dinner?"

"I'll cancel on the other couple. We'll have dinner tonight if you think you'll know something about Christopher. And tell Becky to join us."

"Okay, see you tonight."

Then Max called Becky with the surprising news. "It turns out Christopher is one of us." Silence.

"Becky?" He thought he'd lost the call.

"A wolf?"

"Yeah."

"Ohmigod."

"Yeah, we want to speak with the leaders about it before he sees her. So we thought we could talk to them at lunchtime, and he'll actually meet with Pamela for dinner. I already arranged to have dinner with her tonight and you're to come with me."

Becky couldn't believe that Christopher was a wolf! No wonder he couldn't commit to the marriage and he hadn't wanted to tell Pamela where he'd gone. She suspected he hadn't been able to give her up though, or he would have just told her he was over her.

Becky called Pamela then. "Hi, I guess we're not doing lunch, just dinner."

"You can have lunch with me, if you're unable to have it with Max because he's working the case."

Becky smiled. "I would love to." After they ended the call, she texted Max: I'm still having lunch with Pamela.

Max: Okay. I spoke with Ryan. We're meeting with him at lunchtime.

Becky: I sure hope this works out today.

Max: Me too. I'll let you know how it goes after we talk to the pack leaders this afternoon. Look forward to tonight.

Becky: All right. See you at six.

Becky sure hoped it all worked out. She wished she could be at the meeting with Max, Christopher, and the pack leaders to prepare herself for the dinner engagement. Still, maybe they would have this case resolved tonight. She hoped it was a good resolution for all concerned, and that could mean that Christopher was finally able to tell Pamela he couldn't see her any longer, or the whole truth was going to come out. It was a scary proposition no matter what.

She really hoped Pamela could find true love, but who knew when it would hit? All Becky knew was she had really gotten lucky on her one and only blind date.

Then she went to the mansion and to her office. She called up Pamela and said, "How did you want me to handle the situation with your other dinner guests?"

"Tell them we'll reschedule. You don't have to give them a reason. They're good people."

"Okay, I'll do that." Becky prayed everything would turn out for the best.

Chapter 8

Max met Christopher at the pack leaders' home for lunch, though Ryan had to shift a lunch engagement around that had to do with his mayoral duties. When it came to wolf business, that took priority. Carol was off, having made arrangements to make sure she didn't have any patient appointments. She saw only wolves, so her patients understood if she had to switch appointments around when they had a pack situation she needed to help deal with.

Both she and Ryan were sufficiently shocked to learn Christopher was one of them, but they quickly welcomed him with open arms to join the pack, first thing.

Carol had fixed them roast beef stew that had been simmering in a slow cooker since that morning.

"The way it works is you can join us, but you don't have to," Ryan said. "We don't force anyone to join the pack. Everyone does, because we have so much to offer, but we've had a lone wolf or two who would wait and see, check out the events we're having, and feel if it was right for them or not. We haven't had anyone move on, and we're trying to build up our wolf base here in Green Valley."

Christopher smiled. "You could be a salesman."

"Being a mayor can be like that sometimes. So you can think on it, and even if you do join us and feel it's not right for you, you don't have to stay with the pack."

"We have to tell you how surprised we are to learn you're a wolf though," Carol said. "I imagine Max has brought you up to speed on the business with Becky and how her mother saved Pamela as a child when she was a wolf?"

"Yes. I was friends with Pamela back then. Not as in boyfriend and girlfriend that early on, but we were just friends in school. When that happened, it was all over the school. You know how mean kids can be. They teased her about her story. I told her that it was probably a good idea not to mention the woman was a wolf."

"Because you are." Carol smiled.

"Yeah, and because she couldn't prove the woman was, which meant everyone just thought Pamela had made up the fantastical story. No one wants to be treated that way in school. Anyway, it brought me closer to her because she'd witnessed one of our kind shifting. But another part of me wanted to be with her, to support her when everyone else jeered her. It was so hard for me not to tell her what I was and confirm that what she saw was true. I also wanted to make sure she didn't continue to spread the story."

"So what did you say to her?" Ryan asked.

"Well, I told her anything really was possible. But that she had to remember she'd had hypothermia when the woman saved her, so her brain probably wasn't registering things quite right. Of course I said it in a way that a six-year-old would, as my parents explained it to me."

"What did she say to that?" Carol asked.

"She agreed. But even so, she said the woman was a wolf, shifted, and raced across the ice to save her. That she didn't have any clothes on. That when the woman grabbed her hand just before Pamela went under the ice, she managed to pull her out and made sure she was breathing. Then naked, the woman ran through the snow to reach a cabin beyond Pamela's family's land. Pamela said she should have been frostbitten. Then the woman howled as a human, as if telling her pack she needed help. Pamela never told the paper that a man came running to help them. He was wide-eyed as if he couldn't believe the woman would be carrying a half-frozen, sopping-wet kid, and the woman was naked.

"But he quickly took Pamela from the woman's arms, and then he turned and ran as fast as he could to the cabin. Pamela wanted to see the woman, but she was behind the man. Pamela thought the woman had to have turned back into a wolf. When they arrived at the cabin, Pamela didn't see the wolf again. But sometime later, she heard the woman making hot soup in the kitchen, telling her everything would be all right. The cabin looked normal, no wolf decorations or photos or wolf beds lying around. She did notice that the door had a large doggy door, which Pamela suspected was for wolves, not dogs. She never saw any sign of dogs. So that was the story she had to tell, and I had to listen and assure her everything was all right."

Max was feeling like they just needed to turn Pamela. He couldn't imagine anything worse than knowing about the wolves and having to be quiet about them her whole life. Yet she seemed to have respected Becky's mother for what she had done. Would Pamela feel the same if they turned her? Would she want to be? Would she be happy being one of them?

He doubted she would know the answer to the question until she was one for a time and could process how it felt. She would have problems with wanting to shift during the week of the full moon. She couldn't shift during the new moon.

Then he wondered how Becky was getting along with Pamela while she was having lunch with her.

He was enjoying the meal Carol had prepared, but he wished he could have had lunch alone with Becky. In fact, he was feeling like that all the time. Like during their breaks from work, for any reason—meals, the end of the workday—he wanted to spend time with her. It was as if the lovebug had bitten him hard and he didn't want the feeling to go away.

In the middle of the lunch, Becky called him. "Hey, I hope I'm not interrupting your lunch or anything, but Pamela had an emergency board meeting to go to. I need to meet her there and I'm driving over as we speak."

"Thanks, Becky, I'll let everyone know. She told Christopher when they were kids that she also met your father when your mom was carrying her home. She didn't mention him in the report. He was in his human form. So just something else you should know."

"Okay. I'm thinking Christopher, if he still really loves her, should turn her. But only if she really wants to be one of us and loves him back. If not—which means we need to know how she feels about him before we tell her he's a wolf—then I think we need to rethink things."

"How do you feel about keeping your job there?"

"I'm staying here as long as I can."

"Tell Pamela I've found Christopher and talked to him. If she would like, he could join us tonight for dinner with her, or if she prefers, she could have dinner with him alone." And then Max would wish he could be a fly on the wall.

"Are you sure you don't want to talk to her over dinner first?"

"Yeah, I'm sure. I think the best thing to happen is that we get them together now. If he doesn't want to be with her, or she doesn't want to see him further, or if they're free to date now and they can see how things work out between them, it's for the better."

"What about us? If you've closed your assignment, you won't have any need to come out here." She sounded serious.

"Are you kidding? I just found you on a blind date, and I'm losing you now? Just because the mission might be accomplished, we won't know that for sure until we see if things work out between them. But for sure, I'm telling my coworkers I'm busy seeing a she-wolf every chance I get."

She sighed. "Good. Because I didn't want to have to quit this job so I could see more of you."

He chuckled. "We'll be together. And if things work out between Christopher and her, she's going to be busy too. Though that might be more work for you, come to think of it."

"As long as we can spend time together, I'm game. I'll talk to her after her emergency meeting."

"Okay, you have a deal. Just let me know if Christopher is coming or if we're going to have the night off instead. I'll bring something for us to eat if we're not eating dinner with Pamela tonight."

"All right. Sounds good. After the meeting is through, I'll call you." Then Becky ended the call.

CHAPTER 9

AFTER THE MEETING WAS finished, Becky had several business calls to make, but she said to Pamela, "Max called me with good news. Christopher lives in Green Valley, and if you want, we can make arrangements for him to have dinner with you, with or without us present."

Pamela's eyes filled with tears. Becky probably shouldn't have done it because she had a professional employer-employee image to keep up, but she gave her a hug. "It's up to you. Max and I are happy to do whatever you want."

Pamela chewed on her bottom lip. "Come to dinner, all three of you. We planned it already, and Christopher will be just another dinner guest. Since Max is an investigator, I want to know his professional opinion about Christopher's responses to my questions tonight."

"Okay, sure, thanks. I'll let Max know and he can get in touch with Christopher, if you would like. Or you can if you would rather."

"No, I have too much to do. Max can let him know. It's his case, after all."

Becky smiled. "Sure. I'll see you at the house." She thought Pamela really wanted to call Christopher herself but was afraid to get too emotional over it. Becky hoped she would be fine at dinner. Pamela could put on the most serious of expressions no matter what was going on in her life, but Becky wasn't sure she could when it came to matters of the heart.

Becky called Max. "We're all on. Tell Christopher he's also invited. Six sharp."

"I think he's kind of nervous about seeing her."

"I think she's feeling the same way about him, or she would have called him herself. I've never seen her like this before. I'm sure she still feels something for him. Oh, and why don't you bring an overnight bag. You can spend the night and we'll watch movies, run as wolves, whatever our hearts desire." She always asked and he always said yes.

"You're on." Max sounded thrilled.

Then she ended the call and drove back to the house. She was excited about having Max stay over, but she was still concerned about what would be said between Pamela and Christopher. Part of her wanted to be there to support Pamela, but part of her wanted to leave the couple alone so they could really get to know each other again and she and Max could do the same. She was hoping they could run as wolves tonight—as long as they didn't run into that blasted cougar again.

Becky thought that Pamela was doing a flurry of business, more so than usual, as if she was afraid to think about dinner tonight. Becky wanted to go home and straighten up her place a bit more, though she had cleaned up pretty well. So many things were left up in the air.

That evening, Becky got together with Pamela before Max and Christopher could arrive, running a bit late, and she seemed to be nervous. But Becky wondered if it was about the business with the wolves or it had all to do with Christopher.

She was helping Pamela to set up things for dinner. Sure, the chef made the beef Wellington, and the kitchen staff served the meal, but Pamela was in such a state, wanting everything to be perfect.

"Was Christopher really in Europe?" she finally said to Becky, after readjusting the fresh roses on the side table for the fifteenth time.

"Yes, ma'am. He just started working as a librarian in Green Valley."

Pamela immediately had her phone out and was looking up the library to see if he was pictured as part of the staff. She frowned at first, which Becky took as a bad sign, but then smiled. "He doesn't look much different from the last time I saw him. I wonder why he told me he was an investment counselor." She readjusted the silverware again, so they were completely uniform as they sat on the placemats.

"I think he was. But now, maybe he doesn't believe being a librarian would live up to your expectations. Not that it wouldn't, but you know how men can be. Especially since you're so successful."

"Libraries are important. Librarians are just as important. When I was a girl, I often went to the library. Sure, my parents could afford any book I wanted, but I just loved the children's programs and reading so many different stories, some of which I wouldn't have wanted my parents to know about."

Becky smiled. "Oh?"

"Yes, I read a lot of romance books when I was a teen. My mother…and my father would have frowned on it. It was just silly fluff to them, when I needed to learn all about the business. But we have to have time to enjoy other worlds and, well, I have to admit I ended up reading quite a few shifter stories. I couldn't help it. I just fell in love with them."

The butler announced that Max Browning and Christopher Anderson had arrived.

Pamela's eyes misted when she saw Christopher, and Becky saw the slight curve of his lips as if he was thrilled to see her but didn't want to overreact in front of Becky and Max. Again, she wondered if they should have had dinner alone tonight.

Normally, Pamela would meet guests in the great room, but this time she had them ushered straight to the dining room. She showed them the seats they were to take, and then once they were seated, the salads and wine and bread were served.

"Becky tells me you're a librarian, Christopher."

"Uh, yes, Pamela. I'm sorry I didn't tell you sooner. I only just got the job."

"And the part about being an investment banker?"

He snorted and buttered a slice of bread. "The broker I worked for was picked up by the feds for not paying his own taxes. I was disillusioned by some of the illegal things that were being done, and I just wanted to do something else. I didn't tell you I'd switched occupations because I didn't think you would approve."

"Are you happy?"

"It's a decent job. I was in Europe on business, but once I quit that job, that was the end of Europe for me."

Max was quiet, letting Christopher and Pamela do all the talking. He winked at Becky. She felt her face flush with heat. He was no doubt thinking about tonight.

"I've wanted to see you," Christopher said.

"You wouldn't tell me you were close by. I had to hire Max to locate you."

"I've been only working for three days at the library." Christopher let out his breath. "I just didn't know how to break it to you that I was close by and was afraid to meet with you."

"I…" Pamela smiled. "I'm so glad to see you. I was about to give up on you."

The beef Wellington was served and then Pamela gave the staff the rest of the night off. "I have something to confess," Christopher said.

Pamela's face fell.

"You know when you told me about the woman rescuing you in the pond when you were six?

You said she was a wolf?"

Pamela glanced at Becky. Becky remained quiet, not sure where this was going.

"Yes. I know it was silly of me," Pamela finally said. "It wasn't. I've seen them too."

Pamela's eyes rounded.

"I guess you know that Becky is one."

Pamela looked at Becky as if she was seeing her in a new way. "Uh, I figured she was, but I was afraid I'd said too much already."

"Max is too, but you knew that also, didn't you?"

Her gaze shifted to Max. "Yes. I suspected that might be the case when I had read all about the happenings in Green Valley with the hunters claiming they had shot at wolves and they turned out to be people. How...did you piece it all together like I did? I mean, after I told you about Becky's mother being one. Wait, how did you know Becky is one?"

"I'm one also," Christopher said. Pamela's face lost all its color.

CHAPTER 10

BECKY WASN'T SURE PAMELA was ready for the news that Christopher was a wolf too. That Pamela knew everyone else was seemed fine. She'd known about it for a while. She had come to grips with it. But with Christopher, he had been her boyfriend. And she seemed to still care deeply for him.

"That's why I stuck up for you in school. That's why I wanted to protect you from the others who were giving you such grief. I was one, am one, and I knew you were telling the truth. I knew that they existed—" Christopher said.

"Because you're one." Pamela said the words in almost a hush, like she wasn't sure she should speak the truth out loud now. Not when she was among all wolves and they all knew she knew about them. "So what happens now?"

"It's totally up to you, Pamela," Christopher said. "I've loved you from the day I first met you, even as a young boy, because you had loved the wolf who had saved you. Over the years, I wanted to turn you, but I couldn't. I innately knew it was wrong. It went against everything we believe in, I figured."

"You could turn me?"

"Yes, but while your parents were alive, no. I learned so much from a guy I met in college who was a wolf, and he was surprised I didn't know all this stuff, until I told him my biological wolf parents had died when I was two and I'd been raised by humans. That's when I learned that most wolf kids homeschooled and all the rest of the stuff I should have learned while growing up. If you are turned, you would have trouble shifting without a choice during the full moon. During the new moon, you couldn't shift at all. I'm what is known as a royal. I can shift anytime I want because I have few human roots mixed up with the *lupus garou* roots."

"*Lupus garou*?"

"That's what we call ourselves, or wolf shifters."

"Oh."

"I wasn't part of the Green Valley wolf pack, but now I am. I guess what I'm asking is can you continue to keep a secret?" Christopher asked.

"Or be bitten and become one of you?" she asked.

Becky was trying to see where her employer was coming from. Yes, she wanted to be turned? No, what a horrible idea? She didn't know which it was. She felt bad for Christopher who'd had to hide what he was all those years growing up too.

"If it's something you think you can live with. We live longer than normal human lives," Christopher said.

Pamela's lips parted. Who wouldn't want more longevity? "But—" she said.

"We mate for life. For all time, unless we lose our mate and then we can mate again, but no divorce."

"I–I realized telling Becky about the wolves had been a mistake if I found you and wanted to be with you and didn't want to get you involved in what I suspected. But…well, you're one too. So what do we do now?" Pamela asked.

"I hate to say it, but normally if someone has seen us shift, we have to turn them or eliminate them. We can't hope that they would refrain from telling anyone else about it," Max said.

"Just think of your former maid who was selling stories to the tabloids. What if she had known all about it? It would be the perfect story to sell, only once the press learned it was real, they would have been all over it," Becky said.

"So what does that mean for me? I could have just continued on, knowing but not saying anything. You know how well that worked out when I was a young girl. No one believed me," Pamela said.

"Well, that means that you need to be turned," Christopher said matter-of-factly. As if she had no choice in the matter, and nobody was going to do anything differently.

She arched a brow, he smiled, and the smile was devilishly wolfish.

"I would turn you. I could bite you, or we could do a nonbiting method. I have to tell you that we heal twice as fast as humans," Christopher said.

"Okay, but what about my staff? They're not all wolves."

"That would be an issue," Max said. "If they're wolves, everyone could watch out for you. But if they're not, you're putting yourself and others at risk."

"You could give them huge severance packages, enough to make it worth their while, and generous recommendations for new jobs for their service to you. You wouldn't have to explain why you can't keep them on unless you want to make up a story," Christopher said.

"Do you have any knowledge about investments? Really?" Pamela asked. "I do. I was just unhappy with the crooks I was working for."

"Then you're hired. Will you stay with me, Becky?" Pamela asked. "Absolutely. I love working for you."

"Good. I would be devastated if you left my employ. Max, I would love to hire you on as my personal security advisor and private investigator. You can tell me who in your pack—that you belong to, right?—might be able to fill my other household staff positions—wolf only, of course. Would that be acceptable? You and Becky, if things are working out for you, could have the house she lives in now as a home of your own."

"I'll have to talk to my boss, and I'll have to make sure it's okay with Becky to move in with her, but yeah, I'm all for it." Max reached over and squeezed Becky's hand.

She was over the moon with the news, and yeah, she was ready for it!

"We need to put security cameras up all over the place so that we can be sure your staff, who live on the property, can also run as wolves when they are off duty," Max said.

Pamela nodded. "I was hoping I was right in setting up the blind date between you and Max."

"Why him? And not someone else in the agency?" Becky asked.

"Remember the day when I was talking to you about the kind of guys who appeal to us—physically? I know there's not much to that as far as making a connection, but that was my start. All the men in Ryan's agency had photos on the agency site. I just looked them up, found the three who weren't married, saw that Max had been a Navy SEAL, and because of my near drowning experience—that still haunts me—I just thought he would be perfect to keep you safe."

"What if I had left you instead of any of us telling you about this? What if Christopher hadn't been a wolf?" Becky asked.

"I might have lost you as my personal assistant, though I had hoped not. As far as Christopher was concerned, I knew in my heart I wanted him no matter who he was, what he was doing. It just didn't matter as long as he felt the same for me. Max was really only supposed to find him for me. Beyond that, I wanted to renew our dream. But I'm glad Christopher's a wolf too. It's like living with this secret forever and finally being relieved to know others not only believe it but are some of the same kind and accept me.

"I–I think you and I need to discuss more of this alone, Christopher. Becky and Max, you have a good night. Max, thanks for finding Christopher for me. Becky will have my finance officer pay for your services tomorrow. I hope the two of you have some plans for tonight. I think Christopher and I do," Pamela said.

"There's no charge for the services I provided," Max said. "Just a welcome to our pack."

Christopher smiled and it was truly a happy smile. Becky thought things would work out between them, if they were honest with each other and they showed each other how much they cared. But for now? She and Max were going to have their own party.

And then they said their good nights, and Becky and Max walked to her home.

"I never dreamed I would meet a wolf like you. One who was there to help me with my boss's problems, yet there for me too. Protective. It could have been a disaster when I went to run with you as a wolf if I had been alone and had to face the cougar," Becky said.

He smiled at her. "You are so fierce as a wolf, it scared me. But I would have worried about you if you'd been walking alone as a human. Then you could have been in trouble. Once a predator like that thinks you are supper, you have to be fiercer than it, bigger, scarier, show you will win in a battle between the two of you."

"That's true. It might have turned out differently if I had wanted to strip off my clothes and fight him as a wolf if you hadn't been there for me."

He agreed. "So, about us—"

"When are you moving in? Permanently?"

He smiled and kissed her. "As soon as you say the word."

"I'm ready. It's amazing how many things can fill your life and keep you busy, except for the one thing you *really* need in it. I was so busy doing things for Pamela, I hadn't realized I needed more. You are that for me."

"I feel the same way about you. When we had another PI join our agency, he was seeing a wolf that I thought I might have a chance with. But the two were a couple from the beginning. So when I met you, the feeling was mutual. That we had something going for us that I've never had with any other she-wolf. I feel I can let down my hair when I'm around you."

She chuckled. "If your hair was longer. I can talk to you about anything and I feel comfortable, not judged. I enjoy being with you like this, or just taking walks, eating, playing. It's added a whole new dimension to my world."

"Yeah, if anyone had told me going on a blind date would end like this, when here I thought you were human, I would never have believed it."

"When you were in the service, did you have a lot of dangerous missions to go on?" she asked Max as they entered her house and shut and locked the door.

"Yeah. I stayed in until I retired, then started working for Ryan. As many years as we live, we have to be so careful about exposing the fact we live so long and don't age as quickly as humans."

"Well, I'm glad you left the service, ended up working for Ryan, and Pamela decided you were the one she wanted to have date me. I want you. I love you, Max," Becky said, running her hands over his dress shirt, toeing off her heels.

"I love you, and if you're truly ready for a mating, no more waiting, I'm all for it." He yanked off his shoes.

"I am."

"Good." He cupped her face and began kissing her mouth with gentle presses, then conquering, as if he'd found the one he'd wanted and he was claiming her. But she kissed him passionately right back, letting him know she wanted the same of him—to have him for always. He was smart, wily, protective, and loyal, and she needed that in a man. It was the kind of relationship her parents had and she'd always wanted. Loving, caring, interested in what the other was doing. Yet for her, it was the hot passion between them that stirred her blood too, making her want more. Not just the unconsummated sex but fully committing to a mate—Max, her mate.

He began to unbutton her blouse, but he was still kissing her mouth, and she began unbuttoning his shirt, ready to strip him down and get to the nitty-gritty. She pulled his shirt out of his trousers, bared his shoulders, and kissed his solid pecs. He was so sculpted, like art in the flesh. She licked a nipple as he freed her blouse from her skirt and cupped her silky bra-covered breasts, massaging, kissing her lips again as if he didn't want to be separated from that part of her for anything.

Her panties were wet, her body ready for him, and she began to work on his belt. His hands slid down her skirt, searching for the fastener. "Side," she said, their lips parting for a moment, and he glanced down at her skirt.

The zipper was hidden, and she patted her hip, then resumed work on his belt. He found the button above the zipper on her skirt, unfastened it, and pulled down the zipper. Then he slid the formfitting skirt down her hips and let it fall to her feet. She stepped out of the puddle of blue linen fabric and kicked it out of their way.

She slid his zipper down and pulled his trousers off his hips, and he jerked the pants off the rest of the way and kicked them aside. He slid her blouse off her shoulders, still holding onto her blouse, and kissed each shoulder softly. His tongue swiped over her neck, then her jaw, and he kissed her mouth again, his hands sliding her blouse off her shoulders.

Being with him like this, making love to him was the best ever, but this time it would be different. The first time for a mating, and she couldn't wait, yet she was trying to make it last long too. Max didn't seem to be in any rush either. He was kissing her leisurely all over, her breasts still covered in the bra, her arms, shoulders, breastbone, as if he adored every bit of her. He reached down to whip off his socks, then she pulled off his shirt the rest of the way and ran her hands over his pecs, flicking her thumbnails in a gentle caress over his nipples.

He slid his hands around her back and then unfastened her bra and pulled it off her shoulders. Leaning down, he kissed each of her breasts, then licked the nipple of one and suckled, and did the same with the other. They were peaked and sensitive to his touch, her pheromones and his going wild with anticipation. Even his nipples were hardened pearls, and his erection was straining at his boxer briefs. A beautiful sight.

She moved her hand over his erection, felt it pulsing with need, and she inserted her thumbs slowly beneath the waistband of his boxer briefs and began pulling them off, glancing down to see his arousal spring free.

He quickly kicked off his boxer briefs the rest of the way, and then he did the same to her with her panties, a slow seduction—sliding his thumbs beneath the waistband and then slipping them down her hips, but instead of letting her kick them off, he slid them all the way down until she climbed free of them.

He lifted her on the bed and she quickly scooted over so he could join her—all the way this time. She was so ready for this after years of not finding the right wolf for her.

He climbed on top of her, keeping his weight off her like a wolf on the prowl, leaning his head down to kiss her mouth. And then he spread her legs with his knee. He swept his hand down her body in an erotic caress until he found the center of her and began to stroke her nubbin. Pleasure and need pooled in that region, her channel moist for his penetration. His strokes were gentle at first, working her up to the zenith of the climax, pleasuring her in a way no one else had ever done, making her needy and desperate for completion.

She ran her hands over his muscled shoulders, loving the feel of his hot skin beneath her fingertips, but he stole every thought filling her head—the sexy smell of him, their musky scent arousing her, his stroking her nub harder, faster, in an attempt to coax a climax out of her. His gaze was on hers, hot-blooded, lust-filled, and she knew he felt the same way about her as she felt about him. The need, the want, the craving for making this permanent between them.

Her breathing hitched, her heart beating as she felt the rising crescendo of the climax before it hit. And then she cried out with exaltation, "Ohmigod, Max." She swore he was the greatest lover of all time. But that was before she even knew how he could make love to her all the way.

His smile was strained. "Are you ready?" he asked, his voice drenched with lust. "Yes." They were committing to this, no going back.

He eased into her, slowly, stretching her, making her feel the oneness between them, the connection even greater. He started to thrust, slowly at first, building up steam, deepening the penetration, then he began to kiss her again like he needed to touch every inch of her while he made love to her. To show her how much he cared about her.

She was running her hands over his back in long, sweeping caresses, kissing him, tonguing him, showing him she felt the same way about him.

With that one act of penetration, they had made the commitment to be together forever. He continued to thrust, and she ran her heel in gentle caresses over his leg, and then he was coming, pausing, thrusting, pausing again, as if he was trying to hold on, to experience the wonder of it being their first mating, then thrusting again.

This time he came in an explosive rush, heating her insides, his heart and hers beating hard, but he wasn't finished as he continued to pump into her and rub his body against hers now, kissing her like she was the one he loved most of all.

She enjoyed the closeness, the love they had for each other, and she felt she could stay like this in his arms and never part.

He kissed her finally, pulled out of her, and moved off her. Then they cuddled and their relationship had changed again. From one blind date, not even knowing the other was a wolf, to falling in love and mating for life. She couldn't be happier.

All the rest? Figuring out what to do about his place, telling her folks—oh, she needed to do that right away, well, just a lot of things they had to do. But for now, she wanted to bask in the glow of their lovemaking and snuggle with her wolf.

When they finally woke, they made love in the shower, and then once they were dressed, she wanted to call her parents and her sister and brother and let them know she and Max were now mated.

"I'm calling my parents to let them know about us." Once she called her mom, she said, "Hey, Max and I are mated wolves now."

"Honey! She and Max did it!" her mother shouted to her father.

Becky smiled and kissed Max's cheek while he waited to hear how that went over while she put her phone on speaker.

"You didn't bring him here to meet us first," her mother scolded.

Her dad was on the speakerphone then. "You didn't need our approval. We know you made the right decision."

"That's true. We want you to come over for dinner and celebrate the occasion," her mother said. "Tomorrow evening? Can you both get away?"

"We have the time off." Becky realized she needed to tell her boss it was a done deal. Then she wondered how things were going between Pamela and Christopher.

"Okay, come over for dinner then. Have you told your brother and sister yet?" her mom asked. "Not yet. I need to call them and my boss, and Max needs to let his pack leaders know the good news."

"What goes around, comes around," her mom said to them. "I was telling your dad that the other day. Here we thought we would never get any of you three mated to a wolf. But saving Pamela when she was a girl set the whole thing in motion. It might not have seemed like the right thing to do in the beginning—to some people—but it all worked out in the end."

"I couldn't agree with you more," Max said. "I can't wait to meet all of you." He kissed Becky's cheek.

"We'll see you at six," her mother said. "Oh, and when we can schedule a dinner with Pamela and Christopher"—as Becky had been happy to tell her parents that Christopher was a wolf and Pamela was going to become one of them finally—"we'll have them over as a reunion of sorts."

"I'm sure she'll want to do the same with you," Becky said.

"Welcome to the family, Max," her dad said. "We'll have to get some fishing in with my son, Dale."

"I would like that, sir."

After they congratulated Max and Becky again, they finally ended the call. "I'll call my pack leaders," Max told Becky.

"Afterward, I'll call my sister and brother and then let Pamela know." She realized now that she didn't want to just talk to the parties she needed to by herself. She needed her mate there so he could hear their congratulations too. The same with him talking to his pack leaders.

Then Max wrapped his arm around her and called Ryan. "I'm putting this on speakerphone."

"What's wrong?" Ryan asked, sounding concerned.

Given what they were talking about with Pamela tonight, Becky understood why Ryan might think something was the matter.

"Nothing's wrong. We're mated—Becky and me, so if any single wolves in the pack had ideas, they can forget it."

Becky chuckled. She hadn't expected Max to say that.

Ryan called to Carol and she joined him on the speakerphone. "They're mated—Max and Becky."

"Oh, that's wonderful. I just knew it would work out for the two of you," Carol said. Then they explained about what Pamela and Christopher had agreed to do.

"We're so glad about Christopher and Pamela too. We'll have a pack celebration, and everyone will be invited—your family, Becky, Pamela and Christopher, and of course our pack members. It will be great," Carol said.

Which made Becky think about her family. Would they want to join the pack too?

After they ended the call, she called her sister and brother on a conference call and gave them the happy news.

"We knew it was coming to this," Dale said, "and we're glad for it."

Natalie laughed. "I'm so happy to hear the news. I hope that we'll be seeing a lot of you in the future."

"Now that we have the land to run free on as wolves, you all can come over and join us," Becky said.

"What about the pack in Green Valley? Are you joining it?" Natalie asked.

"Absolutely, and the pack leaders are having a big celebration for us and for Pamela and Christopher, so I'm sure they'll ask you if you want to join the pack too."

"Are there any available bachelors in the pack?" Natalie asked.

Max chimed in then. "Yes, absolutely, and they'll love to meet you."

"What about she-wolves?" Dale asked.

"Yeah, even Rosalind, the pack leader's sister, is available."

Was Max into matchmaking now? Becky hadn't seen Rosalind yet. Max had told her Rosalind had a garden and delivered flowers all over, so Becky hadn't known if she even had a boyfriend.

"We'll see you at dinner tomorrow night at Mom and Dad's," Becky said.

When they all said their goodbyes, she called Pamela last. "Hi, it's Becky. Max and I are mated." She was dying to know if Pamela and Christopher were holding off or if he'd bitten her to turn her.

"Oh, I'm so glad. Christopher is at a business meeting—I know, an emergency night meeting—dealing with some issues I was having. I'll let him know at once. He'll be as thrilled as I am."

"Thanks. If the pack leaders haven't already told you, they'll be having a celebration for you and Christopher and for Max and me with the whole pack."

"I've got an incoming call. That might be them. I look forward to it. Enjoy your day off tomorrow. Your gift from me. And if you need any more time off, just let me know."

"Thanks, Pamela. My parents, Robyn and William, want you to come to dinner one night too, to meet you now that you're all grown up."

Pamela laughed. "I would love that. And when I can have dinner out with your family, I'm paying."

"Did Christopher turn you?"

"Yeah. So you'll need to schedule engagements according to the phases of the moon for me now."

"Yes! Oh, I'm so glad you're one of us," Becky said, Max echoing her sentiment.

"We will do everything to make the transition work as smoothly as it can for you," Max said. "Thanks, Max, Becky. I knew I could count on the two of you."

Then they ended the call, and they were done with business.

"Do you want to run as wolves?" Becky asked Max.

"Yeah, let's do this." He took her in his arms and hugged and kissed her. "Then we return to make love."

"You read my mind."

Before long, they were running through the dark woods, not on the trail that Becky had made and taken for the three years she'd been here, but they were making their own trails now. *Together.*

The next night, Becky took Max with her to meet her parents and sister. Her mother had put on a lavish feast of roast, carrots, potatoes, broccoli, gravy, and she'd even made a cake. Becky's sister, Natalie, was smiling big-time at Max, as if she wished she'd had a blind date with the hunky Navy SEAL.

Her brother, Dale, shook his hand and smiled. "We wondered what made you so special when Becky fell so hard for you so quickly."

"We just hit it off," Becky said. "We chased off a cougar together, like the same movies, enjoy playing with each other as wolves. I love helping him with his cases and he's totally accommodating, which is refreshing. I love him with all my heart, and I couldn't imagine not being with him."

"I never thought I would find a she-wolf who can help me solve mystery cases. I love puzzle-solving and I would never have believed my blind date would be helping me to find a missing dog—one of the cases I was working on. Or that she would be checking me out to see if I could handle a case for her boss, though she didn't even realize that was what she was doing."

"No, I was too busy thinking about next dates and where this might lead," Becky said.

"To mated bliss," Max said. "I couldn't be happier that you chose me."

"I feel the same way about you for me."

"So this all came about in truth because Pamela knew Becky's mother was a wolf and had rescued her, and then hired Becky and thought you were a wolf too?" Becky's dad asked as they sat down to the meal.

"Yeah. It was a mystery I had to keep unraveling. The only thing that wasn't a mystery was my attraction to Becky. Once I'd met her, I just couldn't think of anything else. Well, my job, sure, but I was fortunate that my job often entailed spending more time with Becky. I think Pamela planned it that way."

"We gave Becky such a hard time about going on a blind date, even if her boss was the one who had set it up," her sister said.

"Yeah, you should have seen the last blind date I went on. It was not good," her brother said. "So we thought it would turn out the same for Becky."

"Well, you know I went out with your dad on a blind date. Not the kind like you went on. At least with him, I knew he would be a wolf. We had so much fun. We knew that it was fate," Becky's mother said.

"I still don't want to go on another," her brother said. "The problem is that we need to have a dating service for wolves."

"Oh, yeah, now that's something that you should set up," her sister said. Becky laughed. "Mom, you never told us you went on a blind date with Dad."

"Yeah, it was just something we never thought we would do. After meeting your dad, I ended up rescuing Pamela as a young girl, and after that, your dad and I mated. He thought the world of me for saving the girl. He'd been at my house that day, planning to have lunch. We had the meal cooking in the slow cooker, and he was working on a cake for later when I heard a girl call out that she was 'queen of the ice.' I told your dad I had to go and check it out. He was about to pull the cake out of the oven, but it had to bake just a few more minutes, so he couldn't go with me right away.

"As a wolf, I had watched her before when she'd play on the ice, an only child, no supervision, worried she might fall through the pond during the spring thaw. Running as a wolf was the fastest way for me to get there. When I arrived, she saw me, the ice cracked with a deafening sound to our ears—and she went into the water. I didn't have any time to think. I just reacted. In retrospect, I wouldn't have done anything any differently. In the back of my mind, I knew the danger we were in when I did it, but I figured that she was young enough, and since she had suffered from hypothermia, we could convince her that she hadn't seen what she thought she had. I was trying to run her back to the house, but she was soaking wet, chilled to the bone, and so was I. That's when I howled as a human for your dad to come and help me. He met me three-quarters of the way home and took her from me so I could shift, stay out of sight, and head home and warm myself at the same time."

"Apparently, she knew just what had occurred all along," Becky said, "and in the end, it was lucky for us. She joined our kind and found her mate. And I found mine." The family agreed.

Max squeezed Becky's hand in agreement. "And I found mine."

She loved him and she was glad he loved her just as much in return.

EPILOGUE

When Becky and Max met with her parents and Pamela and Christopher for dinner at her parents' home, it was a tearful but joyous reunion.

Becky's mom hugged Pamela. "I hadn't mated yet when I rescued you in the pond. You don't know how many times I watched you as a wolf from the woods, making sure you remained safe until you returned home. I could never understand how your parents would allow you to roam through the woods on your own and play on the frozen pond or even go swimming by yourself. So I observed you in case you needed rescuing. Then that one day, I heard you playing, calling out to your imaginary friends, declaring you were 'queen of the ice,' and I had to watch over you. I never expected you to fall through the ice!"

"That was her maternal instinct," her dad said, "before her own children were even conceived. I knew she'd make the perfect mate."

"And the perfect mom," Becky said, her siblings agreeing.

"Did you ever wish you hadn't rescued me because of all the trouble I caused for you?" Pamela asked, giving Becky's dad a hug too.

"No, never. I would never have forgiven myself if I hadn't at least tried to save you." Robyn began serving up the chicken legs and baked potatoes while Becky and her sister and brother began pitching in.

Pamela smiled. "I loved you both for it. Truly. All I could talk about was how much you had meant to me. My parents got sick of hearing of it. Even so, my dad wanted to reward you for saving me. They made sure my nanny wouldn't allow me out on my own any further, which was a pain, but I still sneaked out when I could, all because I wanted to see the wolf again who had saved me."

"I was there. Watching. But you never went on the pond in winter again." Pamela smiled. "Nope, I learned my lesson that time."

Everyone was overjoyed to welcome Pamela—and Christopher—to the family, because in Robyn saving her, Pamela had become part of it. Becky realized Pamela was like a big sister to her, and not just her employer any longer.

In the weeks that followed, Becky and Max had set up house at her place, and he had sold his own home to another pack member looking to have a home on the boundary of the pack's property.

Pamela had replaced all her former staff with wolves. Her former staff was happy to receive all the money she had given them to start new jobs, and everyone had found new employment because of her praiseworthy accounts of their service—except for two who were happy to retire.

Becky was thrilled that Pamela had found her husband, her mate, and had become part of a wolf family, finally living the dream that had haunted her for so many years. Even Becky's parents and her sister and brother were glad to welcome her into the family after Robyn and William had saved her life so long ago.

But more than anything, Becky was thrilled to have found her own mate—on a blind date, no less.

Max was so thrilled to be working at the new job for Pamela, another fellow wolf, and so thrilled to be part of the bigger family.

Ryan and Carol had wanted to grow their pack in Green Valley. Instead of losing some of their wolves to work on Pamela's staff in Mountain View, they had effectively extended their pack territory to her city. All of them wanted to take part in celebrations with the rest of the pack. That wasn't something Pamela had anticipated, and she was overjoyed to be included in all these new experiences. Best of all, she was planning her own wolf party to be held at her estate.

Max would always be grateful to Pamela for bringing him together with Becky, the love of his life, his mate forever, and the joy they shared. Not a minute went by that he didn't thank his lucky stars for that first blind date that had changed so many lives. And all in a good way.

He loved Becky and she adored him, and now when they went on runs through the woods, they often saw other wolves of her staff, and Pamela and Christopher themselves, running too. The cougar that had chased them that one day? He was out of there for good. The wolves ruled!

Tangling with the Wolf

A Silver Town Wolf Novella

Chapter 1

If there was one thing that really annoyed Hanna Bridgeman—and as a red wolf, she could get really growly about it—it was when she asked a cute guy out to have a drink and he was late. She was all by herself, didn't know anybody in Green Valley, Colorado, and she was nervous about going for a job interview there tomorrow, so she was hoping for some company, or at least a distraction, not to be stood up.

Maybe he just hadn't had the nerve to tell her no. She'd recently lost her job at the local paper in Loveland, Colorado, and had just arrived in Green Valley when she had met the guy at a service station, pumping gas for his truck, and asked him where a good place would be to go for a drink. She'd needed one, and her hotel didn't have a restaurant, unfortunately.

He was human and had told her about this pub, so she'd asked if he would like to join her there at six and here she was. But the guy wasn't, and it was already six thirty. Traffic jams holding him up? Not likely in Green Valley. Hanna wasn't even sure whether she wanted to live here, but she needed work, and being a news reporter was her job. Rather…*had* been her job. If she hadn't asked the police chief in Loveland some embarrassing questions, she would still have her job.

She sighed. She could be a bit of a rogue wolf when she wanted to do real investigative reporting instead of writing fluff stories all the time.

At least the pub had some fun decorations: a stack of three jack-o'-lanterns on the bar, lighted pumpkins on each of the tables, orange and black lights hanging on the walls, and a sign that had a wood carving of Dracula with the words *Dracula's Pub* beneath it. The bartender was dressed like a pirate with a patch over his eye, and the servers were wearing a variety of costumes ranging from a sexy cat to Superwoman.

Hanna glanced out the window again. The colorful fall leaves were beautiful. Oranges, purples, reds, yellows, and a few evergreens and Colorado spruce trees really set things off. Crisp, cooler night temperatures were great for wolf fur coats and sweaters and jackets. She loved the fall. It was her favorite time of year.

She eyed the parking lot. No blue pickup truck. Lots of motorcyclists were showing up, though.

Then a guy caught her eye as he got out of a shiny, red Corvette. The car was cute. So was he. Or…sexy, rather. Except he had a military haircut. And she'd vowed to stay away from military guys. Two disastrous relationships had been enough for her. This guy was blond and green-eyed, tall and muscular with no fat, not a bodybuilder type but more the kind who could use his muscle when he needed to in a real combat situation.

When he came inside the pub, he glanced in her direction, and she quickly looked away. She wasn't here to pick up some other guy. Not that he acted like he was looking to hook up either. She motioned to the pirate waitress, who was busy visiting with some bikers sitting a few tables away. When the waitress came over, Hanna ordered a glass of chardonnay and a hamburger. She figured she might as well enjoy her dinner even if her "date" wasn't going to show up. Then she would head back to her hotel.

The military-looking guy sat at a table across the aisle and two tables away from hers. He ordered a soda and then pulled out his phone and read something. Maybe a text from a date or a friend he was supposed to meet. Maybe the person was late in arriving too. She couldn't imagine anyone who looked that hot being there by himself. At least she wasn't the only one sitting alone. She hadn't exchanged cell numbers with Joe, the no-show, but at this rate, she was glad she hadn't. She wasn't actually very outgoing. She'd had to work at learning to step out and meet people to interview them. It was something she always forced herself to do so she wouldn't backslide into her shell.

The motorcyclists were beginning to get unruly, catching her attention.

She took a sip of her citrusy wine and glanced at them talking among themselves, ordering beers, and glowering at the bikers at the other tables. The groups were members of different biker gangs, and she didn't think they would play well together. She frowned and eyed them more closely. They looked like some of the outlaw motorcycle gangs that were allegedly into all kinds of criminal activity. She checked her phone to see if she could identify them, and sure enough, there were members of the Bandidos, Hells Angels, Outlaws, and Pagans, all embracing the regalia of their motorcycle clubs.

Corvette Man looked up from his phone and saw her gawking at him again as if she were trying to catch his eye and get up close and personal. What was the matter with her? No matter how much she chastised herself for showing interest in him, she couldn't help it. She envisioned having asked *him* to have a drink with her. He would have shown up—on time even.

She glanced down at the navy sweater she was wearing that was covered in fuzzy pills or balls and pulls. It was her favorite sweater for fall, though she had told herself she should only wear it when she was raking leaves or shoveling snow, not to meet and greet people. Her jeans were just as worn, and her hiking boots had seen better days. Even her hair, clipped back in a French twist, had been tugged and pulled by the chilly breeze, leaving strands dangling about her neck and shoulders. She should have gone into the ladies' room and straightened it out. And why was she even thinking of that?

Hot and dangerous, Corvette Man was the reason. He looked like he could handle any weapon known to man and then some. Her dad had always told her she needed to look her best when she went out because there was no telling who she might run into—relating his own experience when he had looked like the dregs, dropped into a pub, and met her mom. It hadn't turned out badly for them, though her mom always talked about how he'd been dressed in a grass-stained sweatshirt, jeans, and scuffed work boots and was wearing a scruffy, three-day growth of red beard. But she said his green eyes and wolfish smile had won her over, and she had overlooked his disheveled appearance.

Corvette Man left his table, and as he walked past Hanna's, he dropped his paper napkin on her table. She glanced down at it and read the scribble on the napkin: *Get out while you still can.*

Hanna raised a brow as he hurried past, and she smelled the napkin, finding the waitress's scent and a male red wolf's scent. She frowned as he left the pub. He was a red wolf too! Running into gray wolves was a rare enough occurrence, but running into a red wolf like her was unheard of. She looked out the window and saw him on his phone, talking to someone.

A biker at one table shouted something derogatory to a biker at another. Her first instinct should have been for self-preservation and getting out of there like the male wolf had done. But then she thought of her job interview at the local paper tomorrow. Wouldn't it be great if she could write this story and impress the editor? She had a front-row seat to a fight in a pub between biker gangs.

She pulled her phone out of her purse and began to record the beginning of the fight between the gangs.

Suddenly, the male wolf returned to the pub. She thought he

was going to sit back at his table and finish his drink, despite the escalating fight between biker gangs and the fact that he'd warned her to leave, but he targeted her instead.

"Come on. You're bound to get yourself killed in here," he said gruffly.

Before she could object, which she fully intended to do, the wolf grabbed her arm and pulled her out of her seat.

"Hey! What do you think—"

"Saving your ass and keeping you out of jail."

Chairs started to fly. Two men unsheathed knives, and two others had their guns out.

All Hanna could think about was the story she could have written that would secure her a job!

"I'm an investigative reporter," she said, angry at the wolf for forcing her toward the door.

The guy looked skeptically down at her, which irritated her even more.

"Let me go!" she said.

Men were shouting above the piped-in mood music, making it sound surreal.

A chair flew at them, and the blond-haired wolf pulling her toward the exit threw his arm up and blocked it. The chair hit his arm and fell to the floor with a clatter.

"Are you okay?" Hanna asked. Even though he was a wolf and healed faster than a human, he could have broken his arm while trying to protect them.

"Yeah, I'm fine. I'll be bruised, but no problem."

As soon as they were outside, the cops pulled up in squad cars. Several got out of their cars and pointed guns at Hanna and the wolf.

"Get on the ground now!" one of the officers shouted.

"Great, just great. Instead of writing a news report about the fight, someone will be writing about me getting arrested!" Hanna couldn't believe what the guy had gotten her into. Though when she really thought about it, she knew the fight hadn't been his fault and he had been trying to rescue her.

Bryan "Phoenix" Wildhaven glanced at the woman lying on the pavement next to him. She was a red wolf like him—feisty, stubborn, bullheaded like he could be. Instead of being grateful that he had gone back inside to save her ass, she was pissed off at him. She was a tall, long-legged strawberry blond, with beautiful green eyes that had been watching him with interest when he had walked into the pub, looking away coyly after he'd caught her ogling him. And she hadn't even known he was a wolf like her at the time.

If he had just left her at the pub, he could have been well on his way to Silver Town without further incident. He'd been driving for so many hours that he'd just needed a break so he wouldn't fall asleep at the wheel. But she'd been a single woman, wasn't part of any of the groups of people causing trouble, and she was a wolf, so he had wanted to warn her to leave before she got hurt. When she had ignored him, he'd had to return and take matters into his own hands, which had irritated him. She didn't have the good sense to stay out of harm's way, and he couldn't believe a wolf would be that naive.

Now they were being handcuffed and put into a squad car until the police officers could sort things out, while the crisis inside the pub was escalating. Bikers were running out of the building. Police were taking them down. Except for rescuing the woman, Phoenix felt he should have just grabbed a soda from a convenience store and continued on his way to his sister's house.

"I'm Bryan Wildhaven, by the way, though everyone calls me Phoenix," he told the woman as they sat in the back of a squad car together. This was certainly his first time to be arrested, though he knew they would be released once the police had time to check them out. Well, at least he would. What if the she-wolf had had trouble with the law? That wouldn't be good.

"The phoenix rises from the ashes. All right. If I weren't tied up at the moment, I could shake your hand. Hanna Bridgeman, by the way."

Little Miss Hanna had tenacity; he would give her that. "So you knew the guys were going to have a fight in the pub, and you were there to report on it, if you didn't get yourself accidentally killed? Just because a bullet is meant for one target doesn't mean it won't hit another."

"And you know this from experience because you're military, or ex-military, right?" she asked, sounding a little sarcastic. So she didn't like guys in the military?

"Army Special Forces, Green Beret, retired."

"Figures. I wasn't at the pub expecting trouble. I would have had to be an undercover cop or FBI or something to know that." She gave him a sweet but fake smile. "When you dropped the note on my table, I thought it might have been your special way of trying to pick up a wolf."

"Hardly."

"I can't believe we left the pub, didn't cause any trouble, and aren't carrying weapons, but we got arrested. *You* must look suspicious," she said.

He cast her an evil smile. "So what were you here for?"

"A date, but he was a no-show."

"A wolf?" He couldn't imagine a wolf standing her up without good reason.

"Human. What were you doing here? And how did you know there was going to be trouble?"

"I'd been driving for several hours, and I was getting sleepy. So I stopped to get a soda and take a break."

"You're not from here?"

"No. I'm going to Silver Town to visit my sister and her new mate. As to how I knew about the trouble, I realized those were bikers from different gangs and there was bound to be difficulty between them. I smelled your scent when I walked past your table the first time and had to warn you. But you wouldn't heed the warning. So you're from Green Valley and work at the local paper?"

"Uh, no. Loveland, Colorado."

That didn't add up. "And you came all the way down here to get a story? Wouldn't the Green Valley news reporters do the story?"

There was something she wasn't saying.

"I told you. I didn't know the gang members were going to be in the pub."

A couple of gunshots went off inside the building. Both of them instinctively ducked.

Hell, he wished they were out of here now. More shots were fired, and then police were hauling bikers out of the pub with wrists zip-tied. They began loading people in a police van. Ambulances arrived to take injured bikers to the hospital. Then an officer opened the door to the squad car and helped Hanna and Phoenix out.

He questioned them about what had happened, removed their handcuffs, and inspected their IDs. Once he'd run a check on them, he said, "You're cleared. If you think of anything else, let us know."

Hanna rubbed her wrists. "What happened after we left the pub?" she asked the officer.

"Two of the gang members shot each other. Then others began shooting. Three were stabbed. We have to haul them all in for questioning to learn who was involved. Sorry about taking the two of you into custody. We didn't have time to do anything but try to get a handle on things."

"No problem," Phoenix said. "Are we free to go? I'm on my way to see my sister and brother-in-law in Silver Town."

"Yes, Mr. Wildhaven, you're free to go."

The police officer left to help gather evidence from the crime scene. Phoenix asked Hanna, "Are you going to be okay?"

"Yeah, I'm headed over to my hotel."

"Have you had dinner?"

"Uh, no. My hamburger hadn't arrived before all the trouble began."

"There's a place here that has great burgers. You have your own car, right?"

"Yeah."

"Okay, why don't I follow you to your hotel and take you to the restaurant so I don't lose you?"

She hesitated, then nodded. "All right."

They got into their cars and he followed her to the hotel. Once she parked, she climbed into his Corvette. "Beautiful car."

"It was a retirement gift for myself."

"It sure is nice."

"Thanks." He drove her to the hamburger place next. He hadn't planned to eat there, but now it was getting so late that he didn't want his twin sister and his brother-in-law to have to wait on him to eat. He called his sister on Bluetooth. "Hey, Carmela, don't hold up dinner for me. I'll explain when I get in, but it'll be another couple of hours before I get there."

"I hope nothing's wrong. No car trouble?"

"No, I'm good. I ran into a situation here in Green Valley, so I'm close. I'm just grabbing a burger and then I'll head out." He wasn't about to explain he was with a she-wolf, not while Hanna was in the car with him and listening in on the conversation.

"Okay, then we'll see you in a couple of hours."

They ended the call, and he pulled into the parking lot of the hamburger place.

"They have every kind of topping you can imagine," he said as they headed inside.

“Hmm, sounds good.”

“They have wine and beer, too, if you wanted to try again at having a glass.”

“And you?”

“I’m still headed to Silver Town after this, so I’ll have another soda.”

She glanced at the deck with its huge wood carving of Sasquatch holding a rope in his hand, attached to a woodcarving of a fish, and the orange lights draped across it and the building. They had all kinds of clay jack-o’-lanterns set in the windows. Inside, small cauldrons sat on each of the tables holding lit orange candles, and black cats decorated the whole restaurant.

The owner must have cats, he thought.

Hanna smiled at all the decorations. He had thought she might get a kick out of the nine-foot-tall Sasquatch. Plus, the food was great. The restaurant was farther from the main road that would take him to Silver Town than the pub was, which was why he’d dropped in there for a soda and not here.

“Were you going to have dinner with your family?” she asked.

“It’s getting late. It would take me about forty-five minutes to

drive to their place in Silver Town, and I don’t want them to have to wait on me to have dinner.” He opened the door to the hamburger place and stepped inside.

“Besides, you wanted to have a date with me,” she quipped.

He smiled darkly at her. A she-wolf who wouldn’t obey him when he was trying to be gallant and keep her safe wasn’t a wolf he would seriously date.

So that begged the question—why was he having dinner with her?

Chapter 2

"This is the cutest place," Hanna said to Phoenix as she looked at the photos of black bears, brown bears, moose, wolves, elk, cougar, lynx, red fox, bison, and beavers in their natural habitats in Colorado, hanging on the warm, golden-oak-paneled walls. There were also pictures of black cats everywhere. "I love Halloween, so this is fun to see all the decorations."

She and Phoenix sat in a booth that featured a table and seats in the same warm oak as the paneled walls and a picture of two gray wolves howling. They didn't have anything like this in Loveland, and Hanna immediately felt her spirits lifted. Getting a good meal would help too.

"And the food is great," Phoenix said. "So are you dressing up for Halloween?"

"Always. I hand out candy to the kids, wearing something fun. A steampunk outfit this year. What about you?" Smiling, he shook his head.

"Aww, come on. Don't tell me you don't have fun with the paranormal."

He chuckled. "We are the paranormal. That's good enough for me."

"What about when you were a kid?"

"Yeah, sure, but—"

"You're all grown up." And how.

Wearing gray, furry wolf ears, furry wristbands, and a tail, the waitress brought them each a menu and a glass of water and smiled. "Oh wow, a couple of reds. You're new to the area."

"Uh, yeah," Phoenix said, looking at the menu, but then he smiled at the waitress.

"Yes." Hanna knew the woman said *reds* and not *wolves* because everyone else here appeared to be human. The waitress, Carla, was a gray wolf. Hanna was surprised.

"Our leaders are a gray and a red," Carla said.

"Oh wow, really." Hanna smiled. Maybe it wouldn't be such a bad place to live after all. She wouldn't mind being part of a wolf pack, since they didn't have one in Loveland. "I'm going in for a job interview at the paper tomorrow." She hadn't meant for Phoenix to know anything about that or that she'd been fired from her other job. She shouldn't care, but she suspected he'd ask her more about being an investigative reporter and wanting to cover the story at the pub.

"Oh, great! I sure will be rooting for you. Maybe our leaders can put in a good word for you at the newspaper office."

"Wow, that would be super." Hanna told Carla her name and gave her cell-phone number to her.

"If the two of you have had a chance to look at the menu, what would you like to eat?" Carla asked.

"A soda and the Sasquatch Burger for sure." Phoenix handed his menu to her.

"Ohmigod, four pounds of hamburger and one pound of cheese?" Hanna looked incredulously at Phoenix. "For real?" The guy was muscular, but he wasn't bulky in the least. She couldn't imagine where he could pack all that protein away.

"Yeah, I worked up a healthy appetite tonight saving a red from out-of-control biker gangs."

Hanna rolled her eyes at him.

"Oh no, I can't believe they would come to Green Valley of all places," Carla said. "It's all over the news."

"Maybe that's why they did. Because they thought they could get away with it and no one would be able to react quickly enough," Hanna said, wishing she could have had the lead story.

"Ryan McKinley is our mayor, and he takes a personal interest in keeping the city free of crime. He's angry about it. He texted the pack members to ensure none of us had been there, and he's starting an investigation into the pub owner to see if he had anything to do with the biker gangs all appearing there at one time. Not that the pub owner was necessarily involved, but if he was, McKinley will deal with it."

"Wow, your leader is the mayor?" Hanna asked.

"Yeah, he also runs a private investigator business. So he really can check things out in a hurry," Carla said.

Hanna handed Carla her menu. "That's great."

"What would you like to order?"

"A glass of chardonnay and a blue cheese and mushroom burger." Hanna was glad she had come here for dinner instead of just eating the protein bar she'd packed in her bag.

"Okay, I'll have those right up." Carla gave them both a big smile and left.

A guy dressed as a Wookiee walked by them, nodding.

Hanna chuckled. "This is a much better place to have a glass of wine. And it's a lot of fun too. Thanks for recommending it and keeping me company for dinner."

Phoenix drank some of his water. "After what we experienced at the pub, I agree. When I hauled you out of there, you said you were an investigative reporter?"

"Well, a reporter for the paper in Loveland."

"But you're looking for a new job as an investigative reporter in Green Valley?" Phoenix asked.

"Yes."

"And you wanted the gang story to hand in to the editor to help you get the position?"

"That was the general idea."

"But then you were afraid you were going to be locked up by the police, and how would that look to a prospective employer?"

"That's the gist of it."

"Sorry about messing up your gig."

"No, you aren't."

Phoenix shook his head. "Your life is more important than an article for a paper. Believe me."

Changing the subject, Hanna said, "You told me you had retired from the army. Now what are you planning to do?"

"I'm checking out the pack in Silver Town, also run by a red wolf and a gray wolf. Lelandi Silver, the red wolf, is a cousin of mine, formerly with the last name Wildhaven. And, of course, my twin sister, Carmela, and her mate, Michael Hoffman, live there now. He is also special forces, retired. And so is Michael's brother, Daniel. He intends to retire there too. We were friends in the army."

"So you plan on settling in Silver Town?"

The waitress brought them their meals and a soda and glass of wine. "Silver Town is wolf-run, if you didn't know," Carla whispered to Hanna. "But we're trying to build up our pack here in Green Valley too."

"As in, turn it into another Silver Town…or so I've heard," Phoenix said.

Carla smiled. "We're working on it. We just need to get our people into all the key positions, running all the businesses, filling all the vacancies—as long as everyone who takes the jobs is fully qualified, of course."

"Sounds good." Hanna got the impression Carla was trying to sell her on Green Valley.

"I imagine you could get a job as a reporter in Silver Town, no problem, because of who runs the town," Phoenix said, "if things don't work out in Green Valley."

"Okay, so things could be looking up for me." Hanna had never realized two packs were out in this area of Colorado and certainly not that they would be able to help her get a job. She was so relieved.

"Without even having to report on biker shootings at a pub or anything that dangerous," Phoenix said.

"That was something," Carla said. "Were you really there during the fight?"

"Yeah, unfortunately," Phoenix said. "But we got out before the shooting started."

"That's good. I'm glad you weren't hurt. You're military, aren't you?" Carla asked.

Hanna frowned. It didn't matter that she wasn't with him on a date; she was still "with" the wolf, and she was ready to tell Carla to back off.

Phoenix smiled at Hanna, probably because she looked annoyed. "Yeah, retired special forces."

"Wow, cool. Then you were in good hands, Hanna." Hanna smiled lamely at the two of them.

"Did you need anything else?"

"No, I'm good. Thanks, Carla," Hanna said. "I'm good too," Phoenix said.

Then they began to eat their hamburgers. They were divine. When she wanted a burger, this was going to be the place to go if she ended up living here.

Once they finished their meals, Phoenix gave Hanna his cell number. "I've got to get on my way, but if I'm in the area and you ever need help or anything, give me a call."

"Like if I'm at another unscheduled motorcyclists' convention?"

"Hey, if you're going to be an investigative reporter, no telling the trouble you could get yourself into."

She chuckled. "So what? You're volunteering to be my bodyguard?"

"Something like that."

"Thanks for saving me tonight at the pub."

He paid the bill and she opened her mouth to object. She hadn't intended for him to pay for her meal.

"My treat. I invited you. Think of it as a first date, of sorts." She scoffed. "I don't go out with military guys."

Her comment earned her a smile. "Bad experience?"

"Two."

He smiled again. "Okay, not a date. Just a…way to make up for you not getting the story to sell to an editor."

"Thanks then." She gave him her cell number as well. "Just in case you have a story you want to share with me that I can report on."

"I can guarantee you that won't happen."

They said goodbye to Carla, who told them to come back anytime, and left the restaurant. "What are you doing tonight?" Phoenix asked Hanna.

"I planned to see a movie about a woman with superpowers," Hanna said.

He pulled out his phone and scrolled through some pages. "That looks good. Do you want some company?"

She frowned. "Okay. But what about your sister and brother-in-law?"

"I'll send my sister a text telling her I have to keep a friend company and will be there after the movie ends. I can't think of anything worse than worrying about a job interview, staying in a hotel in a town you're unfamiliar with, and watching movies on TV. And then not being able to sleep because of worrying about the job interview."

"So you going with me to the theater will take the pressure off?"

"Yeah. It's a movie I was interested in seeing anyway, if you want the company."

"Are you sure?"

"Yeah. It's great when others have superpowers too."

"Your sister won't mind?"

"Are you kidding? She knows I'll be there after that, and I'm staying with them until I sort out what I'm going to do and where I'll be living. They'll be glad I'm not underfoot for too long."

He texted his sister and then drove Hanna to the theater.

She wouldn't call this a date per se, and she had the distinct impression that reporters weren't on his most favored list of people to get to know. But he was taking her to the movie, and he'd even bought her dinner. Things were looking up.

Chapter 3

"That was interesting," Phoenix said as he and Hanna left the movie theater.

"You didn't like it." She didn't have to be a mind reader to know that. Because of their ultrasensitive wolf sense of smell, she could tell he had been annoyed with the woman in the movie—a reporter like her, who was following the lead on a story out of her assignment zone and got canned for even mentioning it to her editor. The woman ended up saving the world after learning about the trouble the world was headed for. See? Getting fired from a job was the best thing that had ever happened to the superhero *and* the world.

"It was all right," he said.

"But you didn't like it. Why not? I thought it was great. Because the woman got fired from her job, she saved the world."

As they climbed into his car, Phoenix smiled a little at Hanna as if he thought she was being silly for getting so into the movie, which annoyed her.

He drove her to the hotel, where she thanked him for taking her to the movie and buying her popcorn and a soda.

"You're welcome. I hope you have a good interview tomorrow and get the job."

"Yeah, me too. Thanks again." Hanna got out of his car, waved, and headed inside the lobby. Well, she didn't need to worry about getting interested in this guy who had been in the military. His obvious aversion to reporters was enough to make him *so* not her type.

She glanced back at the hotel's covered driveway and noticed he was still there, making sure she got in okay. That was nice of him. Finally, he drove off. She noticed a biker gang member take off from the parking lot headed in the same direction as Phoenix, and she saw another biker watching her. Hadn't the police arrested all of them?

As she walked into the hotel lobby, Hanna thought again about the job interview and sighed. She knew she'd have to tell the editor that she had been fired from her last job. She hoped he didn't hold it against her since she really wanted this job as an investigative reporter. She should have just found a different investigative reporter job before she irked her former boss enough to fire her, though it was a little late for regrets. When she'd heard the police chief openly lying about money from the department that he had spent on home improvements—at his house—she couldn't help but call him on the carpet about it.

Hanna got on the hotel elevator and a man joined her—the gang member who had been sitting on his bike, watching her from the parking lot. He was dressed in a black leather jacket and pants and boots, his brown hair tied back in a tail and his beard well groomed. He eyed her with disdain, and she considered jumping off the elevator. His insignia indicated he was with the Hells Angels—a skull with wings on the helmet and *Hells Angels* written across the top of it.

"You called the cops on us," he said, his voice gruff and dark as the elevator door closed. She should have gotten off when she'd had a chance.

Her wolf instincts were dead-on, and she could smell his aggression, even though he seemed to be keeping his cool.

"If you're talking about the incident at the pub, I didn't call anyone."

"What about the guy you were with?"

"No. And if you didn't know, they stuck us in a squad car and questioned us too."

"But you aren't in jail. My brother is."

She wasn't the one who started the fight either. And she didn't have any warrants out for her arrest. She suspected some of the bikers armed with guns weren't supposed to be carrying them.

"Anyone in the pub might have called the police. The waitstaff, someone else who was there having a drink. It certainly wasn't me." She arrived at her floor and was ready to jump out. The door opened, and she put her hand out to stop it from closing, afraid he would react violently if she tried to bolt because he thought she had lied to him. Now she could have used a military guy as her boyfriend!

"You had your cell out."

Uh, yeah, recording the actions of the biker gangs. Hanna frowned. Despite still wanting to use the video recording in her interview, she supposed she should hand it over to the police so they got the culprits who actually started the fight.

"I was checking messages. Something that many of us do when we're waiting on someone to show up." She hoped he wouldn't realize she was lying. "This is my floor."

He grabbed her arm, and her first instinct was to turn into her wolf and tear into him. Of course there wasn't any way she could do that without stripping and shifting. And there wasn't any way she wanted to bite him and turn him.

"Let me go."

"You'd better not be lying. My friends and I will be watching you, and if we learn you've lied, you'll wish you hadn't." He released her, and she left the elevator, furious with the biker. He'd bruised her arm, not to mention threatened her! The elevator door shut, and she glanced back to see if the hallway was clear. Thankfully, it was. She'd been afraid he might follow her to her room. Wanting to make sure he didn't change his mind and come after her, Hanna raced down the hall, turned the corner, and ran to her room.

She used her key card to enter her room and then called the police.

"Hello, about the incident at the pub tonight? I have a video of some of what happened in the beginning, before my friend pulled me out of the place and he and I were falsely arrested."

"And you didn't tell us before now because?"

"I'm a reporter and I was going to use it for a story, but if it can help you get the right guys, I want to do my part."

"A reporter? That's a first."

Yeah. She sighed. So far, things weren't going well for her. And she wasn't sure Carla, the waitress, would call the pack leader to ask him if he could put in a good word for her at the newspaper office.

The investigative officer told her where to send the video. Hanna held her finger over the send button, sighed again, then pushed it. There went her story.

Phoenix should have known that as soon as he arrived at his sister's home in Silver Town, he'd find her waiting up for him, curious about who had delayed him.

"We thought you might have stayed overnight in Green Valley." Carmela gave him a warm embrace, her green eyes smiling. "What kept you so long?"

He was glad to see her, but sometimes having more privacy was welcome when it came to his love life. Phoenix hugged his sister back. He heard the shower going and figured Michael was getting ready for bed.

"She's a wolf." A wolf who was hiding something. He was wary of her, maybe because of the issues he'd had with reporters before—shoving mics in his face, wanting to know how his team members had died on a mission, how he felt about being the only one who had survived the missile attack.

"And?"

"I'm not staying with her because we're not courting." He explained to his sister how he had met her.

"Ohmigod, we heard all about that on the news. Of course, we thought of you since you were in Green Valley, but we had no idea you would have been in the midst of all the trouble. Why didn't you tell us you had been there? Forget it. I know why. You're special forces and you don't need anyone's help."

"Not that time anyway."

"We'll have to have her over to the house for lunch or dinner.

What's her name?"

"Hanna Bridgeman, and no to having her to the house for lunch or dinner."

His sister's jaw dropped. "Okay, so things didn't work out. I'm sorry. Do you want to talk about it?"

"No."

Thankfully, Carmela changed the subject. "Well, I'm so glad you retired from the army and are here for good."

"Thanks. I'm glad I'm out of the rat race and can settle down."

"Right. Well, it's late and we were headed to bed when I heard

your car pull up. We'll see you in the morning."

"Thanks, Sis." He hugged her again, and she walked to the master bedroom while he carried his bags to the guest room on the other side of the house.

He couldn't believe disliking a movie had rubbed Hanna the wrong way. Was there a deeper reason? Ever since he first saw her, he had been attracted to her, to her feistiness and yet vulnerability. Despite giving him grief, she had seemed relieved he'd wanted to take in the movie with her. She was a mystery, and he was intrigued with her. She was new to the area, no attachments, it appeared, and he was new to the area and wasn't seeing anyone. And they were both red wolves. It certainly wouldn't hurt to get to know her better.

He thought again about the reporter in the movie who had been fired from her job. Phoenix frowned. Had Hanna been fired from her job—and it was personal? He pulled out his laptop and looked her up at the newspaper office in Loveland.

He wondered about the guys she'd dated before and why that had caused her to swear off military men.

He found the web page for her newspaper in Loveland, but she wasn't listed. He frowned. But when he searched for stories with her byline, he discovered she'd written tons of newspaper articles. None of them were investigative in nature. He found an article about her asking the police chief some pointed questions concerning spending department funds for his own home improvements.

Hell, she probably had been fired!

He smiled. She was a bit of a rogue. Like he was. He could imagine himself doing the same thing.

After giving the police her video, Hanna paced across the hotel room floor, unable to stop worrying that maybe one of the motorcyclists had followed Phoenix to his sister's house. Maybe he would be okay because he was retired military, but she needed to at least give him a heads-up. She tried calling his cell number, but it went to voicemail. Afraid he might be in trouble, she found the Green Valley pack leader's phone number, since he was the mayor. She didn't know the names of the pack leaders in Silver Town who would know Phoenix's sister.

"Hi, I know it's late and I'm not a member of your pack, but this is Hanna Bridgeman."

"You're calling about the job at the paper?" Ryan asked. "Carla left a message for me about you."

"Uh, no. Do you know Phoenix Wildhaven? He and I were at the pub tonight that was in the news—the one with the biker gangs causing a shoot-out. One of the gang members approached me at my hotel. He wanted to know if I had called the police, and when I said no, he asked if Phoenix had. I'm worried about another gang member who headed in the same direction as Phoenix on the road to Silver Town. I thought the man might follow Phoenix all the way to his sister's place. I wanted to warn Phoenix, but I haven't been able to reach him. I hoped you would have his sister's number."

"If one of those bikers knows where you're staying, he could be back. I'm sending someone over to pick you up right now. You'll stay with Carol, my mate, and me just to make sure you're safe. I sent word earlier to the newspaper that I was recommending you for the job they have posted. I'll get in touch with Carmela, and she can tell her brother about your concern."

"Thank you."

"Max Browning, one of the private investigators who works for me, will pick you up. He's a retired Navy SEAL so he can offer you good protection."

"Okay, thank you, Ryan. I'm in Room 411."

"I'll let him know. And I'm forwarding you his picture so you will know who he is."

She couldn't believe this was all happening, though she was glad that Ryan had a guy with some muscle picking her up and that the pack leader would make sure Phoenix knew the trouble he could be in. She packed her bags and hoped she wouldn't have any further trouble tonight.

Phoenix heard his sister's footfalls as she hurried toward the guest room, and he got out of bed to see what the matter was.

"Ryan McKinley called. He said Hanna, the woman you were

with at the pub, was threatened by a biker gang member at her hotel."

Phoenix was already yanking on his jeans, ready to go into rescue mode and bring her there.

"Ryan said he's sending Max Browning, one of his PIs and a Navy SEAL, to pick her up, and he's taking her to Ryan and Carol's house. She'll be safe there. But Hanna worried that someone from the gang would follow you here. She said something about the gang member thinking you or she had called the police on them. Ryan said she couldn't get ahold of you." Carmela raised a brow.

"I was in the shower. A Navy SEAL is watching out for her? Hell."

Carmela frowned at him. "Are you sure there's not something more going on between the two of you?"

"No, and just so you know, she doesn't date military men." Carmela smiled. "You never let that stop you before."

Phoenix ran his hands over his hair. "She's a reporter. Well, she *was* a reporter. She was fired from her job for questioning the police chief about some illegal money transactions."

Carmela frowned.

"*Fired*," he repeated, in case she hadn't heard that part.

"Not that you never questioned your former commander when you felt the situation was necessary."

"Not in front of the press." Carmela raised a brow. "Okay, so once."

She folded her arms and cocked her head, indicating she was waiting for him to fess up.

"Well, twice."

"And those are the two times you told me about. No doubt there were others. And your commander didn't fire you because you're good at your job, but someone else? Probably would have been court-martialed. Anyway, Ryan McKinley has it covered. And he said he told her he contacted the newspaper about the job she's interviewing for tomorrow. She—and he—just wanted to give you a heads-up if any gang members showed—"

They heard a couple of engines rumbling as two motorcycles drove into Carmela's driveway and parked.

"Speak of the devil. I'll wake Michael and call the sheriff. Don't answer the door until the cavalry arrives." Carmela hurried off down the hall to her bedroom.

Phoenix finished getting dressed. Hell, he never thought a gang member would go after Hanna at the hotel. He should have walked her to her room at the very least.

Michael was soon heading into the living room, shirt and shoes and a couple of Glocks in hand. He set the guns on the back of the couch and pulled on his T-shirt. "Hey, Phoenix, good to see you. This reminds me of some of our earlier days." When Carmela rejoined them, Michael kissed her and said, "Go back to our bedroom, honey. We'll take care of this."

"Don't the two of you dare do anything. Wait for the sheriff and his men to arrive!" Then Carmela headed back to the room.

Phoenix watched her and realized his sister had gained a bit of weight since the last time he had visited with them, six months ago. "Is she—?"

"Yeah, she is. Babies are due next year." Michael pulled on his boots.

"She never said anything to me about it."

"She miscarried after three months the first time, so she didn't want to say anything this time until she was more sure they'd be okay. She's five months along now."

Phoenix slapped Michael on the shoulder. "Congratulations, man. How many?"

"Twins. We're thrilled."

Someone banged on the door, as if telling the occupants they'd better open up or their callers would huff and puff and blow the house down. The problem was that the wolves were on the inside, and more of the pack would be arriving shortly.

Michael handed Phoenix one of the Glocks. "Let's do this."

Just as Michael was about to pull open the door and jump aside so Phoenix could confront them, the sheriff and a couple of deputies were running their sirens and headed straight for the house. The next thing they knew, the motorcycles had taken off and were racing out of Silver Town.

"Well, now you see firsthand what a great pack this is," Michael said, and then he and Phoenix went out to meet the sheriff and deputies.

"Good to see you have finally come to stay," said Peter Jorgenson, Silver Town's sheriff, shaking Phoenix's hand.

"Yeah, I'm glad to be here." But all Phoenix could think about was the she-wolf in Green Valley who'd had to face a gang member all on her own when he should have protected her.

Chapter 4

At the McKinleys' home, Hanna had just showered and thrown on a long, purple T-shirt featuring a black cat sitting in a pumpkin. She was climbing into bed when she got a call. She grabbed her phone from the bedside table and saw the call was from Phoenix. Worried about him, she said, "Hello, are you okay?"

"Hell, I was worried about *you*."

She smiled. "I'm fine. I'm staying with the Green Valley pack leaders while I am here to do the interview. Did you have any trouble with the bikers?"

"They were just here. Good thing you called us about them. The gang must have had someone follow me to my sister's house in Silver Town, then wait until another biker joined him to provide more muscle. They both drove up into the driveway. But our sheriff 's department was here in no time to back us up."

"Oh good. I tried calling you."

"I was in the shower. I got your message after the fact. I'm sorry.

I should have walked you up to your hotel room."

"It wasn't necessary. At least I didn't think it would—" Suddenly, the door to her bedroom opened. Hanna eyed it warily, then saw Carol's tabby, Puss, saunter into the room and jump onto the bed. She laughed and started petting the cat.

"Is everything all right?"

"Yeah, Carol's cat, Puss, decided to come join me in bed."

He chuckled. "Well, I'll let you go then. Tell me how the job interview goes."

"I will. Thanks."

They ended the call. A few minutes later, he called her back, surprising her. "Do you want to have breakfast with me before you have your interview?"

She closed her gaping mouth. She figured she would be having breakfast with Carol and Ryan in the morning. So why did she tell Phoenix sure?

"Okay, I'll meet you at the Waffle Makers on First Street. My treat. They have all kinds of different food if you don't like waffles—omelets, sausages, hash browns. All kinds of breakfast foods."

"My interview is at ten. So at nine?" She was stroking Puss, who was happily purring, her little motor rumbling under her supersoft fur.

"Yeah. I'll meet you there then."

"Night."

They ended the call and she set her phone on the bedside table, smiled, and closed her eyes. Maybe she could give another military man a chance.

Phoenix rested his head on his hands on his pillow as he thought about dating—really dating—the she-wolf. Hell, Hanna was a reporter! And reckless! But damn if she didn't fascinate him on several different levels. What if the Navy SEAL Ryan had sent to pick her up at the hotel and take her to the pack leaders' home had already caught her attention?

He closed his eyes, determined not to borrow trouble. Before long, it was time to get up and tell his sister and brother-in-law he was having breakfast with the woman he told his sister he wasn't interested in getting to know. He knew she had figured differently.

Carmela always seemed to know him better than he knew himself.

"Hey," he said to his sister as he walked into the kitchen and gave her a hug. "Congratulations on the twins."

"Thanks! We're excited."

"I'm going to get breakfast in Green Valley."

Carmela laughed. "But you're sure you don't want to invite Hanna home for lunch or dinner?"

"Lunch is okay. Let me ask her. We're having breakfast together, and then she's having her interview. After that, I'll bring her home for lunch if she would like it. She may need to return to Loveland to take care of business."

"Does she have family?"

He tilted his chin down and looked at his sister with exasperation. He had no idea. He and Hanna hadn't spent time with each other as if they were really getting to know each other. But now he did want to know about her.

"Oh, right, you aren't dating her."

Michael came in to get some coffee. "Give him a break, Carmela."

Phoenix chuckled. He was going to like having his brother-in-law in his corner.

"Remember who you're sleeping with," Carmela said, giving Michael a kiss and then starting to scramble some eggs.

"Okay, I'm off. I'll check in with you later, one way or another," Phoenix said.

Carmela seasoned the eggs with lemon and pepper spices. "Ask her what she likes or doesn't like to eat."

"Right. See you both later." Phoenix drove off to Green Valley, hoping Hanna got the job there. Though if she ended up in Silver Town, that would be good too.

What he hadn't expected was to see Max Browning with Hanna at the Waffle Makers restaurant, and he realized his mistake.

Phoenix should have told her he was picking her up at the pack leaders' house and brought her to the restaurant. Though he had assumed she would drive herself. He was ready to go tell the retired Navy SEAL to take a hike.

Phoenix went inside, and Max smiled at him as he approached the table. "I'm here, per Ryan's orders, to watch out for Hanna, but if you're going to be with her until she has her interview—"

"I am. You can leave. Thanks for watching out for her." Phoenix was more abrupt than he had meant to be.

"If you want to stay and have breakfast with us, Max—" Hanna said, giving Phoenix a look that said he was being way too wolfishly possessive.

"I'm sure he's got important PI business to conduct." Phoenix lifted a brow at Max, signaling him to go and he would take care of matters.

Max smiled at him. "I want to wish you well on your interview, Hanna. I do have some urgent business to take care of. Otherwise, I would stay and have breakfast with you." He glanced at Phoenix as if to tell him the Green Beret wasn't chasing off the SEAL.

"Thanks so much, Max, for watching over me."

"My pleasure." Max said goodbye to both of them and then left the restaurant.

Hanna glanced at the menu. "You could have been nicer to him and let him stay to have breakfast with us."

"I *was* being nice. I didn't want us to keep him from his urgent business and stress him out."

Hanna laughed.

He smiled, glad she wasn't annoyed with him for sending the SEAL away.

They both ordered blueberry waffles and blueberry syrup.

"So why don't you like reporters?" She drank some of her coffee and then took a bite of her waffle.

"Who said I don't like reporters?"

"Oh, I don't know if you realize this about me or not"—she leaned across the table and spoke low for his ears only—"but I'm a wolf."

He laughed. "Okay, so you sensed it. Honestly, I want you to have every success in your field of endeavor."

"What happened to you that makes you not like reporters?" She was tenacious and not dropping the issue. She might just make a good investigative reporter.

"On one of our missions, all the members of my team died except me. It was bad enough that I had to deal with inquiries from all over from military officials about how I managed to survive, but reporters had a field day with me. After it happened, I was numb. I couldn't get over what had occurred. I couldn't believe my buddies were all gone. I'd been injured, too, but once I had recovered, I kept wondering why I had lived when they had died. For months, reporters hounded me. You can see why I'm not that fond of them."

"Oh, I'm so sorry. That must have been horrible for you."

"It was. What about you and military guys?"

"Not as devastating as your story. The first guy had a secret wife and was seeing me when he went to training in Colorado. His wife was in Florida."

"A wolf?" He didn't think she would be shook up about a human she'd been seeing, but he was surprised the cheater had been a wolf.

"Yeah. Unreal, right? We mate for life."

"Very few of us are like that. Most of us believe in the wolves' ways." He drank some of his coffee. "What about the other guy?" He cut into his waffle and took a bite. "What was his problem?"

"Oh wow, well, he acted so into me whenever he returned from an overseas assignment, and we weren't supposed to be seeing others while we were dating. We had an agreement. If we decided to move on, we would. I kept my part of the agreement. He didn't."

"So you think all military men are cads."

She smiled. "I'm beginning to think I might give one more guy a chance, if I find one who—"

"Wants to date you? Hell, put me on the list before any other military guy gets there."

She smiled brightly. "I don't know any other military guys—"

"Max."

"Oh. Him. Yeah, well, if you hadn't saved me from the motorcycle gangs fighting at the pub, he might have been on my list."

"I knew I had done something right when I went back inside to drag you out, no matter how pissed off you were at me. So I'll be waiting for you at the newspaper office, and my sister wants us to have lunch with her and Michael later. If you're agreeable, I'll let her know."

"Yeah, I would like that. I, um, need to tell you that I was fired from my last job for going against my boss's instructions."

"I got lucky with my boss. If I hadn't been so good at my job, I would have been fired any number of times."

She chuckled. "I doubt that."

"Oh hell yeah. I'm a bit of a rogue wolf."

"Like me."

"Yeah, that's exactly what I was thinking." He glanced at the clock. "Are you ready for your job interview?"

She let out her breath. "Yeah." She was going to pay for their breakfast, but he did. "Thanks."

"Is there anything you would like or don't like to eat at my sister's house?"

"No, anything is fine."

"Are you nervous?" he asked.

"Yeah. They always say to have a job to get a job, and being fired from a job isn't the same as leaving it. I have to be honest with the editor, though."

"I agree. You wouldn't want that to backfire on you." He walked her out to his car. "I guess Max brought you here and didn't follow you from the pack leaders' home."

"Right."

Phoenix drove her over to the newspaper office, and she took a deep breath before they went inside. He sat in the lobby while she went to the receptionist, spoke with her, turned and gave Phoenix a small, worried smile, then headed to an office.

Phoenix texted his sister: We're on for lunch. Noon?

Carmela texted: Sure. What would she like to eat?

Phoenix: Anything is good with her.

Carmela: Okay, see you then.

Phoenix figured he would show Hanna around Silver Town and check with the newspaper office there if she didn't get the job at the Green Valley newspaper. He watched the door to the office, hoping she did well with the interview, and he swore he felt as nervous for her as she had been.

Hanna shared her résumé with the editor, who frowned at her work. She didn't have a good feeling about this, even though the mayor had spoken on her behalf with the editor.

"I have to tell you that I was—"

"Fired from your last position? We're a newspaper office, Ms. Bridgeman. We are all about the news." He didn't smile, and she figured this wasn't going anywhere.

"Yeah, I saw where the police chief is under a lot of scrutiny now. Maybe they'll make him pay for his crime," she said, hoping the editor would realize she was right.

"I have to be honest with you. I have three other candidates applying for the job," he said.

Oh, naturally. Why hadn't she realized she wouldn't be the

only one? "Two have worked as investigative reporters for a few years with larger newspaper offices. They wanted a slower-paced town like this one to relocate to… Families, you know." He flipped through her résumé, as if he was really seriously looking over all her journalistic awards and other credentials. "You don't have any investigative experience."

"I'm a quick learner."

The editor smiled.

Okay, just end the interview already. There wasn't any sense in prolonging the inevitable.

"I have another interviewee in just a few minutes."

"Of course. Thanks so much for your time." She rose from her seat and shook his hand, smiling graciously.

"If you don't get this job…" As if she would—"Don't give up on your dreams, Ms. Bridgeman."

"Thanks, I won't." When she left his office, she saw Phoenix seated in the reception area, but he immediately rose to his feet. She didn't smile. She couldn't help but be disappointed. A rejection was a rejection. Then she thought of Silver Town. There, she might get a fair shake because it was wolf-run.

"Hey," Phoenix said and drew her into his arms.

"Sorry." She wiped away a tear, damn it. She hadn't wanted to fall apart in front of him just because she didn't get the job.

"Max told Ryan I'd brought you here, and Ryan knew you were in the interview, so he called me."

"Yeah, well, now I have to tell him I'll have to try in Silver Town.

Ryan and Carol really want me to stay in Green Valley."

"That's what he called about. He said if the editor didn't hire you, he would."

Hanna stared up at Phoenix. "Doing what?"

"Communications staff. He learned the mayor in Knoxville

was hiring newspaper veterans to be his communications staff, and Ryan thought it would be a great idea. He didn't want to mention it to you unless you didn't get the job because he knew how much your heart was set on being an investigative reporter. And the icing on the cake?"

"Yeah?"

"He wants you to help him with his PI agency—doing some investigative work. You'll have to get some additional training for that, but what do you think? A communications officer for the mayor's office and a PI so you can do some investigating to really help him out?"

"Ohmigod, yes." She threw her arms around Phoenix and kissed him as if *he* had hired her and put her out of her misery.

He kissed her back, but it was much more of a heated and passionate kiss between wolves than a glad-you-feel-better kiss. And she was really beginning to warm up to the idea of dating the Green Beret and taking the chance that he wouldn't be anything like the last two military wolves she'd dated.

"We're supposed to go to the mayor's office next, if you liked the idea of working for him. I think he was afraid Silver Town would hire you in a heartbeat, when he's trying to increase the wolf population in Green Valley."

Hanna smiled. "Let's go see him, shall we?" She was thrilled. And she was glad Ryan had called Phoenix to have him give her the news so she wouldn't feel bad if she didn't get this job.

When they arrived at the mayor's office, Ryan ushered them right in, even though Phoenix didn't need to be with Hanna to learn about the job. But Ryan said, "I can offer you a job too, Phoenix."

Phoenix raised his brows.

"If you're looking to join our pack. I know your sister is in Silver Town and you might want to get a job there, but we are really trying to expand our pack and our influence over the town. If you want to work here, we would be delighted."

"What's the job I would be doing?" Phoenix asked.

"Private investigator, communications, anything you could do that would help the pack."

"Okay, sure. I'm interested." Phoenix glanced at Hanna as if telling her he was sticking around, so they could do some things together.

"As for you, Hanna, if you want to be one of my communications officers and work on getting your PI license and do investigative work, I would be glad to help you out."

She smiled. "Yes, thanks so much. I would love it."

"You can stay with us until you can find a place to live. Phoenix, you too. We have plenty of room for guests."

Hanna thought Phoenix might want to stay with his sister and brother-in-law since they were family.

But he just nodded. "That'll be great. Then I won't have to commute."

She couldn't believe it.

"We have a fall festival going on tonight, if the two of you would like to join us. Hayrides, cornfield maze, pumpkin patch, face painting, costumes, food, and fun," Ryan said.

Hanna smiled. "I would love to go."

"It has been set up on the acreage behind the house. And we have plenty of woods to run in as wolves, so you're welcome to strip and shift and run at any time."

"All right." Hanna thought this was just what she'd needed. A real change of pace. She hoped she would do a good job for Ryan.

"Sounds good to me. I'm going to show Hanna around Silver Town, and we're having lunch with my sister and her mate. After that, we'll come back here," Phoenix said.

Ryan shook his head. "Don't convince her to stay there."

Phoenix smiled. "No problem. I think she's looking forward to her job here, and I wasn't sure what I wanted to do so this works for me. We'll get out of your hair then."

"Thanks to both of you for joining our pack." Ryan rose and shook their hands. "We'll see you when you return. Feel free to pick any guest room to stay in at our house when you arrive, Phoenix."

"We'll be there," Phoenix said.

"I'll need to pack up my things and move them," Hanna said, not wanting to delay getting moved. Her apartment lease was coming up for renewal, and she needed to clean out her place.

"You can have all the time in the world to get moved. We can help you."

"I can help you too," Phoenix said. "Being in the military, I have moving down to an art."

She smiled. "I don't. So thanks."

Chapter 5

"I can't believe Ryan hired both of us at the same time," Hanna said as Phoenix drove her around Silver Town to see the sights in the downtown area and then took her out to the ski resort.

"I do. My sister, Carmela, had told me Ryan was checking out the Silver Town pack to see how he could make Green Valley more like it, more wolf-run. Silver Town had the advantage of being built by wolves from the ground up, and they didn't let others settle in their town unless they were wolves. Ryan took over the pack in Green Valley and has been trying to change things ever since."

"That's great. We need more wolf-run towns. I love Silver Town. I love all the wood carvings of wolves at the entrances to several of the establishments. And that old ghostly Victorian inn is pretty neat. Too bad somebody hasn't renovated it."

"I agree. Do you ski?" Phoenix drove her to his sister's house. "I do. So the resort will be close enough to Green Valley to go skiing. What about you?"

"Yeah. That's another reason I liked the idea of moving into the area. By the way, my sister's going to think there is more going on between us than there is, so ignore her if she makes any mention of it."

Hanna sighed. "Here I thought you took the job in Green Valley and are staying with me at the pack leaders' house because there *is* more between us."

He chuckled, but he didn't agree or disagree with her. He

needed a job. He got a job. What more could he ask for? Dating the she-wolf? Once he had met her, that was inevitable, despite all his denials to the contrary. He couldn't imagine dating a shy, retiring wolf. If he had any say in it, Hanna was not dating Max, the Navy SEAL.

She smiled as if she knew just what he was thinking.

When they finally arrived at the house, Carmela welcomed Hanna as if she were her long-lost sister. "I'm so glad to meet you. I was worried about what happened to you and Phoenix last night at the pub. I'm relieved he was there for you."

Hanna sighed. "I had hoped to get a news story out of it."

"Oh, sure. If I was in your line of business, I would too. How did the job interview go? If you didn't get the job, I was going to contact our own editor and see if he needs an investigative reporter," Carmela said as she set plates of spaghetti on the table and Michael brought them glasses of water.

"Thanks so much, Carmela. In truth, I didn't get the job, but Ryan McKinley gave me one instead. I'm really looking forward to working for him. And he gave Phoenix a job too."

Her mouth agape, Carmela abruptly shifted her gaze to Phoenix. He smiled, knowing just what she was thinking. He'd taken the job to be with Hanna.

"Ryan wants to expand his pack," Phoenix said.

"Well, I'm glad about it. We were going to ask the Silvers what kind of jobs they had that you could do, but that works too. You'll be close by anyway." Carmela set a platter of garlic toast on the table. "And we're staying with the McKinleys while we find a place, um, places to live," Hanna said.

Carmela smiled brightly and brought over a bowl of salad while Phoenix poured them glasses of tea. Then they all sat down to eat.

Michael finally said, "That sounds like a really good deal."

Phoenix knew they would have been happy to have him stay

with them, but he was eager to start on a new job and get settled in, especially with his sister expecting twins.

"So where are you from?" Carmela asked, and Phoenix knew poor Hanna would get the third degree.

"Fresno, California, but my parents and my sister and I moved to Loveland, Colorado, when I was three. My dad is still in charge of the post office there. My twin sister, Susan, runs a day care. She loves it in Loveland and doesn't plan to move. My parents are the same way. There are no wolf packs in Loveland, so I'm excited about joining the Green Valley pack."

"It would be a good pack to join," Carmela said. "You must be a royal."

"Yeah. I take it you are too."

"Yeah, we were all in the military, no time to take off for shifting when we didn't want it to happen," Phoenix said.

"Oh, I bet. Same with me as a reporter. The meal is delicious," Hanna said.

"Thanks. I figured I would make it because it's both Michael and Phoenix's favorite dish," Carmela said. "I'm glad you like it too."

"Well, we're really glad you both got jobs," Michael said as they finished up their meal.

"We are too," Hanna said. "We're going to the fall festival that the pack leaders, Ryan and Carol, are putting on for their wolves. Do you want to go with us?"

"Oh, I would love to, but the cooler fall weather and nausea from the pregnancy are keeping me from doing a lot of extracurricular activities right now," Carmela said.

"How wonderful. Do you know how many? Their sex?"

"Twins, but we don't know the sex yet. I think Michael is sitting on pins and needles more about it than I am." Michael and Phoenix chuckled.

"When are they due?"

"February next year."

Hanna smiled. "Congratulations to both of you."

"Thanks," Michael and Carmela said.

They cleaned up after lunch, and Phoenix repacked his bags in the guest room where he was staying. He couldn't believe he would take Hanna to a job interview and end up with a job of his own and a new pack to join.

Before he left, he gave his sister a hug and shook Michael's hand, then gave him a warm embrace. Carmela hugged Hanna, too, and she looked like she appreciated it.

Then Phoenix and Hanna drove back to Ryan and Carol's house in Green Valley. "Are all your things out of the hotel and at Ryan and Carol's place?" Phoenix asked.

"Yeah. I checked out completely." Hanna frowned. "I wonder who called the cops on the motorcycle gangs at the pub. And why they thought we had something to do with it."

"I phoned them."

"What? You never mentioned it to me when we got arrested. I told the biker you hadn't notified the police."

"Anyone at the pub could have called the police." Phoenix let out his breath. "So you're irked that you didn't tell the gang member the truth?"

"Of course not. I thought that *was* the truth. I wouldn't have said you had, if I had known. You could have told me that you called them, though."

"You had your phone in your hand when I pulled you out of there. I thought you had called the police and that's why the biker came after you and me, because I had been with you. Wait, you were recording the fight, weren't you?"

"I'm sure several people were."

He passed another car on the road to Green Valley. "And you're irritated with me for calling the police. What if one of the gang members had seen you documenting their illegal activities? And captured their faces in the event the police had warrants out for their arrest?"

"I had to get my facts straight."

"And you didn't turn it in to the police when they questioned us."

"No. I did later, though."

"And?"

This time, she let her breath out in exasperation. "They were grateful."

"What did they say about the delay in turning it over to them?"

"I told them why I had and they understood. You know, if you're going to date me, you're going to have to get used to being with a—"

She hesitated to say anything further, and he figured she remembered being a reporter was no longer her job.

"Well, you're just lucky I'm not," she said.

He smiled. "Sorry." He didn't comment any further about her taking the video.

She smiled. "Okay, now that's been said and done, I like your sister and her mate. That was fun. And I can't wait to go to the fall festival."

"With me." He wanted her to be with him. Yeah, he'd done about a one-eighty from the first time he met her, but she was the kind of woman who made things exciting for him. He'd been waiting a long time for someone like her who could keep him on his toes.

She chuckled. "Yeah. With you."

"Maybe we could get a place to rent together so we won't be on top of Carol and Ryan at their place," Phoenix said. "I mean, when we feel we like our jobs well enough and plan to stay."

She glanced at him. "You're moving awfully fast."

"I've waited a very long time to meet a she-wolf like you. You're the one I never saw coming."

She smiled. "Thanks, Phoenix. I guess you saw me ogling you at the pub when you first arrived."

"I did."

"So tell me, why do you have the name Phoenix?"

"Uh, that. When I was on a mission, a bomb hit a building we were checking out, and when it did, the place exploded in flames. Everyone but me had made it out, and when I finally managed to get to my feet and exit—luckily—I got the nickname Phoenix, for rising from the ashes."

"Wow. Okay, I truly need you by my side if I have any trouble with bikers or anyone else. Let's see about the rental after we've been at the jobs for a while. I feel like we don't want to overstay our welcome."

"Yeah, I agree."

They arrived at the pack leaders' house, and she helped him move his bags in.

It was brisk outside, and they pulled on their jackets and were ready to have fun at the festival.

"What do you want to do first?" he asked.

She looked like she was excited about this, her gaze glancing around at the pumpkin patch, the sign for the cornfield maze, the booths of food, the bobbing for apples, craft booths, and a bounce house for the kids. She grabbed his hand and hurried him to the maze. "I have never been in a cornfield maze before."

He laughed. "Then the maze it is."

"Bobbing for apples after that."

He smiled. "I want the apple with the longest stem."

"You're a Green Beret. You can have the shortest one." Then she was pulling him through the maze at a run.

"We'd better slow down or we'll find our way out of it too quickly."

"The sooner we're out of here, the sooner we'll get to bobbing for apples."

He had to admit he was having fun with her and felt more lighthearted, like when he'd been a kid on an adventure. He was having nothing but pure fun with a she-wolf, and he felt he was making memories with one who might one day be his mate. He pulled her to a stop and kissed her.

Hanna couldn't believe she was kissing such a rare, mythical bird as Phoenix again. He was cupping her face and kissing her mouth in a way that was both precious and memorable, and it made her think that perhaps moving into a shared apartment sooner rather than later would be something they would have to do.

She was giving the kiss her all just as passionately. Well, maybe she pushed for more, making sure that he knew she was all in when it came to showing him some intimacy. They heard voices of people coming toward them in the maze. She pulled her mouth away from his and kissed his cheek, then took off running with him, her hand in his.

Phoenix smiled at her. "I think we're going to have to get our own place very soon."

"Oh yeah, I believe so too." The way their pheromones had jumped in to tell them just how much they were interested in each other was a clear sign of their deeper attraction.

While they were racing through the maze, they ran into several dead ends, entered another path, turned a corner, and found yet again a dead end. Others behind them somewhere in the maze were laughing at their own folly. If others had found the right path and stayed on it, they all could have gotten right out of there just by following the first wolves' scent. But everyone was having as much trouble making their way out of the maze, and Hanna loved it.

"This is so much fun."

"Yeah, I don't think I've had this much fun in a good long while." Phoenix seemed to be enjoying this as much as she was, which was important to her.

No stick-in-the-mud wolves for her.

When they finally found the exit to the maze, she hugged and kissed him. "Yes! We made it."

He laughed and kissed her back. It was chilly out, though they were wearing jackets, but she was full of energy, and he was warming her right up. "Bobbing for apples next." She took his hand and led him to the activity's station.

He let her go first, and she tried and tried and finally got hold of an apple and pulled it out of the water. When he tried, he had to struggle to get his apple out of the tub for much longer than she had. Hanna was glad that she outdid the special forces guy, and then they were off to ride the horse-drawn hay wagon that took them all over the property while they sipped hot apple cider and were covered in a pretty green-and-black-plaid blanket. She snuggled up next to him, his arm wrapped around her shoulders.

"I'm glad I went to the pub," she said. "Because it led to a job."

"Because I met you."

He smiled. "Yeah, you know I had thought of just stopping to get gas and grabbing an energy drink there, but I saw the pub and something just drew me in."

"Me?"

He laughed. "I couldn't help but notice you sitting there all alone, looking like you needed some company, but then I saw the bikers, learned you were a wolf, and things worked out differently than I had planned."

They ended the ride, and he asked her what she wanted to do next.

"We should have worn costumes. But I didn't bring mine with me," she said as she looked at participants dressed as everything from superheroes to cats, witches, elves, and warlocks.

"Yeah, I don't have one either yet. So what's next?"

"They have guided trail tours. Since I've never seen the property, I'd love to do that. How about you?" she asked.

"Sounds like a great idea. And then we'll know where to run."

"Oh, and they're having a howling contest. I want to do that too." She saw little kids making wolf masks on paper plates, with others face painting or striking at a wolf piñata.

They took the walk on the hiking trails hand in hand, which was fun, the trail lined with battery-operated candles in orange sacks, while their tour guide gave them a nature talk about how long the property had been owned by the wolves and how they had expanded the acreage to allow for their pack members to run.

Hanna loved the river and all the forested land. "We can come here and run later tonight."

"Yeah. That would be good. After we have apple cider, turkey legs, and pumpkin pie, or whatever else appeals to us, we'll have to work some of those calories off."

They headed back to the main activity area and watched a man dressed in a skeleton outfit being dunked.

"Have you got a good arm?" she asked Phoenix. "Yeah, the rest of me is good too."

She chuckled. "Go win something for me."

"You got it." He started throwing the ball at the target and knocked the skeleton into the water.

"Betcha can't do that again," the skeleton taunted.

Phoenix smiled and threw another ball. He hit the target and sent the skeleton into the dunk tank again.

Hanna clapped her hands. "Yes! I want the big stuffed wolf."

"Ten shots without missing," he warned.

"I'll go home with you tonight if you get it for me."

He chuckled since they were staying at the pack leaders' home together already. He threw the next ball and sent the skeleton dropping into the water.

"You can't make the next one," the skeleton said, climbing back out of the water.

Phoenix threw the next four balls and dropped the skeleton every time.

"Okay, give someone else a chance," the skeleton said. "Sheesh."

Phoenix smiled and threw another ball. A crowd was gathering to watch now and cheered when he dunked the skeleton an eighth time.

Ryan joined them and folded his arms and smiled. "Next time we choose teams for baseball, you're on mine."

Phoenix laughed. Two more times, he hit the target and won the prize for Hanna.

"My hero." She hugged and kissed him and then took her stuffed wolf in a hug. It was four feet long and she loved it. The wolf toy would make it an even more memorable night.

Everyone clapped, and the skeleton said, "Anyone else? You there, Robin of the Hood. Why don't you try?"

Robin Hood looked like he was about five. The skeleton must have needed a break from being dunked in the water.

Phoenix and Hanna grabbed some turkey legs and wandered around. They saw the ladies and their handmade quilts and the maple-syrup booth where pack members were demonstrating how to produce syrup from the maple trees. They watched a man doing hand-tooled leatherwork and a woman carving small animals, predominantly wolves, from wood. Another man was carving animals from soapstone.

Others were carving pumpkins, and Hanna and Phoenix had to try that. He carved a phoenix flying. She carved a bear, to do something different. They carried their pumpkins to the McKinleys' deck and set them there to decorate it. Afterward, they stopped by a booth for sugary pecans, bottled water, and pumpkin pie. Hanna had thought of leaving her stuffed wolf on the deck, but she didn't want it to wander off, and she was enjoying cuddling it. Though while she ate her treats, Phoenix was good enough to tuck Wild Thing under his arm so she could have her hands free.

They finally sat by the bonfire where a man was telling ghost stories.

"This is the best." She had her wolf on her lap, and she was snuggled up to Phoenix.

"Yeah, I agree, but it wouldn't be this much fun without you." He leaned down and kissed her cheek.

Hanna should have known that it was all too perfect and trouble would turn up.

Some of the pack members had motorcycles, so Hanna really hadn't paid attention to the sound of additional motorcycle engines rumbling out in front of Carol and Ryan's house and cutting out.

Soon, they saw that six members of the Hells Angels had come to their pack fall festival. Only the wolves were allowed to be there. Their wolf-pack parties weren't open to the general public. Hanna worried the reason the members of the biker gang were there was because of her, and maybe Phoenix too.

Sure enough, the men began walking through the activities, looking like they owned the place, and headed straight for the bonfire where Phoenix and Hanna were sitting.

Phoenix was on his feet in an instant.

She was worried, but she needn't have been. Women and children had suddenly slipped away like wolves in the woods seeking safety, all but her. She was sticking by Phoenix. If she had brought the trouble here, she didn't want to lead any of these men to the women and children.

Ryan and several armed men in the pack headed to the bonfire to speak with the gang members. "This is a private party," Ryan said, his voice razor sharp. "You're trespassing on private property."

"I want to talk to that woman and her boyfriend," one biker said, pointing at Hanna and Phoenix.

Phoenix moved forward to confront the biker. "You've already spoken to her, threatening her. We have security video of it. We know who you are—your background, your brother's, and the reason he's in jail—and you and your gang are under surveillance at all times while in Green Valley."

She loved that Phoenix would be a PI and could do that kind of work, even though he hadn't been involved in it yet. She knew Ryan would have had his men on the case from the moment she'd called about the trouble.

The man looked like he wanted to kill Phoenix right then and there. But one of the men slapped him on the shoulder. "Come on. We can't afford to end up like your brother."

The blond was still staring Phoenix down as if he hated to give up the confrontation, like one alpha wolf to another. But Phoenix wasn't backing down, and more of the male wolf-pack members showed up with guns to emphasize the point that they had the firepower to end this confrontation in their favor.

"Come on," the other man said to the blond again. "Anyone could have called the police on us. And your brother knew what would happen this time if he got caught."

The blond scowled at Phoenix and Hanna. Then he growled, turned on his booted heel, and left with the other men. Ryan's men followed them to ensure they left the property peacefully.

The party resumed after that, and Ryan said to Phoenix and Hanna, "I'm glad you told them the PIs have been investigating everything there is about those men. Rest assured, the sheriff is just waiting for any excuse to throw them back in jail. None of this group are innocent, and we don't want them harassing anyone, wolf or otherwise, in Green Valley."

"Thanks," Hanna said. "I was worried they might have been after me because I turned over the video to the police that showed who started the fight."

Ryan smiled. "You two will fit right in."

Chapter 6

With the full moon shining brightly in the night sky, orange lanterns lighting all the paths and trails, a couple of wolves getting a start on being wolves by howling in the woods, a band playing in the background, and the man telling stories as Phoenix warmed Hanna up at the bonfire, this couldn't be more perfect. Not to mention he'd really lucked out when he'd managed to knock the skeleton into the tank ten times in a row without a miss to win Hanna her stuffed wolf. He knew he'd made her night.

Hanna made his. He hadn't done anything like this since he was a kid, and certainly not with a she-wolf wrapped in his arms. He couldn't think of a more special way to spend the night with her in Green Valley.

He was glad that they had Ryan for a pack leader and the whole pack to back them if they had trouble with motorcycle gangs or anyone else who might cause trouble for them in the future.

"Hey, are you ready to run as a wolf?" Things would be winding down soon, and he really wanted to run as a wolf with her before it got to be too late. He realized they hadn't even talked to Ryan about when they would start work.

"Oh yeah, I'm ready," she said.

He stood and helped her up, then they walked to the house and she dropped off her stuffed wolf in her guest room.

"You're staying with me, aren't you?" she asked. "Yeah, sure." Hell yeah.

He began stripping off his clothes, and she was doing the same. They were eyeing each other with small, appreciative smiles. Then she shifted, and she was a beautiful red wolf with white fur legs, chest, and under her chin. He had a black fur band around his chest, red and gray fur under his chin, and a darker tail. But she was just beautiful.

She licked his face, and he nuzzled and licked hers. Then they pushed through the wolf door and ran toward the woods where they heard other wolves barking and playing.

At first, they ran and were just having a great time, and then they began play fighting, nipping each other, tussling with each other, biting, growling, having a blast. He couldn't believe his timing in meeting Hanna like he had.

She liked to play rough, but he was easy on her, not wanting to injure her.

She suddenly stopped playing and lifted her chin and howled at the moon. He smiled at her and howled with her. Now he knew her lovely wolf voice. They'd missed the wolf-howling competition, but this was just as much fun.

Then she tackled him again—when he was off guard. Phoenix wanted to laugh. They were suddenly joined by other wolves, and he could smell Carol's and Ryan's scents, Max's, and the others he didn't know. But they greeted him and Hanna, welcoming them to the wolf pack, and he was really glad to be part of a pack after not having been for so many years while moving around with the army.

Hanna nudged Phoenix and then raced off. He chased after her and figured she was heading to the house.

As soon as she barged through the door, he followed her inside, and they raced to the bedroom. She shifted and shut the door behind him.

He shifted and pulled her into his arms and began to kiss her.

Her hands were all over his back, her body rubbing against his growing erection, their mouths fusing together with long, dreamy kisses. Her green eyes had darkened, and she kissed his neck and cheek. He pulled away to kiss and lick her taut nipples, her breathing growing ragged.

He breathed in her sweet, wild scent: the fresh woods, apple cider, and cinnamon. Their tongues tangled together again, stroking, passionate, wanting more. Her hands ran through his hair, and he combed his fingers through hers, their bodies rubbing against each other.

"I knew you were hot the first time I saw you," she whispered, licking his chin.

"Did you 'see' me like this then?"

"Hmm, in my dreams that night after the pub incident." Then they were kissing again, and he slid his hand down her backside and pulled her against his thigh, raising her leg a bit over his.

He began stroking her between her legs and she was groaning. He stopped and she moaned, but he wanted her in bed with him. He released her and jerked back the covers, then swept her up in his arms and set her on the bed. He followed her there, stroking her again, and she was practically purring as she arched against his fingers. He enjoyed this with her, everything he'd done with her, but this ended the night perfectly.

Phoenix was all lean muscles, his erection reaching out to her, and she wanted him to bury himself in her, but for wolves, it was a mating for life. So for now, they had to be satisfied with going as far as they could without consummating the relationship.

His strokes on her feminine nub were magnificent, his tongue entering her mouth and dueling with hers intoxicating, and she was wet with arousal. He smelled musky and feral, a wild wolf ready to mate. Heat filled every cell in her body as he kept stroking her nub until she felt the end coming. Relief, anticipation, expectation, and then mind-blowing release.

"Ohmigod, yes!" She kissed him and he kissed her back, as if she was the most important wolf in his life.

She rubbed her body against his steel-hard erection.

"Are you ready?" she asked, as if she needed the confirmation. "Hell yeah. For you, yeah."

She chuckled and began to stroke him, his breath hitching. She was kissing his mouth at the same time, his hands gently combing through her hair. He had such a wonderfully, kissable mouth, and his hands were strong yet gentle too. His body was taut with need, beads of sweat forming on his brow. She smiled, loving how she could make the tough Green Beret sweat.

She ran her free hand over his nipples, then leaned over and licked one and gently nibbled it. His hand tightened on her hair, and he lightly groaned. Then she kissed his other nipple and licked it.

But she didn't let up on stroking his erection. The way he was tensing, she knew he was about to come, his face grim, his green eyes darkened, lust-filled, and then he exploded.

"Hmm." She kissed him soundly. "Should we check the shower next?"

He chuckled darkly. "Yeah."

She'd heard Carol and Ryan head for their bedroom earlier, so she and Phoenix grabbed some nightwear, and naked, they raced each other to the bathroom. They were trying to be quiet about it, but they were laughing when they got there.

This was just what she needed in her life. A hunky military guy.

Chapter 7

A month later, Phoenix was serving as a private investigator for Ryan in his firm and loving his job. He'd had a four-year criminal justice degree when he went into the army, and now he could finally use it for something. He and Hanna were trying to agree on an apartment to rent, so they were still at Ryan and Carol's house. The McKinleys were glad to have them stay there, but Phoenix and Hanna needed their own place.

Phoenix had decided they were getting a house, instead of bothering with an apartment, if Hanna would agree to it.

She was working as a communications member of Ryan's team, and she was loving her job too. Best of all, they'd had so much fun with the pack activities. It was nearly Thanksgiving, and Phoenix had lots to be thankful for. Hanna topped his list.

He left the PI office and headed over to the mayor's office to pick up Hanna for lunch and drive her to the house he thought she might like. She'd shown him pictures of homes that really appealed to her, but they wouldn't know until they actually walked through it whether the home was the right fit for them.

Ryan was releasing her early from work, though she didn't know it, so she and Phoenix could look at homes. He was getting tired of their indecisiveness in finding an apartment. Phoenix knew they couldn't decide on one because they really needed a home, one with a wolf door. A place near Carol and Ryan's vast acreage. Someplace where they would feel safe as wolves. They could always go to the pack land and run no matter where they lived, but wouldn't it be better if they could just run through a wolf door and be in the woods?

There was one place that would border pack land once Ryan had bought up more of the land, and it had just gone up for sale.

"Hey, honey," Phoenix said, "are you ready for lunch?" Hanna smiled at him. "I sure am. I'm starving."

"Okay, great."

She got into his car, and he drove her out toward the pack's land. "Wait, there aren't any food places out here."

"There's a house that I wanted to look at with you. It's on the border of the pack's territory." He was certain Ryan was hoping they would buy it to keep the pack's territory more secure, but no one else in the pack needed a home. Phoenix had even wondered if Ryan and the pack had had anything to do with the people wanting to sell the property.

"Really? Is it what we wanted?"

He motioned to his phone. "You can look at all the pictures and the specs of the place."

Hanna lifted his phone and found the house he'd been looking at on the Google search. "Oh, this is nice."

"With my salary, retirement, and savings…"

"And mine," she said.

"We can get it, if it suits us."

"The property butting up to Ryan and Carol's property is great, and it does have ten acres with it," she said.

"Just think, anytime we want to run as wolves, we can. No driving to the pack's lands."

She sighed. "We have to feel connected to the house. We've looked at so many apartments, and all of them were—"

"On top of other apartments. That's not how we live."

"Okay, well, I hope this is it then."

When they finally reached the property, they found a pretty log home, about twenty years old, treed property, a wraparound deck, big windows, and a two-car garage.

"I don't know about you, but I like the look of the house and the property already," Phoenix said, hoping they could agree on something.

"Don't mention you like it to the owners." He glanced at her after he parked.

"So we can get them to come down on the price."

He smiled and took hold of her hand and squeezed. "Right."

Then they got out of the car and headed for the front door. "It's for sale by owner, so the owner said he'd be here when we wanted to look at it."

"Okay, great."

They walked up to the front door, and Phoenix smelled Hanna's nervousness.

"I want to like it. I really do," she whispered. But she was frowning.

"What's wrong?" He hoped she wasn't already feeling bad vibes about the house.

"I smell a familiar scent that I've smelled before." Then she snapped her fingers, and just then the door opened and she said, "Joe."

When Joe, the human who had stood her up her first night in town, saw her, his jaw dropped.

Phoenix was frowning at the two of them, having no idea what was going on.

"Hey, uh, I'm sorry about missing seeing you at the pub that night. Something came up." Joe sounded like he hoped he hadn't screwed things up with them buying the house because of that little incident a month ago. "Then I heard about the motorcycle gang incident there, and I was glad I hadn't gone."

She arched a brow. "I mean, well, sorry."

Yeah, the guy was sorry all right.

"Can we take a look at the house?" Phoenix asked, ready to sock the guy for standing Hanna up. He figured if he hit him, it wouldn't help in asking Joe to reduce the price of the house if Hanna loved it.

They looked at the large living room area and the stone fireplace, and Phoenix was already thinking of setting up a Christmas tree near it the day after Thanksgiving, if they could get moved in that quickly. The place was devoid of furniture and household goods, so it looked like it was ready for the new owner to move right in.

"So why are you selling the place?" Hanna asked, looking over the kitchen.

"My mother died years ago, and my dad just died. I inherited the property three months ago, but I had to have it probated, sell everything else off, and then put the place up for sale."

"I'm sorry about your parents," Hanna said.

The cabinets in the kitchen were honey oak, and the appliances all had wood-grained paneling. The counters were granite and the floors tile. And they even had a wolf door. Well, large dog door, but it would be their wolf door.

At least Phoenix was ready to settle in. All his furniture was in storage. Hanna had moved her household goods into the same storage unit, so they would just need some muscle to help them move it all, and they would be all set up in their very own home.

One wall in the den was covered with built-in bookshelves, a nice touch. The master bedroom had a walk-in shower and a Jacuzzi tub. Hell, Phoenix was sold on the house already.

But Hanna was looking into closets and frowning, glancing out the windows and frowning. She hadn't said one nice thing about the house. He was dying to buy it.

"She and I haven't agreed on anything so far," Phoenix said, sounding like this was another lost cause. He hoped his words would convince Joe to push to sell it to her by lowering the price.

"It's not exactly what I want," she said, peering into the fridge. "I mean, we'd have to replace all the appliances."

"They're only two years old," Joe said, sounding exasperated. "She loves to cook, and she knows just what she wants in a home," Phoenix said, though she really hadn't cooked much, not at Carol and Ryan's house. Carol and Ryan both loved to cook.

Joe folded his arms. "Okay, make me an offer."

He'd listed the property at $295,000. Phoenix was going to offer $280,000, but Hanna took hold of Phoenix's hand and said, "We've got some other homes to check out."

Phoenix looked at her in disbelief. What if some other interested couple saw the property and bought it outright? He would still be dreaming about being with Hanna in this house, making it a home for Thanksgiving.

"Two hundred and eighty thousand," Joe said.

Hanna looked at the kitchen again, frowning, and let out her breath in exasperation. "Two sixty-five and you have a deal. I can use the money we didn't spend on the asking price to renovate the kitchen, and you aren't going through a real estate agent, so you don't have that cost."

Joe rubbed his bristly chin. Phoenix knew he was dying to sell the house as much as Phoenix was dying to buy it. But would he drop the price that much?

"You think about it. We're going to look at the other homes now," Hanna said and pulled Phoenix toward the door.

Hell, if they missed the opportunity to buy this house and the land that went with it—

"Okay, two seventy."

"When can we move in?" she asked.

Joe smiled. "Now, today, any time. I just need a down payment—"

"Let's get a contract written up. We have the funds for a home, so we'll be good to go," Phoenix said, relieved beyond measure. "We can move in now, if you allow it, and we'll get the title transfer and all the other paperwork done as soon as we can." He knew it could take thirty to sixty days to close on a home, but they weren't taking out a loan, and Ryan had told them one of their wolves owned the title company, so they'd expedite the transfer of title.

Hanna smiled at him and squeezed Phoenix's hand. He realized she'd played both of them. Here he was a PI, and she was a con artist! He loved her.

Chapter 8

Hanna and Phoenix were so excited to move in that once they had paid the down payment, signed the contract, and had the appointment for the title company, they were ready. Joe had deposited the check and left them the keys to the home, glad to be rid of the property after the house was signed over.

Phoenix called Ryan with the good news. They needed pack help to move their belongings to the house, but the title company had already let him know that they were closing next week. The pack couldn't be happier that the property would belong to pack members.

"I've already made arrangements for a moving van, a driver, and a bunch of guys to help you get moved."

"Thanks, Ryan. For everything," Phoenix said.

"Thank you for adding that land to our property. You can be one of our outer guard posts."

Phoenix laughed.

"But really, thanks for buying it. And I know you'll love being there."

"We will." Phoenix rubbed Hanna's back.

She was smiling up at him. When they ended the call, she laughed and twirled around with exuberance. "It's ours. Don't you just love it?"

"I love you. And yes, I love the house too. I didn't think you cared for it all that much." He pulled her into his arms and hugged her.

"That was the ploy. Pretend it wasn't exactly what we wanted and we were going to look at other places that might suit our needs better. But oh, this is just beautiful."

"No renovations on the kitchen then?"

"No way. We probably will need to get some furniture, but I couldn't have said that to help convince him to reduce the price on the house."

"True. You really like it?"

She kissed Phoenix. "Yeah. I know you were totally exasperated with me when you thought I didn't like it. I could smell your tension and saw it in your face. It was a good thing Joe didn't recognize it."

"It wouldn't have mattered. All that mattered was what you wanted. He was sure you wore the pants in the family."

She laughed. "We both do. Come on. We need to get our bed moved here and then we need to—"

"Mate?"

Smiling, she nodded. "I was beginning to think we would never agree on a place to live and this wouldn't work out between us."

"Are you kidding? An apartment? No. We needed a home in the woods. And we'll make it *our* home. I love you." He was even thinking about when they had kids and how this would be perfect for them. The home had five bedrooms and three and a half baths. Perfect for a family. And no more moving. He was ready to settle down permanently.

"I agree. And I love you too. Let's go and get our stuff."

After moving their belongings to the home, they spent the rest of the afternoon setting up their house, but they didn't have any groceries to make dinner. It would still take them days, weeks, to get everything the way they wanted and to find things too.

"Let's go to the pub where we met and celebrate," Phoenix said, "and we can buy some groceries in town after that."

"Let's invite the pack, in case we have trouble again there."

He laughed. "It wouldn't be a celebration without them. Besides, if any motorcycle gangs show up, we'll be safe. I'll invite my family too."

That evening, they had dinner and drinks at the pub with close to thirty pack members, several of whom had brought them housewarming gifts. Both Hanna and Phoenix were overwhelmed by the generosity of the pack. Michael and Carmela were there, too, promising them a housewarming gift in a few days.

"We'll have everyone over for a barbecue one of these days," Phoenix said, though they needed to get set up for it first.

"In the spring," Ryan said. "You two need to get your household set up the way you like it."

A couple of motorcyclists drove up and parked at the pub, and Phoenix and Hanna eyed them speculatively through the window, but they didn't belong to any gangs and grabbed a booth inside. Hanna sighed with relief. Not much later, Joe drove up in his blue pickup and entered the pub with a woman. When he saw Hanna and Phoenix, he almost looked like he wanted to leave.

They smiled and said they were getting all moved in, and he looked relieved.

After dinner, a number of pack members piled plants and small appliances and other presents into Phoenix's car and wished him and Hanna the best on their first home together. Phoenix and Hanna drove to the grocery store for one last trip before they settled into their house for their first night out in the country.

He got steaks; she got fixings for s'mores.

"I thought you were going to dump me if I didn't agree to buy the house," she said while they were trying to remember everything they needed to set up housekeeping.

He was pushing the basket, and she was grabbing flour, sugar, and spices. "I should have known you really wanted the house. You would make a terrific poker player."

She chuckled.

Then they were finally home, ditching their jackets, scarves, gloves, hats, boots, and socks, unpacking their groceries and gifts. Other than putting the refrigerated goods away, Phoenix figured none of the rest of the stuff mattered for now. Not when they had other business they needed to attend to.

They still hadn't hung pictures, boxes were filled with their household goods, and they had to make their bed. But when he swept her up in his arms and headed into the master bedroom, he discovered she'd found the sheets and made the bed just for them. He'd figured they would be making love on the bare mattress, floor, anywhere would do, but he was glad they had a made bed for their mating.

"You planned this all along, didn't you? Seducing me?" he asked, kissing her cheek.

She laughed. "Yes, while the guys were putting the bed together and you were helping to unpack the rest of our furniture and household goods, I was frantically searching for our sheets and pillows, and when I finally found them, I made the bed. Just for this."

He glanced down at the green comforter decorated with pink hearts and the pink sheets and smiled.

She shrugged. "We can get something else later. This will have to do for now."

"Pink works for me as long as you're the one in between the sheets."

"Hmm, and you're there with me."

He started removing her sweater and pulled it over her head and kissed her cheek. "At the rate we were going, I never thought we'd get to this."

She laughed. "Of course we would. I know, I know, we couldn't agree on an apartment, but that didn't mean you and I weren't meant for each other." She smiled at him, pulled his shirt out of his waistband, and ran her hands underneath and up his shirt and over his ripped abs. "I wouldn't give you up for anything."

"The same here with wanting you. Hell, if we'd had to live with Ryan and Carol forever…" He kissed her cheek, his hands rubbing over her shoulders.

"No. Way."

He chuckled. "My feeling exactly."

She found his nipples and gently tweaked them with her fingers. He moaned deep in his throat, then kissed her mouth, leisurely, lovingly. His large hands tenderly rubbed her shoulders, and he made her feel amazing. *He* was amazing. His mouth was incredible on hers as he brushed kisses against her lips, his green eyes mesmerizing.

She sighed as he unbuttoned her blouse and found she was braless. His masculine lips smiled against her mouth in a predatory way. She shrugged. "If you weren't going to ask me to mate with you, I was going to ask you…and fewer clothes work better."

"All day at work—"

"I had a shirt and sweater on." She smiled up at him.

"Vixen." Then he lowered his head to kiss the swell of her breasts, one and then the other. He kissed a nipple with his hot mouth, then licked and moved across, pressing kisses against her skin, leaving a sizzling path in his wake before he began to lick the other nipple, suckling.

Heat enveloped her and her breath grew ragged. She breathed in the scent of him, her wolf forevermore, maleness personified, hot testosterone, enticing pheromones, the human and the wolf, desire filling her with each passing second. Wet with need, she pulled off his shirt. She began to work on his belt, unfastening it, unzipping his trousers. Reaching down as he was kissing her mouth, she ran her hand down, and what she found shocked her.

Her heavily lidded eyes shot wide open as soon as she touched his penis and short, curly hairs, and her mouth curved up. "You weren't wearing boxer shorts today?"

"I was going to ask you to mate with me, and the fewer clothes, the better."

She laughed. She loved him. "Great minds." She hurried to pull his trousers down his lean hips and kissed the tip of his penis before his trousers fell to the floor and he kicked them off.

He hurried to pull off her trousers and he smiled, ran his hand over her lacy boy-shorts, and pulled them off.

She wrapped her arms around his neck and pressed her naked body against his. She loved the feel of his hard, muscled body against hers as he ran his hands down her back and cupped her buttocks and squeezed.

"You're a wild one," he whispered against her cheek. "Wild and mine."

"Shy and retiring, in truth." Of course she was teasing him. He did bring more of the wildness out in her, though.

"No way. You're just the one for me." Then he was kissing her again, and she let him in all the way, tongue to tongue, greeting him in a way that said there would be no holds barred this time.

"Hmm, so hot and wolfish." She rubbed against his arousal and he groaned low.

She savored every bit of him: his touches, groans, scent, taste. He was just divine, and she was so glad they had a place of their own where they could be themselves, be a couple, enjoy the intimacy in total privacy, and become mated wolves.

He slipped his hands under her buttocks and lifted her so that she wrapped her legs around him, and he carried her to the bed. She already felt the white-hot ache for his touch. Then he was finding her wet, swollen nub with his finger, teasing the center of her pleasure. He pressed his advantage, stroking her, making her feel wondrous, lusty, and in love.

Scarcely breathing, she felt awash in rising pleasure, the need for fulfillment, the craving to have him inside her now filling her with urgency. Her heart and his were beating wildly, and she was heading for the stars and the moon, ready to release. And then she shattered in the most exquisite way, cried out, howled, and clung to the love of her life.

He was pressing the head of his shaft between her thick, slick folds and began to thrust after that, not waiting for an invitation, her howl enough to say she was all in on the union between wolves. "Love you so much, honey."

She kissed him with drive and enthusiasm. "I love you right back," she said, breathless. He took her breath away, filled her with joy, and meant everything to her.

She wrapped her legs around his waist, deepening his penetration, wanting him desperately to climax inside her this time. This was what it meant to be wolf mates, the consummated sex between wolves, the driving need to be as one, a mated pair forever.

She couldn't be any happier as his body slammed into hers, thrusting, undulating, sexy, hot, and hers. Seeing the tension on his face, the straining of his neck muscles, the way his body tightened, his ragged breathing, and lust-filled, beautiful green eyes, she knew he was near completion. But so was she. Again.

He growled as he filled her with his wet heat, and then he howled like she had done, thrusting until he was finished, but she ground out, "Not yet." And he smiled and slid his hand between them, coaxing another climax out of her, stroking, kneading, bringing her to the precipice and orgasm.

She cried out, feeling wondrously fulfilled, satiated, hearts beating as if they'd been racing through the woods as wolves, and that was just what she wanted to do next. As a newly mated wolf pair.

She pulled him to her, held him tight, her legs still wrapped around him, hers forevermore.

"Hmm, you aim to keep me," he said, his voice rough and sexy, needy even.

"You bet," she said. "I'm only letting you out of my grasp to run as a wolf tonight."

"I was hoping you would say that. Running with you as a wolf means we'll be ready for more bed play when we return home."

"I knew you were the only one for me." She shifted and he chuckled. He should know that about her by now. She could be totally unpredictable.

He shifted and she raced down the hall. He raced right after her, though they had to maneuver around a few packing boxes before they reached the door. They'd unpack more tomorrow, but for now, they were going to enjoy their newfound mated status.

Wolves in lust and love—the only way to be.

Epilogue

The holidays were upon them. Instead of visiting Phoenix's family or Hanna's, their families came from Loveland and Silver Town to see them for Thanksgiving, and so did the Green Valley pack leaders. Phoenix and Hanna were so grateful for all Ryan and Carol had done for them.

"You know we love having families join the pack in Green Valley," Ryan said to Hanna's parents and Hanna's sister, Susan.

"We're sure you could take over the post office here as soon as the postmaster retires, and Susan could be a teacher for our wolf children if you ever want to move out here and be part of our pack," Carol said.

Hanna smiled, but Phoenix knew her family had no interest in uprooting themselves from Loveland, as much as she hoped they would. He thought if they could convince Susan to move here, the sisters' parents would follow.

That was when Max Browning arrived late to dinner. It was Carol and Hanna's idea to have the retired Navy SEAL come to dinner, in hopes he and Susan might hit it off. But Michael had the same idea with his Green Beret brother, Daniel, who was visiting him and Carmela, so naturally they brought him to Thanksgiving dinner too.

"Sorry I'm late. I got a flat tire on the way over here," Max said, making a detour to the kitchen to wash up first.

"No problem at all," Hanna said as Max took his seat at the table next to Susan and introductions were made.

Maybe something would spark between Max and Susan. Or Daniel and Susan. All that mattered to Phoenix for now was that *he* had found his mate in Hanna during one big motorcycle-gang brawl close to Halloween.

Hanna was thrilled all the families could be together. Michael's twin brother was sitting on the other side of Susan, and Hanna hoped one of the two men, Daniel or Max, would interest her. She truly wanted her family to move to Green Valley before she and Phoenix had kids, but her parents wouldn't move unless Susan did. Hanna squeezed Phoenix's hand and smiled at him. No matter what happened between her sister and the men, Hanna had her own loving mate. Dating a military guy had finally worked out, and she'd ended up with the job and a pack that she couldn't have been happier to be with. She and both their families and, of course, her mate couldn't have been more pleased or thankful for this holiday season.

ACKNOWLEDGMENTS

To my mother, daughter, and son, who cheer me on and believe all my books should be made into movies. And to my editor, Deb Werksman, who inspires me every step of the way. Thanks to all the help my Rebel Romance Writers give as they encourage my writing daily. And to my fans who write to me and encourage me to continue creating more wolfish tales.

About the Author

USA Today bestselling author Terry Spear has written over sixty paranormal and medieval Highland romances. In 2008, *Heart of the Wolf* was named a *Publishers Weekly* Best Book of the Year. She has received a PNR Top Pick, a Best Book of the Month nomination by *Long and Short Reviews*, numerous *Night Owl Romance* Top Picks, and two Paranormal Excellence Awards for Romantic Literature (finalist and honorable mention). In 2016, *Billionaire in Wolf's Clothing* was an *RT Book Reviews* Top Pick. A retired officer of the U.S. Army Reserves, Terry also creates award-winning teddy bears that have found homes all over the world, helps out with her granddaughter, and is raising two Havanese puppies. She lives in Spring, Texas.

Made in the USA
Columbia, SC
25 March 2023

14266032R00212